NOW SERVING DRAGON

DAVID R. MICHAEL

Also by David R. Michael

Novels
Closing Crew
Gunwitch: A Tale of the King's Coven
Gunwitch: The Witch Hunts
The Door to the Sky
The Summoning Fire

Novellas
Alligator Bait (Gator-man #1)

Collections
Brain Freeze & Other Stories
Demon Candy
Dragons of the Stars
The World Wears Thin

NOW SERVING DRAGON

DAVID R. MICHAEL

Published By
Four Crows Landing

For Allison

1. Dragon Drop Soup

The Queen

THE QUEEN OF THE KITCHEN readied Herself for the arrival of the Devourer. Her family, both drones and workers, readied themselves, as well, for they would be the appetizers, after the designated *amuse-bouche* Opened the Door.

The Queen and Her family had been preparing the World for Devouring for more than a century, seasoning and leavening and just generally adding flavor. She had not expected the End to come quite so soon, however. Still, after a century, what difference did a week or two make?

Also, the Queen had not expected company. She had expected to Devour the World Herself, Her and Her as-yet unborn Sisters, and had flavored to Her Own tastes. She hoped the Devourer did not mind.

If the Devourer had merely let Her know It had been Planning to attend the End of the World, She would have been more than happy to address any special seasoning requests or dietary needs. At least She knew the Devourer was not vegan. That was a relief.

Still, the Queen had been hoping to acquire a Final Ingredient before Devouring the World, and had set in motion Her plan to capture a specimen of said Final Ingredient. Of course, the Final Ingredient would be Devoured along with the rest of the World, but She had wanted a chance to prepare it first. To get the flavor just right, and to spread it across the World like mayonnaise across a slice of pumpernickel.

No time for that now, though. She and the Devourer would just have to make do with the World as it was.

She told Herself it would be nice to have company for Dinner.

The Only

The Only of His Kind shook snow from his wings and allowed the banked heat inside him to bloom forth in a great white spray of fire that erupted into the heavens. Then he leaped from his mountaintop, found the wind, and soared away from the rising Sun.

The Only had awakened on his mountaintop when he sensed the changing direction of the winds. When he had felt the stars being pulled from their constellations to cast strange, new shadows on the Earth. When he had felt the odd sensation of someone perusing a cookbook with his picture on the cover.

The Only swooped, gaining speed as he sought the next thermal updraft to carry him higher. Normally, the jet-stream winds would have fought him, attempted to push him back the way he came. Not tonight. Tonight, he knew, he could be flying from any corner of the globe, and the winds would carry him to his destination.

The Only had been sleeping. He did not know for how long. If there were any time left after this night, there would be time enough to find out how long he had been asleep. How many decades or centuries had passed. Maybe it had been a millennium or two.

However long it had been, the End of the World was ahead of schedule, and the Only wanted to know what was going on.

The Bug

WITH MORE THAN A TINGE of jealousy, the Bug regarded the bright orange sticker that had been affixed to the windshield of his sibling rival. The Second Ugly Replacement did *not* deserve a special trip.

The Bug didn't understand why the Second Ugly Replacement attracted the orange stickers more frequently than either he or the First Ugly Replacement. The Second Ugly Replacement was so *generic* looking. No distinctive curves on its fenders, no particularly interesting lines along the hood or across the top of the cab. The Second Ugly Replacement wasn't even as ugly as the First Ugly Replacement, though both did have hatchbacks, a feature the Bug found especially disturbing. Hatchback aside, the Second Ugly Replacement was just *bland*.

The Bug glared at the Second Ugly Replacement, whose generic, bland face looked so smug.

The Bug wanted his own orange sticker.

The Driver was never happy when any of her Outdoor Babies were taken on outings, but the Bug thought the trips were grand. Mostly. Except when the tow truck drivers scratched his undercarriage or took turns fast enough to dent his frame or pull his tires over the curb. The trips gave the Bug a chance to see how the world was progressing, at least those stretches of it along the route to the impound.

The Bug's only consolation was that the Driver would almost certainly show up soon, see the orange sticker on the Second Ugly Replacement's blandly ugly face, and remove it.

1

THARA GOLD SAT AS STILL as she could on the uncomfortable contours of the plastic bus seat, willing her Episode to wait. Wait. WAIT. Please, wait. Please? The urgency of her silent pleading ebbed and flowed with the cycle of intensity that pulsed within her.

Her left hand, clenched into a fist and pressed against the worn black cotton of her trousers, seemed to vibrate, the edges blurring, fraying, the human material straining to maintain itself. One portion of her brain read and reread her DNA chains to remind herself that, yes, yes, look-at-that, she was *supposed* to have fingers, knuckles, skin, and fine little blonde hairs on the back of her hands.

Another portion of her brain, though, kept reviewing the other option she had available.

She kept her fingers curled, the tips out of sight, hiding those tingling bits of her extremities that might already be giving the alternative a try.

Outside the window, past the uncertain reflection of her face with its heavy eyeliner and gold-blonde hair in a pixie haircut, the winding tour of south Rio Cruces's ugliest apartment complexes, strip malls, and commercial districts passed with her paying even less attention than usual. With each stop, the weeks-delayed Episode built up inside her, pushed against the bonds of her willpower and threatened to break free.

It was worrying to think she might have an Episode in public. She glanced at the other passengers. Except for Denny, the bus driver, no one looked familiar. Not that she had paid much attention before tonight. In the months she had ridden the bus to and from this particular job, it was possible she had seen all the current passengers and just never noticed anyone sufficiently to recognize them. Still, maybe none of them, including Denny, would connect the twenty-something-looking, probably-a-waitress-from-the-way-she-was-dressed young woman with the creature that might suddenly appear in the middle of the bus—

But that wasn't going to happen. Thara gritted her teeth. She was going to hold herself together—literally—hopefully—until she got home.

Her Episode was twenty-three days late. A new record, made even more unusual after the six seasons of mark-your-calendar, steady-as-clockwork, night-of-the-solstice Episodes that had preceded it.

The Autumnal Equinox had been inconsiderately scheduled for a Tuesday this year. Trading a Tuesday shift had not been easy. Tuesdays were always slow at the Bottomless Breadsticks Family Restaurant, with tips to match. She had had to give up a prized Thursday night and agree to work the following Tuesday to make it happen. She had even gone to bed early that evening to offset the late night Episodes tended to bring, curling up in her favorite old sleeping bag in the corner of her bedroom, under the window, which had been unlocked for her Episodic egress convenience.

And nothing. No Episode. It had been nice to sleep late the next morning, and to wake up not smelling like cheesy breadsticks, but also somewhat frustrating to have given up a Thursday night for nothing.

Nothing happened the next night either, which she had worked. She had been ready to claim food poisoning and throw up on a co-worker—in the back, out of sight of customers, because she hadn't want to get fired at the time—then rush home. The theatrics had not been needed. She was off the next night, the precious, lost Thursday, but there was still no Episode.

Nothing had been the continuing story, night after night, twenty-two nights in a row.

It was a chicken-or-the-egg question. Did she quit because she had subconsciously felt her Episode coming on? Or had her Episode decided to show up three weeks and two days late because she had finally quit her job? Walking out had certainly felt freeing at the time.

She had worked at Bottomless Breadsticks for almost a year. Not her shortest stint at a restaurant, but definitely part of a trend of ever-shortening terms of employment. Maybe she was finally getting tired of the food service industry.

As she rode the bus, wiggling her toes inside her shoes to remind her feet she was *supposed* to have toes, she couldn't think of anything that happened tonight, before walking out, that hadn't happened at least nightly during the previous year. Tonight, though, something had happened, or someone had finally gotten to her, as it, or someone, always did, eventually. Sooner or later, every job—every boss—every co-worker—got to her.

For the past few years, *sooner or later* seemed to be getting sooner and sooner. Whatever it was, she had taken off her little apron, thrown it and her waitress pad in the face of Wes, the current titleholder for World's Worst Manager, and walked out.

Then she had walked back in, picked up her apron and her waitress pad, and left again. Because those were hers.

Maybe it was Wes, the World's Worst Manager, putting his arm around her shoulders and giving her a good-natured squeeze as he told her he had moved her from dinner to lunch for the next two weeks. Maybe it was Carlos and the other cooks on the line making rude and suggestive comments on her way into, out of, and during her short-as-possible stays in the claustrophobically small and disgustingly unsanitary staff bathroom. Maybe it was the customers who kept assuming she wanted to date customers who asked out waitresses—who then assumed, because one assumption wasn't enough, that her turning them down meant they, male or female, had incorrectly guessed her sexual orientation.

Except all that was any given Thursday. Nothing special or unusual about any of those things.

Which made her wonder, and not for the first time, if the real question she should be asking was, *Why she had continued to work there for so long?*

She had been pondering both questions—*why tonight?* and *why not long ago?*—as she always did, post-quitting, while waiting for the bus. She would need to find a new job, of course, because there was rent to pay. She had a lead on a job, of a sort, and she still had a roommate—

As soon as she set foot on the bus, though, her thoughts, like the rest of her, had been nearly overcome by the onslaught of her Episode. She had held herself together, but only just, and doing so required pausing on the first step of the bus, trembling.

"If you're going to be sick," Denny the bus driver had said to her, looking concerned, "could you do it *before* you get on? I'll wait."

Thara managed a low wattage hi-my-is-Thara-and-I'll-be-your-server-tonight smile as she pulled herself the rest of the way up the steps. "No, you wouldn't," she said as she swiped her bus pass through its slot.

"No, I wouldn't," Denny replied, shaking his head and smiling with far more sincerity than Thara thought was necessary. "You know who gets to clean that shit up? Here's a hint." He leaned toward her and tapped himself on the chest. "It's me." He paused and his smile became a concerned frown as his eyes searched her face. He held up his hand to stop her from moving past him. "Are you sure you're alright?"

"I will be," Thara said, trying to make it sound like she wasn't talking through clenched teeth. "Fine," she added. "I'll be fine."

Denny frowned, but he moved his arm. "If you think you're going to hurl, just pull the cord. I'll stop and let you off."

"And leave me there to catch the next bus, I'll bet."

"Maybe," Denny agreed with a nod, but his expression was still more concerned than jovial. "But maybe not. You look a bit... scaly... around the gills. That can't be good."

Thara hunched her shoulders to cover her tingling neck with the collar of her white button-down shirt. "Thanks," she said. "You're a true friend."

"I am your friendly neighborhood bus driver."

Thara scurried past him, before he could see her neck more clearly, and maybe notice it was longer than usual. She found the first open window seat and occupied it with extreme prejudice.

She normally dozed through the long trip back to the bus stop in front of her apartment complex. She lived and worked—well, *had* worked, until a few minutes before—at the extreme ends of Denny's bus route. There would be no dozing tonight, though. If she fell asleep, her Episode would begin post haste. What would Denny make of *that* kind of mess in the back of his bus? She didn't want to find out.

When the bus reached her stop, she didn't have to pull the cord. Denny even waited for her as she took a lot more time than usual to stand, walk carefully, humanly, and non-Episodically up the aisle and down the steps.

"You take it easy," Denny said to her back. "And if you're contagious, you stay home tomorrow, you hear?"

Thara managed a wave with her left hand but didn't turn around. She focused on putting one foot in front of the other as she made her way through the semirandom maze of three-story buildings and parking lots that made up her apartment complex.

The sky overhead had gone from sunset pink to twilight blue on her bus ride, but the dingy gray paint of the apartments looked as dingy gray as always, immune to illumination. Even under the mismatched yellow and white lights that shone on the motley collection of vehicles in the parking lot, the paint was dingy gray.

The night was cool, but she didn't feel it. Her Episode had stoked her body temperature to the point she expected to see steam lifting off the exposed skin of her clenched fists and wrists. It had happened before.

Her apartment was all the way in the back, as far from the main entrance of the apartment complex as possible. She had chosen that apartment years ago for precisely that reason. Tonight, though, it seemed like an eternity before she walked past her Outdoor Babies. They were all still there, as they should be, but a bright orange tow sticker had been slapped on Nova's windshield. Thara kept walking. She had no time to take care of that now. Then she entered the final breezeway and walked to the end, to the front door of her apartment.

Which was locked.

A growl started in the back of her throat. Her nose was still human, but she was pretty sure she had just seen a wisp of smoke emerge, and could smell her roommate on the other side of the door. Cucumber and melon body wash, with more than a hint of stale buffet restaurant.

For six months, Tina had never paid any attention to Thara's admonition to always keep the front door locked. Night after night she had left the door unlocked when she came home. Tonight, though, of all nights, the words had finally sunk in.

Thara took two deep breaths and let them out, waiting for an ebb in the chaos lapping at the edges of her consciousness, a lull when it would be safe—or at least safer—for her to unclench her left hand, reach into her pocket and retrieve her keys. Then she took two more breaths before inserting the key in the lock, turning the knob and opening the door.

She opened the heavy door with amazing calm, she thought, but still startled her roommate when the door slammed against the doorstop.

Tina, who had been sitting on a pile of Thara's clean clothes on the couch, eating a bowl of breakfast cereal while watching TV, jumped to her feet with a shout. Milk and Cinnamon Toast Crunch sloshed from her bowl and splashed on the carpet. Tina was a mousy girl, shorter than Thara's five-foot-seven but also curvier. She wore the shapeless yellow shirt and brown trousers of her uniform at the Yellow Sign Buffet.

"I thought you were going out with Ricky tonight," Thara said, pulling on the door to close it.

"We have to work—"

The front door slammed closed behind Thara, startling Tina again. The girl was as jumpy as a cat, and had similar bad habits around fresh laundry.

"—sort of."

"Don't sit on my clothes."

Thara rushed through the living room, past Tina, and around the corner to the door of her bedroom.

"And clean that up."

She started simultaneously kicking off her shoes and unlocking the three deadbolts that secured her bedroom door. She had had the deadbolts installed when she first moved into the apartment, after she had had the bedroom door replaced. The original door had been a hollow excuse for a barrier, thin paneling over an unimpressive wooden frame, painted white. The door she had replaced it with was much more substantial. She had wanted a stainless steel door, but couldn't afford one. So she had settled on a single piece of solid oak. She was reasonably sure her bedroom door was the strongest door in the apartment complex. It was certainly stronger than the heavy front door of her apartment. At the moment, though, both the deadbolts and the heavy door seemed to be conspiring to frustrate her, to keep her out.

"Work?" she managed to say through clenched teeth, trying to maintain at least a facade of friendly roommate. She growled again when she almost twisted the key off in the second lock. "Sort of?" Second lock open. She focused on the third. "You need a new boyfriend. Or a new boss."

"Ricky is my boss."

"My point exactly."

She opened the third lock and extracted the key in one piece. She put her hand on the door lever she had chosen because it was a lot easier for claws to open than the original tiny, round doorknob.

"Don't open my door. In fact, don't spend the night here. Say hi to Ricky for me."

Again she thought she had been the epitome of calm in the face of the storm that was her oncoming Episode. But when she leaned to her left and glanced around the corner, Tina's wide eyes and open mouth seemed to indicate that she might have shouted her advice, instructions, and meaningless pleasantries. Or said them too fast. Or roared them.

She smelled a faint scent of burning plastic and noticed a new scorch mark blistering the latex paint on her bedroom door.

"Are you OK?" Tina asked.

Thara thought her smile had been reassuring, and not as frightening as Tina's expression would indicate.

Then she was in her room, slamming that door closed too. As she turned all the deadbolts back into position with fingers that thought they had better things to do, like stretch and grow golden claws, she heard Tina say, "I never open your door. It's always locked." Then, "Is something burning?"

The walls were so thin in this apartment Thara wasn't entirely sure why she bothered to lock the doors, either the front door or her bedroom door. Other than she had to. Because not locking the door of her bedroom, whether she was in it—and especially if she was out—was an unbearable thought.

If any of her long parade of roommates had ever *really* wanted to get into her bedroom, they could have bypassed her sturdy, replacement door and its many locks and come through the walls with a couple good kicks and a hai-yah-karate-punch. So far, though, no roommate had made that particularly poor decision. Which didn't mean she hadn't run them off, intentionally or unintentionally, for other reasons. She hoped she hadn't just run off Tina, though. The girl had only paid rent through the end of October.

Then Thara stopped thinking about Tina and rent and the curiosities of roommates as her Episode began in earnest.

She stripped off the black trousers and white shirt that comprised her waitress uniform, then her sports bra and panties. Unfortunately, she didn't have time to pull her phone out of her pants pocket and duct tape it to her bare leg.

Her new, golden claws wanted to shred her waitress uniform, because Thara the Golden Dragon had no use for clothes and hated the smell of breadsticks. Thara the Out-of-Work Waitress, though, still needed her waitress clothes, and kept that from happening. Even if she agreed about the breadsticks.

2

THARA'S FIRST EPISODE OCCURRED ON her tenth birthday. Which was, coincidentally, also a Thursday.

There was no birthday party, as such. She and her parents had gone to Harden's Hamburgers for birthday burgers, onion rings, and chocolate shakes, a special treat for her. Had she realized how many years of her adult life would be spent serving birthday meals at restaurants and singing obnoxiously upbeat, royalty-free happy-birthday songs, she probably wouldn't have been so excited.

She didn't remember much about the burger or onion rings, though she had no doubt they were excellent, as always. She remembered the shake.

Mostly, she remembered it was cold. And brown.

Poppa had made a joke about her nose. She didn't remember the specifics of the joke, but remembered giggling as she lifted her chocolate shake to take a sip. The paper cup had collapsed in her grip as if she were circus strongman with a grudge instead of a ten-year-old girl with her favorite drinkable form of chocolate ice cream. Cold, cold chocolate shake dumped down the front of her new dress, the one her mother had only let her wear to school that day.

When they got home, she hardly protested when her mother sent her take a bath. Thara wasn't especially fond of baths, and this was her second bath in as many nights. Momma had sweetened the deal, though, by letting her squeeze liquid dishwashing soap in the water, creating a bubble bath.

Thara might have gotten carried away with the amount of liquid soap she put in the water, but she was sure Momma wouldn't mind. It was still Thara's birthday. By the time she slipped in to the tub, eight inches of shimmering, twinkling bubbles capped eight inches of hot, soapy water. She had thought dumping chocolate shake on herself had ruined her birthday, but now she felt incredible. Warm and bubbly. Even the chemical smell of the dishwashing soap seemed the height of luxury.

She sighed and rested her head on the edge of the tub and let her body float, invisible under the bubbles. After a long, luxurious moment, she lifted her left leg so she could see it rise from the bubbles—

She screamed at the sight of the gleaming, golden-scaled—and, frankly, knobby—appendage that rose from her bath. What should have been her foot with what Momma assured her were the five cutest toes in the world was instead a monstrous claw with incredibly long, jointed finger-like phalanges, each of them tipped with a curled, golden hook.

She scrambled backward, climbing the back of the tub and the wall behind her to get out of the water. Her fingers and toes scritch-scritched against the smooth porcelain of the tub and the ceramic tiles of the wall.

She screamed again as she looked down at her body.

Instead of her naked chest covered in bubbles she saw a soft—but still scaly—underbelly, pearly white, running from under her chin down her torso. Her arms weren't her arms, and her hands looked like the clawed feet that couldn't have been hers. She twisted and noticed the thick tail attached to her spine as it sloshed in the water between her legs.

She braced herself, then held her left hand up where she could see it. Like the toes she had seen on her left foot, her fingers had become longer, though not as long as her toes. Her fingernails, trimmed and buffed by Momma after last night's bath, were gold, an inch long, thick, and hooked.

She tried not to think of how she got out of the bathtub as *crawling over the side*, but she could hardly call it standing and stepping out in the more normal fashion of a ten-year-old girl.

She soaked the towel she had placed on the floor by the tub, then dripped water on the hardwood floor as she went to the sink.

She tried not to think about how she was on her belly as she reached up with her left arm, gripped the edge of the sink and pulled herself up to look in the mirror. Her rear legs—no, her *only* legs, she reminded herself—spread and bent in a way that felt unnatural as her feet—not her *rear claws*, her *feet*—splayed. She tried to ignore the feel of her ten long finger-toes on the polished boards of the floor.

She screamed again at what she saw in the mirror, except by this point it was beginning to seem only natural. *Of course* there was a dripping-wet, golden-scaled lizard face looking out of the mirror at her. She wanted to cry more than scream. She used her left hand-claw—very carefully—to wipe away the bubbles that remained on her cheeks and forehead so she could see more clearly how hideous she had become.

She jumped as her mouth parted and a long, forked tongue slicked out, licked her cheek, then slicked back in. She grimaced at the taste of dishwashing soap.

She turned her head to the right, then the left, so she could see with both eyes, one at a time. Trying to focus with both eyes at the same time made her head hurt.

Her head was a wedge, with twin humps for her eyes and for her nostrils. Under her chin was a fluttering flap of skin. Her bright yellow blonde hair was gone. A ridge of gold spikes started between her eyes and extended down the back of her head and her spine.

Someone knocked on the bathroom door.

She jumped again, and her right eye swiveled in a disturbingly inhuman way to look at the bathroom door while her left eye continued to examine her new facial features.

"Thara?" Momma said, sounding worried. "Are you OK? Is everything alright?"

Her tongue flicked out, then back in again, as she considered how to respond.

"Thara?"

The jiggling of the doorknob made up her mind. She didn't want Momma to see her like this.

"I'm fine," she said. Or tried to say. The words came out a lot more breathy and hissy than she intended.

She skittered-scurried-crawled across the wet floor and towel and up and over the side of the bathtub. She slipped in to the water in a way that reminded her of the alligators and crocodiles she had seen in the old Tarzan movies at the cinema.

She rolled over in the bathtub—her tail proved quite useful for this—keeping herself below the still-impressive blanket of bubbles as she heard the door open.

"Is everything OK?" Momma asked.

Thara considered holding her breath until Momma left, but if she did Momma might think she was drowning and look closer at whatever it was floating in the water. She poked her head up, but kept it low, hoping the bubbles would cover her.

"Momma!" she said. A little less breathy this time, but still hissy. Except hissy seemed to work for this. She opened her eyes. The bubbles stung for an instant, then she closed her eyes. Or thought she did. She felt her eyelids close. She even saw something move across her eyes as it happened. But she could still see. She resisted the urge to rub her eyes with her knuckles.

Momma stood just inside the bathroom door with her hands on her hips, looking at Thara, then at the floor.

"Thara! You scared me! Have you been splashing? There's water everywhere."

"Sorry, Momma," Thara said. She let herself sink back into the water. In case the spikes on her head were sticking up out of the bubbles.

"You're going to have to clean that up. Hurry up and finish. Birthday or not, you still have school tomorrow."

Thara considered arguing with Momma about school. She wasn't sure her fifth grade classroom was the right place for a lizard-girl. She said, "Sorry, Momma. I will, Momma."

She didn't come up out of the bubbles again until Momma had left and pulled the bathroom door closed.

She sat up in the tub and her hands went immediately to her face to wipe away the bubbles.

She stared.

Her hands were hands. She dipped them back into the bathwater and pulled them out again. Still hands. With normal skin and fingers with perfectly rounded and buffed fingernails.

She touched her face and felt normal skin there too. And her normal nose. And her hair was wet on the back of her head and down her neck.

She finished her bath in a daze, wondering as she did if she had dreamed the whole thing. Had she fallen asleep in the warm, bubbly water and had a nightmare?

She told her best friend, Nancy Chisum, about it the next day at school. Nancy, a whimsical girl who still believed in fairies, had immediately declared that Thara had turned into a dragon.

Thara had laughed and decided it was all a dream. Until it happened again at the summer equinox, three months later, at Nancy Chisum's first—and only—slumber party.

That was 1958.

3

THE DAYS WHEN EITHER FORM of Thara, human or dragon, had been able to lay down in a bathtub and hide under the bubbles were long gone. Thara had never officially measured herself during an Episode, but she knew she was at least half again as long as a Cadillac Escalade. And while she could look at that Cadillac Escalade and estimate to within a few hundred dollars what the sticker price had been, when new, before it ran into her—and before she ran into it, repeatedly, in retaliation—she wasn't as good at estimating feet and inches. She was pretty sure she was about twenty-five feet long. That had been during her previous Episode. She might have grown. When she was younger, her dragon form had sometimes grown as much as a foot between Episodes. The last few years, though, she seemed to grow only a few inches each time.

If she grew much longer—or wider—she would need to find a new lair and a new cave for her hoard. As it was, when she transformed, she had to twist and contort herself to fit among and around her accumulated belongings. She also had to take special care to end up with her wedge-shaped head and her forelegs near her bedroom's only window. Turning around inside the crowded space wasn't impossible—she was a flexible dragon—but it was awkward, and used up precious Episode time.

The bedroom window of her ground floor apartment didn't overlook the parking lot, nor did it open on the breezeway. Instead, the window gave her a view of the empty, sloping bit of grass behind the apartment complex that bordered on the highway that ran behind the complex. She saw that view, though, only during the few minutes after the start of an

Episode when she had pushed the venetian blinds aside on her way out of her bedroom. The rest of the time, the blinds were down. Thara had taken the screen off the window long ago, and several times since, when some overachieving apartment managers had replaced it.

Her back half was still stretching and flexing, such as it could within the close confines of her hoard, while her front half was raised, head turned so she could get a clear view with her left eye. Her right foreclaw held up the venetian blinds while her left foreclaw, index claw extended, worried at the human-sized locks that kept the window from opening. Under normal circumstances, she would have opened the locks before transforming. That hadn't been an option this time.

She had opened the second lock when the earthquake struck.

She roared in surprise and frustration as the ground tried to escape from underneath her. During the long seconds of the world shaking, she was able to keep most of her floor-to-ceiling shelving units and bakers racks upright, but with only four claws it was impossible to stop those shelves and racks from dumping their contents on her. Nor was she able to stop the pillars of stacked boxes and plastic containers from toppling, first at the top, then at the bottom, as those normally universal positions tried to reverse themselves.

When the shaking finally stopped, her forward ten feet or so were still upright and aligned with the normal gravitational pull. From her elongated waist to the tip of her tail, though, was twisted around. Her rear legs were holding up separate shelves, one containing her mother's collection of 45 RPM records among other invaluables, while her tail managed to keep a rack of vintage high-fidelity components, including her father's old turntable, from becoming a pile of spare parts and broken vacuum tubes.

"The old female grows adroit," she muttered, quoting a novel she had read long ago. Her hardcover, first edition copy of *West of Eden* by Harry Harrison, complete with original dust jacket, was on a built-in shelf in her bedroom's walk-in closet, along with every other hardcover book she had ever purchased. At least, she hoped the books were still on their shelves.

She would check on her books in due time, straighten them, dust them if they needed it. First, though, she had to do the same thing for everything else she owned. Including her Outdoor Babies.

She waited a full sixty seconds after the shaking subsided before she trusted *terra* to again be *firma*. Then she began the slow, careful process of realigning the twisted portions of her long body without causing any additional damage to her belongings. In dragon form, her back legs and claws were as flexible and prehensile as her front. So she was able to use her feet as well as what she would normally consider her hands to put things back on their shelves at the same time as she maneuvered herself back into position to go out the window.

She hooked her front claws in the frame of the window and—

The window was jammed.

She tried again, a little more firmly.

She stopped trying when she felt the metal in the window frame want to buckle.

She stopped herself from roaring again, this time in frustration, since frustration roars usually came with fire, and there were a lot of flammables packed in around her. Then she stopped herself from ripping the window out of its frame or smashing her way through the glass. Getting the manager to replace the glass in her bedroom window wasn't a chore she wanted to face again.

There was no help for it. She was going to have to be flexible. And she was going to have to hope Tina had already left for work.

She turned her head around so she was facing backward, then began flexing her body, from the base of her neck to the tip of her tail. She preferred not to think she was crawling like a snake back over her own body, though she was pretty sure that was exactly what she was doing. She also hated when the spikes of her crest rubbed against the ceiling and created a dribbling, dusty rain of bits of popcorn ceiling on her face. The nictitating membranes of her eyes snapped closed. Her nostrils snapped closed as well after the first inhalation of dust. She snuggled her head down into her own back, so she wouldn't be damaging her ceiling further. And so she could breathe. She could hold her breath quite a while during an Episode, but it tended to cause her internal temperature to rise, which tended to make her breath explode when she started breathing again. There was nothing in her hoard she wanted to burn.

It took her ten minutes to turn around, with her head at the bedroom door and her body twisting behind her through the suddenly messy maze of her hoard. She would be back to straighten up after she had checked on her Outdoor Babies.

She had to squeeze the claws of her "index finger" and "thumb" to turn the deadbolts back. The door lever, though, was easy, she only had to put her claw on it and push down, like the velociraptors in the laserdisc copy of *Jurassic Park* that she hoped was still in its cardboard sleeve, on its shelf with the other laserdiscs, in the walk-in closet.

She paused before she opened the door, listening for Tina.

For the first time she realized how noisy the world had become since the earthquake. She heard sirens and car horns and car alarms. She heard people shouting. She heard dogs barking, cats meowing, and... somethings... skittering. She didn't hear Tina.

She couldn't wait any longer. Her Outdoor Babies needed her. Tina, if she was still around, would just have to come to grips with having a dragon walk through the living room.

She pushed down on the door lever, then pulled the door open. She flowed around the door and out of her bedroom, then around the corner and into the living room. When her rear legs were clear of the door, she whipped her tail out of the way and used her left rear claw to pull the door closed. There was no time to finagle the keys and lock the doors. She didn't plan to be gone long.

She saw no sign of Tina. Which was good. She wasn't sure she could have handled having the girl stand there screaming while she did the two-finger tweezer-claws thing on the deadbolt of the front door. Then try to wrap two twelve-inch-long, golden-clawed "fingers" around the doorknob and pull it open. Someday she needed to swap out the interior doorknob of the front door for the more useful door lever.

She rushed out into the breezeway, pulling the door closed behind her, this time with her tail. She didn't care if she slammed her front door.

Her claws made scratching noises on the concrete of the breezeway. She nosed a woman out of the way and ignored the resulting screams as she went to see her Outdoor Babies.

Something small, with more legs than she expected, jumped at her as she emerged from the breezeway. Whatever it was, she caught it with her mouth and crunched it as she ran. Then did the same thing with another one. She had no idea what the things were. Eating them had been instinctive, a reflex. She hoped they weren't dogs. Or cats. They didn't taste like either, but she didn't have time to stop and consider the culinary possibilities.

Her Outdoor Babies were her most vulnerable possessions, since she couldn't fit them in her bedroom with the rest of her hoard. The apartment manager she had approached, twenty years ago, with the idea of converting one of her two bedrooms into a garage had been very closed-minded about the idea.

Louie and Howie were parked together in the two spaces closest to the breezeway. Nova had been parked with them, but the car's most recent from-and-to towing had left her farther away. Thara had been planning to have Nova pushed back into place, next to Howie, but hadn't arranged that yet.

Louie, the 1964 Volkswagen Beetle, had been her first car, and the last gift her father had given her. While Louie's original light blue paint had faded to a blueish white over the years, his white interior had gone the other direction, becoming darker with age. His engine hadn't turned over since 1992, but she no intention of ever giving him up. She had driven him until 1983, when the cost of repairs had finally exceeded the cost of a used car. Maybe if she had taken shop class in high school instead of home economics, she might've become a career mechanic instead of a career waitress, and maybe Louie would still be drivable. Such maybes accumulated with the decades, of course, and she tried not to dwell on them.

Howie, the 1979 Mercury Bobcat, somehow managed to look older than Louie. The scratches on his hood had rusted, and the brown paint had taken on a similar color. The once-sporty pinstriping had faded from orange to a dusty pink. Howie had come into her life as a used car, and from the sloppy bodywork done on the front right fender, he had been in at least one accident before she took him in. As a means of transportation from one place to another, Howie had lasted six years, until the cost of his daily quart of oil became prohibitive. Howie's engine had probably rusted itself solid. The last time he had been started had been 1991. Like Louie, though, she had no plans to get rid of him.

The two cars were still in their herringbone parking spaces, though they looked like they had been parked by a cross-eyed valet with inner ear issues. She nudged both cars back into square with the diagonal lines of their parking spaces, crunched and swallowed two more of the many-legged things that threw themselves at her—by the fourth one, she was reasonably certain the creatures weren't dogs or cats or any other typical pet—then went to check on Nova.

She had found Nova, a dark red 1985 Plymouth Omni, the day after Howie last sputtered into smoky silence. Nova's dark red paint had become a sort of maroon over the years, but was rust-free. The driver side window used to be noticeably less marred than the others. That window had been smashed in a robbery before Thara owned the car. These days, though, there was no discernible difference between the windows. Except the bright orange tow sticker on the windshield.

Like Louie and Howie, Nova had been shifted out of alignment with her parking space. Thara fixed that with a few gentle head bumps, then focused on the tow sticker.

All of her Outdoor Babies attracted tow stickers and generated complaints from the apartment management and other tenants. Nova attracted the most attention, though, her boxy body shape and fading paint job giving her that most-hated of car looks: 1980s subcompact. Most of the time, Thara could either get rid of the stickers or bribe the tow truck drivers when they appeared. Sometimes, though, she had to have the vehicles retrieved from impound. Not this time, though.

Thara pulled the front half of her body onto Nova's hood, her claws carefully placed so they wouldn't scratch the paint, and so the weight of her upper body wouldn't dent the hood. Then she licked the orange tow sticker off Nova's windshield.

With a grimace at the taste—the paper and its sticky glue tasted much better than the layer of dust and grime underneath it and around it, but combined with the taste of whatever kept jumping into her mouth, it was all nasty—she turned to her left and spit the sticker out. It left a stream of smoke in the air and puffed into ash before it reached the next car.

There would almost certainly be a new tow sticker soon, but Thara had a razor blade scraper in her apartment to take care of it when it happened.

She had ignored the shouts and screams as she took care of her Outdoor Babies. She was used to those. Once she had stopped screaming at her horrible visage, it was easy to stop paying attention when other people did it. They would get over it. Or go away. Or—

It was the flashes from camera phones that caught her attention.

Or, these days, people would pull out their phones and start taking pictures and videos. No one stood near her, but there was a circle of people standing along the edges of the parking lot, cowering behind cars but holding their phones up.

She roared for the cameras, letting a bit of blue-and-white flame leak out to light up the night and create flares in their video. From seeing a handful of such videos, she knew the streetlamps of the parking lot were hardly generating enough light for their video to show much more than a dark, glittering shape. The sound of her roar would be like static, and the light of her flame would give a quick, tantalizing glimpse that they could freeze and blow up and use to amaze their more gullible friends.

Usually, though, when she was caught on camera, she wasn't so close to her lair. And her hoard.

She roared again, less entertainingly and far more convincingly, and charged away from her apartment, toward the main entrance of the complex.

She had been careful to leave no scratches on Nova, but she had no such reservations about other people's cars. She gleefully ran up their hoods, over their cabs and down their trunks, leaving scratches and dents in her wake. People scattered, screaming again, some of them dropping their phones in their hurry to get out of her way. She ended up following one poor guy because he chose the wrong direction to flee. When she caught up to him, she tucked her head down, swept his legs from under him, and tossed him to one side. After that, no one and nothing was in her way.

4

THERE WAS LESS TRAFFIC ON Fifty-first Street than Thara expected. What cars and trucks there were had stopped in the middle of the street or pulled to the side. More than a few had run into each other. Their drivers were outside their cars, talking and shouting about non-dragon-related issues when she showed up to change the subject.

She didn't have much of a plan. She just wanted to put some distance between where she was causing a commotion and where she slept and kept her belongings. Ultimately, she wanted to disappear into the shadows, then sneak back to her bedroom and straighten her stuff. She hated it when her bedroom wasn't tidy, when her belongings weren't exactly where she wanted them. Her Outdoor Babies had been taken care of, it was time for the rest of her things to get some post-earthquake tender-dragon-care. First, though, she needed to disappear.

She had expected more attention from the nondriving drivers at her appearance on the street, but they weren't looking at her any longer. They were looking up at the sky, and had their phones pointed the same direction.

She came to halt in the middle of the street as the spikes on her head went rigid.

The first thing she noticed was that the stars overhead weren't as stationary as they should have been. Instead, the stars swirled and trailed comet tails in a slowly shrinking orbit around a black funnel that filled the sky to the south and east. The black funnel seemed to reach down from the cosmos overhead, the spinning black finger of a god reaching out to touch the Earth.

Her saucer-sized eyes blinked all their layers of eyelids at the sight and the tiny bones of her inner ear struggled against the sense of disorientation generated by forces that tried to interrupt the rotation of the Earth itself. She gripped the asphalt of the street to steady herself.

The wind picked up. With the wind came the sound of voices, chanting. There were no words, only sharp, staccato bursts of sounds, almost white noise. Human voices, but touched with inhuman meanings. She found herself surprised that any sounds were able to escape that vortex. These voices, though, seemed to be feeding the vortex, adding to it. Preparing the way. Offering the world to the god of the vortex. Inviting the end of the world.

She thought she heard gunshots in the direction of the black funnel.

Run away, little one! Hide!

Like the voices on the wind, these words bypassed her ears. She heard them only in her mind. A man's voice, shouting at her with surprise and fear, hope and terror.

Go! I will find you after!

Thara pulled her eyes from the swirling black funnel. She looked around, but saw no one even looking at her. Everyone was staring up at the impossible night sky, the same as she had been.

Then all she could hear was a roar that hit her like a physical blow, a hammer falling on her from the sky.

She looked up at the sky again and roared back, the automatic reaction of an apex predator surprised to discover competition. Inspired by the roar that surprised her, but also needing to show she was not as impressed as she knew she was, she let her own roar loose in a way she never had before. The bladder under her throat swelled, her chest expanded. She let the blue flame of her internal fire go white hot.

The sky above her shook. The insulation of the power lines that stretched over the street melted under the onslaught, then the twisted copper strands melted and fell away. Sparks flew.

She almost scared herself.

The voice in her head was not as impressed.

This is not your time, little one! Go! Hide!

She heard the words in her mind just as the creature that sent them to her appeared in the sky above her.

Silver wings stretched wide enough to block her view of the vortex and the stars it had captured. The wings, each of them the length of two Cadillac Escalades, beat against the air, creating a flurry. Her eyes twisted in their independent sockets trying to take in what they could see. Something she had never expected to see.

A dragon.

Silver, at least twice her length and four times her mass, but unmistakably a dragon. Defying the physics of unpowered flight and—literally—flying in the face of everything Thara had been told and believed. The dragon tucked its wings and swooped at her.

I said GO!

The roar that accompanied the words shook the asphalt free of Thara's grip. There was no fire in the roar, but Thara's nostrils twitched at the hints of methane and sulfur in the rush of air.

Thara went.

She ran away from the street, toward the nearest office buildings and the shadows their multistory superstructures provided. As she ran, she could think of only two things: the dragon flapping and roaring in the air overhead, and her father.

She wasn't alone.

Poppa was wrong.

5

"It's OK, Goose," Poppa said, as they drove away from Nancy Chisum's house. "It will all be OK."

Thara sat on the front seat of Poppa's 1957 Chevrolet Bel Air Sport Sedan, feeling very small. She stayed close to the car door, looking out the rolled-down window but not seeing the houses that passed. She doubted anything was going to be OK ever again. The summer had been fresh and new the night before, a long, warm vacation from school. Less than twenty-four hours later, summer had been ruined.

"Nancy hates me," she told the open window. "Everybody hates me."

"They don't hate you, Goose," Poppa said. Poppa always called her Goose. She was Golden Goose some days, and Silly Goose others, and on the days when *he* was feeling like a silly goose, he called Momma Mother Goose. Most of the time, though, Momma was Momma and Thara was just Goose. There was nothing silly in his tone that day. "You just... caught them off guard. They weren't expecting... what happened."

Thara hadn't been expecting it either.

Nancy Chisum's pajama party had come to an awkward end that morning. The other girls had decided that Nancy and Thara's "little joke," as Lorraine Reed put it before she left with her parents, had been in "very poor taste."

Nancy had been just as scared as the rest of the girls when it happened. For that matter, so had Thara. Thara had convinced herself that the incident in the bathtub on her birthday had been only a dream. She had told Nancy about the dream, because she told Nancy

33

everything, and Nancy told her everything. They were best friends. Which was why all the other girls thought Nancy had been in on the surprise. So she and Nancy had been ostracized together, but they had not been together.

Yesterday, Thara had been feeling funny all afternoon, even before Momma left her at Nancy's house. Tingly, all over. Almost itchy. Momma had frowned when Thara told her this, and checked Thara quite thoroughly for a rash or other allergic reactions. Finding nothing, Momma asked if Thara wanted to stay home. But Thara most definitely was not going to miss her best friend's first pajama party of the summer, so she told her mother it was nothing. She was better. Completely fine.

Except she wasn't fine. The tingling only got worse. It was especially bad on her fingertips, and her toes. And down her back. She could hunch over and wiggle to make her shirt rub against her spine, but how do you scratch your fingertips? She settled for rubbing them against her shirt too.

She made herself stop scratching during the short walk to Nancy's house with Momma. Later, as the evening continued, she had to make herself stop again. At least she wasn't leaving scratch marks on her skin. The other girls would have definitely noticed that and wanted to know what was up, especially when they changed into their one-piece swimsuits and splashed in the wading pool in Nancy's backyard.

The water had been deliciously cold, and they had splashed it everywhere, the little droplets sparkling in the nearly horizontal sunshine just before dark. Little girl laughter and screams had echoed between the nearly identical white houses of the neighborhood. No matter how much water poured into the plastic wading pool, the girls splashed it out. Mr. Chisum gave up trying to regulate how much water the girls used. He left the water running, with Nancy in charge of the long rubber hose, and went inside.

Then, as the sun disappeared, leaving only a yellow-blue twilight behind, had come the breath-holding contest.

Nancy borrowed her father's watch, and the girls took turns lying in the wading pool and letting the water cover their faces. When it was Thara's turn, the time to beat was Lorraine's one minute and thirteen seconds.

Thara lay back in the water. She let her hands float alongside her body. For the first time that night she felt no tingling urge to scratch. The cool water soothed away the itch.

She opened her eyes underwater and was surprised at the clarity. The world above her swayed and bent with the motion of the water, but she could see almost as clearly as she could normally. She could see the metal end of the water hose where it hung over the side of the pool. She could see the mild distortion that indicated water was still flowing out of the hose.

Above her, the twilight sky had become a deepening blue, and the first stars glinted like tiny sparks. No matter how still the water became as she held her breath, the stars continued to dance, though always staying within the confines of their gradually appearing constellations. The Milky Way was so bright it actually looked as if God had splashed a cup of cold milk across the curtain of the sky.

The faces of Nancy and Lorraine and the other girls formed a ring above her, looking down at her in the water. Nancy held her father's watch in her right hand, her eyes moving from Thara's face to the face of the watch, back and forth. Slowly at first, but with every increasing frequency.

Thara realized some portion of her brain had been counting seconds, and she knew when she had been holding her breath for a minute. She noticed Lorraine Reed frowning down at her as that girl's record time approached then passed. Thara smiled up at her.

Thara's first sign that something had happened, just before the tingling returned to her skin, was Lorraine's petulant frown disappearing into a look of open mouth confusion. Just before the water in the wading pool began to boil around her.

Thara pushed herself up with her hands and feet and came out of the steaming water like the eruption of an underwater volcano.

She heard the screaming of little girls again, but this time there was no joy in the screaming, and no laughter. The girls ran away from her as she fell forward, her body half in and half out of the pool, the plastic ridge of the pool pressing against her stomach.

Then she screamed as she saw the knobby elongated, golden-scaled and golden-clawed fingers of her hands on the ground in front of her. Her eyes swiveled in their sockets and she could see almost 360 degrees around her. Her tongue flicked out and she could taste the sweat and fear of the girls she could see running away. In the pool behind her, her tail thrashed back and forth, spilling more water over the sides as the hose next to her tried to keep it full. She curled her neck to look down at herself and saw she still wore her swimsuit, but it had been stretched and distorted by the new shape of her body.

She spun around, getting back into the pool.

Nancy still stood by the side of the pool, holding her father's watch, staring at Thara with her eyes wide and her jaw trembling.

"It's me!" Thara said, but her voice was both hissy and bubbly and steam came out of her mouth as she spoke. "Nancy! It's me, Thara!"

The tingling washed over her body again, from crest to tail tip, and she *was* her again. Thara, ten-year-old girl, propped on her arms in the swimming pool, her legs behind her. She felt her swimsuit relaxing back into place, though still uncomfortably tight between her legs, and the water too hot on her skin.

"It's just me," Thara said. This time with her normal voice.

She pulled her legs under her and stood, though somewhat shakily. "See? It's me?"

She tugged on her swimsuit to adjust it. At least it hadn't torn.

"What's going on?" Mr. Chisum stood inside the big sliding glass door that opened into the kitchen. "What's all the screaming?"

Thara turned around, suddenly self-conscious. She saw that the other girls had stopped running away and were coming back, if slowly.

"I," Thara started. "I guess I scared them. I... I came up out of the water like... like Godzilla. King of the Monsters." She had seen the movie at the drive-in with her parents.

Mr. Chisum's expression softened and his lopsided grin appeared. "Oh, OK then. It sounds like you got them pretty good."

Thara glanced back at Nancy. "Yeah, I did."

Mr. Chisum looked up at the sky. "I guess it's time this party moved indoors," he said. "Come on in, Nancy. Your mother's got the living room ready."

Nancy managed a nervous laugh, and nodded. None of the other girls laughed, though, as they went inside. They kept looking at Thara and walked wide of her.

If it had just been the incident in the wading pool, the pajama party might have still been considered a success.

Nancy's mother had pushed the furniture of the small living room aside to make space for all the girls' bed rolls and sleeping bags. Lorraine moved hers from beside Thara's and took up position on the loveseat.

Thara wanted to take Nancy aside, to apologize, but her friend would only shake her head when Thara got her attention.

During the short-lived game of Monopoly, Lorraine looked at Thara and said, "You were wearing a mask, right?"

Thara nodded, seizing on the idea with more enthusiasm than it deserved. "Right. I was wearing a mask. I put it on while I was under the water. Then... it was funny, right?"

Some of the other girls forced a laugh, but Lorraine's tight-lipped expression didn't look like much of a smile.

Thara was the last of the girls to nod off to sleep. She thought—she hoped—that was the end of it.

She remembered a nightmare. She was a fifty foot tall lizard-dragon, trying to get her family and friends to stop running away as she accidentally crushed their houses and cars by stepping on them and set fire to everything with the fire that kept spraying out of her mouth when she tried to explain—

She awoke to Lorraine Reed's screaming. She opened her eyes to Lorraine pointing at her and stumbling away backward, tripping over Nancy.

Thara tried to stand, but her arms and legs were all the wrong lengths and bent the wrong way. Plus, coming suddenly out of the dream, she was disoriented. She seemed to think she was bigger than she was, much bigger, and the living room around her and the girls beginning to wake up looked tiny, almost toylike.

Her back legs were caught in her pajama bottoms. The golden hooks that should have been her toenails had pierced the fabric of the pant legs and threatened to shred them if she moved too quickly.

The claws on her hands scratched the hardwood floor of the living room, then got caught in Nancy's sleeping bag.

She shook the sleeping bag off her claws, leaving little hoops of snagged thread dangling from the material.

More girls screamed.

She managed to pull herself along the floor, heading for the short hallway that connected the living room to the three bedrooms and the only safety Thara could think of: the bathroom.

She made it, without causing additional damage to her pajama bottoms, and only trailing one calico print bedroll—she could never remember whose it was—into the bathroom with her. She had to push the bathroom door closed with her head.

She lay on the linoleum floor of the bathroom with her head still propped against the door so no one could open it. No one tried.

She heard Mr. and Mrs. Chisum leave their bedroom.

After a few minutes, there was a knock on the bathroom. "Thara?" It was Mrs. Chisum. "Is everything OK?"

"Yes," Thara managed to say. The hissing in her throat extended the 'ess' sound, making her sound like a cartoon snake. "Yes," she lied again, with better, more human-like enunciation. "I'm fine."

Thara flexed the elongated fingers of her left hand in front of her face. She hoped her claws hadn't scratched either the hardwood floor or the linoleum.

After asking her again if everything was OK, and being lied to again, Mrs. Chisum went back to her bedroom. Thara heard her talking softly with Mr. Chisum. She realized she could have listened to what they said, but if she did that, she would also hear what her friends in the living room were saying. So she let the whispers and murmurs remain whispers and murmurs as she cried hot tears that steamed when they dripped on the floor.

She didn't come out of bathroom until Mr. Chisum woke her at the first light of dawn by almost walking in on her. She was human, at least, and still wearing her pajamas when that happened.

Under Mr. Chisum's curious gaze, she straightened her pajamas and went back to the living room dragging the borrowed calico sleeping bag with her. She dropped the sleeping bag, then stepped over the sleeping forms of the other girls. Several of the girls huddled in one sleeping bag, as if seeking safety in numbers. Nancy slept alone on her bed roll, with a space of bare hardwood floor around her, as if the other girls had dug a moat and put her on the far side. Thara picked up the dark green sleeping bag Poppa had loaned her for the pajama party. She wrapped the heavy blanket around herself as she sat on the overstuffed chair. She pulled her legs up to her chest to be as small as possible, and dozed off again.

She only picked at the breakfast of pancakes, eggs, and sausage that Mrs. Chisum prepared. None of the girls ate much, and all of them kept glancing at Thara, looking away before she could meet their eyes. They also looked at Nancy, but less furtively.

It seemed like forever before Poppa arrived in his car to pick her up. She hadn't expected that, since they lived only a couple blocks away. As they got in the car, Poppa explained that he had a couple errands he had been putting off, and it was probably time he took care of them.

"It'll be OK," Poppa said again as he drove. "By the time school comes around again, this will all be a wild story. Even if some of the girls still believe it really happened, no one will believe them. And I'm willing to bet you, Goose, right here, right now, on my bottom dollar and my mother's grave, that you and Nancy are best friends again before the end of next week."

Thara was more than dubious, but Poppa proved to be right, as he always was. Lorraine Reed was never her friend again, nor Nancy's, but Thara and Nancy were talking and playing together again before three days had passed.

Lorraine Reed and the other girls convinced themselves that Nancy and Thara had scared everyone with Godzilla movie masks and monster claw gloves. Nancy, though, embraced her friend Thara-the-part-time dragon with enthusiasm. Their games around the neighborhood that summer prominently featured dragons and knights in armor, sometimes battling it out, sometimes fighting side by side against the evils of Communism. When he learned about their interest in dragons, Nancy's father let them read his original copy of *The Hobbit*.

But that was all in the future. That day, on her way to the hardware store with Poppa, Thara was convinced she was going to be alone and friendless for the rest of her life. Then she realized no one had told Poppa what had happened. He had merely appeared, knocking on the front door, and after greeting the Chisums with a smile and a handshake, Poppa and Thara had left.

Thara looked at Poppa. "Did... did they call you?"

"No," Poppa said. "I saw it in your face, and the faces of everyone there. Something happened."

Thara nodded. Something had happened. Something had definitely happened.

Poppa sighed. "I should have been paying more attention, especially after your birthday, but it's been 'summer' for weeks now. I forgot about the Solstice."

"You know about what... happened... on my birthday?"

Poppa smiled and glanced at her as he navigated a turn. "Well, now I do. It was just a suspicion before. Since you never talked about it, Momma and I weren't sure." He paused. "You know, you can talk to Momma and I about anything, right? Anything at all?"

Thara nodded again. She knew. Because they kept telling her. They never told her *how* she was supposed to talk to them about "anything, anything at all," though. For example, how did you tell your parents, *I just turned into a lizard, but I'm all better now?* They had never included that part.

"Good," Poppa said. "So, Goose," he added after a long stretch of silence, "this may come as something of a surprise, but you're a dragon."

Thara sighed and slumped.

"That's not the response I expected."

Thara sighed again. It seemed more final when Poppa said it, even if she already knew. "That's what Nancy said. Not last night, but when I told her about what... what happened on my birthday, in the bathtub. I told her I turned into a lizard. She said I turned into a dragon."

"So you told Nancy?"

Thara nodded.

"But not us?" Poppa sighed this time. "I shouldn't be surprised. In any case, I guess she got to see it firsthand last night? Bit more of a surprise in person?"

"She's never going to speak to me again."

"She'll get over it, I promise."

"I don't want to be a dragon."

"If that's true, I have bad news for you, Goose." He turned to look at her. "You're still a dragon."

Thara crossed her arms over her chest and looked straight ahead. "It's not fair, Poppa."

"I'm sure it's better than being a lizard," he said. "Who wants to be a lizard?"

She didn't talk as she considered the implications of being a dragon. She was still a month away from reading *The Hobbit*, and Walt Disney's *Sleeping Beauty* wouldn't come out for another year, so she didn't have a lot of mental references for *dragon* at that time. She could only think of the fairy stories Nancy liked, and dinosaurs like Godzilla in the drive-in movies Momma and Poppa liked, and the regrettable fate of the dragon killed by St. George.

"Are you and Momma dragons?"

Poppa's smile became pensive. "No, Goose. No such luck."

Thara sat up straight and turned to face him on the big front seat. "Was I adopted?"

"Being a dragon makes you sad, but being *adopted* gets you excited?"

"Was I adopted?"

The smile disappeared as Poppa's lips pressed together into a thin line. "No," he said. "We have been your parents since... the beginning."

"Then how am I dragon?"

The smile made a comeback and Poppa looked at her from the side of his eye. "There's still some magic left in the old world, Goose, even now."

Thara's eyes got wide. Not being adopted was something of a disappointment, but Nancy talked about magic all the time. She more than talked about magic. She *believed* in magic. Maybe, if Thara really was magic, Nancy would talk to her again. Momma and Poppa, though, had never said anything about magic. Or, for that matter, dragons.

"Are there more dragons?" she asked.

"No," Poppa said. His smile faded as he sighed. His voice became wistful as he added, "Unfortunately, Goose, you're the last dragon."

Through nearly sixty years of Episodes, Thara had never encountered another dragon, so there had never been any reason to think Poppa was wrong.

6

MISSING POPPA MORE THAN SHE had in years, and more frightened than she had been in decades, Thara made her serpentine way back to her apartment. A second earthquake struck as she sneaked through the shadows behind the lights that illuminated I-44, but she hardly felt it. This earthquake was at least a category below the first, and as a life event hardly compared to discovering that Poppa was wrong *and* seeing another dragon. Especially a dragon like that one. No one would mistake that dragon for a big lizard.

Once the initial shock of becoming a dragon every few months wore off, Thara hadn't been scared of much of anything. Even when she had been a smaller dragon, less than ten feet from nose to tail, she had known she was the scariest thing on four legs. She could breathe fire, she could shred steel with her claws, and if she ran into the street, oncoming traffic was in more danger than she was. The last time she had flinched had been at a spray of gunfire from a semiautomatic pistol in 1977. The bullets had stung, and left welts still visible the next day on her human form, and she had suffered indigestion from eating the handgun, but that was it for consequences.

Tonight, though, she had been reminded of what it was like to be afraid. And not just that someone might be stupid enough to steal her stuff.

She saw no shame in being afraid. Who wouldn't be afraid of a fifty-foot-long dragon with a seventy-foot wingspan?

Besides the fear, though, there was the total readjustment of her mental model of the universe. Poppa was wrong. She was no longer the last dragon. The ground beneath her physical feet was shaking less than the ground beneath her mental feet.

Poppa was wrong. There was another dragon—

And that dragon was *male*.

Or at least, the voice in her head had been male. She hadn't noticed anything gender-specific about the roar, but the voice in her head had been male. Or seemed male.

She had not had time to properly examine the huge, flying beast that had roared and swooped at her, so she couldn't be one-hundred percent certain. On the other hand, she wasn't one-hundred percent certain she even knew what to look for. Until she encountered definitive proof, though, she would assume the big, silver dragon was male.

Which opened up possibilities that had never existed, and made her more than a little uncomfortable to consider.

As a human, she had been sexually active since the mid 1960s. As a dragon, she had been asexual by default. There had been a couple instances early in her sexual history that might be considered crossover events, but just because she had partially transformed into a dragon before, during or after the act of intercourse didn't mean she had had dragon sex. That the other side of that equation might not agree was irrelevant. She didn't know what the two men—and the one woman—had called what happened or how they remembered it. She had simply called the events embarrassing and never seen any of those people again. Or, in the case of one of the men, he had run away, screaming, and she had never seen him again.

She was pretty flexible as a dragon. Serpentine, even. More than once she had wondered how that might come into play. Or foreplay. Or masturbation—

As a child of what might have been the last generation of American adolescents frightened into abstinence with threats of blindness and hairy palms, she had tried not to think about it too much.

She wished Poppa were here—

She shuddered, uncomfortable again. She wanted to change the topic of conversation in her head, but was also uncomfortable shifting from thoughts about sex, human or dragon, to thinking about Poppa, so she focused on slinking in shadows and not being seen.

Traffic on the interstate was picking up again, post-earthquake. She listened for the sound of huge, leathery wings beating at the air, but could never be certain she heard them again.

A pair of the many-legged, suicidal creatures she had eaten in the parking lot jumped at her from the shadows she wasn't using. She crunched and chewed the one that came at her head, catching it automatically. The other landed on her right hip. She turned her head, flicked her tongue and pulled the creature into her mouth. As she chewed, she glanced at the sky.

Had the dragon tried to follow her? The black funnel was no longer visible, and the stars were drifting back to their regularly scheduled astral positions. Some of the stars appeared to be moving back more reluctantly than others. She wondered if the second earthquake had shaken some sense into the cosmos. As if the first earthquake had tipped over the Cosmic Snow Globe, and the second had picked it up and put it back into its proper place on the Universal Knick Knacks Shelf. Whatever had happened, the visual effect made Thara's head hurt, but not so much that she would have missed seeing a fifty-foot dragon if it were there. It wasn't.

Would it bug her if the dragon had been up there, winging around, following her? Was she disappointed that he wasn't?

She dodged both questions by noticing she was almost home.

She came around to the rear of her apartment complex, which was "guarded" by a six-foot metal fence, a feature added about twenty years ago as both a pretense of security and, more importantly, as a way the new managers could charge more rent. She followed the line of fence to the hole she had created during a particularly pissy Episode not too many weeks after the fence had been put up. Apartment management had inspected the damage, assessed that it couldn't be seen from the parking lots, and decided they didn't care enough to fix it. Which spared Thara the trouble of having to wreck it again.

As she passed through the hole in the fence, she realized she had grown thicker in the intervening years. She was going to have to widen the gap soon. She opted for exhaling and holding her breath as she went through, because she was still at least partially running away from the very large dragon.

She reached her ground floor bedroom window and tested it. The second earthquake must have reshifted whatever structural warping had occurred in the first earthquake, because the window rose smoothly.

She climbed into her bedroom, stepping carefully around her fallen belongings as she twisted her way between the shelves and racks and columns of boxes and containers. Once she was fully inside, she swung her tail behind the venetian blinds and used the tip to push the window closed again, cutting off the sounds of traffic and people in the parking lot. She used the tip again to flick the locks into place. Then she maneuvered so she could reach the deadbolts of her bedroom door and tweezer-twisted those locked, as well.

It occurred to her that the front door of her apartment remained unlocked, but she felt no urge to leave her bedroom. Not yet. As always, her bedroom felt like the safest possible place she could be. Even if the flimsy walls of her apartment suddenly seemed more flimsy than ever, they surrounded her. She was wrapped in a security blanket of drywall and two-by-fours and panel siding that was more blanket than security, but it was home.

Her heart still pounded in her chest, from the exertion of her run home and from the lingering fear and excitement that had sent her running home. The familiar—if messy—environment of her bedroom, even with its flimsy security of window locks and deadbolts, calmed her. Some.

She stood still and took stock, sniffing at the air of her bedroom as her eyes swiveled in their sockets, trying to see everything. The second earthquake didn't seem to have added appreciably to the mess.

Her Episode was less than an hour old, and would probably last until sunrise, but she had no intention of going back outside. Not tonight. Not with the stars wandering around the heavens like lost gods. Not with a dragon that shouldn't exist flying around, probably looking for her. And certainly not with her hoard in such a state.

She had expected an unusually intense Episode tonight. Three weeks and two days late was a lot of pent up dragon steam to blow off. She wouldn't have been surprised to wake in the wreckage of a biker bar on the outskirts of Rio Cruces, hung over and naked, wishing she had taken the time to tape her phone to her leg because she was going to have to find a pay phone to call her a cab. Or hope one of the county firefighters hosing down the wreckage would let her use his phone. They usually did, but she liked using her own phone.

But tonight she was staying in. In a manner of speaking.

She sighed and picked up the white shirt and trousers she had discarded at the beginning of her Episode. They still smelled of sweat, marinara sauce, and, of course, yeasty breadsticks. She folded them and placed them in a stack on the floor by the door. Then she started picking up the rest of her hoard.

She tried not to wonder if the other dragon would be impressed by her hoard. That is, if she ever met him again. And if she decided to let him see it.

2. Chopped Dragon

The Queen

THE QUEEN IN HER KITCHEN felt the presence of the Devourer fade, then disappear, like the winking of a star collapsing in on itself after a brief, unimpressive attempt at going nova.

The Queen had been ready to welcome the Devourer as the God It was—and still, presumably, continued to be behind the Door that had been shut in Its face. She would have been happy to feast on the crumbs that might have dribbled or otherwise escaped Its maw, to gorge Herself alongside the Devourer until, finally, as the final curtain of night was drawn, the Devourer devoured Her. The End of the World, after all, was Her Goal. Her Purpose.

The Queen had been more than willing to share. The World was a big World, and She was only one Queen. She could not possibly eat the whole World by Herself. Not all at once. There would be leftovers. Then there was the rest of the Universe. All those other Worlds, warm and breathing and waiting to be Consumed.

The Devourer certainly would have been a welcome guest, but It was gone now. Even if It might return, the Queen had Her own Plan. Though, after sacrificing so many resources to the Devourer's... (She couldn't bring Herself to consider the Devourer to have *failed*; God's do not *fail*, They *lay the groundwork for future success*)... attempt, Her Plan had suffered setbacks. She would have to rebuild.

The Drones would be happy, of course. She had been holding them off, saving Herself for the Devourer. But the time had come for Her to get back to Her Work. And that meant Making Babies.

She hummed a short song to recover some of her scattered resources before they could slink away. They misunderstood the... unexpected outcome... of the Devourer's attempt. All was not lost, and neither should they be. She needed them to do Her Work.

The Queen flexed her jaws, readied Her ovipositor, and started humming that song that always drove the Drones wild.

The Eldest

The Eldest of His Kind stood in the last shadows after the dawn and blinked against the glare of the Sun as it rose over a World that had not Ended. A World in which he was no longer... the Only.

The Eldest had been the Only for so long he had only the vaguest memories of what it was like to be... not the Only.

That the World had not Ended, though, was not from any direct effort on his part. Until he had seen the Child, he had only circled the End, allowing its influence to keep him in its orbit, using his strength only to maintain his distance. This was not the End he had known was Coming. It was too early. But it might have been *an* End.

An End to a World the Eldest did not recognize. A World where the Eldest had been the Only for too, too long. A World the Eldest had decided he was content to see End, if only because the End would mean he would not be the Only.

Then the Eldest had sensed the Child.

The Eldest had not stopped the End of the World. That had been accomplished by others, without his assistance. But he had been ready to help, if needed. Because of the Child.

The World had not Ended. And he was no longer the Only. Avoiding the gaze of the Sun, the Eldest set off to find the Child.

The Bug

WHEN THE SHAKING AND SLIDING of the earthquake subsided, the Bug enjoyed his new view. The same cars and buildings, of course, including the Two Ugly Replacements, but in a new, more chaotic configuration that appealed to the Bug in a way he didn't completely understand. Plus, he almost never saw this many drivers anymore.

The First Ugly Replacement's discomfort in the aftermath of the earthquake was as plain as the scratched and faded tan paint on his hood. The Second Ugly Replacement was further away, her blank and bland face no longer in the Bug's direct line of sight. Which was OK with the Bug.

The Bug also enjoyed the slightly naughty thrill of being parked so obviously out of skew with the fading white lines that delineated his parking space. The Bug had been left in gear, with his emergency brake engaged, but the shaking had managed to spin him a bit to the left, causing his driver side front wheel to almost touch the white line and encroach on the First Ugly Replacement's parking space. His arched wheel well and curved bonnet were mere inches from the First Ugly Replacement. The Bug always looked like he was smiling, no matter how he really felt. Now, though, he actually was smiling, inside and out.

Most of the cars in the parking lot had been moved around the same way, which took away some of the nonconformist thrill. In fact, the entire lot looked as if the various drivers had simply pulled in and parked wherever and however, and were now standing around trying to figure out who was to blame.

The parking lot was usually such a boring place, and the Bug had been in this parking lot for a while now, looking at the same cars and buildings, watching the same infrequently seen drivers come and go, with only brief, irregularly timed outings to and from the impound lot.

Or maybe the whole shaking thing just reminded the Bug of his long-passed California youth. It had been decades since he had been in a real earthquake.

1

"Dragon Hunter Wanted! No Experience Necessary! Call..."

Marcus Nelson leaned back in his chair and dialed the phone number that accompanied the job listing, wondering as he did how much he was about to be punked by whoever answered. If anyone answered. The listing, which had shown up only moments before, had to be someone's idea of a joke. After nearly six months of job hunting, though, Marcus decided he could use a joke.

Marcus sat in the tiny second bedroom of his mother's apartment, surrounded by the stacked boxes filled with his high school and junior high school paraphernalia, squinting into the too-bright depths of the huge, old CRT monitor that had come with the ten-year-old computer. His mother had purchased the computer for him during his first year of junior high, thinking it would help him become the next Bill Gates or Sergey Brin—or at least a white-collar professional.

"Then I can live off you for a few years," she had said. "Get under your feet for a while, drink your beer out of your fridge. For however long I have left when that finally happens." Then she had added, as she settled in to her spot on the old sofa to watch her shows, "You know I love you, Baby Boy."

It was the middle of the afternoon, but the miniblinds on the bedroom's single window were closed, as always, so the old monitor and the display of his phone were the only sources of light. His old bedside lamp was perched on a shelf with his small collection of trophies, dust-free, but not plugged in.

He rubbed his left hand back and forth over his freshly shaved head and glanced from the phone in his right hand to the monitor again, making sure he had dialed the right number. On his old clamshell phone, the buttons had been actual buttons, so he always dialed the correct number. When the "button" was just a circle drawn on a high-resolution display, though, he had to be more careful.

He had purchased this new phone as a graduation present for himself. The phone had more pixels in its tiny screen, as well as a faster processor, than the old computer with its tower CPU and CRT monitor. He had told his mother to give the computer away the last time she moved, but she had told him then, as she had told him many times before, that she had paid "too damn much" for "that computer" to get rid of it while it still worked, even if no one was using it.

"Besides," she had added, "how am I going to do my taxes if I don't have a computer?" She had said that in the spring of every year for the last ten years, but she still did her taxes by hand.

She hadn't even unpacked the computer after she moved, just like she hadn't plugged in the lamp or even put his old twin bed back together. She had told him he could do both those tasks himself when he moved back in with her after graduation.

"You weren't here then, Baby Boy, but you're here now. Knock yourself out. Put that college diploma to some kind of use."

His mother called the apartment's second bedroom "his" room, but in reality it was just storage, for both his past and hers. Marcus hadn't been that eager to revisit his past, so all he had done was set up the computer. In the months since he had come home after graduating from college, he had been sleeping on the sofa in the living room, using one of the old pillows to even out her spot in the middle. His mother didn't mind. Too much.

"Reminds us both this isn't supposed to be permanent," she said. Except for those weeks, like the current week, when she was on the late shift and he was still asleep when she came home. On those mornings, he moved himself and his blanket to the recliner, because after a long shift she desperately wanted to sit in her spot, lift her feet, and watch some TV.

The fan on the old computer was loud enough to drown out the sounds of his mother in the living room and the TV she had running all the time she was home. He preferred to use his laptop, but at the moment his laptop was open and running on the coffee table in the living room, where it was mining diamonds, emeralds, and rubies for his mother, in blocks of three, four and five. He should never have introduced his mother to match-three games. Certainly not on his laptop. When he reminded her that he needed to be looking for jobs, she reminded him that the computer she paid so damn much for was in his bedroom and he could use that one.

"And it's not like you paid for this one," she would add. Because she could remember his scholarships when it suited her.

He sat up as he listened to the call connect, and positioned his left hand back over the old computer's keyboard. He doubted anyone would even answer the phone, but if someone did, he might need to use his one-handed typing skills to make notes. He could type one-handed as fast some of his former classmates could hunt-and-peck with both hands. Computer keyboards like this one were still mechanical enough that his fingertips could find their way on their own.

He was sure, though, the number would be some kind of automated voice messaging system wanting to let him know about the exciting benefits of male enhancement supplements or something equally stupid. Or some sales job, where the only "dragons" he would be hunting were old friends he could convince to help him out by listening to his pitch for a combination water filter, invisible dog collar, and torture-free squirrel repellent. He more than half hoped it would be some local click-farming recruiter who wanted him to play some fantasy game for twelve hours a day. Make-money-on-the-internet-while-having-fun! "Fun" meaning clicking on the same four spots on the screen over and over doing some ridiculously simple task that was the modern equivalent of picking cotton and being paid by the bale at the end of the day, but without the heavy bags. At least it would be a job doing something with a computer and the internet. At his current job, the closest he came to working on a computer was when he rang up a customer using the store's point-of-sale system.

To his surprise, the call was answered on the first ring.

"Yes? Hello?"

Not a voice messaging system then, but not much better. The voice sounded like a middle-aged white man. The kind of man who would be on the other side of a desk in a bland cubicle or small, bland office, blandly smiling as he pretended to review Marcus's resume while both of them knew he was just trying to pick which version of don't-call-us-we'll-call-you-thank-you-for-coming-in he would recite. So far, then, this punking call was exactly like every other job interview Marcus had been on in the past five months. But he had to try. To at least pretend to take it seriously.

Marcus sat up straight. "I'm calling about your job posting," he said, keeping his voice positive and businesslike. Negro white. Bright, educated and articulate. As if this whole thing wasn't a joke and he didn't know how it was going to end. "The one on Craigslist," he added. In case this was a punking, he wasn't going to actually *say* he was calling about a "dragon hunter job" into a microphone.

"Do you have the experience we requested?"

Marcus glanced at the job listing on his screen again. His sense of *déjà vu* was increasing, as was his sense that he was being punked. "It says no experience necessary."

He waited for the male enhancement supplements pitch to begin.

"So it does," the void said, sounding oddly amused. "Do you believe in dragons?"

Marcus paused. Maybe he was wrong about the male enhancement supplements and the pimp-your-friends sales job recruitment. Maybe this was some lonely podcaster's attempt to generate content, recording the stupid people who will dial any number they find on the Web next to the word "dragon."

"Sure," he said. He would play along, for now, but he still wouldn't say the word "dragon." Just in case.

"Very good. Excellent, in fact. Can you begin work immediately?"

Marcus paused again. Should he joke about needing to shine his armor first? Or sharpen his sword, wink-wink-nudge-nudge? Should he ask about the type of dragons he would be hunting, because he didn't want to be hunting any black dragons. Professional courtesy and all that. Or...

"Can you begin work immediately?" the voice asked again.

"Sure, man, I can show up tomorrow, if you want."

"Tomorrow isn't good for us."

Marcus could almost see the apologetic smile. Of course tomorrow wouldn't be good for him to start. This whole thing was a joke. Marcus waited for the punch line.

"There are other preparations in progress," the voice went on. Before Marcus could ask what kind of preparations, the voice asked, "Do you live in Rio Cruces?"

"No, but—" Marcus stopped himself before saying he could borrow his mother's car and drive the two hours to Rio Cruces. Because that would work for punking him almost as well as admitting he had called to apply for a job hunting dragons. Marcus had been thinking of moving to the city, anyway, which was why he happened to be looking at job listings in Rio Cruces when this one showed up. "I can get there."

"Do you have your own transportation?"

"I can get there," he said again. "When do you want me to show up?"

"Friday morning, if you would," the voice said. "If the World has not ended by then, the restaurant will open at eleven, as always. Ask for me."

"Restaurant?" As a punking or a podcast prank call, this wasn't going anything like he expected. Maybe it was some kind of performance art. That bit about the world maybe ending before Friday certainly seemed like a weak attempt at absurdist comedy. "Ask for you? If you don't mind my asking, who are you?"

"My apologies, I was so excited to get your call I forgot to introduce myself."

Marcus continued to refuse to introduce himself.

"I am August Neuland," the voice said. "I am the owner of the Yellow Sign Buffet."

"Buffet, huh?" Marcus said before he could stop himself. "And you need a dragon hunter? What kind of food are you serving at that buffet?"

"Only the best kind. Are you still interested in the job, Mr.... Nelson?" No hint of emotion in the voice. No impatience. Maybe a touch of hesitation before saying his name. Otherwise, just a middle-aged white guy asking a twenty-two-year-old black guy if he wanted to be a dragon hunter. As if the question made perfect sense.

"Well, I'm going to need to cover my transportation costs, and..." Marcus decided to go for it. "And we haven't talked about my rates, or my per diem, or— Wait. How did you know my name?" Even as he asked, the answer came to him. The man must have done a reverse lookup of his phone number while talking. Marcus should have done the same thing before he called, but he had been distracted by the job title.

"A lucky guess, Mr. Nelson." No hesitation in saying his name this time. "Just another indication, a sign, if you will, that we were meant to have this conversation."

"What?"

"The job is yours, Mr. Nelson, if there is still a job to have come Friday morning."

Marcus considered various responses, still trying to process "a sign." He settled on, "Right. If the world doesn't end."

"Exactly, Mr. Nelson."

He decided to roll with it. See where this went. "So is there anything special I should bring?"

"Whatever you choose to bring with you will almost surely be appropriate, Mr. Nelson," the man said. "That is the nature of Fate."

"Fate? What?" He didn't wait for the explanation. "Don't you even want to see my resume? My references?" Not that either one was anything special, but every other job interview had insisted he bring both, and promised they would keep them "on file." Half his one-page resume was projects he had done in college, the other half was the short list of after school jobs he had had while still in high school. His references were much the same. A couple college professors and two bosses, one current, one retired.

"Yes, you're right," the voice said. "Bring both. We will discuss your rates and your per diem when we meet on Friday."

"OK," Marcus said. He wasn't sure what else to say.

"I will see that some money is deposited in your bank account this afternoon," the voice said, "to help with your transportation costs. I look forward to meeting you, Mr. Nelson," the voice added before Marcus could tell the man that he wasn't going to be giving out his bank account information. "Have a great week. If the world ends before we meet in person, please know that it has been a pleasure speaking with you."

The call ended.

Marcus had his mouth open to say something, though he wasn't sure exactly what.

If the world ends before we meet... ?

He hit redial. Once again, the call was answered on the first ring.

"Hey—" Marcus started.

"Thank you for calling," said an automated female voice, "but this position has already been filled."

The call ended.

Marcus got the same message the next three times he called.

He stared at his phone, then noticed his Web browser had automatically refreshed the job listings page he had been looking at before. The dragon hunter job listing was no longer there.

His phone buzzed and showed him a text message from his bank. The message informed him that the sum of $500 had been deposited into his account from BORCOK***YELLOWSIGNBUFF.

Marcus put his phone down on the desk next to the keyboard and leaned back in the worn desk chair his mother had purchased with the computer. A reverse lookup of a phone number was one thing. What had just happened was even more outside of "normal" than a job posting for "Dragon Hunter, no experience necessary." And much scarier.

Marcus looked from his phone, to the monitor, then back.

Joke or job? Some kind of elaborate prank by an eccentric millionaire? Some off his rocker hacker?

Who could have found his bank information that quickly? Who would casually throw $500 at him? Or was it all, as the man had said, just Fate?

Either way, Mom Nelson would be happy. For however long the joke went on, Marcus had a job in Rio Cruces, and would be, as she put it, out from under her feet. She would probably tell him she would drive him into Rio Cruces for less than a bus ticket. She might even let him borrow the car for the weekend to drive himself.

On the other hand, Morgan might be willing to drive out and give him a ride back to Rio Cruces. She had already done so, once, over July 4th weekend. That no such weekend road trip had occurred since July 4th was on him, not her. He wouldn't even have to pay Morgan anything. If he covered gas, she would be more than happy. She would also be excited to hear he had a job in the city. Though he wasn't sure how she would respond when she heard the details, such as they were, for this particular job.

He would have to think about that.

He grabbed his checkbook from where it sat next to the monitor, and found a pen. If this was a joke, he thought as he wrote a check for $500, or a prank, and if whoever August Neuland was wanted his money back, let them try to get it back from Mom Nelson.

2

THE WORLD DIDN'T END AS the week moved through its normal sequence of days, so Friday dawned on schedule. Marcus decided that meant his Friday morning appointment with Mr. August Neuland at the Yellow Sign Buffet in Rio Cruces, made Monday afternoon, was still on.

As expected, when Marcus told her about the job—though he left out the part about dragon hunting and the possible punking—and, more importantly, had handed her the check for $500, she had agreed to drive him to Rio Cruces. She had Friday off, anyway, and Saturday. And she wanted to see what kind of restaurant offered $500 signing bonuses to new busboys.

"I'm not going to be a busboy, Mom."

"Then what is this job you're going to go get?"

He wasn't going to lie to his mother, but he wasn't going to tell her *dragon hunter*, either. If he told her, he was sure she would snort in derision, then ask what they were calling "dragons." Then probably suggest they had some kind of infestation and he would be an exterminator, which was definitely not what she had put him through college to be.

"I'm not entirely sure," he said. He had looked up the restaurant online, but found little besides standard business listings with hours of operation and a phone number. He didn't mention that either.

"Uh huh. And you're sure it's not to be a busboy?"

He nodded. "Positive. They couldn't pay me enough to be a busboy."

"I should hope not," she said, scowling. "I put you through four years of college, that ought to land you something better than busboy."

63

Scholarships and a few loans had been far more instrumental in putting Marcus through college, but he knew better than to correct Mom Nelson about anything related to money or his education.

Instead, he said, "Five hundred dollars seems a step in the right direction."

"It's a start," she said. "But just a start. It'll be more of a start once this check clears," she added, folding the check and putting it into her wallet. "I'll stop by the bank when I get off shift tomorrow."

The check had cleared by Wednesday.

He talked to Morgan on Wednesday, too, but the conversation never came around to him maybe having a job in the city. When she asked if there was anything new for him, he told her about the blue 1969 Pontiac GTO that had come into the store that day with a For Sale sign in the back window. Unimpressed, she talked about her own new job, working as an entry-level programmer analyst for a health insurance company. Still, when they ended the call an hour later, he said, "Love you." And she replied, "Love you too, Baby Boy." Because she thought it was funny to call him Baby Boy, just like Mom Nelson.

The world didn't end, but it seemed to have tried that Thursday night.

His mother had been getting ready for her shift Thursday night when they heard about the earthquakes in Rio Cruces. They hadn't been able to feel the earthquakes, the news said, because the epicenter was too far away. But for the sake of those who had missed out, the news was more than happy to show jerky, blurry camera phone video of the world shaking and the damage caused.

Earthquakes weren't something Mom Nelson was prepared to deal with, even if she couldn't feel them. So the plan was changed. She would let him take the car to Rio Cruces by himself the next morning, after she came home from her shift.

So at nine in the morning on Friday, with the world not ended, Marcus headed off to Rio Cruces on his own, to see what life would be like as a dragon hunter. Or as a punk who had been lured two hours away to be made fun of. Leaving at nine was cutting it close, but his mother didn't get off her shift until eight, then had to drive home. And she had refused to let Marcus pack the car the night before.

"I am not going to drive around with your dirty underwear in my car," she said.

"I'm not taking any dirty underwear with me."

"Well, don't leave it here. I'm not going to wash it."

Marcus had been doing his own laundry—and hers—since he was ten and was big enough to push quarters into the washers and dryers of the nearest Laundromat. He had forgotten to put soap in once, but Mom Nelson had never forgotten and didn't let him forget. She had had to wash her own clothes while he was away at college, and she hadn't let him forget that either. He resumed family laundry duties the day after graduation.

"Love you, Mom," Marcus said as he kissed her good-bye.

Her hair was escaping the bun she had pinned it in eleven hours before. Her nurse's uniform looked rumpled, and she smelled of antibacterial hand liquid and antiseptic cleaning products, with just a hint of the bodily fluids of the sick and dying. She reached up and put her hands on his cheeks, intensifying the smells enough to make his eyes water.

Her big brown eyes peered into his. "Love you too, crybaby," she said. Then she pulled him close. She hugged him, kissed him on the cheek, and tweaked his nose. "Don't forget," she added, releasing his head to resume his normal height, "I need my car back by noon on Sunday. I'm on evenings next week."

She waved at him from the door of her apartment, but was gone inside and the door closed before he got the car started.

His mother's car, a faded, gunmetal gray Ford Focus from 2003, was four years older than his computer. She had taken reasonably good care of the car, which mostly meant letting Marcus change the oil when he told her it needed doing and agreeing to buy new tires when he pointed out that the previous set had gone bald.

Marcus remembered the day she had bought the car. At only two years used, it had seemed like a brand new car to twelve year old Marcus. Excited, he had learned how to change the oil, rotate the tires, and do other basic maintenance tasks, like his daddy used to do. The Focus hadn't spoken to him the way the old cars his father worked on used to, but he had still felt the connection of man and machine, even if the machine wasn't "pure."

That had been his father's word for the old cars with their rotating distributors and mechanical breaks and accelerator pedals. *Pure*. The Focus hadn't been pure, but it was a car, and Marcus liked to work on it. His mother had been more than happy to let him save her money on oil changes, tire rotations and the occasional break adjustment, but she had been adamant in her refusal to let him become a mechanic.

"I didn't pay so damn much for that computer," she had said, "so you can drop out of school and be a mechanic, like your daddy."

"I'm not dropping out of school, Mom."

"That's right, Baby Boy," she said, nodding. "You're going to graduate, just like I did. But I am not sending you to college to become no mechanic."

"You're not sending me to college. Mr. Ward is confident my test scores will get me a scholarship anywhere in the state I want to go."

"Well, I'm certainly not sending you to some vo-tech school to learn how to take care of a rich man's cars."

"You're not sending me anywhere. It's a scholarship, Mom."

She shook her head. "Your daddy was a mechanic. And look what it got him."

"He died in a car accident, Mom."

"He died poor, Baby Boy, and he left us poor. That's what being a mechanic got him. A poor widow and a poor son."

"We're not poor, Mom. You're a nurse—"

"I am a certified medical assistant," she said, emphasizing each word, the way she did for anyone who made the mistake of calling her a nurse. "And I want better for my only son."

So he attended a nearby four-year university and, as his mother described it to her friends and coworkers, "studied computers." The university was close enough she didn't mind driving him there and back, infrequently, but far enough away he could live on campus. Or off campus, with enough roommates to pay the rent.

As he drove away from the apartment, navigating the streets of his hometown on the way to the highway north, he kept trying to remember if the university had offered a course in How to Get a Job After College. Had he missed that one? All he knew how to do was post his resume, which was mostly just a declaration that he had completed a Bachelor of Science Degree in Computer Information Systems, and send emails to the addresses given in the job listings. He had been doing that for nearly six months, and the result had been a handful of phone interviews with pleasant-sounding human resource employees that asked him about experience he didn't have. The highlights of the endeavor had been three in-person interviews. All the interviews seemed to go great, with lots of positive energy that evidently dissipated as soon as the interviews ended. The one man who had said he would "definitely" call Marcus before the end of the week, had definitely done no such thing.

Still, Marcus hadn't given up. Mom Nelson wouldn't let him.

Even when he landed the part-time job at the local Pep Boys, not as a mechanic, but as a register clerk, so he could help with the rent, she had kept at him.

"You will not get any of the jobs you don't apply for," she had said. "So get in there and apply for more jobs." Then she would monopolize his laptop matching gems.

When Marcus changed the oil, checked the air pressure of the tires, and checked the various belts under the hood on Wednesday, in preparation for Friday's trip, his mother had commented that it was good he knew how to work with his hands, since his mind seemed to be going to waste on her couch. Marcus had ignored her.

The previous week, when he had mentioned an opening on the garage side of the Pep Boys, and since the owner knew him—and had known Marcus's father—he could probably get that job—

"I didn't pay too damn for that computer," she had said, "so you could jockey a register or bend a wrench. You get one of them computer jobs, then you talk to me."

Dragon hunting wasn't looking to be a "computer job," but since it had already paid $500, Mom Nelson was willing to at least not discourage him from seeing how it went. He had also already given up two shifts of work over the weekend, so he was committed. Mostly.

Once he was on the highway, heading north, Marcus switched to one of the Rio Cruces radio stations. The second half of a song was playing. He listened as he drove, and watched the road through the windshield. He kept his speed steady. He never needed to look at the dashboard when he drove, except to adjust the radio station.

He had his father's knack and affinity for cars. Like his father, he "just knew" how fast he was going when driving, and how fast he was being driven. If he was in any car, even lying down on the back seat half asleep, he knew how fast that car was going. He could even give a good guess as to the numbers on the odometer if he was riding in the car or just looking under the hood.

When he was little, the old cars his father worked on had spoken to him, just like they spoke to his father. That had ended when his father died, but he had never lost his affinity for cars. Mom Nelson had never encouraged that in him, except when it was saving her money on oil changes, so it remained just a knack, something he could use to win small bets with his friends. Sometimes it even impressed a girl.

"Listen to this," said the radio station's morning show funny DJ as the song faded away. "You won't believe this."

"I already don't believe it," the morning show's straight DJ said.

"You and me both," Marcus said. "Here I am, driving into the city to see a man about hunting dragons." That alone seemed to cover his "unbelievable things before breakfast" quota.

"You don't even know what I'm about to tell you," the funny DJ protested.

"Let me guess," the straight DJ said. "There was a gas leak last night, caused by the earthquake—"

"Aren't there always gas leaks after earthquakes?" the funny DJ asked. "But that's not what this is. Look at this video that's going around."

"This is radio," Marcus said.

"We're on the radio," the straight DJ said. "We can't look at anything."

"Well then listen to this," the funny DJ said. "Which is what I said, isn't it? 'Listen to this.' Everybody out there, listen to this. Hang on. Now."

Marcus reached over to find another radio station, but paused when he heard white noise come through the car's old speakers. The white noise resolved into people shouting. "Oh my god!" "What the hell is that?" "Are you getting this?" Then there were screams. Then the speakers rattled as something roared, drowning out the voices and the screams.

The noise ended abruptly.

"Did you hear that?" the funny DJ asked. "Did you hear that?"

"What?" asked the straight DJ. "Hear what? I think I'm deaf now."

"That was amazing, wasn't it? And it wasn't any gas leak or an explosion. It was a roar, I'm telling you."

"A roar?"

"More than a roar. Check out the video, man—"

"We're still on the radio, dude."

"Ha ha, funny man. All of you listening to us this morning should check this out. It's amazing. We have a link to the video on our web page," the funny DJ added, and gave out the web page address. "Check it out. Watch this video and tell me that's a gas leak."

"Fine," said the straight DJ. "I'll watch your stupid video and tell you it's a gas leak. But first, you tell me, what do you think you see?"

"I don't know what I'm seeing, man. But it's big—"

"And blurry. And shaking. Did I mention it's blurry?"

"—and it puts its front legs on the hood of that car. Then it licks the windshield."

"That is amazing, yes. Amazingly gross. Are you sure it's not a Great Dane?"

"Shut up, man, this isn't any kind of dog. It's obviously a lizard of some sort."

"Like an iguana?"

"Shut up and I'll tell you. But, yeah, something like the biggest iguana you've ever seen. Its tongue darts out and it licks the windshield."

"That's still pretty gross."

"Then it turns to face the camera, spits, and roars—"

"I'm pretty sure I know why it was spitting."

"—and then fire comes out of its mouth."

"Fire? Right. You mean the display goes white and the video ends."

"No, man, I'm telling you, that's fire. And it's coming out of that thing's mouth."

"So you're trying to tell me," the straight DJ said. "Wait! Let me finish. You're trying to tell me there's a dragon running around Rio Cruces?"

"I'm telling you to open your eyes, man, and watch this video."

"You know Halloween is coming up, right?"

"If that's a costume—"

"Or a movie prop. It could be a movie prop."

"If that's a Halloween costume, or a movie prop, I will eat my phone."

"I think that's probably more gross than licking the windshield of a car. I've seen where you take your phone—"

Marcus turned off the radio and settled back in the worn driver's seat. He stared at the road in front of him. He noticed the knuckles of his left hand were going white from his grip on the steering wheel. He relaxed his grip, putting both hands on the steering wheel in the driver's education proscribed ten-and-two positions.

It was October, almost Halloween, just like the DJ said. A hoax. A prank.

It was a coincidence, that was all. He was driving to Rio Cruces to accept a joke job as a dragon hunter the day after a dragon was spotted in the city and, supposedly, caught on video. Just a coincidence.

He resisted the urge to pull over and visit the radio station's web page to see the video for himself. He didn't need to see the video. It was fake. It had to be fake.

There were no such things as dragons.

3

THARA GOLD WOKE IN HER bedroom, which didn't always happen after one of her Episodes, and could be considered a good thing. Walking home naked was never as much fun as it sounded the night before.

Indirect, late-morning sunshine created a glow around the venetian blinds that covered her window. With the blinds closed, the window provided enough light for her to see, but not so much she needed to worry about a headache—which wasn't an issue this morning, as last night's Episode had been alcohol free—or that it might fade the vintage sleeping bag she had wrapped around herself when she finally went to sleep the night before. Or, more accurately, earlier this morning.

She and the dark green sleeping bag were curled up on the floor under the window. After the previous night's earthquakes, both physical and mental, she had found herself missing her father. She wanted to hug him and curl up in his lap. His old sleeping bag, the same one he had loaned her for Nancy Chisum's first-and-last pajama party in the summer of 1958, had been the closest she could come. She could almost imagine how surprised he would be when she not only told him he was wrong—Poppa was never wrong about anything—but told him about the huge dragon that had flown in the night sky and roared at her and spoke in her mind. He would be skeptical at first, but he would believe her. Poppa was used to not being wrong, but on the rare occasions when it happened, he accepted the new information and went on to be even more never-wrong in the future.

She wondered what Poppa would think of there being another dragon—and a male dragon, at that. She could imagine his face looking at her with his I-have-no-comment-to-make-about-that expression, and maybe a hint of a wink.

She tried to snuggle back into the sleeping bag, to recover the illusion of Poppa being there, listening to her—or even just pretending to listen as he continued to read a book—but there was just her and her hoard. In dragon form, she could still—just—smell him in the old fabric. Back in post-Episode human form, though, she could only imagine his scent. She sighed.

After a few minutes of memories that didn't lull her back to sleep, she yawned a deep, stretching-and-popping post-Episode yawn. She wiggled her fingers and her toes to make sure they were all still there. She started her habitual, post-Episode check for unusual bruises, then remembered she had stayed in, more or less. Any bruises this time would have come at the beginning of the night, when the first earthquake picked up her stuff and dropped it on her.

She yawned again, but to less of an extreme. The odd taste in her mouth made her want to gargle an entire bottle of Listerine, and not the new, less intense flavor. This taste—dusty windshield, tow sticker glue, and whatever the suicidal creatures with all the legs had been—required the full strength and intensity only the original, full-antiseptic Listerine flavor could deliver. Or maybe a bottle of Scotch. Not that she liked Scotch, but if she had some, the whiskey might burn the taste out of her mouth.

"Bleh."

She didn't remember seeing Tina, her roommate, on her short jaunt last night, either going or coming back, so she probably hadn't eaten her jumpy, laundry-lounging roommate. She would feel guilty, though, if any new "Have You Seen My Eight-legged Dog" posters went up in the next few days. Except the aftertaste didn't seem dog-like. More like stale sashimi. Or calamari. She was glad she couldn't smell her breath.

She threw off the sleeping bag and sat up. Time to face the morning. Whatever time it was.

She grimaced. Despite her best efforts not to, she smelled her breath.

She pressed her lips tightly closed and tried not breathe as her eyes watered. She waved her hand in front of her face, but it didn't help. She held her breath as she went to the window.

The window slid up and the breeze reluctantly drew out the vile cloud of her Episode breath. When the room was safe, the mélange of French fries, fried fish, and sweet-and-sour sauce emanating from the nearby restaurants, plus the smell of exhaust from the highway, ventured in with the sounds of the late-morning traffic. When she could breathe again without her eyes tearing up, she pushed the window closed, and locked it.

As she folded the sleeping bag and put it away in its plastic storage container, she surveyed her work from the night before. There was no longer any sign of an earthquake in her hoard. Her accumulated belongings, those that would fit in her bedroom and its walk-in closet, had been resorted, repacked, and restacked. And, while she was at it, dusted. Nothing had been irreparably damaged or broken, for which she might owe a favor to some god somewhere. If she met a god today, she would be sure to thank Her. Or Him. Or It.

She made her way to the bedroom door through the maze created by gleaming stainless-steel bakers racks, black wooden bookshelves, and pillars of boxes and containers stacked to the ceiling. Every day she took a different route. Today, she ran her fingers along the hardback books and long play vinyl records in their worn covers on one shelf, then across the array of high fidelity turntables, and amplifiers on a rack, and finally, briefly, with a faint smile, the Bakelite case of the AM radio that had, like all those other things, been Poppa's.

She picked up her keys and the clothes she had taken off last night before her episode. They still smelled of doughy breadsticks, overcooked marinara sauce, antiperspirant and sweat, but she had, while straightening the rest of her room, folded them neatly and placed the keychain on top, the keys spread as evenly as spokes in a wheel. She couldn't abide disarray in her hoard.

The clothes reminded her that she needed to look for a new job today, and she sighed. Then she shrugged. There were always more crappy jobs out there for her to find.

With the folded, smelly clothes tucked under her arm, she unlocked her bedroom door. She pulled the door open, slipped out, and closed it again quickly in case Tina was there.

Standing naked in the small "hall" that connected her bedroom with the bathroom and the rest of her apartment didn't bother her. She had gotten over nudity long ago, but she hated strangers—and roommates, and apartment staff, and coworkers who came over before or after work, and, really, anyone at all—looking into her bedroom. Looking at her stuff.

She used the keys to lock the collection of deadbolts. Then she dropped yesterday's work clothes on the growing pile of dirty clothes in the corner of the "dining room" and tossed the keys on the kitchen counter. Now that the clothes and keys weren't in her bedroom, she didn't care if they were folded or symmetrically arranged. Her bedroom was sacrosanct. The kitchen, "dining room," and living room were too public to bother.

The back wall of the "dining room" was a floor-to-ceiling mirror that attempted to make her apartment and the pile of dirty laundry look bigger than they were. And she was pretty sure the mirror was also exaggerating the disheveled state of her short, blonde hair. The pixie cut she had paid for only a week ago looked far less Tinkerbell and more street urchin. Or sea urchin. The smudged eyeliner raccooning her light brown eyes didn't help. She resisted the urge to either mess with her hair or rub her eyes and looked away from her reflection to see how the rest of her apartment had survived the earthquakes.

"Well, crap."

Most of the cupboard doors in the kitchen were open, as were several drawers. The counters were remarkably clear of dirty dishes, though. Even the bowl and spoon Tina had been eating from the night before were gone. All the takeout trash was, of course, still scattered on the counter and the floor. Tina had always demonstrated a blind spot when it came the big, white, plastic trash can with the white trash bag in it. If the earthquakes had made any difference, Thara couldn't spot it.

The door to the apartment's second bedroom was open, as well. It looked like that room had been cleaned out too, loosely speaking. The bed had not been made, but there were none of Tina's clothes on it.

Thara's clean clothes from the couch had been tossed all over the living room, probably from Tina looking for that camisole she had tentatively accused Thara of stealing.

Thara sighed. Not only was she going to have to find a new job, she was going to have to find a new roommate. Again.

She wondered if that meant Tina had seen her last night, during her Episode. It had happened before, with previous roommates. Those roommates had left just as quickly, though often with considerably less decorum, thoroughness, or honesty. Tina hadn't taken the TV, for example. Not that the TV was Thara's, except by default. The thirty-two-inch flat screen TV had been left by another roommate in more of a hurry. Another former roommate had left the bed in the other bedroom, because roommates seldom came back once they fled.

"Crap," she said again. November rent was going to be due soon.

No help for it, of course. What was done was done, and what was seen could not be unseen.

Before she could look for another roommate, though, she needed to find a new job. She already had a place in mind. It was another restaurant, and probably paid less than she had been making at Bottomless Breadsticks. But she wouldn't have to take the bus to get there, she wouldn't have to wait tables, they provided a uniform, and there would be a counter between her and any handsy customers with strange ideas about her sexual orientation. It wouldn't be a step up, or even a step over, but it would be a step toward simpler. And, suddenly, simpler seemed better than well-paid.

As she picked up her clean clothes in the living room and returned them to their piles on the couch, she picked out a pair of white underwear, a bra, and, because she owned almost nothing else, a pair of black trousers and a white button-down shirt.

She pulled on black socks and her current pair of sensible shoes and thought about breakfast. She wasn't as hungry as she normally was after an Episode, which made her wonder again what she had eaten the night before. And how many. She touched her stomach. She didn't feel anything moving, so at least she hadn't swallowed anything whole.

She found Tina's key to the front door balanced on the narrow top of the flat screen TV, so she added that to her keychain. If Tina *had* seen Thara last night, the girl had handled it remarkably well. Seeing Thara mid-Episode had rattled tougher-seeming former roommates than Tina. Few of them had kept it together long enough to so thoroughly get all their stuff—and only their stuff—*and* leave the key. So maybe Tina hadn't seen her. Thara was sure there were other reasons for a roommate to suddenly pack up their stuff and run away in the middle of the night. But seeing Thara the Golden Dragon still seemed the most likely explanation.

She made a quick visit to the bathroom for an overdue, post-Episode floss and gargle. Then she brushed her hair, washed her face, and reapplied her eyeliner. When she passed the mirror in the "dining room" again, she looked much less urchiny. She looked like a twenty-something waitress. Or maybe a caterer. Which was almost funny, because she had been either for far longer than twenty-something years.

After locking the front door behind her, she walked to the parking lot to check on Louie, Howie, and Nova.

She noticed, then ignored, an old man in baggie, blue-collar work clothes. He was walking, stooped, between cars on the far side of the parking lot as she patted each of her Outdoor Babies on the hood and wished them a good morning. The second, smaller earthquake didn't seem to have moved them, and there were no new tow stickers that needed to be scraped off. She noticed, then ignored, the forked-tongue smudge on

Nova's windshield, but took the time to wipe away the very clear dragon claw prints in the dust on Nova's front fenders.

She was wiping the dust off her hands, turning away from Nova, when she almost ran into the old man. Or ran over him. She hadn't heard him walk up to her.

The old man had been taller than her at one time, but now, with his hunched shoulders and stooped posture, his eyes were even with her collarbones. But he wasn't looking at her collarbones. He was staring at the narrow strip of asphalt between her feet.

"Those were some unusual tracks," he said, drawing out each word with both age and accent. "On your car. Just then." He glanced at the dust-free fenders of Nova, then at her hands, then back at the parking lot.

"Kids today," Thara said, and sidestepped to walk around him. She had never officially met the man, but she recognized him. She knew who he was. She had encountered him in the past, usually after Episode-related indiscretions.

She couldn't see his name stitched into the left breast of his shirt because it was swallowed by the wrinkles of fabric. It was like he had shriveled inside his Rio Cruces Animal Control Center uniform. The name she couldn't see stitched on his shirt was Jimmie, and he was called "Jimmie the Wrangler" by his animal control colleagues. Thara had never called him that. Or anything. She had, so far, avoided an official introduction.

Jimmie nodded, somehow still standing in front of her without having seemed to move. "Kids today," he said. Then he shook his head and stepped out of her way. "But what can you do?"

Thara offered only a shrug as she walked away. She had no idea what to do with kids today. She had been one of those "kids today" since she was a teenager in the 1960s. Fifty-plus years of being lumped in with the current generation, first by her parents' generation, then by her own, and counting.

She resisted the urge to look back at Jimmie. She could do that so much more surreptitiously as a dragon, just swivel one eye. As a human, though, she had to swing her whole head around, expose her face as well as her interest. She assumed Jimmie was still looking at the asphalt near his feet, where she had been, but tracking her with his peripheral vision. He might look like an old man, but she knew he was more than that. He was an old hunter.

She was going to have to be careful. Earthquakes, huge dragons, and now Jimmie the Wrangler poking around her apartment complex. Maybe she had stayed in Rio Cruces too long. Except—

She had lived in Rio Cruces her whole life. She had no idea where she would go if she left. Louie always seemed to be suggesting California, but she was pretty sure he just missed the scene in San Francisco. And the earthquakes.

Still, today was a new day. The sun was shining. The earth wasn't trying to throw her off. Her Episode had finally come and gone, so she shouldn't have to deal with dragons, known or unknown, for at least a couple months. And she was off to apply for a simple job taking orders and handing out food at the Buffalo Burger Pit. Maybe things were looking up.

4

"WELL, CRAP," THARA SAID, AND stopped walking.

She felt betrayed. It was as if the flawless blue dome of sky overhead and the soft, cool breeze at her back—the kind of perfect day that Rio Cruces offered up only a few times in any particular year—had been the smiles and encouragement of a special, new friend playing a practical joke, luring her on stage before dumping pig's blood on her head.

She stood at the corner of Fifty-first and Harvard, two blocks north of what remained of the Buffalo Burger Pit. Only the statue of a buffalo on the restaurant's roof seemed untouched as it stared calmly over her head. If the buffalo was in on the joke being played on her, he hid his guilt behind his bovine serenity.

Below the buffalo, though, there was nothing serene. Every window of the restaurant's dining room had been broken, either burst in or burst out. From this distance, Thara could see no consistent pattern to the debris. The dining room itself looked as if there had been a riot. Tables and chairs were overturned, even thrown out or through the broken windows. The far side of the dining room, clearly visible through the lack of windows, was only a gaping hole.

A bouquet of emergency, utility and city vehicles surrounded the buffalo and the heavily damaged structure below it. There was a red firetruck, a yellow hazmat truck, a white gas utility truck with a blue flame painted on its side, a black-and-white RCPD police cruiser, and a sand-colored Humvee with the logo of the Rio Cruces Animal Control Center painted on its doors. There was also a rusting red dump trunk with a black tarpaulin pulled over whatever it carried.

As Thara watched, the dump truck's engine escalated from a rumble to a roar, belched a cloud of black smoke, then pulled out of the parking lot, into traffic, heading north. The smell lurking under the diesel smoke the truck left in its wake reminded her of the stale squid-taste that lingered in the back of her throat. She wrinkled her nose.

On the far side of the intersection, a white Chevrolet Suburban blared its horn at the small Ford Focus in front of it that had also been distracted by the passing dump truck. Thara blinked against the reflected sunlight that bounced off the windshield of the Focus as it executed a curb-jumping right turn, followed closely by the Suburban, whose driver was still leaning on her horn.

Thara looked back at the restaurant. The damage looked like far more than would have been caused by an earthquake. Thara had vague memories of an Episode where she might—*might*—have left a roadhouse in a similar state, but what had happened here couldn't be blamed on her. Even if it had happened just down the street, only a few blocks away. She had stayed in last night, straightening.

Whatever had happened, the Buffalo Burger Pit looked closed forever. So much for Reemployment Plan A.

"Crap."

Men in firefighter uniforms and holding a hose connected to the nearest hydrant turned on the water and began giving the north parking lot of the Buffalo Burger Pit a high-pressure wash. The water frothed and foamed in an unpleasant, unsettling way. When the water flowed into the city drains along the street, it did so sluggishly, rolling less like water and more like molasses. Thara felt as if her simple dream of simple, nearby, nonchallenging employment were being washed away too.

Tina, her now former roommate, had worked for the Buffalo Burger Pit when she first moved in with Thara. She had quit a few months ago when she broke up with her night manager boyfriend. What had caught Thara's attention had been the husband-and-wife owners of the restaurant, Gil and Barbara Houck. She had met them once, just after the lunch rush on the same day she had met Tina, who had heard, somehow, that Thara was looking for a roommate.

Barbara, short, plump, blonde and obviously the mother-figure-matriarch of the restaurant, had misunderstood why Thara stood at the counter and offered her a job. Thara had been amused. She had been a waitress for so many years that working a counter or, even more amusing, flipping burgers on a grill seemed like a step down. She hadn't said that, of course. She had just smiled and thanked the woman for the offer.

"Well, if you ever change your mind," Barbara had said.

Thara had remembered Barbara's offer yesterday, though, and thought maybe it was time to take that "step down." To change her mind, and maybe change her life in the process. Or at least stop being a waitress for a while. Fifty-one years was probably long enough.

Thara sighed.

She turned away from the broken skeleton of what had once been the Buffalo Burger Pit and her plans for the future and considered the restaurant directly across the street, the Yellow Sign Buffet.

The Yellow Sign Buffet was a simple rectangular cinderblock structure, maybe forty feet wide across the front and twice that extending back, away from the street. The restaurant looked as if it had been built in the 1940s, with all expenses spared. Even from two blocks away, Thara could see that no attempts beyond repeated coats of brown paint had been made to hide its humble origins. The only windows stretched across the front, facing the street. A short, slanted roof of gray wooden shingles, unpainted and untreated, extended around the building. On top of the restaurant, closer to the back than the front but level with the serene, unperturbed buffalo across the street, was a large rectangular sign, yellow, with tall black letters. The sign said, redundantly, "Yellow Sign Buffet." Beneath the sign, the rough texture of the shingles and the flat roof made the building look like a medieval monk, complete with brown robe and tonsure haircut. Or like Moe Howard of the Three Stooges, with the top of his head shaved and a sign mounted on it.

Thara had never eaten at the Yellow Sign Buffet. She seldom ate at any restaurant unless she worked there. Sometimes not even then.

She mentally considered the reasons she shouldn't apply at the Yellow Sign Buffet. First, Tina worked at the Yellow Sign Buffet. That could be awkward if she had witnessed Thara's Episode last night. It could be awkward even if Tina didn't see her last night, because Tina was dating one of the managers at the Yellow Sign Buffet. Or had been dating one of the managers before last night's day off became last night's evening shift. Who wanted to be in the middle of that kind of drama? Finally, Thara hated the Three Stooges. She always had, going back to her childhood and watching them on a tiny black-and-white TV. But she needed a job.

With a shrug, Reemployment Plan B was launched. She looked both ways before crossing the intersection, in case that white Suburban had come back and was still in a horn-blaring hurry.

5

Marcus followed the navigation instructions on his phone through the spaghetti of crisscrossing highways outside of Rio Cruces to the final exit off Interstate 44 and onto Fifty-First Street. He had made good time and expected to arrive on time for his job interview. For the job of dragon hunter.

If they hadn't already paid him $500—and he hadn't already handed the whole sum over to Mom Nelson—he wouldn't have made it past the halfway point of his trip. That was when driving two hours to a job interview that was almost certainly a punking stopped seeming like a good idea and started feeling insane.

But he had taken the money, and he had driven the whole distance. There's was nothing to do now but finish it. Get to the punchline, laugh about how much fun the whole thing had been, and go home to spend the money. Assuming he could get any of it back from Mom Nelson.

More than once, riding in the relative silence of the Focus with the radio off, he had considered calling Morgan. To let her know he was headed into Rio Cruces, and might need a place to spend the night. She would be at work, doing whatever programmer analysts did in the hours before lunch, and that should limit how long they could talk. If he played it right, she might think he was making a long-distance booty call and think he was driving up just for her. But he didn't call.

As reluctant as he had been to talk about the job with Mom Nelson, that was nothing compared to how little he wanted to talk about the job with Morgan LaVoi. Once he got as far as picking up his phone and bringing up her contact information. He was one thumb press from calling her. Instead, he tossed his phone into the floor of the back seat so he couldn't almost do it again.

Morgan had been able to walk off the stage after graduation and into a job that matched her degree, while Marcus had had to ride home with his mother and was still looking. Morgan had been even less enthusiastic than Mom Nelson when he took the cashier job at Pep Boys. He had, at Morgan's insistence, sent his resume to the company she worked for. He only realized later that he had misspelled the name of the manager she had told him to contact and his resume had ended up in the Human Resources slush pile. At least he had received an email rejection. Most companies didn't bother.

If this job interview worked out, he would call her after. Because he might need that place to stay. And if she interpreted his request as a celebratory booty call, that worked too. If the job didn't work out, he would just go straight home. A pity booty call just didn't appeal to him, especially if he had to tell her he had driven two hours to be turned down for a fictional job at a buffet restaurant.

As he waited at the stoplight to make the right turn onto Harvard Avenue, a large, red dump truck passed, heading north in front of a dark cloud of exhaust. The truck bumped noisily over a fresh patch in the asphalt, jolting its tailgate and rattling its chains. What looked like the end of an octopus's tentacle flopped and dangled over the top of the tailgate. As Marcus looked, telling himself it had to be the end of a vine or something that made a lot more sense than an octopus's tentacle, the narrow end curled, then uncurled and twisted, revealing a double row of suckers. Then the truck was gone and the SUV behind Marcus was leaning on its horn, letting him know the right arrow had come on.

Startled, Marcus jerked on the steering wheel and gave the accelerator a nudge. At the same time, he noticed the woman standing on the far corner, looking at him as he was turning. Just another blonde white girl, tall-ish, maybe a couple years older than him, dressed in black and white. Probably a waiter on her way to work. If it wasn't for the way her hair flashed gold in the sunlight, he wouldn't have noticed her. Then he forgot her hair as two heavily outlined eyes met his. The little wingtip flourishes of her eyeliner, highlighting the corners of her eyes, were visible even as far away as she was. So were the tiny flecks of gold that made her light brown eyes so distinctive—

He cut the turn too short. The Focus's rear passenger side tire went up the curb, then down, in a way that made him wince in shared pain with the car. The SUV behind him hit the horn again, in case anyone in a mile radius had missed Marcus being a jackass.

He straightened the car in the right lane and resisted the urge to look back over his shoulder at the woman who had just seem him take a corner like a moron. The SUV honked at him once more as it passed him on the left.

In his embarrassment he almost missed the Yellow Sign Buffet. Then, when he did see it, with its brown cinderblock walls, aging gray shingles, and ugly yellow sign, he almost missed it on purpose.

At the last second, though, he hit the brakes and made the turn in to the restaurant's parking lot. He had come this far, he might as well see it through.

6

THE YELLOW SIGN BUFFET WAS even less impressive on the inside. The front counter, just inside the door, had a beige cash register with bright red LED numbers on it that might have been as old as Mom Nelson. The walls were paneled and hung with yellowing black-and-white photos. Combined with the fluorescent lighting in the dingy drop ceiling, walls and photos created an ambiance that reminded Marcus of his grade school lunch room. Though with far fewer diners.

Beyond the close-packed booths just inside the front door, the steam tables that should have been loaded with whatever it was the Yellow Sign Buffet served for lunch were mostly empty. The few patrons that had shown up for an early lunch stood in a line, waiting with more patience than Marcus would have been able to muster.

The smells in the air teased Marcus's nose, but not in a playful, tasty way. Instead, the scents hinted at such dishes as pepper steak and fried chicken, green beans and mashed potatoes, *suggested* those dishes, without actually being any of them. No such dishes were visible on the steam tables, at least.

A middle-aged white man stood behind the counter. He met Marcus's eye and smiled as Marcus entered.

Marcus had to stop himself from staring. Average height, graying auburn hair in a comb over, pale, slightly jowly, and wearing glasses with vintage frames, August Neuland, as the nametag pinned to the man's yellow shirt identified him to be, looked exactly as Marcus had envisioned him. The yellow and brown manager's outfit was a surprise—Marcus would never have imagined anyone wearing the combination, not in his lifetime—but Marcus had known the man would be wearing something similar, including a matched set of pins in the breast pocket of his shirt. The gold Rolex on the man's wrist was the only indicator that owning a restaurant might spin off *some* extra cash. Marcus tried to pin down the man's age more specifically than "middle-aged," but failed. August Neuland could be anywhere from forty-five to sixty-five.

"Good morning, Mr. Nelson," August Neuland said before Marcus could introduce himself. He came around the front counter and held out his hand.

Marcus's eyes went straight to the watch and he reassessed how much extra cash the Yellow Sign Buffet might spin off from *some* to *wow*. As old as it was, that Rolex had to be an heirloom, and very well cared for.

"You're right on time," August Neuland added, "which is a pleasant surprise."

Marcus drew up. He had been about to reach out his hand, but stopped. "What?"

"There was a bit of a catastrophe last night," August Neuland said, still smiling. He nodded to indicate the rubble and emergency vehicles across the street. "Earthquakes, as I'm sure you heard. The World almost Ended," he added, his smile becoming oddly rueful.

Marcus clearly heard the capitalized words, he also heard the somewhat wistful nature of the statement. He extended his hand and August Neuland grasped it firmly.

"It is good to meet you, Mr. Nelson," the man said, still smiling, as he shook Marcus's hand.

"Likewise," Marcus said, then added, "Mr. Neuland."

The handshake ended amicably. Not too long, not too fast. Not too warm, or too moist.

"Come this way, please, Mr. Nelson," the man said, turning. He picked up a manila folder from the counter.

"Call me Marcus."

Somehow, the man's smile became even brighter. Smilier. "Alright, Marcus, and you can call me August. Probably for the best, now that I think of it. If we went around calling each other Mr. Nelson and Mr. Neuland, people might get confused. Our family names are surprisingly similar."

Marcus nodded, unsure how else to respond.

"We're an informal bunch here at the Yellow Sign Buffet," August Neuland went on. "It's hard to be pretentious when you run a buffet.

Simple food for simple people, that's the Yellow Sign Buffet." He pointed with the manila folder to indicate the booth nearest the front door. "Here, please, Marcus, have a seat. We have so much to discuss."

Marcus took the indicated seat. The window on his left offered a clear view of the lunchtime traffic on Harvard Avenue, and of the ruins of what had been another restaurant across the street. On top of what was left of the structure, an oversized buffalo stared north, ignoring Marcus as completely as it ignored the emergency crews picking through the wreckage below it.

Marcus heard the door of the restaurant open. August Neuland smiled and nodded to a woman who walked past the table on her way to the buffet line in the back, then placed the folder on the table and slid into the seat across from Marcus. He leaned forward and rested his forearms on the table. "Please excuse me if I have to get up suddenly," he said. "We're very short staffed today. We lost some of our own last night."

Marcus faced the man. "They died? In the earthquake?"

The man leaned back and held up his hands. "Oh, no, nothing like that. Well, almost like that." He rested his hands on the table top again and looked out the window. He sighed. Before Marcus could ask what he meant, the man turned to him again, and said, "Are you hungry, Marcus? Would you like anything to eat before we get started?"

Marcus almost asked if eating the food was a requirement for the job, but he stopped himself. He shook his head. "No, I had a late breakfast."

"Something to drink then? We have fresh coffee. Or are you an iced tea man? Sweet or unsweet?" August Neuland looked ready to push himself to his feet and quickly fetch Marcus a drink.

So Marcus let him. "Tea. Sweet."

"One sweet tea, coming up." August Neuland rose and went for the drink. The perfect host, in a yellow shirt and brown trousers.

Marcus used the opportunity to glance at the folder on the table. "Nelson, M" had been written in heavy black ink on the folder's tab. The edges of a few sheets of paper showed, but that was all.

Behind him, the front door opened. Marcus turned to glance over his shoulder—

He turned away quickly, before the girl with the golden hair and the light brown eyes looked at him. Before she could recognize the jackass who couldn't make a right turn.

She looked both younger and taller from his seat in the booth. Something about her also said, *Her*.

He made a point of not looking at—

Her.

A single word he could almost hear, whispered in the back of his mind.

He risked another glance over his shoulder. So far as he could tell, she hadn't even noticed him. She was dressed like a waitress, but she hadn't moved past the front counter. She stood just inside the door, looking around the restaurant with an expression of... It wasn't distaste. It was... odd-taste. Marcus recognized the look because he was pretty sure that had been his expression when he walked through the same door a few minutes before.

Her.

Marcus found himself studying her, and his response at the sight of her as well. What was it about the girl that made some part of his mind point her out, draw a circle around her, and insist she was what he was looking for? Because she really wasn't. She was pretty enough, for a white girl, with her long face and angular facial features. Her nose had just a hint of an arch, adding character. Her light brown eyes were her best feature, and they were almost hidden behind her bangs and eyeliner. Close up, the black eyeliner that emphasized the shape of her eyes was even heavier than he had thought. The wingtips that adorned the corners of her eyes curled around like hieroglyphs. Her body was like her face, long and angular, with whatever curves she had mostly hidden by the blousy white shirt and the baggy black trousers. Plus, she was at least three or four years older than him. Twenty-five, at least, maybe as old as twenty-seven or twenty-eight.

Marcus knew he had a type. Morgan was his type. Counting from high school, Morgan was the fourth girl of his type. His mother went so far as to pretend she couldn't remember which girl went with which name, which Marcus sometimes thought was funny. Whoever this white girl was with her striking eyes, she wasn't his type.

And yet, there she was.

Her.

She turned toward Marcus, and he looked away again. He felt his face get warm with embarrassment at being caught staring—

Except she hadn't been looking at him. August Neuland was coming back to the table carrying a tall, plastic glass of iced tea.

"How may I help you, young lady?" he asked, placing the glass on the table in front of Marcus.

"I saw your sign—"

"Splendid!" August Neuland said, and Marcus almost expected him to start clapping. He held up his right hand, index finger extended. "Hold that thought, young lady." He looked at Marcus. "Do you mind? I think Fate has just sent me another lifeline."

Marcus shrugged. "Do you what have to." He picked up the glass of tea and took a sip—

He forced himself to swallow, and very calmly set the glass back down. There were hints of traditional brewed black tea flavor in the drink, and hints of sugar, but only hints. It was like the drink was *supposed* to be tea, in that it was brown, and, to some extent, sweet, but the resemblance quickly faded after those points.

August Neuland didn't seem to notice Marcus's poorly disguised grimace. The man pushed the folder in front of Marcus, then pulled one of the pens out of his shirt pocket and placed it on top of the folder. "If you don't mind, go ahead fill out these forms. Fate may have brought you to my door, but it didn't provide some of the details Uncle Sam insists on. I'll be right back." Then he was walking past Marcus toward the girl. "Can you start today, young lady? Right this minute?"

7

FROM THE SUN OVER HER left shoulder, Thara knew it was after eleven. The Yellow Sign Buffet had to be open. The lunch crowd had begun to arrive, parking in front of the restaurant. As she walked down Harvard Avenue toward the restaurant, she watched more than one car arrive, disgorge drivers and passengers, who then disappeared into the restaurant. Including, she noticed, the gray Ford Focus that had jumped the curb back at the intersection.

The parking lot behind the restaurant, though, where she had no doubt employees were instructed to park, had only two cars. An aging beige Cadillac Eldorado that dated back to the 1990s would be the owner's car, she decided. Or maybe an older manager. The much more recent, but in far worse shape, red Chevy Tracker parked several spaces away from the Eldorado would be an employee's car. That was it. Unless the Yellow Sign Buffet employed a disproportionate number of public transit passengers or carpoolers, Thara was pretty sure the restaurant was short-handed. Which boded well for Reemployment Plan B.

Now that she was closer to the restaurant, she could see the coat of brown paint that covered the cinderblock walls was not as smooth as it looked from a distance. Layers of brown paint had been added over the years by painting over the previous, peeling, flaking coat. The effect was most prominent near the corners, where the Oklahoma wind and rain had been most effective in their attacks.

She still could not see into the restaurant. The windows were tinted a darker shade of brown than the bricks. They reflected the street and the traffic, but with curving distortions like funhouse mirrors. According to the reflections, Harvard Avenue wasn't flat. It rose and fell like a roller coaster in both directions. And the Buffalo Burger Pit wasn't across a mere five lanes of city traffic, but across the universe, a tiny, broken spot in the infinite distance. Thara blinked and glanced away before the effect could give her a headache.

She took in a breath through her nose, sorting through the various restaurant smells that always permeated this area. She tried to isolate the particular scent of the Yellow Sign Buffet. The smell of French fries was weaker today, without the Buffalo Burger Pit's usual contribution. The fried fish and overcooked hush puppies smell was there, if fainter here than near her apartment, and so was the tangy scent of sweet-and-sour sauce. Underneath those smells, though, was... nothing specific. There were hints of soy sauce and ketchup, a strong note of stale frying grease, and a soupçon of caramelized onions, toasted white bread, and overcooked bacon.

Her eyes watered and she wrinkled her nose.

Thara had worked in restaurants of one ethnicity or another, presumed or actual, for her entire adult life. She had smelled kitchens preparing dishes ranging from a simple burger-and-fries to *coq au vin*, from classic chop suey to mee siam, and many, many unholy variations in between. She had learned the word *soupçon* while dating a chef in the 1970s who wanted to be the next Julia Child, complete with TV show and outsized cultural impact—and who had left his knives behind in his panic and sudden need to get away from her and find a new career. Thara Gold, lifelong waitress, knew what restaurants smelled like.

The Yellow Sign Buffet smelled like none of them.

Instead, the Yellow Sign Buffet smelled like... all of them. But not specifically. The mathematically precise. but usually mythical, *average*.

The Yellow Sign Buffet should not exist.

This certainty impressed itself on her mind and echoed through her head, sounding like the voice of the dragon she had heard the night before. She stopped walking in surprise.

She looked around, suspiciously eyeing the blue sky overhead, in case it proved to be hiding more bad news, as well as between cars parked in the nearest lots and behind short, droopy hedges. There was no place visible where a fifty-foot dragon could be hiding. She saw only a few places a dragon half that size could hide, at least when it was a dragon. When she was Thara Gold, human, she had plenty of options. Which thought made her wonder if the dragon she had seen last night even now be walking around in human form? Would she recognize him if she saw him? Would he recognize her?

She started walking again, away from thoughts of the other dragon.

She decided the certainty the Yellow Sign Buffet shouldn't exist was *her* certainty. The Yellow Sign Buffet should *not* exist. No question about it. She had always known that, but never really formed the thought. It was as obvious—and as invisible—as the air she was breathing.

The Yellow Sign Buffet should be destroyed.

She stopped walking again. This time, though, she checked her fingers and touched her face, suddenly needing to be reassured that she hadn't begun to transform. She ran her hand down the back of her neck, making sure it was still the appropriate length, and smooth. She still looked and felt human, or as human as she ever felt, but...

There was a part of her that wanted to charge the Yellow Sign Buffet's brown, Moe Howard look-a-like manifestation and tear it apart. Blast the cinderblocks and light the wooden shingles on fire. Pull down the big, yellow sign on top and cast it into the street—

She clenched her fists and took deep breaths in an effort to calm herself. As she did, she tried to think of any past Episodes where the Yellow Sign Buffet might have gotten on the wrong side of Thara the Golden Dragon.

She had never visited the Yellow Sign Buffet. Not even after Tina started working there. The Yellow Sign Buffet had barely existed in her world until today.

And now she wanted to get a job there. And, simultaneously, to wipe it from the face of the Earth.

One of these goals clearly had to go away. Or the two of them needed to at least come to some sort of understanding.

When she was certain she wasn't about to have an unscheduled Episode and attack the Yellow Sign Buffet for surviving the earthquakes when the Buffalo Burger Pit had not—and for the audacity of accomplishing a perfect-if-hideous culinary average—she started walking again. Toward the restaurant. Because her rent was still due.

A beige minivan of indeterminate make and model pulled into the parking lot as Thara approached. On the rear window of the minivan were stick figure decals showing two adult figures of indeterminate gender, two similar smaller figures, and a dog-like creature that might also have been a cat, as if the family the decals represented was as generic as their vehicle. As if to prove the point, a nondescript woman wearing a beige pantsuit with her dishwater blonde-brown hair held back with a beige shawl stepped out of the minivan and walked to the front door of the restaurant. The woman didn't seem to notice Thara, or even glance across the street.

When the woman opened the front door of the Yellow Sign Buffet, though, the glass in the door reflected the scene across the street, showing Thara the wreckage of the Buffalo Burger Pit with perfect clarity, in case she needed a reminder of why she was here.

A small gray Toyota Corolla at least as old as the Eldorado in the back lot, and in almost as good condition, came up behind Thara and pulled into the parking lot in front of her, missing her only by inches. She started to raise her left hand to express her negative opinion of the driver's inability to see pedestrians, but stopped herself. At first because she thought the driver might have been a customer—or worse, an employee—at the place she was about to ask for work, then because she recognized the car. She had seen that car parked near Louie, Howie, and Nova several times over the past couple months. Seeing it now gave her pause. And perhaps another reason to turn around and walk home.

She watched as the car drove to the rear of the building and pulled into the spot next to the Eldorado. Ricky, Tina's manager boyfriend had just arrived.

Thara reconsidered, again, how badly she needed a job.

No, there was no doubt she needed a job. The question was, did she need *this* job? There were other restaurants within walking distance of her apartment. She could walk to any one of them just as easily as she could walk here. In fact, if she left now, she would pass three of them on her way back to her apartment. But she didn't leave.

She watched as Ricky, a young man in his late twenties, got out of the Corolla. He disappeared behind the restaurant, entering through a rear door Thara couldn't see.

When it became clear that Tina hadn't come to work with her manager boyfriend, Thara continued walking. Maybe the two hadn't had time to talk that morning. Or maybe Tina was already at work.

When she reached the front door, she saw a plastic sign in the corner of the window next to the door. The sign said, "Help Wanted Apply Inside." Encouraged, but not exactly happy, Thara pushed the door open and stepped inside the Yellow Sign Buffet for the first time.

8

THE INTERIOR OF THE RESTAURANT showed its midtwentieth century origins. A few nods to modernity had been attempted, if not exactly committed to. The dining room was the front half of the structure, dimly lit by the banks of fluorescent lights in the dingy drop ceiling. The pale, yellowing paneling that extended around the interior perimeter of the dining room almost certainly dated back to the original construction. Thara had no doubt that if she pulled away the paneling she would see naked gray cinderblocks. Her fingers twitched with the urge to do exactly that.

Just inside the front door was a wooden counter fronted with the same paneling as the walls, and topped with a cash register that might have been salvaged from Alice's Restaurant. Mounted on the front of the counter were two more plastic signs. The first said, "No Tipping." Something about the sign reminded her of "Please Don't Feed the Animals" signs at the zoo. The sign below it said, "Please Seat Yourself." Thara remained standing.

Starting above the counter and extending to the back, the north wall was covered with aging photographs. The largest photograph was a yellowing black-and-white image of the restaurant surrounded by cars from the 1940s and 1950s. Except for the sign on top and the cars, Thara had seen the same view on her walk. In the photograph, the sign on the roof of the restaurant said only, "Buffet." Thara could only assume the sign in the photograph was, in fact, yellow.

There were no standalone tables with chairs, only booths pushed together into long blocks that stretched across the dining room. The booths had dark brown faux wood grain Formica tables and yellow vinyl seats. Despite their obvious age, the Formica and vinyl were in good shape, taken care of. One line of booths extended along the front windows. Only one of those booths was occupied. The lone occupant, a young black man dressed in charcoal slacks and a red pullover wasn't eating anything. Another line of booths went down the wall in front of her, behind the front counter. The rest were in blocks in the middle. There were no separators between the booths, allowing diners to watch each other eat, if they so chose, and she could see all the way back to the built-in steam tables and past them to the twin doors of the bathrooms and the swinging double doors that led to the kitchen.

With their scratched sneeze guards, the two banks of steam tables that made up the buffet line glowed like lanterns in the shadows at the back of the dining room. Despite the proximity of lunchtime, none of the serving tables was fully stocked. One had only empty dark holes where basins of food should be. Five customers in business casual, plus the nondescript beige woman with the shawl, waited in line at the nearest steam table as an employee in an ugly brown and yellow polyester uniform, complete with hat, slid a stainless-steel basin of something that might have been pepper beef into place.

Along the far wall on Thara's left, the south wall, was the drink station, with a soda fountain, stainless-steel dispensers for sweet and unsweetened iced tea, coffee, and more, and a hulking chrome soft-serve yogurt dispenser with twin spouts, one off-white and the other dark brown. A middle-aged man in an ecru shirt and brown trousers was filling a clear plastic cup with tea.

The only employee Thara had seen so far left the steam table and went into the back through the double doors.

No cashier or greeter stood behind the counter. Except for the sounds of customers spooning the contents of chafing dishes onto heavy ceramic plates, and the chorus of hums from the fluorescent lights, the soda fountain, and the soft-serve yogurt machine, the dining room was quiet, and had been quiet since she entered. There had been a brief sound of a man's voice in the back when the double doors opened, but it had ended when the doors sprang back into place.

As the front door closed behind Thara, the man at the drink fountain turned around. He noticed her, gave her a nod and a smile, then started walking to the front carrying the glass of iced tea. The nod and the smile as much as the name tag pinned to his ecru shirt announced him as the owner, or at least a manager.

Thara returned the nod, and waited. The man smiled at her the whole way. After the first few steps of that, Thara looked away. She pretended to look at the big photo on the wall, then at the old cash register. The cash register, with its beige plastic shell and red LED display with square, segmented zeros, had been the pinnacle of modern, hi-tech, point-of-sale machination when she first joined the food service workforce.

When Thara looked at the man again, he was still smiling at her, but closer. She triggered her hi-my-name-is-Thara-and-I'll-be-your-server-tonight smile, but it flickered and her mouth became a line closer to did-you-need-another-minute-to-read-the-entire-menu-again?

The lone employee came back into the dining room through the double doors with another chafing dish, this one loaded with a mound of what might have been deep fried chicken or pork. Thara's nose still smelled nothing specific, however, not from the steam tables with the food already available, nor from this new heaping helping. It was like watching a silent movie with her nose, exaggerated shapes and colors attempting to convey scents and aromas locked behind the viewing screen.

She noticed the man at the booth near the door looking at her. She glanced at him, but only had time to notice he was younger than she had first thought and wonder if he was applying for a job too. Then the manager with the glass of iced tea was there, placing the glass on the table.

"How may I help you, young lady?" the manager asked.

"I saw your sign—"

"Splendid!" the man said, cutting her off with an even bigger smile and enough enthusiasm she thought he was about to clap. Instead of clapping, though, he held up his right hand, finger extended. "Hold that thought, young lady." He looked down at the customer in the booth. "Do you mind? I think Fate has just sent me another lifeline."

As he instructed the young black man to fill out some forms, Thara noticed the manager's clothes for the first time. Though the ecru shirt and brown trousers were obviously his manager's uniform, they weren't off the rack. Both shirt and trousers were custom-made, with perfect seams supporting a perfect fit. The shirt was twill cotton, the trousers were lightweight wool, and the silk tie was identical in color to the trousers, but adorned with swirling yellow paisleys. She found herself wondering if there was more to the Yellow Sign Buffet than first impressions implied.

The manager finished and turned back to her, his smile as big as ever. "Can you start today, young lady? Right this minute?"

"Yes—"

"Wonderful!" The man put his hands together in front of him, as if this time he really was going to clap. But he still didn't. Instead he only put his hands together and gave a slight bow in her direction. Then he held out his right hand. "Forgive my poor manners, Miss—?"

Thara introduced herself as they shook hands. His grip was firm, if fleshy, and still a bit damp from carrying the cup of iced tea. She had to resist the urge wipe her hand on her trousers when he released it.

"Miss Gold," he said, repeating her name, using *Miss* again, instead of the *Ms.* she had clearly enunciated. "Again, please forgive my poor manners. My name is August Neuland, the Fifth, owner and manager of the Yellow Sign Buffet, and I am very, very happy to make your acquaintance. And to hire you and put you to work." His smile amped up the wattage as he spoke. "As you can no doubt see for yourself, we are quite understaffed today. Come with me. I'll introduce you to Mr. Lampley." He turned to lead her back the way he had come.

Thara followed him. She felt the man in the booth watching her, but she ignored him. "You want me to start right now?" she asked the manager's back.

"Oh, yes, absolutely. Poor Keenan has had to serve lunch all by himself."

"What happened to everyone—"

"We lost so many in the events of last night."

"Lost? They died in the earthquakes?"

"Oh, no, nothing like that. Let's just say their faith in the future was shaken. Some of them will return, I'm certain of it. Most of them, given time. Maybe even today, but that won't help poor Keenan with lunch, will it?"

"Faith in the future?" Thara tried to decide how she was supposed to interpret his words. "So they just didn't come in? Because of the earthquake?"

"More because of what didn't happen *after* the earthquake, but that's enough about the past. Let's focus on the future, shall we, Miss Gold? Here at the Yellow Sign Buffet, we are very generous to our loyal employees, and we want that loyalty to go both ways."

They reached the double doors. August Neuland pushed through without checking if "poor Keenan" might be coming from the other direction. Thara followed him through. She stopped just inside the door.

She had expected a steamy, brightly lit kitchen and prep area, crowded with cooks in front of grills and burners and prep stations, all of them boiling, frying, sautéing, chopping, grating, and otherwise doing those things cooks do when they aren't bragging about the size of their penises and making rude comments to each other and the wait staff and busboys.

Instead it was like walking into a stainless-steel cave. Bare bulbs overhead gave off a yellow light. The room stretched all the way across from left to right, but was only half the depth of the dining room. On the left, a conveyor belt emerged from a dark, curtained alcove on the far wall and extended most of the way to the other wall, then curved back to disappear into another, similar alcove. A procession of covered steam table insert pans were backed up on the conveyor belt. As Thara watched, "poor Keenan" picked up the rightmost pan from the conveyor belt with large oven mitts. Then he carried it past her, through the doors to the dining room.

To the right of the conveyor belt, an office with a big plate-glass window was obviously the manager's office. Tina's manager boyfriend sat on one of the chairs in front of the desk, his back to the window. He held a phone receiver to his ear. Outside the office, boxes of syrup for the soda fountain, napkins, and more were stacked in a corner. In another corner, a line of stainless-steel sinks and shelves filled with empty chafing dishes and other kitchen containers.

"I see Mr. Lampley is on the phone," Mr. Neuland said, "so you'll have to meet him later."

"We've met," Thara said.

"Oh, splendid!"

Before the man could start talking about loyalty again, Thara asked, "Where does the food come from?" Unless there was a door in the manager's office, there was no visible way to reach the real kitchen from where she stood.

"From the back, of course," Mr. Neuland said. He pointed to the conveyor belt. "If you would pick up the next pan and take it to the front, that would be a great start. Keenan can tell you where it goes."

Thara glanced around for a clock. The walls were bare. "You want me to start work right now?"

"Yes."

"What about paperwork?"

"We can do it later. The same goes for your uniform." He gave her a quick looking over. "What you have on now is acceptable."

Thara looked down at herself. "Thanks, I think. Should I wash my hands, at least?"

"Absolutely," Mr. Neuland said, still smiling. If he noticed her sarcasm, he showed no sign of it. "In fact," he added, "I believe that's the law these days. Oh, and you might want to get yourself a pair of oven mitts, Miss Gold. Keenan can show you where those are when he returns. The chafing dishes can be quite hot."

"How do I clock in?"

Mr. Neuland pulled a phone with a large display from his pants pocket. He tapped the screen, then spelled her name incorrectly.

"There's an 'h,'" she said.

He stopped tapping and looked up at her. "Hmm?"

"In my name, Thara, there's an 'h.'" She spelled her name out for him. "I was named after my parents," she added. "Thomas and Lara." Poppa had found it endlessly amusing that no one spelled her name right on the first try.

Mr. Neuland tapped more in rapid succession, then said, "Thara with an 'h'." He paused. "I'm assuming Gold is gold?"

"Gold is gold," she said, nodding.

"And you are clocked in, Miss Thara-with-an-h Gold. Please excuse me, I must go back and see to our other new employee." Mr. Neuland left her standing in the middle of the big room.

Thara frowned. Obviously, the "other new employee" wasn't going to be hauling hot stainless-steel pans of food from the back to the front. Or, like Thara, he would already be doing that. How many managers did the restaurant need? Until she showed up, management outnumbered front of the house staff by two-to-one. She had no idea how many cooks were in the kitchen, though there was evidently no shortage there, since more food was being conveyed from the back. Then she realized she hadn't discussed how much she was being paid, either.

The double doors opened and Keenan walked through.

"Hey," Thara said.

He didn't seem to hear her as he walked past her to the conveyor belt.

"Hey," she said again, waving a hand in front of his face.

He stopped and stared at her hand, then turned as his eyes followed her arm back around to her shoulder then up to her face. His eyes focused on her.

"Where are the oven mitts?"

"Eat me," he said.

The distracted look in his eyes, combined with decades of experience as a waitress, kept her from taking it personally. Obviously a cook in training. She could see he was about to say it again, with the same lack of conviction, and held up her hand to stop him.

"Never mind." She shook her head as she turned her back on him. "I need to wash my hands, anyway."

He made no comment as she walked away from him, which just showed how new he had to be in the cooks training program. She heard him turn back around and get on with hauling hot chafing dishes.

She went to the big sink to wash her hands. Instead of a soap dispenser mounted on the wall for employees to use, there was only a small, generic bottle of soft soap next to the faucet, and a roll of rough brown paper towels. The soap dispenser was nearly empty, which Thara took as a positive sign.

"Mr. Lampley" emerged from the office while she was ripping off a paper towel to dry her hands. Ricky's rumpled ecru shirt and brown slacks were a far cry from Mr. Neuland's bespoke clothing but still conveyed his status as manager.

"Is Tina," he started. He paused, looked confused, then focused on her again. "Did you see Tina this morning? Thara?" As he spoke, he recovered himself, suppressing his innate humanity and emerging as the manager she knew he could be. His eyes went to her breasts—or where her the curve of her breasts would be visible if she weren't wearing an oversized shirt buttoned all the way to the neckline—then to her hands with the paper towels, then back to her face.

"No," Thara said, dropping the damp paper towels in the trash. "I haven't seen her since last night, when she said she was supposed to work, instead of go out."

Ricky's face fell and his shoulders slumped. "So... she's not coming in?"

"I have no idea, Ricky. She moved out last night."

"Moved out? She's... gone?"

"Didn't you see her last night? Here? At work? Instead of on your date or whatever?"

"She was... here, yeah." As he spoke, Ricky's hands fluttered in approximations of actual gestures. Like his sentences, though, they couldn't quite commit. "Something... came up. We had to work. But... she left. After... I didn't see her..."

Thara held up her hand to stop him from rambling further. "She left her key, Ricky. And since she took all her stuff, I don't think she's coming back."

Ricky sighed, then said, "I... I know we're friends and all... Thara, but... I kind of need you to... call me Mr. Lampley. Now. While we're at work."

Thara met his gaze, or tried to. It was hard, the way his eyes kept moving, glancing at everything around her, only landing on her every few seconds. Each time it was like he was surprised to see her there. She had never liked Ricky. She had never disliked him either. Suddenly, though, she could understand why Tina might have run off without warning. "Can you fire me, Ricky?"

"What?" The surprise on his face became much more plain, then became lost in the muddle of other expressions. Like his hands doing impressions of gestures, his facial muscles only seemed to do impressions. "No... not today... I'm not even sure you're... I'm not even sure you're really working here."

"Me either. But I'm working here today, Ricky. So how about you show me where the oven mitts are? 'Poor Keenan' could use my help."

9

Marcus watched as August Neuland escorted the blonde waitress out of sight into the back of the restaurant. He still had no idea why she drew his attention. He knew her name now, because she had given it to August Neuland. Though when he thought of her name, Tara Gold, it made his head hurt. As if he were mentally pronouncing her name wrong.

He had watched her walk past him with some interest. The belt around her waist was cinched tight enough to indicate she wasn't as shapeless as her clothes, but, unfortunately, not enough to really fill out her pants. After the double doors swung closed and blocked his view of her, he turned his attention to the paperwork August Neuland had left with him.

The forms in the folder were typical new employee tax forms. Nothing unusual or suspicious. Still, Marcus was reluctant to fill in the blanks for his Social Security number and his home address. Which seemed silly after the man had been able to wire him $500. He was almost surprised the forms hadn't already been filled out, just awaiting his signature. He was signing the last of the forms when August Neuland returned and sat across from him.

"Tara with an 'h,'" the man said without preamble.

Marcus started to ask him what he meant, then the double doors to the back opened with a bang and the girl came out carrying a covered stainless-steel pan. So he hadn't been mispronouncing her name. He had been spelling it wrong. In his head. And that had bothered him. The day was only getting weirder.

105

"Thara," Marcus said, because he felt he had to, to correct the imbalance he had created earlier. He watched her slide the pan into an empty slot on a steam stable and take the cover off, revealing what might have been egg noodles and cheese with cut green beans. "With an 'h.'"

August Neuland nodded and shrugged, then spotted the completed forms on the table. "Excellent!" he said, gathering the papers into a neat stack and putting them back into the folder. "So do you think you can start immediately?"

Marcus wasn't ready to discuss his actual job. Not just yet. Neither of them had even once said the word *dragon*, and he wasn't going to be the first. He managed a smile. "You don't waste time, do you?"

August Neuland's smile faltered, but only for an instant. The neon wattage was back up to full so fast that Marcus wasn't sure he had seen anything different. "We try not to, Marcus, but, of course, no plan survives contact with the enemy." He gestured with his hands to indicate the entire restaurant, and maybe the entire world. He looked out the window toward the ruined restaurant across the street. "As you can see, we suffered a bit of a setback last night."

Marcus followed his gaze. "What happened over there? That looks like more than an earthquake."

"It was much more than an earthquake, Marcus. Much more than two earthquakes, actually." August Neuland looked at Marcus. "But let's focus on the future, Marcus, the future we can build together. Here at the Yellow Sign Buffet, we are proud of our long history. We have been serving lunch and dinner, seven days a week, fifty-two weeks a year, on this very spot, for over one hundred years. Can you believe it?"

Marcus looked around. He could believe it.

"My great grandfather Neuland," the man went on, "built this building where my great great great grandfather Neuland first pitched his tent. My family," he added with a conspiratorial smile, "was one of the original Sooners."

"Did I hear you say were August Neuland the Fifth?"

"Way to pay attention, Marcus. I like that in my employees. Yes, I am the fifth generation of August Neulands. The fifth incarnation, if you will. But that's the past. All of it. Done, gone. The future is what concerns us now, and that future is just waiting for us to do our parts." Still smiling, he asked again, "So do you think you can get started immediately?"

"We still haven't discussed my rates—"

"Name your price, Marcus. Hit me with your best shot, then tell me you can get started today. Because the future waits for no one, be they man or goddess."

"Fifty thousand," Marcus said. He felt his face get warm again, and his heart thudded in his chest, but he kept his face straight. Serious. Businesslike. He had considered different openings on his drive up, then settled on a price that—he hoped—would bring this whole joke to an end. "Plus expenses," he added.

"Done and done, Marcus," August Neuland the Fifth said. His smile never faltered. "A singular price for a singular service. But let me be the practical businessman for a few seconds and offer you ten thousand up front, with the rest due on delivery. As for expenses, let's handle those on a case by case basis, once we know what they are."

"I was," Marcus started, then stopped as his throat got tight. His head felt light. He hadn't expected his bid to be accepted. His mind raced. "I was thinking half up front," he managed to say. "Twenty-five thousand."

August Neuland didn't blink. "How about fifteen, fifteen and twenty? Fifteen to get you started, another fifteen when you think you're getting close—and can provide proof—and the final twenty thousand when you hand over one dragon on a leash."

"On a leash?"

August Neuland nodded. "That's why I'm willing to meet your price, Marcus. That's why we advertised for a dragon *hunter*, and not a dragon *slayer*. We need our dragon alive, Marcus."

A crash at the back of the restaurant drew both their attentions. The blonde girl stood just inside the still-swinging double doors that led to the kitchen. At her feet was a stainless-steel chafing dish that had fallen and spilled what might have been mashed potatoes with sliced ham. The girl's heavily outlined eyes met Marcus's and once again she became all he could see.

Her. Thara-with-an-h Gold. Her. Her. Her.

The girl's expression changed, as if she had also heard the voice in Marcus's head. Her brow furrowed and her jaw clenched as her eyes locked hard on his. She frowned. Then she turned away and went back through the doors, nearly knocking a second chafing dish out of the hands of the only other employee Marcus had seen.

"I see our newest employee is having some first-day jitters."

August Neuland turned back, and Marcus reluctantly met the man's gaze again, but his mind was still focusing on the girl. He wanted to ask about the girl. For no reason he could think of, he started to get up. To follow her.

"Don't you worry about the mess, Marcus," the man said. "Mr. Lampley will see that it's taken care of."

"Right," Marcus said, settling back in to his seat. After another glance at the double doors, he forced himself to look at August Neuland, to meet the man's eyes. "Of course. And, yes." He made himself nod. "Fifteen, fifteen, and twenty sounds... reasonable." It sounded a lot better than reasonable. And it didn't sound reasonable at all. The idea that he was about to be given fifteen thousand dollars made him want to smile—except that it wasn't like August Neuland was just *giving* him the money. "And, yes," he added before the man had to ask again, "I can get started immediately. Today."

"Wonderful, Marcus. Just wonderful!"

"My... my laptop is in my car," Marcus said, since that seemed like a good way to show he was, in fact, starting immediately. "Is it OK if I bring it in? Set up here?"

"I will do you one better, Marcus. Feel free to consider this booth your office away from the office. I will reserve this booth for you every day, for as long as you need it."

"Great." Marcus noticed the girl had reappeared and was scraping mashed potatoes back into its dish. Their eyes met once, briefly. If she was embarrassed by dropping the mashed potatoes, he saw none of it in her light brown eyes. Instead, she looked... wary? She looked away before he could be sure.

"It will be better than great, Marcus," August Neuland said, pulling Marcus's attention back to him. "It will be perfect. We'll get a chance to check in with each other every morning, or afternoon, depending. And if you need anything, anything at all, you let me know."

"I will," Marcus said.

"Was there anything else?"

Marcus wanted to ask if this whole thing was a joke. He desperately wanted it to be a joke. Even if that meant he wouldn't be getting fifteen thousand dollars. Or fifty thousand.

"Forgive me, Marcus," the man said. "I forgot. Just a second." He leaned to his left, reached into a pocket, and took out his phone.

Marcus's eyes went to the phone. He had never seen one of those before, except on TV, and behind thick glass. Those phones weren't put out where people could actually touch them. Either you could afford one, or you just looked. Marcus kept his hands to himself and just looked.

"It's a beauty, isn't it?" August Neuland held the phone in front of him, and started tapping and sliding. "I got mine as soon as it was available."

Marcus nodded. In his pocket, his phone vibrated to let him know he had received a message.

"There you go," the man said. "We are in business." He slipped the phone back into his pocket.

Marcus resisted the urge to take out his phone and read the message. He could guess what it said.

"It's a pleasure doing business with you, Marcus," August Neuland said, standing.

Marcus stood too, since it seemed like the thing to do. He shook the man's hand again.

"If you don't mind my asking," Marcus said, "what made you... choose... me? For this job?"

"I believe in the future, Marcus."

"The future." Marcus glanced across the dining room. The girl had finished scraping up the mashed potatoes. She was mopping the floor by the double doors. "The future?" Marcus said again, looking at August Neuland.

The man nodded with an enthusiasm that made Marcus's world sway. "Call it Fate, if you will, or just faith that the World, the Universe, everything, Marcus, runs in a certain way, and that what is meant to happen, will happen." August Neuland pointed to the plastic sign in the corner of the window. "When I need servers, I put up my sign, and servers show up. Like Miss Gold back there, or Keenan, who I found the same way last week. That works for simple jobs that can be filled with the local talent pool. But when I needed a dragon hunter, a somewhat more specialized occupation as I'm sure you will agree, I had to think bigger. I put up my sign, like I always do, but this time I put that sign where the whole world could see it, including the hunter. You saw the sign, and you called. That makes you the hunter. So here we are."

"I was the first one who called?"

"I took only one call, Marcus. I only needed to take one call. The hunter's call." He poked Marcus in the chest. "Your call." He took his finger back. "That's the way the World works, Marcus, if you know what you're doing, and I've been doing this a long time." August Neuland smiled and gave Marcus a light slap on the shoulder.

"One more thing," Marcus said. "Do I... should I keep this secret? The job you're paying me for?"

Still smiling, August Neuland shook his head. "Not at all, Marcus. Not at all. Who would believe you?" He gave Marcus's shoulder another light slap, then he picked up the manila folder and his pen. "I'll check in on you in a bit, after the lunch rush. And speaking of lunch, you feel free to help yourself to anything on the buffet, OK? Everything's on the house."

Marcus nodded. Who would believe him? He wasn't sure he did.

"Great!"

He watched the man walk away, then went out to his mother's car. Still thinking of his phone in his pocket and the message waiting for him, he popped the trunk, grabbed his laptop and its power supply, and walked inside. Then left his laptop on the table and walked back outside to close the trunk.

When he returned to the table the second time, his tea had been replaced with a new glass that had fresh ice, and a small, triangular black sign with "RESERVED" in gold letters had appeared. He put the laptop on the table and sat down. He would look for a power outlet when he needed one. Right now it was everything he could do not to take his phone out of his pocket, check the message, and faint.

His hand went automatically to his glass of tea and lifted it to his mouth. He stopped himself before taking a sip, and set it down. Then he pushed it away from him as far as could be managed on the tabletop. He looked around.

More lunchtime diners had appeared. Men and women in suits and pantsuits, business casual and blue collar uniforms of various types, stood in line or sat eating in booths. Seeing people eat caused Marcus's stomach to remind him that he hadn't eaten since breakfast. Seeing *what* the people were eating, though, convinced his stomach it could wait.

In the back of the restaurant, Thara Gold had finished mopping and disappeared into the back again.

Marcus carefully took his phone out of his pocket and placed it on the table. Casually, as casually as he possibly could, he activated the display and reviewed his waiting message.

The message informed him that the sum of $15,000 had been deposited into his account from BORCOK***YELLOWSIGNBUFF.

He opened his laptop with shaking hands. He didn't know how he was going to explain his new job to his mother. Or Morgan. Or anyone. He wasn't sure he could explain it to himself.

He picked up his phone and nearly called Morgan before he placed it on the table again.

He jumped as his phone buzzed. The displayed told him Morgan was calling.

He wondered if this was more of August Neuland's "Fate" at work.

His hands shook again as he picked up the phone and took the call.

3. Dragon Dumplings

The Queen

IN THE WARMTH OF HER Kitchen, The Queen's mandibles cracked open the brain case of the last drone and munched contentedly. The drones always tasted better when they died happy.

She surveyed the ring of still-twitching bodies that surrounded Her, each one headless and swollen with Her eggs. One egg each, because She had loved each of Her drones equally.

How long had it been since She last Made Babies? Too long.

The Queen sighed a happy, satisfied sigh, then belched a happy, satisfied belch, and settled down for a happy, satisfied nap. She looked forward to a dream of Devouring the World with Her new Daughters by Her side.

The Seeker

THE SEEKER STALKED THE SHADOWS, avoiding the gaze of his old enemy, the Sun. The Sun could not hurt him, directly, but he didn't want the Bright Bastard to know where he was.

By now, the Sun had surely spotted the broken mountaintop that had been the Seeker's bed for so long. From His place in the Heavens, the Sun peered down constantly, ever vigilant, ever watching, always poking His Rays in where He was not wanted. Meddling when He could, selling the information He collected to others when it suited His Purposes. Who had the Sun already informed?

Did any of the Seeker's old enemies still walk the World? Was there anyone left for the Sun to gossip with?

At least one new enemy had been born while the Seeker slept, and grown powerful. Not quite a God, but on Her way. Did the Sun know about this new God? Would it be worth enduring the gaze of the Golden Eye to see if there might be more to learn in this new world?

First, though, the Seeker needed new clothes. His old clothes no longer seemed in vogue. Fashions were so fickle.

The Bug

THE BUG ENJOYED THE AUTUMN sunshine, and the blue sky overhead. In earlier days, his paint had been the pale blue of the early morning sky, just after the sun had risen. Now, though, his paint had faded, due in no small part to the long years he had spent exposed to the bright sunshine he currently enjoyed. His paint was now more like the last minutes of twilight.

New colors had blossomed among the cars that came and went around the Bug on a daily basis, then faded. It was the nature of Nature. Flowers bloomed, then faded, season after season, year after year.

The Bug knew he had faded, but he didn't mind. He didn't envy the new cars with their rose golds and their moss greens just like he hadn't envied the black golds and champagne beiges that came before.

The Bug looked vintage, and he was proud of it. And he had certainly held up better than the First Ugly Replacement. No one had ever made the mistake of trying to remove snow and ice from the Bug's hood with a screwdriver. The poor First Ugly Replacement's hood looked as if he had been in a fight with the bobcat it had been named after, and lost.

It was on days like today that the Bug most missed driving. Even a tow would have been nice.

1

MARCUS PICKED UP HIS PHONE.

"Hey," he said, trying to put as much player into his voice as he could. "You at lunch—"

"Hey, Baby Boy," Morgan said. She sounded sweet. "Guess who I just talked too?" Too sweet. "I'll tell you in a minute. First, guess who I just found out is in town? You'll never believe it."

"I was going to call you—"

"I know you were, Baby Boy." Honey dripping. "How did your job interview go?"

"Mom told you about that, did she?"

"Not exactly. Not in so many words. You know how she is when your girlfriends call."

"Did she call you Daisy again?" Marcus asked, trying to lighten the mood. "You know she thinks it's funny—"

"Mikayla, but who's paying attention? It's just her little joke." Still pouring the honey. "So did you get that busboy job?" A bucket of honey, with the buzzing of angry bees just beginning to be heard. "The one you told Mom Nelson about on Monday? The one you drove two hours to interview for today, Friday? In Rio Cruces? Where your girlfriend—whose name is *Morgan*, by the way— Did you know Morgan lives in Rio Cruces, Baby Boy?"

Marcus resisted the urge to look around, to make sure no one was watching him. And to make sure Morgan wasn't about to come through the front door of the restaurant with a swarm of bees in her wake.

He lowered his voice. "It's not a busboy job—"

"Is your phone not working, Baby Boy? Oh, right. We're talking on your phone right now. So it must be working. Was it working earlier this week? Why, yes, I do believe it was working during our little talk on Wednesday. Two days after you knew you were coming."

He could almost see her. Her eyes looking up, her head tilting back and forth as she spoke. "Morgan—"

There was much more buzzing now, much less honey. "So I'm going to guess it's not the phone having the problem. This one I'm going to chalk up to user error. No. Player error."

In the back of the restaurant, the girl with the eyes—*Thara*, the voice in his head supplied—came out of the back bearing a new chafing dish. He noticed her looking at him. Saw her notice him looking at her. He hunched over his laptop, almost putting his head against the screen.

"I was going to call you," he said into his phone, his mouth just above the laptop keyboard. "I didn't want to tell you until I knew for sure. And, really, it's..." He paused. "Wait. Why did you call my mom?"

"What difference does that make, Baby Boy?" She didn't wait for him to respond. "If you have to know, I was going to surprise you by driving down there tonight, after work. So I called your mother to ask what your schedule was."

"You were going to drive down here? I mean, there? Why?"

"To see you, silly. It's been so long. I was going to drag your shapely ass back up here for a weekend of dancing, sexing, more dancing, more sexing, and maybe even some talking."

"No eating? A man can't live on dancing and sexing alone."

"Oh, you weren't going to be doing them alone, Baby Boy. But don't try to change the subject. Tell me about this job."

"Not much to say, really, except, well, I just got it."

"Yay!" she screamed into the phone and his ear. "That's great, Marcus! That's really great. So what is the job."

Dragon hunter, he didn't say. He went on to not say, *I'm being paid fifty grand—with fifteen grand up front—to find a dragon and deliver it to the Yellow Sign Buffet.*

He said, "I'm not really sure how to describe it."

"It's not busboy, is it? Or a waiter? Or a cook?"

"Hell, no. It's... well, I'm being hired to look for... something."

He raised his head just enough to see over the top of his laptop.

"What do they want?" Morgan asked.

Her, said the voice inside his head as he spotted the waitress again. He ducked back down.

"I can't tell you over the phone." He wasn't sure he'd be able to tell her in person, either, but that could wait.

"Oooh, so it's a secret then? Did you have to sign a nondisclosure agreement?"

"No, not exactly." *Who would believe you?* "It's just... hard to explain."

"Uh huh," she said. "What can you be hired to find, Baby Boy, that's so hard to explain?"

"I have depths, girl, depths. You only met me in college, you know."

"You were pretty boring before I met you, Baby Boy."

"And yet you're the one who asked me out. So I think you must have sensed the depth."

"Something's getting deep in here, that's for sure."

Marcus decided to press his luck, and change the subject. "You still up for all that dancing and sexing? I got a signing bonus," he added, "so ice cream's on me."

"A signing bonus?" He could almost see her pulling her head back, as if he were right there in the room with her and she needed distance to get a better look at him. "You got a signing bonus? How much?"

"I'll tell you later."

"You're definitely buying."

"It'll be my pleasure."

"It'll be a first."

"Ouch. That's mean."

"Just keeping it a hundred."

"I was going to call you."

"And I believe you more every time you say it, Baby Boy."

"Ouch again, girl. Ease up, or I'm going to have to explain all these bruises to my girlfriend."

"Oh, yeah? When does your girlfriend get off work? Maybe she and I should have a talk."

"When do you get off work? Maybe I can watch."

"Five o'clock, like a woman with a real career, but don't think you're going to pick me up in your mother's car. You just meet me at my apartment and we'll pick up the thread from there."

After agreeing to meet her at five-thirty and swapping a "Love you" for a "Love you, Baby Boy," Marcus ended the call.

He put the phone back on the table and spent a few minutes trying to think about what he would tell her later, over dinner. *Hey, baby, who's your dragon hunter?* He shook his head.

For now, he had to figure out how to do the job he had been hired for. At least he had a place to start. He typed in the URL for the radio station's Web page. The so-called dragon video had to be a hoax. But it was a place to start.

2

SOMEONE STANDING NEXT TO THE window, outside the Yellow Sign Buffet, made Marcus look up, away from the screen of his laptop. He had just found the Web page for the radio station and clicked on the video link with the blurry picture of beat up cars. He hadn't noticed anyone walk past the window.

Him, said the annoying voice in his mind before he even had a chance to register it was, in fact, a man standing less than three feet from him, separated only by the tinted window. Marcus began to wonder what it was about the Yellow Sign Buffet that made him notice people he would otherwise hardly see.

The sun had passed zenith, and the man stood in the narrow shadow cast by the roof of the restaurant. The man seemed to be his own shadow, barely a silhouette against the brightly lit parking lot, city street, and wrecked restaurant behind him. What Marcus could make out of the man's black on black clothes was... incongruous. Unless the man had come straight from a Renaissance Faire or a live-action roleplaying game, or was a particularly devoted cosplayer.

The man's mane of shaggy black hair deepened the darkness that surrounded his face, so only his silver eyes were visible, but what Marcus could see of his features seemed vaguely Asian. As if Genghis Khan had decided he was a LARPing goth.

A bulky black leather trench coat with a high collar draped down to the man's knees. The coat hung open, revealing a shirt of black scale armor, the silver edges of the scales glinting like overlapping fingernail

125

crescent Moons in the night sky. A studded leather belt with a large black metal buckle was strapped to his waist. The hilt of a sword poked out from under his left arm. Baggy black leather trousers ended in heavy black leather boots. Marcus wondered how many cows and pigs had been slaughtered just to clothe one man.

The man looked, Marcus realized, like what a dragon hunter was *supposed* to look like. A warrior. Armored and armed. Marcus suddenly felt very unqualified for his new job. And underdressed.

Him, agreed the voice in his head, causing Marcus to have his first-ever incident of gender attraction confusion.

As if the man had also heard the voice in Marcus's head, he stopped looking past Marcus and looked down at him.

The distance above Marcus that the man looked down at him from telescoped vertiginously, as if Marcus were sinking to a distance more appropriate to their relative stations, or as if the man were rapidly rising above him to take his proper place in the order of things. That neither of them was actually moving at the center of the swirling maelstrom that surrounded them made Marcus's inner ears want to bleed and his eyes to cry foul.

He would have blinked. He would have looked away, but the silver eyes held him. He was being looked at, and he would sit still and be looked at until—

The man turned to his right and...

Marcus's mind desperately wanted to believe the man had walked away, the tails of the trench coat fluttering around the point of the sword in its sheath. It would, his mind insisted, have been a cool image. His eyes *had* seen the man begin to take the first step. After that was where his mind didn't want to go.

The man took a step. That was all that happened. He didn't... extend into black infinity, or become one with the shadow cast by the noonday sun, or... vanish.

The man had just taken a step, and was about to open the door behind Marcus and bring the Ren Faire inside.

Except the man was no longer visible, and the door behind Marcus did not open.

The speakers of his laptop erupted with a roar that suddenly seemed all too real, making him jump. On the screen, the image of the video went white and came to an end, cutting off the roar.

3

EVEN WITH THE MAN IN black no longer looking down at him, Marcus didn't feel like much of a dragon hunter. With each minute that ticked by, the euphoria of having fifteen thousand dollars in his bank account leached away, replaced by a growing sense of panic. Panic that August Neuland would want his money back. Panic about what he was going to tell Morgan in a few hours. Was this what people meant when they talked about "impostor syndrome?"

August Neuland's words still echoed in his head. *You saw the sign. You called, and here we are.*

Here he was, and he had no idea where that was.

How did one find dragons in the modern world? Or, more precisely, how did one find mythical beasts in the real world?

He almost wished "dragon" had just been a fancy, misleading word for "Norwegian brown rat" or "big-ass-scary cockroach," and that he had been hired as an exterminator, no matter what Mom Nelson thought was an appropriate job for a college graduate or what Morgan would think. But it wasn't and he hadn't.

He watched the video from the radio station's Web page over and over, with the sound turned down, trying to spot anything that would make it clear, beyond any shadow of a doubt, that what he was seeing was fake. He started with the assumption that it was fake because, despite August Neuland's faith in the Future—call it Fate, if you will—despite the coincidence of a dragon sighting in Rio Cruces the night before he took a job as a dragon hunter in Rio Cruces, the video had to be fake.

It *had* to be. Dragons weren't real. They had never been real. No one knew what St. George had slain, or even if he had slain anything. For all anyone knew, St. George, or his publicist, had made the whole story up.

The creature in the video wasn't a dog, not even a big dog in some kind of a costume. The creature moved too much like a lizard. In fact, it moved *exactly* like a lizard, with its wide-splayed front legs and long claws. With its head jerking around and its crest spiking and its eyes swiveling. With its long tongue shooting out to hit the windshield and lick away the bright orange spot that had to be a tow sticker.

Not that the video was *clear*. The lighting was terrible, coming only from streetlamps that flared when they came into frame, their yellow-white coronas wiping out the rest of the image. The lights that could be seen in some of the apartment windows weren't enough to make any difference. Focus jumped back and forth between the buildings, cars, and people beyond the creature and the various parts of the creature nearest to the camera at any given time.

But it certainly looked like an iguana scurrying lightning fast into frame, head butting a tire, then stopping to look around, before slowly climbing on the angular hood of a car that had to date back to the 1980s. Then licking a tow sticker off the car's windshield. A really big iguana, the size of a car, with gleaming scales, that roared and breathed white fire at the camera.

Marcus wondered if this was some kind of forced perspective special effect, like monster movies used in the 1950s. Film a normal-sized iguana in close-up as it crawled over model cars with tiny rear fins and miniature dance halls with even more miniature neon lights.

He *wanted* it to be some kind of special effect, but he couldn't spot any flaws. Nothing he could point at and say, with certainty, *This is fake*.

While he was watching the video for maybe the twentieth time, he noticed a new video had been posted to the radio's Web page under the headline, "More DRAGON Video!!! CHECK IT OUT!"

This video showed the same scene as the first, but from almost the exact opposite vantage point. The car-sized lizard raced out, head butted the tires of the same car it climbed on—Marcus now recognized the car as a Plymouth Omni—did the tongue thing, then turned away from the camera, spat, and spewed a cone of fire. Then ran away from the camera to disappear into the darkness, the tip of its tail the last part of it that was visible.

Marcus watched this video over and over, as well, then downloaded both videos to his laptop so he could watch them side by side. He found video editing and playback software so he could sync up the two feeds and watch them both frame by frame.

This wasn't what he had thought he would be doing with his CIS degree when he graduated, but it seemed close enough. Mom Nelson would be proud. That is, after he took an hour or two to explain to her what he had done, and that, no, not everyone would know how to do what he had done, or at least not as fast. Except he knew Mom Nelson would never sit still for the explanation.

When he looked up from his screen, the lunch rush was over. There were still a few diners, but no one on the buffet line, and no sign of the waitress or the other employee who seemed to be doing all the work that didn't involve greeting customers on the way in or taking their money on the way out.

He looked back at the screen with the side-by-side videos playing in slow, synchronized motion. He had not spotted anything that could prove either video was a hoax.

The radio station, when it posted the second video, had included the name of the apartment complex where the two videos were made. Marcus did a quick map lookup and saw that he was sitting a mere few blocks from where multiple people reported seeing a dragon the night before.

Marcus shook his head as he heard August Neuland's words in his head. *That's the way the World works, Marcus, if you know what you're doing, and I've been doing this a long time.*

4

THROUGHOUT THE LUNCH RUSH, SUCH as it was, hauling food, such as it was, out to the steam tables and bringing back empty chafing dishes and stacks of dirty trays piled with dirty plates and half-filled cups, Thara kept an eye on the young man who had been hired as a dragon hunter.

He didn't *look* like a dragon hunter. He looked like a kid just out of college. More like the kind of kid who was hired to be her next World's Worst Manager than the kind who would do a St. George routine.

Was dragon hunter a college degree or a vocational course? Thara had never gone to either college or vo-tech, but she was pretty sure she would have noticed if any school of either type had offered classes in how to find her and bring her down.

The summer fantasies she and Nancy Chisum had played out suddenly seemed to be coming real.

She wanted to ask Mr. Neuland what the young man's name was, but the owner and manager of the Yellow Sign Buffet had gone into his office and closed the door. And stayed there, presumably owning and managing for all he was worth. She knew Ricky, the so-called Mr. Lampley, didn't know, so she hadn't asked him. Or called him Mr. Lampley.

So far, the only positive thing she could note about the restaurant's new dragon hunter was that he hadn't eaten anything from the buffet.

She had stopped trying to identify the dishes that came out of the back on the conveyor belt. What might have been "sushi casserole"— some kind of twisted, shell-like pasta covered with bright yellow cheese and containing strips of raw fish—was the last straw. After that, she picked up the steam table pans with her ovenmitted hands, hauled them through the swinging double doors, and placed them in the steam tables, holding her breath the entire time. She didn't want to know what anything was called, or whether it was intended as an entree, an appetizer, or a dessert.

During a lull, when she and Keenan were standing behind the swinging doors, looking through the tiny windows, watching for booths that needed busing or empty chafing dishes to bring back to throw on the heap growing around the dive station, she asked, "What kind of cuisine do they say they serve here?"

Keenan looked to be twenty, plus-or-minus a year or so. He had curly brown hair tucked under a poofy polyester brown hat the same color as his polyester trousers. His face was spotted with both acne and freckles.

"That black guy in the front asked me the same thing," Keenan said. "I told him I don't know, just what's on the tables." He paused. "What does cuisine look like? Is it good?"

"Never mind."

No one else had shown up to help with the lunch rush, neither existing employees like Keenan nor newly suckered recruits like Thara, and the so-called Mr. Lampley alternated between greeting customers at the front door, taking the customers money as they left, and telling Thara where to put the trays of so-called food on his way to the back to hide in the manager's office with Mr. Neuland. So the dirty dishes had become a cheese- and sauce-smeared monument to Midwestern appetites. More than once Thara had considered volunteering to wash the dishes, because then she wouldn't have to hold her breath and blank her mind so often, but if she did that she wouldn't be able to keep an eye on the so-called dragon hunter.

"Gold," Keenan said, interrupting her thoughts. "You're up."

"Call me Thara," she said for the fifth time.

Keenan tapped on the window in front of his face. "Booth two needs busing, and it's your turn."

"Which one is booth two?"

"The one that needs busing," he said, tapping the window again.

Thara pushed through her half of the double door and walked past the steam tables with their slowly congealing leftovers to survey the booths. No one had explained how the booths were numbered, and she had seen no map, but it didn't matter. Of the three tables that actually needed busing, only one of them could logically be booth two, and it was the booth adjacent to the dragon hunter.

"Excuse me, miss," said a woman with red hair held up with enough hairspray it glistened under the fluorescent lights.

Thara smiled her no-I'm-not-too-busy-to-stop-what-I'm-doing-to-answer-your-question smile and said, "Yes?"

The woman gestured to the still overflowing plate in front of her. "Can I get a to-go box?"

"No," Thara said, still smiling, "this is an all you can eat buffet. We don't offer to-go boxes. Can I refill your drink?"

She walked away before the woman could answer.

She managed to avoid making eye contact with any other customers on her way to the front, which wasn't hard. The lunch crowd had thinned, and most of those still eating were focused on transferring the food on their plates into their faces.

The dining room had been surprisingly quiet throughout lunch. There was very little conversation, and the woman's failed attempt to take all-you-can-eat home in a to-go box had been one of the only times a customer had actually spoken to her. The regular customers of the Yellow Sign Buffet seemed to be interested in only two things: eating and leaving. They knew what they wanted—even if Thara had no idea what that was—and they left after they got it. No unnecessary conversations with the staff, or even each other. Most of them didn't even go back for seconds. That part Thara could understand.

The booth next to the dragon hunter was typical of what she had seen during the lunch rush. One dirty place setting for each of the three people who had sat there. A one-plate-to-one-customer ratio was not typical for an all-you-can-eat buffet. Two plates to one customer, at least, was more common, and Thara had witnessed ratios as high as four-to-one and five-to-one. That the food at the Yellow Sign Buffet might be more satisfying or filling was not an answer she was prepared to accept.

Three plates with crumpled paper napkins, three forks, and three plastic cups with surprisingly similar levels of leftover soda and melting ice. Thara remembered the two men and the woman who had sat there, because all of them had been wearing navy suits with white shirts and red ties. She hadn't realized the old "IBM Uniform" was still a thing after "casual Fridays" had conquered the rest of the week in the 1990s.

She glanced at the dragon hunter as she stacked the plates. He had spent the last two-and-a-half hours hunched over his laptop, typing and clicking, except when she had noticed him looking at her. Like now.

When his eyes weren't looking at her, she found them attractive. When she caught him looking at her, though, he mostly looked confused.

It wasn't a good look on him. Lines appeared on his smooth forehead, his mouth went straight, and the corners of his eyes became serious. As if she were a riddle he couldn't quite figure out.

She gave him the same smile she had given the woman with the red hair. "Can I refill your drink?"

His lips tried to smile, as if he heard the wilting sarcasm she knew she had kept out of her voice, but he only shook his head. His head was shaved, which made Thara wonder if she would look as good with her own hair shaved. She had never tried fully bald. She had shaved the left side of her head during the post-punk, New Wave period of the 1980s when girls just wanted to have fun, but most often she wore a version of her current pixie cut. Aside from a trim every six to eight weeks, it was low maintenance.

She turned back to the table and was dumping the two less-full cups into the third so she could stack them, when he spoke.

"I did have a question, though."

"Yes?" She switched her smile back on as she looked at him again.

"What," he started, then glanced toward the steam tables. "If you don't mind my asking, what kind of cuisine do you serve here? I haven't noticed any real... theme. I guess."

"It's a buffet," Thara said. She put the two cups together, then put them on the stack of plates. "They serve whatever's on the steam tables."

He leaned forward. "What *is* on the steam tables?"

Thara tried not to smile for real as she picked up the plates and cups with both hands, then transferred the load to her right hand. She picked up the cups with their slurry of sodas. "I have no idea," she said. Then she turned her back on him and walked away.

He was waiting for her when she came back with a wet towel to wipe the table.

"Does holding your breath help?"

Thara gave him a genuine smile this time. She nodded. "Yes, it does."

"Wait," he said before could walk away. "Again, if you don't mind my asking—"

"So polite," Thara said. "You realize I work here, right?"

"I just don't want to come off all creepy," he said. "I was going to ask if you lived around here."

Thara let the smile fade. "Why?"

"Have you seen these?" He pointed to his laptop. "There's these videos of... of a something like a big lizard, or a dragon. Or something. And they were taken really close to here."

"How close?"

"Like, around the corner close. You gotta see these." He twisted his laptop so she could see it.

Still holding the damp towel, Thara stepped closer. Two videos played side by side on the screen. One started before the other, but both showed her in dragon form running through the parking lot, pushing Nova back into place, then climbing on Nova to lick the tow sticker off. Both videos ended with her breathing fire and running away.

It was more fascinating than she expected to see herself as a dragon. Neither video would win the Oscars for best special effects or cinematography, but they were clearer than any amateur footage that had caught her before. Those had been grainy 8mm footage or blurry snapshots. Nothing like this. Technology had caught up with her, and she had almost let it catch her. She was going to have to be more careful.

"Isn't that something else?" he asked.

Thara nodded. The videos replayed automatically. She watched herself run, stop, push, climb, lick, spit, roar, and run away again. With the two videos side by side, it was a lot like the way she saw when she was in dragon form, with two independently moving and focusing eyes.

"Do you know that apartment complex?"

Thara nodded again. She tilted her head to the left. She had never before wondered if her butt looked big as a dragon. Dragons were supposed to be beyond all that body image nonsense, right? Or maybe having two bodies made the issue twice as bad. She had never seen another dragon's butt, though, not before last night. Then she had been more distracted by the wings and the roar and the simple fact that there was another dragon to notice the other dragon's butt. At twice her size, though, his butt had to be much bigger.

"So how do you know where this is?" she asked. "I don't see any signs."

"Whoever posted the second video forgot to take out the location tagging."

"Great." She was going to have to move.

"Why do you have to move?"

Thara hadn't intended to say that last bit out loud. She pulled her eyes away from the videos. "Now it's going to be like living in Bigfoot Central, or Roswell, New Mexico. So much for the peace and quiet."

She turned to walk away, but he asked her to wait. She did. She was a waiter. It's what waiters did, though usually she tried to do it with a friendlier expression on her face.

"Did you see it?" he asked. "Did you see the dragon last night?"

"No," she said. Because she hadn't. There weren't any mirrors that big. "Would you like me to refill your drink?" She could see his drink didn't need refilling, but when he told her *no*, as he inevitably would, she could use that as an excuse to walk away.

He ignored her offer, his brown eyes never leaving hers. A hint of a smile tugged at the corners of his lips. "You did, didn't you? You saw something."

"I stayed in last night," she said, which wasn't a lie if you started the stayed-in-last-night clock at the right point. "I had a lot of stuff to pick up after the earthquake."

His head turned slightly, but his eyes stayed steady. "You didn't even hear the roar?"

"Oh, I heard a roar." She could still *feel* the other dragon's roar. "I heard lots of roars. Lots of shouting too, and a few screams. Plenty of sirens, as well. But since no dragon crashed through my front door and asked to borrow a cup of kerosene, I didn't assume any of it had anything to do with a dragon. Or me."

"Uh huh." His lips were in full smirk mode now.

"Fine, you caught me. The dragon sneaked in my bedroom window and helped me clean up before curling up in a corner to sleep it off."

"Is he still there?"

"She," Thara said, "and, no, she left this morning."

"A lady dragon?"

"You didn't think there would be both kinds?"

He shrugged and smiled. He let his eyes leave hers, finally, and twisted his laptop back to face him. "So you think this is a lady dragon? How can you tell?"

"So that's a 'no' on the drink refill?"

Then she turned and left him again before he could respond. And before she could start to like him. It was never a good idea to start liking customers, and it was completely pointless here at the Yellow Sign Buffet with its prominent "No Tipping" signs. She felt him watching her all the way across the dining room, then all the way back to the double doors.

Once past the double doors, Thara went to the big sink and started moving plates, trays, and cups out of the way. The hot water steamed as she turned it on. She rolled up the sleeves of her shirt, then found the industrial-sized bottle of industrial dishwashing liquid under the sink and dumped an industrial-sized quantity of the pink liquid into the water.

"If you don't mind, uh, Gold," the so-called Mr. Lampley said as he came out of the office behind her and continued his audition for World's Worst Manager, "could you, uh, get all these dishes washed? We're going to need them. For dinner."

She didn't bother to turn around. "Wash the dishes," she said, brightly. She made no attempt to hide the sarcasm. He wasn't a customer. "Thank you."

As expected, he didn't seem to notice. "Keenan, make sure all the tables are bussed, then check the drink stations. Oh, and, uh, we need you both to stay and help with dinner. Thanks, guys, we really appreciate what you've done for us. Today." Then he was through the double doors and into the dining room.

Thara turned to look at Keenan. He was still standing at the double doors, looking out the window.

"That's it?" Thara asked.

Keenan visibly jumped, then looked at her. "That's what?"

She nodded after Ricky. "That's it? No getting friendly with his hands? To either of us? No pep talk about teamwork where he tells us we can't leave because we owe it to ourselves? No standing around to stare at us to make sure we actually do what he tells us?"

Keenan looked confused. "We're short staffed today."

"Never mind."

Keenan pushed through the doors and Thara turned back to the big sink and the amorphous blob of shimmering soap bubbles growing out of it. The so-called Mr. Lampley was going to have to step up his game if he was going to be the World's Worst Manager. She had faith in him, though. She knew he would come around. He might even be coming back now, to do all those things he had obviously forgotten.

Thara took one of the brown plastic aprons from the hooks on the wall by the sink and tied it on. As she started tipping plates into the hot, soapy water, she made a point of not thinking about the dragon hunter with the big brown eyes.

5

THARA WAS STEAMING FROM THE hours spent washing, rinsing and stacking clean plastic trays, ceramic plates, plastic cups, and plain, blunt silverware when she finally peeled off her apron. She looked around, but there was still no clock on the walls of the stainless-steel cave. There were no windows either, but she could feel the autumn sun was beginning to set beyond the cinderblock walls. She hung the apron back on its hook. The apron hadn't been especially useful, except to catch a sampling of the splatters of leftover food and drinks. The parts of her the apron had ostensibly kept dry were damp with sweat instead, and she wasn't sure if that was better or worse. She felt hot and soggy. Her bangs drooped in front of her eyes. She wondered if she had worked through her break.

The so-called Mr. Lampley had walked past her several times, but other than a few meager *Good work, Gold*'s and *Keep it up, Gold*'s he hadn't said much. He had certainly never said *Take your break, Gold*. She had been listening for that one.

The so-called Mr. Lampley must have said something to Keenan, though, because the boy was taking a teetering stack of plastic trays to the dining room.

At one point, Keenan had dropped off a single plate and cup for her to wash, so he had been given a break. And, for some reason, he had chosen to eat from the buffet. Thara never expected to get that hungry.

She pushed her bangs out of her eyes and glanced at the manager's office. Neither Mr. Neuland nor the so-called Mr. Lampley were visible through the big window. She was dimly aware that the so-called Mr.

Lampley had just passed through into the dining room. Mr. Neuland must have left through the special manager's escape hatch in the office.

The conveyor belt from the kitchen—wherever that particular pit of Hell was located—was empty and still. She decided that meant she could take her break now.

The dining room was empty, except Keenan restocking the trays and plates on the buffet line, and the so-called Mr. Lampley standing behind the front counter with his back to her. There was no sign of the dragon hunter. She surprised herself by being both relieved that he was gone, and a bit disappointed. She was in no fit state to be seen, and she didn't want to see him anyway.

The steam tables were empty, which she had expected, since she had washed more than enough empty chafing dishes to fill the tables twice, but the drink stations were all still humming. She hadn't seen anyone making the tea, so she opted for a soda on the basis that it was probably safe. There were boxes of soda syrup stacked in the back, so she knew no one who worked at the Yellow Sign Buffet was responsible for anything other than connecting hose A to valve B.

She felt a bit light-headed from the extended standing, the steam, and from not having eaten since the day before, but she still had no intention of eating anything she might find in the restaurant. Not even the soft serve yogurt, white or brown. She wondered if she would have enough time on her self-assigned break to walk down to the seafood restaurant around the corner on Fifty-first Street—

With a loud hum and a whiff of ozone, the conveyor belt lurched into motion.

She sighed, then took a sip of her drink as she watched the rollers of the conveyor system spin. No, there was not going to be time. If she were going to continue working here, she was going to need some way to eat. She wondered if Mr. Neuland would object to her bringing a bag lunch, or having pizza delivered.

Four stainless-steel pitchers full of something steaming and, presumably, liquid, were the first things to emerge through the plastic curtain, followed by nearly spherical glass pitchers with the traditional black and orange handles of regular and decaf coffee. Then the first of the chafing dishes laden with steaming food emerged. She deliberately refused to think what might be in the pitchers or waiting under the stainless-steel cover. She also made a point not to think about the cooks she had never seen since entering the restaurant but who had to be hiding in the darkness behind the split plastic curtains.

She stood and watched the conveyor belt with no interest whatsoever until the so-called Mr. Lampley came back and told her and Keenan to start loading the steam tables.

Keenan immediately picked up a stainless-steel pitcher in each hand and took them into the dining room. He came back a few minutes later with empty pitchers that he dropped into the sink she had just emptied. Thara watched him do that twice more. Then she put her plastic cup into the sink with the pitchers, found a clean set of oven mitts and did as she was told.

The so-called Mr. Lampley stepped out of the office. "And, um, try not to drop any of the, uh, dishes, this time, Gold," he told her before he went back to manning the front counter.

Thara wanted to say she wasn't being paid enough to not drop anything, then remembered she had no idea what she was being paid. She was pretty sure it wasn't enough, though. But since she would be the one cleaning it up, she decided to not drop anything.

Then she barreled through the double doors into the dining room, using the chafing dish like a breaching ram, more than half hoping Keenan was in the process of coming the other way. He wasn't.

6

MARCUS WAITED UNTIL THE LAST possible minute to leave the restaurant, because he wanted to talk to Thara-with-an-h before he left. But she never reappeared. For all he knew, she had left after the lunch shift, through some back door he hadn't been able to see.

Since Thara lived in the same apartment complex where the dragon videos had been shot, he thought he might offer her a ride home in exchange for a quick tour. He could triangulate out where the videos had been shot on his own, but it would be faster if she just showed him. Or, at least, that's the reason he gave himself for sticking around, waiting to see her again.

The waitress wasn't his type, he told himself again as he drove away from the restaurant. Morgan was his type, personified. Refined through years of dating in high school and college. He doubted the waitress had been to college. Which was another strike against her, aside from being a white girl and a waitress.

He had to use his phone to find Morgan's apartment. He had been there only once before, and he hadn't been driving. She lived across the river from downtown Rio Cruces, with the skyline visible from her third-floor patio—if you leaned to the right to look past the next building in the complex. You could even see a thin, vertical sliver of the midcentury twenty-floor office building she worked in.

She lived close enough to her work that Marcus knew she would beat him there. Still, he had meant to arrive on time, not fifteen minutes late.

He wasn't late because he waited too long for the waitress, though. He was late was because he missed the change in the street name that happened as he crossed the bridge from downtown, then missed the tree-shrouded right turn he should have made after the bridge. He had to drive past, find a place on the left side of the street he could use to turn around.

Then he had to figure out how he was supposed to get through the gated entrance as a mere visitor. When Morgan drove, the gate just opened for her. He pulled up beside the hooded keypad and looked for instructions. He punched in the supersecret four-digit code clearly posted "For Deliveries Only," then drove through the gate when it opened. The whole process had seemed a lot cooler and less of a hassle when he was a passenger.

Mom Nelson's Ford Focus felt drabber and more antiquated as he drove deeper into Morgan's apartment complex. Not all the parked cars were shiny new sedans and crossover SUVs, but few of them seemed as old as the Focus. When Morgan had driven him up over the summer, she had still been driving the Volvo her parents had used to shuttle her from volleyball to ballet in her tween and teen years. They had given her the car when she started college while they upgraded to something with less of a soccer mom vibe. Marcus looked for the Volvo, but saw no sign of it, even when he pulled into a parking spot next to Morgan's building.

He started to grab his duffle bag and his laptop, then opted to leave them in the trunk. He could come back to get all that later. He didn't want to show up for a booty call looking like he was there to move in.

He paused in the breezeway at the top of stairs to catch his breath. He looked back across the parking lot. The poor Focus stood out even more from up here. A dull gray patch in an otherwise brightly colored garden of shiny metal. With his new job, he would be able to have his own car. He wouldn't buy anything new, though. Like his father, he preferred cars with a bit of history to them.

Morgan opened the door. She still wore her office clothes, a button up ivory blouse and gray wool slacks, but she held a half-full wineglass in her left hand.

"Hey, Baby Boy," she said, smiling.

Marcus stepped in and put his arms around her waist. He pulled her to him, enjoying the feel of his hands on the curve of her waist and the soft roundness of her breasts pushing against his chest—

"Whoa, hold on," she said, pulling her face back from his.

"What?"

"You smell like..." She wrinkled her nose. "Some kind of food, I guess?"

He smiled and leaned toward her again. "That's the smell of a man with a job—"

"No no no," she said, twisting out of his arms and walking away from him. "That's the smell of a man who needs a shower."

He followed her into the apartment and closed the door. He stood on a square of tiles just inside the door that marked the entryway. To his right was the back of an overstuffed blue sofa that faced into the living room. The sofa was new. Or, at least, different and newer from the worn leather couch that had been there on his last visit. He noticed that the flat screen TV on the wall above the gas logs fireplace seemed to have grown a good fifteen inches in the intervening time as well. He saw the gray wool jacket that matched her slacks draped over the back of the sofa.

"Morgan—"

She held up her empty hand, palm out, to stop him. She took a drink from the wineglass. "Not yet." She took another drink. "I think I need to sit down."

Marcus watched her walk past the sofa to the breakfast bar that separated the living room from the galley kitchen. She set the now-empty wineglass on the bar next to an opened bottle of wine. She picked up the bottle and filled the glass again.

Instead of coming back toward him to sit on the sofa, she went to the small dining table in the corner, next to the glass double doors that led to her patio. Like the sofa, the dining table was new. She pulled out one of the chairs and sat.

"Don't just stand there." She waved him over with her right hand as she took a sip from her glass. "Come on over. Sit down."

Marcus looked from the indicated seat to the sofa, which looked a lot more comfortable. He said as much.

"There's plenty of time for getting comfortable," she said. "We have all weekend. Now sit down and tell me about your new job."

Marcus noticed an opened bottle of Corona on the breakfast bar next to the wine bottle. Beads of condensation had formed on the clear glass and begun to pool at its base. He grabbed the Corona on his way by. Not because he liked the beer so much as because he needed a drink. He sat and took a long drink from the beer, then set the bottle on the table between them.

"I'm sorry, Baby Boy," Morgan said. "It just caught me off guard." She managed a smile and batted her eyes at him as she took a sip from her glass. "You smell like a waiter, or a busboy."

"Since when was that so bad? I remember when you liked it that I smelled like pizza."

"That was long ago, Baby Boy, in college. And this... whatever it is... is nothing like pizza."

Marcus sniffed at the sleeve on his shirt. "I don't smell like anything a shower wouldn't cure."

Morgan returned his smile, but made no other indication she was ready to get up from the table. "Tell me."

"You won't believe me."

"Tell me anyway."

He took a drink of his beer and decided to go for it. "You, Morgan LaVoi, are dating a dragon hunter."

Her smile started to become a grin, then fell away. "Hunter? I don't know what you mean."

"Dragon hunter," he corrected her as he tipped the bottle of the beer in her direction. "See? I told you. You don't believe me."

"Just tell me."

"I have been hired," Marcus said. "Or, more properly, I have been retained. To find them a dragon." He added, "For some reason. They didn't specify the why, just the what."

She still looked confused. "Is that some kind of new recruiting term? Dragon hunter? Like headhunter?"

"No. Literally. I've been retained—"

"To find them a dragon," Morgan finished for him. She took another sip. "You said that. I'm just trying to wrap my head around the idea."

Marcus nodded. "Me too."

"You've never hunted anything in your life."

"True, but I'm really good at finding things."

"On the Web, Baby Boy. That's hardly *hunting*."

"It's hunting. You got to know where to look. You got to know *how* to look."

"Whatever you say." Then she asked, "Are the benefits good?" Something about the way she asked told Marcus she didn't believe him. She was just playing along.

He shrugged. "The signing bonus was OK." The signing bonus had been more than *OK*, but he played it cool.

She shook her head. "They did not give you a signing bonus."

"Do you want to spend all night arguing about it? Or you want to help me start spending it?"

"Why won't you tell me what your job is?"

"Why won't you believe me?"

She laughed. "You're silly, Baby Boy." She waved him away. "I think you should go take that shower now."

"I thought you were going to help me with that." He drank the last of his beer and set the empty bottle down on the table. He smiled at her.

She shook her head. "I don't remember saying anything about any shower helping." She touched a finger to her chin as she looked thoughtful. "I remember sexing," she said, "and dancing. And maybe eating. Besides, I notice you didn't bring any clean clothes."

"I brought clean clothes," Marcus said. "They're in the car."

"Your mom's car."

"Hey, don't you be saying anything bad about my mom's car."

"Still, it's poor planning on your part."

"Bringing my mom's car?"

"Not bringing your clothes. Unless you're fetching those clean clothes naked?"

"I could go get them—"

"No time for that now, Baby Boy. We have an agenda."

7

THE SO-CALLED MR. LAMPLEY WAITED until Thara had finished washing the dishes for the dinner rush before poking his head out of the manager's office.

"Could you, uh, come in here? For a minute? Gold?"

Thara had been about to hang the dripping plastic apron on its hook. She paused, midhang, and considered her options. She could drop the apron to floor. She could let the tingling in her fingertips become hooked claws and shred the apron on its way to the floor, for added effect. She could...

She had often wished that her fingers could become claws at any time. Usually when the general mood or a situation seemed as if it would benefit from the addition of claws. But she had never actually had her claws come out on any day that wasn't also hosting an Episode. The tingling in her fingertips, though, seemed to promise more. Maybe last night's Episode wasn't over yet?

She stopped that line of thought because it would only lead to more messes that she would have to clean up.

There were still no clocks visible, and she didn't want to reach into her pocket to get her phone. She couldn't reach for her phone, anyway, until she decided what to do with the apron.

She figured it was at least nine o'clock. The restaurant had closed the dining room about an hour ago. She and Keenan had been working since then to get the front and back ready for tomorrow's lunch. She felt like a damp, dripping pillar of sweat. She was tired. She was hungry.

149

She finished the motion of hanging the apron with only a hint of how she was imagining the peg was the so-called Mr. Lampley's neck, then turned to face him. She didn't say anything. She just met his gaze. Or tried to. His eyes touched hers for only an instant, then he was turning around in the doorway and walking to the far side of the manager's desk. She watched him sit, then followed him. She looked at the two office chairs, but didn't sit. She wasn't one hundred percent sure she would be able to stand again if she did, and she still had to walk home. She leaned against the office doorway.

The manager's office looked much the same as any restaurant manager's office Thara had seen, except larger. The office had the same paneling on the walls as the dining room. A large metal desk dominated the room, with a padded leather chair on the far side, where the so-called Mr. Lampley sat, and two cushioned office chairs positioned in front of it. The walls were covered with photographs like those on the wall in the dining room, as well as small, framed five-by-seven portraits of what had to be past and present employees arranged around a larger portrait of Mr. Neuland. The so-called Mr. Lampley's photo was on the periphery, just above Tina's. Beyond the desk were a bank of metal four-drawer filing cabinets, all of them painted brown. Neat stacks of stainless-steel pans, chafing dishes, and bowls were on top of the filing cabinets. There were only two doors. The one Thara stood in, and the door that led to the rear parking lot.

A faint odor of chickens made Thara look over the entire office again. She saw no sign of chickens, but the odor was definitely there. She had been born and raised in the city, but long enough ago that she had had some contact with farm life as a child. Plus, she had invaded more than one chicken coop during more than one Episode. She knew what chicken coops smelled like, and the manager's office smelled—faintly—of a chicken coop.

"Why does it smell like chickens?" she asked.

The so-called Mr. Lampley almost looked at her, but caught himself just in time.

"Mr. Neuland, uh, he wanted you to..." He pointed at the top of his desk.

Thara recognized the tax forms and other paperwork of the newly employed, and a neatly folded stack of brown and yellow polyester uniforms. This gave her one more chance to reconsider her employment. Until she signed anything, she could just demand they pay her for the day and walk home. Or maybe just walk home, and let them keep their day of free labor. There were other restaurants within walking distance of her apartment, where the food was recognizable, at least marginally edible, and the cooks could be both seen and heard. She had never been fond of cooks, but they were part of her world. Not the best part, to be sure, but still there, where she could despise them to their faces.

"You must have, uh, really impressed Mr. Neuland," the so-called Mr. Lampley said, looking at her quickly, then looking away again.

He seemed to expect her to say something, but she really didn't have anything to say to him. There were no words. She made her decision, though.

She stepped around the two office chairs to the desk. She took one of the yellow pens with "Come Eat at the Yellow Sign Buffet" printed on them in brown letters, then leaned over and pulled the papers to her. She didn't sit. She filled out her home address and Social Security number and other information, then signed each sheet.

"Yeah, you, uh, must have really impressed Mr. Neuland," the so-called Mr. Lampley said again.

"Did I?" she asked, so he would get to the point.

He nodded, glancing at her as he did. "He, uh, yeah. He hired you for, uh, three times the, uh, normal... three times minimum wage. Which is what we, uh, normally pay the, uh, you know, the servers. Minimum wage."

Once she had processed out all the *uhs* and *you knows*, and the math had time to percolate through her tired, soggy brain, Thara looked at him. "Did he?" She estimated she had worked more than nine hours today. "Hourly or salary?"

He nodded again, then said, "Uh, hourly." He didn't glance at her this time. "Yeah. That's, uh, yeah. That's more than I make."

She calculated the overtime. It made her dizzy. The thought that she might not need a new roommate outweighed her cynicism about what Mr. Neuland really wanted for his unexpected generosity. "And he, Mr. Neuland, told you to tell me? Now?"

"Yeah. He, uh, said you were busy. Before. He said I shouldn't get in your way."

She wasn't sure how Mr. August Neuland not telling her that himself worked for or against her opinion of the man. "That's actually really good advice in general, Ricky."

"Call me—" He stopped and sighed. "Is he, uh, is Mr. Neuland going to give you my job, Gold? Thara?"

"God, I hope not."

Thara turned to walk out of the office.

"You, uh, forgot your uniforms."

Thara shook her head. "No, I didn't."

"Oh. Well, I can, uh, let you out the back door. If you want."

Thara turned back around. A shorter path was a better path right then.

She waited while he stood and pulled a bundle of keys out of his pocket. He twisted a key in the deadbolt that was the poor cousin of the three deadbolts on her bedroom door, then pulled the door open. He held the door as she walked through.

The coolness of the night air felt refreshing at first, then it chilled her clothes and made her wish she had brought a jacket.

A single yellow bulb in a frosted sconce above the door was the only light illuminating the rear parking lot. Ricky's Corolla sat by itself next to the parking spot reserved for Mr. Neuland.

"Do you want me to give you a lift—?"

"No." After a second, she added, "Thank you." Because it suddenly felt like punching down to make fun of Ricky, the so-called Mr. Lampley. Ricky would never be the World's Worst Manager. She didn't think he had it in him. But she wasn't going to get into a car with him. Chilled or not, dead on her feet, she would rather walk.

Thara looked to her left. There were no other doors on this side of the restaurant. She had seen three sides of the restaurant already today, but only two doors, the front door and this one. It wasn't a shorter path, but she needed to know. Despite how tired she was, she turned left to walk along the west side of the building. There had to be another door.

"I thought you, uh, lived the other way—?"

"Good night, Ricky." When she turned the corner, she glanced back to see he was standing by his car, watching her.

Thara didn't stop walking, even when she could clearly see there was no third door into the restaurant. There wasn't even a single light on this side of the restaurant. The only illumination came from the yellow glow of the redundant sign mounted on the roof, and a distant streetlamp from the front parking lot. This side of the restaurant was bordered by an eight-foot-tall holly hedge that looked as if it were pruned only a couple times a year. Just enough to keep it from totally blocking the walkway under the overhang of the roof.

She emerged from the cinderblock and holly bush tunnel into the front parking. She walked across it at an angle.

For the second time that day, Ricky nearly clipped her with his Corolla. This time, at least, he stopped, rolled down his window, and said, "Sorry, uh, Thara. I didn't... I'm sorry."

Thara waved to indicate that she accepted his apology, and resumed walking to show that she was unhurt.

"Are you sure about that ride?"

"Good night, Ricky."

He might have said something else to her, but she was still walking, and doing math in her head. It wasn't money math this time, so she didn't put that much effort into it. She noticed Ricky drive past her, heading north, on the other side of Harvard Avenue.

By her rough estimate, at least one-third of the total square footage of the Yellow Sign Buffet was inaccessible, from either the inside or the outside. Except maybe through the portals of the conveyor system that delivered food from that part of the restaurant.

Thara shivered from more than the cold and renewed her resolve to never eat anything from the Yellow Sign Buffet. Ever.

The Yellow Sign Buffet should not exist.

The words from this morning sloshed out of the recesses of her water-logged brain. The litany didn't echo this time. It was too damp in there for echoes.

Thara pushed the thought—the *need*—to destroy the Yellow Sign Buffet out of her head. Let Mr. Neuland pay her three times minimum wage for a couple months, *then* she could destroy the restaurant. If she still thought it needed destroying. Maybe she could find a way to see what was in that walled-off area, and maybe free the kitchen slaves if it seemed like a good idea. Maybe with her next Episode. The Winter Solstice was coming.

The so-called seafood place was already closed when Thara walked past. She wondered if Tina might want to split a delivery pizza, then remembered Tina had left.

She had enough of her tips left from the first half of the week, working at Bottomless Breadsticks, that she could pay for the pizza on her own. Just. She wondered if the generous Mr. Neuland would be open to giving her an advance on her first paycheck, so she didn't starve before then.

She ordered the pizza with her phone as she walked. Even giving the pizza a head start, she had no doubt she would reach her apartment before the delivery guy did.

She gave each of her Outdoor Babies a quick pat on the fender on her way through the parking lot. None of them had sprouted new orange stickers, which was good. She was too tired to be scraping windows.

At her front door, as she took out her keys, she felt an odd sensation at the base of her neck, as if someone was looking at her. Thinking it might be the pizza delivery guy, she looked back down the breezeway, toward the parking lot. The streetlamps that lit the parking lot threw triangular shadows toward her that looked darker than usual, but she saw no one.

The tips of her fingers tingled again and she almost dropped her keys. She shook her head.

She unlocked her door and walked inside. The apartment felt emptier than normal. Since she had no idea how long she could stand to work at the Yellow Sign Buffet, no matter how much they paid her, she decided she still needed to look for a new roommate.

She locked the deadbolt on the front door, then started peeling off her clothes. She wondered how many showers it would take to get the smell of the so-called food of the Yellow Sign Buffet out of her hair.

4. Dragon Tail

The Queen

THE QUEEN'S MANDIBLES SMACKED AS She consumed the sweet nectar prepared by the workers. Even a Queen could be allowed a few smacks and dribbles when She was this hungry. There was no need to stand on ceremony all the time. Laying Her Sister-eggs had made Her hungry. More hungry than a few drone heads had been able to satiate.

Deep within the corpses of the drones, the Queen's Babies coalesced around the nuclei of Their egg sacs. They were each like tiny stars forming in the darkness of space. When They were ready, Her Babies would glow and burn their way through the empty husks of the drones that had died in Their conception. When They did, She would be ready to vomit into their mouths the royal jelly that would take Them from squirming, twitching larvae to Daughters, then to full Sisters.

The Queen sighed. It would be beautiful.

She accepted the next offering, daydreaming as she did, imagining the World devoured by Her and Her Sisters and Their Sisters, a Swarm that would, in Time, Consume the Universe.

There was still much to do, though, before that beautiful day could dawn when no more days would dawn. Her Labor was not yet finished. The final ingredient had yet to be procured and prepared.

Distracted, She ate both the nectar offered by the next worker, and the next worker.

If She had not been the Queen, She might have been embarrassed.

The Queen's proboscis flicked and knocked the still-twitching, inedible bits of the consumed worker from Her face. There was no need to stand on ceremony all the time, but it was unseemly for a Queen to have food on Her face.

The next worker stepped up with its offering.

The Lonely

THE LONELY, WRAPPED IN SHADOWS and his new, more modern garments, watched the Child as she left the lair of his new enemy. He had been prepared to go in and rescue the Child, but the Child emerged on her own.

He followed the Child as she walked.

He told himself he was watching over her. Protecting her.

But he could not stop himself from noticing the Child was a her. And she was not so much a Child as he had first thought.

Oh, there was no doubt the Child was a Child. Compared to the Lonely, few things in this World were not children. After the first few millennia, there had been very few entities he could not call "child." He called everyone "child" at this point.

Dragons, though, matured quickly. Not as quickly as humans, but human lives were puffs of smoke compared to the Lonely, and just as quickly lost to the winds of time.

He followed the Child back to her lair and saw her close and lock the flimsy door behind her. From the shadows, he stared at the door, trying not to think how easy it would be for him to knock it down. Desires he had not felt in centuries stirred within him, but he kept them in check.

A young man arrived with a satchel of food. He walked straight to the Child's door and knocked. The door opened and the Child stood there, naked. She handed the young man bits of folded paper and took from him a flat box that smelled of spicy meats and dairy. Then she closed the door in the young man's face.

Suddenly feeling more protective than procreative, the Lonely waited, claws ready, until the young man, looking stunned, moved away from the door.

The Bug

THE BUG DIDN'T LIKE THE way the shadows moved around him. Shadows weren't supposed to move like that, or be so dark. And they certainly weren't supposed to grow wings and leap into the air.

The shadow took a form much like that of the Driver, but bigger, and with extra accessories. Like the wings.

1

MARCUS WOKE BEFORE MORGAN AND slipped out of bed. The slipping part was easy. The out part was more challenging. Morgan's royal blue satin comforter and satin sheets were as smooth as warm Jell-O, and just as hard to get traction on. He felt like a desperate, drowning swimmer trying to reach the edge of the pool while not alerting or alarming the lifeguard.

Morgan woke as he was pulling on his pants. They were more rumpled than when he had taken them off the night before, but that was to be expected, considering how they had come off.

"Where are you going so early?"

Marcus watched as she gathered her hair and pulled it to one side. She didn't quite expose her breasts as she did this, but he had no complaints. He knew she was naked under the covers. Then she pulled the comforter to her chin, and rolled on her side to look at him.

"First," he said, looking around for his shirt, "I'm going to get my overnight bag from my car."

"From your mom's car," she said, smiling.

"From my mom's car," he agreed. He spotted his shirt on the far side of the room, draped over the cheval mirror. "Then I'm going to take another shower."

She followed him with her eyes as he retrieved his shirt. "I'm with you so far."

"That will make the shower take longer," he said, pulling the shirt over his head, "but I'm good with it."

She rolled her eyes. "That's not what I meant."

He grinned at her. "Yeah, it is."

She met his gaze, then grinned too. "Yeah, it is. I like this plan so far. Then what are we doing?"

He ran his hands down his chest and torso, straightening the shirt, then unrolled the sleeves. "Then," he said, "I'm going to go earn some more of my signing bonus."

"That mythical signing bonus again," she said, rolling back over so she was looking at the ceiling. "Weren't we supposed to be spending that last night?"

"We would have, if you had let me go get my clothes."

"I said you could go get them."

"Naked." He sat on the edge of the bed next to her. Carefully. He wasn't sure he trusted the sheets not to dump him on the floor. Or pull him back in. "You said I could only go get them if I did it naked."

Her right hand came out of the covers, exposing her shoulder. She touched him on the nose as she said, "Yeah. Gives a whole new dimension to 'walk of shame,' doesn't it?"

"No shame here," he said. "But we were comfortable. I didn't want to disturb you."

"Uh huh." She ran the tip of her finger down his chin and gripped the collar of his shirt. "You were scared I was going to lock you out."

"And why would I think that?"

"Because I said I would, if you disturbed me. I was comfortable." She tugged on his shirt. "Kiss me."

"Mmm-hmm." He let her pull him over and they kissed.

After a long, warm, wet moment, she let him take a breath, but she still held his shirt so his face hovered over hers. "I'm still comfortable." Then she pushed him away. "But you smell like a waiter again. A stale waiter."

"What's this sudden venom against waiters?" he asked, still smiling. He went to lean over and kiss her again, but her hand stopped him.

"Go away, stinky stale waiter." She pulled her hand back under the comforter.

He sat up. "I'm not a waiter. I'm a dragon hunter."

"I think that might be the weirdest thing anyone's ever said to me in the morning." She turned away from him. "You go hunt dragons. I'm sleeping in."

2

Mom Nelson's Ford Focus was far from the oldest car in the parking lot when Marcus pulled into the apartment complex where the dragon videos had been made. The relative newness of her car increased as he went from sublot to sublot on his way to the back, until the gunmetal gray of the Focus seemed to take on a showroom floor gleam in the late morning sunlight.

He didn't know which of the sublots was where the dragon had been caught on camera, so he cruised them all. When he spotted the angular front end of a 1985 Plymouth Omni, he knew he was close. He pulled into an available space and got out to investigate.

Not even the Omni was the oldest car in the parking lot. That title went to the light-blue VW Beetle faded almost white, which Marcus estimated as a 1964, but there were more contenders. The yellow AMC Gremlin with the brown pin-striping was also older than the Omni. As was the rusty brown Ford Pinto-looking car that claimed it was a Mercury Bobcat.

If someone had compiled a highlights reel of cars from the 1970s and 1980s, this parking lot was the opposite of that. Less a testament to the hardy durability and forward-thinking designs that used to roll off Detroit assembly lines, and more a concession to the need for people to get to work as cheaply as possible.

The Omni, though, hadn't driven anyone to work in a long time. The car had once been dark red, but after thirty years of sun and at least a few weeks of rain-speckled dust, the color looked more like cheap wine, complete with sediment.

The dust in the center of the car's windshield had been... he decided
licked was the best word, since *smudged* would hardly have left what could
only have been an impression of a forked tongue. The video played back
in his mind, the dragon's tongue shooting out of its mouth to lick away
the orange tow sticker.

He looked at the front fenders, where the dragon had placed its front
feet. The fenders had been wiped, obscuring any dragon-specific traces
that might have been left.

The rest of the car had a thin film of dust showing a few random
hand prints. He wasn't surprised to find layers of "WASH ME" and other
messages inscribed in the grime on the hatchback window. One message
might have been "TOW ME," but it was hard to be sure as an effort had
been made to obscure that one. The chrome OMNI nameplate on the
hatchback door was chipped.

He walked back to the front of car and touched a clean spot on the
hood where he wouldn't leave a handprint. He wasn't sure what a car
could tell him about a possible dragon, but—

Nova.

The word—no, the *name*—appeared in his mind, bursting into his
awareness like its namesake. He drew his hand back and stepped away
from the car. He looked at his hand. His fingers tingled. He had only
expected to get a quick mental feel for how long the car had been parked
there, and maybe a reading of its odometer. It had been a long time since
a car had spoken to him, much less given him its name. Not since his
father died.

He could almost hear his father telling him, *Not every car has a name,
Baby Boy. It takes a special car to get a name.*

Thinking about his father made him look at the cars around him in a
different light. His father had never met a car he didn't like. *Your Daddy,*
Mom Nelson had told him so many times, *never saw a car he didn't want to
pop the hood of and start having relations with right there on the spot.*

Even dusty, faded Nova looked almost pretty. He just had to look at
her from the right angle. Marcus could almost hear Daddy telling him that
too. Maybe Daddy had. From that right angle, though, Marcus could see
the sporty lines that must have attracted some mid-1980s up-and-comer.

"OK, Nova," Marcus said, taking out his phone. "How about a smile for
the camera?"

He used his phone to take pictures of the car from various angles,
starting with the forked-tongue-shaped smudge on the windshield. Then
he took pictures of the smudges on the fenders, just in case. After that,

he backed away from the car, trying to replicate the angle seen in both videos. He wanted to get an estimate of where the person with the camera had been standing.

"If you're a repo man," said a man's voice behind Marcus, "you're about twenty years too late. Probably not worth taking back."

Marcus turned to see a man in a gray shirt and matching trousers. The man's graying brown hair stuck out at all angles from beneath a gray ballcap. His face was grizzled with at least two days of not shaving, and his skin showed he had spent those days—and many years of days before those—working outside. His clothes were rumpled but clean. On the ball cap and on the left breast of his shirt were matching patches with the logo of the apartment complex. Stitched above the patch on his shirt was the name Johnathan.

"Or do you work for the city?" Johnathan asked, giving Marcus a quick once over, including the camera.

Johnathan pushed up the brim of his ball cap with right hand, exposing heavy eyebrows that continued the theme of graying hair sticking out in odd directions. He wasn't smiling, but he wasn't frowning either. He looked curious.

Marcus nodded toward the Omni. "You know who owns that car?"

"Sure. She's the only person who's been here longer than I have." He scratched at the grizzle on his chin. "In fact, that car's been here longer than I have. And in almost that exact same spot, if you can believe it. You here to see it gets properly towed this time?"

"No." Marcus tried to think of how to describe why he was there. He decided not to bother. "It doesn't run?"

Johnathan's face contorted with a lopsided smile. "Did you expect it would?" His eyes sparkled with genuine amusement. "I think that pee-oh-ess been sitting right where it is now for most of the last year. Before that, it was parked over there." He pointed to a parking space a few spots down currently occupied by a Toyota Tercel. "Before that it was over there." He pointed to another spot, this one held by an Isuzu Rodeo. "But it never got to any of those places under its own power."

Marcus felt himself get defensive when the man called Nova a POS. He wanted to argue the point, to defend the poor girl's honor. But that made as little sense as telling Johnathan he was a dragon hunter. Instead, he asked, "So why hasn't it been towed?"

Johnathan laughed. Like the sparkle in his eyes, his laughter was genuine. No hint of malice. "Oh, it's been towed. I've lost count of how many times it's been towed. She always has it towed back, though."

"She?" Marcus glanced back at the car.

"Yeah. That's what I call her. *She*." Still smiling, he leaned toward Marcus and actually winked. "Not sure it's safe to actually say her name out loud, if you know what I mean."

Marcus had no idea what the man meant. He didn't say so. He just waited.

"It's a game we play here," the man went on. "Me or the manager calls the cops when the stack of complaints about her cars reaches a certain height. Then the cops come when they think she's least likely to notice, and they put tow stickers on her cars and run away. But she's not so easily fooled, and she comes after them and scrapes the stickers off. The manager, he hasn't been here as long as I have, so he still takes the whole thing personally. Doesn't see the humor."

"Aren't there fines?"

Johnathan shrugged. "Probably. I don't have to pay them. Sometimes, though," he added, "she keeps the cars from being towed, sometimes not. I forget what the current score is, but as you can see, she's winning."

"Cars? As in more than one?"

"Sure." Johnathan turned to point at the faded Volkswagen Beetle. "She also claims that Bug over there. She told me once her father gave it to her— Well, she yelled it at me once, along with a string of good old-fashioned obscenities, to make sure I got the point. So I can almost understand not wanting to give that one up. If I had my father's 1979 Pontiac Firebird, I'd be right there with her. But then there's that ugly-ass Pinto-thing over there, and this box on wheels here." He pointed in the general direction of the Mercury Bobcat and nodded at the Omni.

Nova didn't seem to mind being called a box on wheels, so Marcus let it pass. "And none of them run?"

Johnathan shook his head. "I've never seen anyone drive them, or even start them up. They only move when the tow trucks arrive, so far as I know. That is, if they manage to show up when she's not home, or if she can't bribe them off. I've never looked under the hoods, though, so who knows? Maybe she's keeping them as project cars? Not that I've ever seen her get under their hoods either. She's not a mechanic, so far as I know." He shrugged again. "Truth is, I think she's a hoarder."

"A hoarder?"

"You know," Johnathan said, "like those weirdos on TV. Keeping everything, piling it up in their houses so deep you have to crawl over a mountain of newspapers and greasy pizza boxes just so you can reach the bathroom. They say she's lived in her apartment for something like twenty years. Or twenty-five."

Marcus had never watched any such TV show, but it sounded like the kind of show Mom Nelson would watch. "Which apartment does she live in?"

"Down that breezeway there," the man said, pointing, "the last door on the right, just before you reach the highway." He leaned toward Marcus again, and added, "Don't tell her I told you." He walked away before Marcus could either assure the man or ask him why.

"Thanks," Marcus said to the man's back.

The man only pulled his hat back down to shade his face.

Marcus put his phone away. He had enough pictures. Probably more than enough. He had no idea how the pictures were going to help, but he would study them later.

He went to stand in front of the Omni, his knees almost touching the bumper. He held up his left hand and pantomimed putting it on the left front fender. Then did the same with his right hand, mimicking as best he could what he had seen the dragon do in the video as it propped itself—or herself, if the Thara-with-an-h waitress lady was to be believed—on the front of the car. Doing so gave him a new appreciation of how large the dragon had to have been. He leaned his torso forward, over the hood. The beast had a huge head too—

"What are you doing to my car?"

3

FORTIFIED FOR THE DAY WITH leftover pizza, Thara left her apartment. She walked out of the shade of the breezeway into the late morning sun. She had been about to run her hand along Louie's fender, wishing him a good morning on her way to work, when she saw a man standing in front of Nova. He had his arms outstretched and was leaning forward. It wasn't the oddest thing she had ever seen a man do in front of a car—at least he was wearing clothes—but this was one of her Outdoor Babies, and her little girl, to boot.

She walked as quickly as she could, zigzagging through the parked cars.

"What are you doing to my car?" she asked as she got close. Her left hand clenched into a fist, ready to defend Nova's remaining honor.

The man jumped at her shout, and turned to face her.

"Oh, it's you," she said, recognizing the so-called dragon hunter from the Yellow Sign Buffet. He was wearing black jeans today instead of slacks, and a pink pullover shirt. She relaxed, but kept her fist ready. "What are you doing here?"

"This is your car?" he asked, pointing.

"Why?" She moved to get between Nova and Marcus. She put her right hand on Nova's fender, to comfort her. "It's OK, girl," she said. None of her Outdoor Babies had ever responded to her when she spoke to them, but that wasn't the point.

"What?" He stepped back.

"What yourself. What were you doing?"

171

He pointed at Nova. "Did you call her a her?"

Thara squinted at him, then glanced up at the sun. "Maybe you should wear a hat," she said. "Or let your hair grow out. I think the sun is getting to you. What else would I call her? Besides 'her?'"

His hand went to his head, then dropped back to his side. "I thought women always called their cars 'he' or 'him.'"

"She's not a he, or a him. And why are you bothering her? Why were you doing... whatever it was you were doing? To my car?"

"This is the car," he said, pointing at Nova again. "This is the car the dragon climbed on."

Thara had been about to tell him to stop pointing, it wasn't polite, but his statement stopped her. She squinted at him again and took a more defensive stance. "How do you know that? There's probably lots of cars just like this one, all over the place." Then she patted Nova on the fender to let her know Thara was just making a point. Nova was special.

"I know cars, Thara-with-an-h," he said. "And this is the car in the video. And, no, there probably aren't a lot of these left. Anywhere." He reached into his pocket and took out a phone. "I can show you, if you want." He pointed to a lime-green 1997 Chevrolet Cavalier. "That car was parked next to Nova in the video—" He stopped. "Why didn't you tell me it was your car yesterday? When I showed you the video?"

"Maybe I didn't recognize it—" She stopped. "You called her Nova. She's an Omni. A Plymouth Omni."

"From 1985, yes," Marcus said, "but her name is Nova."

Thara felt more exposed that he knew the name of her car than from being caught on video as a dragon. "I know that's her name. I gave her that name. How do *you* know her name?"

Marcus looked as if he were going to try to change the subject, to ask her again why she hadn't told him it was her car in the video, but he stopped. He looked thoughtful for a few seconds, then said, "Because she told me."

Thara stared at him, then she turned to look at Nova. "You little tramp. You never talk to me, but you tell a stranger your name right off?"

Nova at least had the decency to look embarrassed. Though that may have just been her faded paint.

Thara turned back to face Marcus. She pointed at him. "You leave her alone."

"She talked to me," he said, holding up his hands between them. "But that's not the point. I know you recognized her in the video. That's why you said you were going to have to move."

Thara decided that admitting she recognized her car in the videos might distract him from her own part in those same videos. "Fine, yes, I knew it was Nova."

"Why didn't you tell me?"

"Why would I? Some kids film a prank that involves my car, and you think I want to get involved? Do you think I want a bunch of people hunting Bigfoot where I live?"

"Bigfoot?"

"Tall guy, needs a shave and a haircut? Doesn't live anywhere near here? You should go look for him somewhere else."

"I know who Bigfoot is—"

"So tell him 'hi' for me." She held up both her hands and made shooing gestures. "Go. Nothing to see here." When he didn't show any sign of shooing, she added, "Look, I need to get to work. So how about you run along and leave poor Nova alone?"

Marcus shook his head, then sighed. "I think we got off on the wrong foot. Look, I saw you walking to work yesterday—"

"Are you stalking me?"

"No. But even if this is your car—"

"Why wouldn't it be my car?" She crossed her arms. "Is little Nova too classy for a waitress who walks to work?"

"I know it doesn't run—"

"Who told you that? Was it Nova?" She glanced at Nova, but the face of the car revealed nothing. "You know, she just wants the attention."

"How about I give you a ride to the restaurant?"

"What?" She hadn't expected him to say that.

"How about I give you—"

"Fine," Thara said, because it would mean he was leaving. And for no other reason. Then she added, "Thank you."

Marcus looked surprised. "'Thank you,'" he said, mildly mocking. "Wow. So formal. So nice. So... sudden."

"I can be nice."

"Uh huh. So you're not going to give me any shit if I tell you this is my mom's car?"

He led her to the gray Ford Focus she had seen yesterday, parked at the Yellow Sign Buffet.

"You're giving me a ride," she said. "I don't care if you stole it. Unless we get pulled over on the way there. That would be awkward. Oh, and try to do a better job on the right turns than you did yesterday."

Marcus looked at her across the car. "You saw that, did you?"

"I didn't see who was driving. You could have told me it was your mom." She opened the door.

He shook his head again. They got in.

Thara sat in the passenger seat and watched him as he put on his seat belt, then put the key in the ignition and started the engine. He looked over at her, obviously waiting for something.

"What? I already said 'thank you.' Or do you need directions?"

"Seat belt," he said.

Thara met his gaze. "My father never wore a seat belt."

Marcus's expression darkened. His lips pressed into a line. He looked away from her as he put the car into reverse. "Neither did mine."

He pulled out of the parking spot with enough speed that Thara put her hand on the dash in front of her. She changed her mind about the seat belt, and pulled it across her. As she clicked it into place, she asked, "So does your mom's car have a name?"

Marcus shook his head. "Not according to my Mom."

"What do you call her?'

Marcus glanced at her as he navigated the parking lot. "What makes you think it's a she?"

"She's a she," Thara said. "So what do you call her?"

"My Mom's car."

Thara nodded and looked out the window. "Yeah. You can't go around naming other people's cars."

She felt Marcus glance at her, but she continued to look out the window. She didn't often get to be a passenger on her way out of the apartment complex. Sadly, the view through a car window wasn't any better than the view as she walked. She just saw less of the sidewalk, and didn't have to feel awkward about not saying *Good morning* to anyone they passed.

4

"Not all cars get names, Baby Boy," Marcus's father told him. "Takes a special car to get a name. A special car, and a special driver."

"Special like how?" Marcus asked.

Marcus was five, and he loved coming to the cavernous garage where Daddy worked. The thick smells of the different oils and lubricants, from black gold fresh to burnt black sludge, the heady fumes of gasoline, the rumbling sounds of the compressors and the ratcheting staccato beats of the impact drivers, the roar of an engine being fired up and revved to red line. Daddy's world in the garage was the opposite of Mommy's sterile, chemical-washed world at the hospital where people whispered to each other. Mommy liked to say that she and Daddy were both in the business of fixing white people's problems, but that she was able to do it without getting those problems all over her and in her hair and under her fingernails. Then she would add, "Most days, anyway."

Marcus sat cross-legged on the stained concrete floor of the garage while Daddy changed the oil in a silver Toyota Corolla four-door. The hood was up, with an electric light hung on a hook, exposing and illuminating the black and silver transverse block of the engine. Marcus held the cube-shaped white box that held the new oil filter Daddy was going to install. He bounced the box from one hand to the other, sometimes tossing it into the air and catching it.

"Just hold onto that, Baby Boy," Daddy said. "You drop it and I'll have to pay for it. Then you'll have to pay for it."

Marcus caught the box and held it tight.

Daddy nodded, then went on. "There's no one type of special, Baby Boy. That's what makes it special. And it's not always what you might expect. Take this Corolla here." He paused and looked at Marcus. "What year is it? Don't touch it," Daddy said as Marcus reached out his right hand. "Just look at it, and tell me."

Marcus pulled his hand back. If he could touch the car, just one finger on the bumper, he would know immediately what year it had been made. But Daddy wanted him to learn how to look at cars, to really see them. He looked the car over. "1990?"

Daddy nodded approval, then said, "Good guess, but you're a year off. It's a 1991. The next year they changed the body style to what they have now. I think they're about to change it again, which will mean all new manuals and probably some newfangled computerized sensors to cause new problems, but that's beside the point. The point is, Baby Boy, that this little Corolla goes by Zachary." As he said it, he put his hand on the block of the engine. "Don't you, boy?"

"Boy?" Marcus asked. "Zachary? I thought they were supposed to be girls names. Like Lilith," he added, naming Daddy's two-door Lincoln Continental.

Daddy grinned. "Can't all cars be momma cars like Lilith, Baby Boy. But that's not what I'm talking about. Zachary here has a twin sister, born the same day off the same assembly line and sold from the same dealership in the city. Both of them come in here, which is pretty unusual. They are as alike as two cars can be, even if one of them is a he and the other's a she. She comes in every few months, just like clockwork, to get her oil changed, fluids checked, her tires rotated and so on. Do you know what *her* name is?"

Marcus shook his head. Twins usually had similar-sounding names. He had no idea what the twin sister of Zachary would be called.

Daddy shrugged. "Me either, Baby Boy. The guy who drives her just calls her 'the Corolla.'" He shook his head in disbelief. "That's a case where the special car gets saddled with someone who doesn't appreciate her."

"Maybe her name is Corolla?"

Daddy chuckled. "No, I think she's still looking for her name. Her driver just hasn't helped her find it yet."

"Maybe you can give her a name. Like Lilith."

"There's only one Lilith, Baby Boy," Daddy said, grinning again. "Only one. But a man can't go around naming another man's car. Be like naming his children for him. No, Baby Boy, that little girl and her driver will just have to work it out on their own. Or, more likely, her next driver will name her. She and Zachary here are both more than five years old. Zachery isn't likely to go anywhere, but his sister is probably close to being traded in. Plus, her driver bought her new, and that seems to be the way of it. Brand-new cars don't get names. Their drivers take them for granted. They don't appreciate the personality of the car. They can't even *see* the car beyond the shiny new paint job, the chrome points, and the painted bumper. They don't hear the car whispering to them. They just hear the purr of a brand-new engine and think that's all there is. And when the new wears off, they start looking to replace a perfectly good car."

"Mommy wants a new car," Marcus said.

"Yeah," Daddy said, nodding, "she does. And maybe someday we'll be able to get her that new car."

"But you won't trade in Lilith, will you?"

"Hell, no, Baby Boy. No chance of that."

"Two cars?" Marcus had trouble thinking of his family having two cars.

"One for your mother to park at the hospital all day, and Lilith, to keep me company here at the garage."

"We would name the new car, though. Right?"

"That would be up to your mother."

"Maybe she'll call it Lilith Junior."

Daddy smiled and chuckled. "That's highly unlikely, Baby Boy. Your mother is no fan of either Lilith, or her name."

"What would she call it?"

"I don't know." Daddy shrugged. "New cars can be tough to name. It's not their fault, though, Baby Boy. New cars are like new baby humans. There are only hints of the person inside, waiting to come out."

"But you named me right when I was born."

"I named you as soon as I saw the ultrasound, Baby Boy. Marcus Antonio Nelson was your name. I could see that right away. I could have filled out the birth certificate right then and there. I would have too, but your mother made me wait."

"So can I touch him?" Marcus asked. "Zachary?"

"Yeah, go ahead. Just don't leave a greasy handprint I have to clean off. And just say hi."

Marcus touched the black bumper of the Corolla with one finger. As soon as he did, he heard the name *Zachary* in his mind, almost as loud as Daddy would have said it, but Daddy hadn't said anything. Daddy was rolling under the car on his creeper.

"Hi, Zachary," Marcus said. "I would like to meet your twin sister. Maybe we can think up a name for her."

"Now what did I just say about naming another man's car?" Daddy asked from beneath the engine.

"I'm just talking to Zachary."

Marcus never met Zachary's sister, and it was the small life-insurance payout from the crash that purchased his mother's first and only new car, a 1998 Ford Tempo that was traded in seven years later for the gunmetal gray Ford Focus. Neither Daddy nor Lilith survived the crash, and Mom Nelson never named either car.

5

MARCUS PULLED INTO THE PARKING lot of the Yellow Sign Buffet. The restaurant wasn't open yet, so he pulled into the spot closest to the front door. He left the engine running.

"Doesn't it just make you want to bulldoze the whole place down?" Thara-with-an-h asked as she took off her seat belt.

Still thinking about Daddy, and Lilith, and seat belts, Marcus asked, "What?"

Thara nodded at the front windows of the Yellow Sign Buffet and the warped world reflected in them, with its infinitely wide five lane street and, beyond that, the ruins of the other restaurant across the street with its unperturbed buffalo.

"Every time I look at it," she said, "part of me wants to smash the windows, then pull it apart brick by brick."

"Not much of a morning person, are you?"

Thara-with-an-h paused with her hand on the door handle. She noticed that he hadn't removed his seat belt, and the car was still running. "And why aren't you coming in to work today?"

"Why?" Marcus asked. "You going to miss me?"

"So far, you're my favorite customer. You refill your own drink, and you don't eat the food."

"Maybe you've been a waitress too long," Marcus suggested.

"You have no idea," she said and opened the door. "Thanks for the ride."

"Yeah, no problem. Wait. How long have you been a waitress?"

Thara stepped out, then leaned over to look at him again. She was wearing the same kind of blousy, button-down shirt as the day before, buttoned all the way to the collar, so her leaning over showed him nothing. "I have been serving people their food," she said, "or at least charging them for the privilege of eating their breakfast, lunch or dinner in my place of work, since I was sixteen. I started out as a bellhop," she added. "Roller skates, bobby socks, and a pleated skirt."

"Bobby socks?" Marcus's gaze dropped to her knees. Since he had never seen her legs, he had no idea what she might look like in bobby socks and skirt. Not that he cared. He looked in her eyes again. "How long ago was that?" He knew he was pushing his luck, asking her age, but he already knew she was older, and he wasn't trying to make time or get lucky. Still, he decided to be generous. "Six years ago?"

She shook her head. "I don't feel like doing math this morning. How long ago was 1964?"

Before he could respond with anything except a confused look, she straightened and stepped clear of the door as she swung it closed.

He watched her walk to the front door of the restaurant and pull it open.

1964? What was that about?

When the front door had closed behind her, he pulled out of the parking lot and drove back to the apartment complex. Maybe Nova the 1985 Plymouth Omni would be easier to talk to than her owner.

6

THERE WERE MORE OPEN SPACES in the apartment parking lot when
Marcus pulled in for the second time that morning, but not one next
to Nova. He parked next to a green-and-white 1976 Chevrolet Silverado
pickup that he didn't remember being there before, and got out. An
aura of sunbaked roadkill greeted him. He made a point of not looking
into the bed of the pickup truck as he walked past it.

In spite of the smell, he stopped beside the gate of the pickup and
watched as an old man crouched next to Nova, then duckwalked away
from her, head down, hands on his knees, following the trail of something only he could see in the asphalt of the parking lot. The old man
wore baggy jeans and a baggy blue shirt, a uniform of some kind.

The old man paused after three awkward ducksteps and leaned
forward. Marcus wondered if the old man would fall on his face, but
that didn't happen. The old man reached forward and held his right
hand over the surface of the asphalt. He spread arthritic fingers as
wide as he could, as if matching his hand to something Marcus couldn't
see. Then he resumed his duckwalk. After three more ducksteps, he
paused and reached out his left hand the same way. Then he continued
until he was face-to-bumper with the rear end of a brown 1991 Buick
LeSabre.

Marcus leaned against the tailgate of the pickup, watching the old
man.

Lassie! said a voice in his mind. Then there was a lot of panting, and
Marcus thought he felt a wet lick on his right cheek.

181

He pulled himself away from the pickup. He brought his right arm up to block the dog that had jumped—

The bed of the pickup was... not empty. There were a handful of what must—at some time in the past—have been squirrels, and what might have been an opossum. All were in various states of decomposition, flattened, skinned and gutted, along with some deadfall tree limbs. Mixed among the roadkill and the branches were a variety of aluminum cans. There was no dog, though.

Careful not to touch the pickup again, Marcus turned back to see what the old man was doing.

Still squatting, the old man leaned to his right to look under the LeSabre. He extended his right leg, reached into a pocket and came out with a small flashlight. He clicked the flashlight on and aimed it under the LeSabre. After a long minute, he grunted, then pushed himself up. He rose slowly, and with enough popping of joints that he almost seemed to be ratcheting up, as if he were being helped by old-fashioned car jack. He stopped in a stooped position, then turned to see Marcus watching him.

The old man nodded a silent greeting, then walked around the LeSabre without paying Marcus any additional attention. The LeSabre was parked facing the narrow strip of grass and sidewalk that bordered the parking lot. The old man squatted again, in front of the LeSabre, and resumed his duckwalk, his path curving around to pass between two three-story apartment buildings.

Still watching the man, Marcus walked toward Nova. He paused to look down at the asphalt at the approximate location where the old man had held out his left hand. The sun overhead made it hard to see, but he eventually made out five shallow scratches. He squatted and held out his left hand. His hand was less than half as wide as the claw that had made the scratches. He had seen rakes that weren't as wide as that claw had to be.

He did his own duckwalk, backward, to the first spot where the old man had stopped. He spotted the scratches faster this time, because he knew what to look for. They were the mirror image of the other scratches.

He remained squatting, resting on his heels, as he replayed the video in his mind again. The dragon had backed off Nova's hood, then come straight at the camera. The dragon's first two steps, right foot then left foot, had made those scratches. Then it had climbed over a car and disappeared along the path the old man was following.

Since the old man was still duckwalking, Marcus caught up to him quickly. The old man was slowly moving down the center of the sidewalk that passed between the two buildings.

"Hey," Marcus said as he came alongside the old man. "What are you doing?"

The old man's head swiveled on its skinny neck as he looked up at Marcus. The old eyes swept up and down Marcus, then he faced forward again. "Nothing."

"You're tracking."

"If you knew," the old man said to the concrete surface of the sidewalk in front of him, "why did you ask?"

"You're tracking the dragon."

The face swiveled again to look at him. "Ain't no such thing as dragons, probably. At least, that's what kids today tell me."

"Then what do you think it was?"

The old man looked at the sidewalk again. "Might be a dragon. Kids today don't know anything."

"You saw the videos? Do you think it's a dragon too?"

"Took the calls. More than one, probably."

"What calls? More than one what?"

The old man didn't answer. He took another three duckwalk steps forward.

Marcus caught up to him again. He reached out to put his left hand on the old man's shoulder, but a low growl that could only have come from the old man stopped him. He pulled his hand back and did a quick count of his fingers to make sure they were all still there.

"Seen it before, probably," the old man said. "Seen her before, too."

"Seen what? Who? You're not making any sense."

"Kids today wouldn't know sense, probably, if it walked up and breathed fire on them. Too busy taking pictures of their own pouting faces and sharing them." The old man made a sound in the back of his throat, a mixture of a derisive *hmm*, another growl, and a lifetime of smoking. "Kids today."

The old man duckwalked away again. This time, Marcus let him go.

Marcus turned to go back to Nova. As he walked, he leaned over and peered at the sidewalk, looking for whatever signs the old man was following. He spotted a few scratches similar to those in the asphalt, but they weren't as obviously claw marks. Again, if it weren't for the old man pointing them out, indirectly and unintentionally, he would never have noticed them.

He glanced back at the old man, who had managed only another two duckwalk paces. If he decided to catch up with the old man again later, that shouldn't be difficult. The man wouldn't have gone far.

Marcus stood in front of Nova's faded red hood, then reached out and put his hand on the sun-warmed metal.

Nova! echoed through his mind.

"Hey, Nova," Marcus said. "What have you got for me?"

7

"TALKING TO A CAR, BABY BOY," Daddy told Marcus as he drove, "is a lot like talking to your cat."

"I don't have a cat," Marcus said.

Four years old, Marcus wasn't tall enough to see outside the passenger side window of Daddy's big car, Lilith. Only if he stood in the seat, which even Daddy didn't let him do. So he sat and watched the sky and stoplights passing over him through the windshield. His feet dangled over the edge of the seat, and Mommy's Spot, as Daddy called the visible indentation in the seat cushion, nearly swallowed him.

On the rare occasions when Mommy drove Lilith, she never let Marcus ride in the front seat. She made him ride in the back, and put his seat belt on. Daddy, though, said, "My little wingman always rides shotgun." Daddy liked to talk as he drove, and he didn't like talking into the rearview mirror.

"Or like talking to your dog," Daddy said, smiling.

"I don't have a dog, either."

Daddy feigned shock. His eyebrows shot up and his mouth opened in surprise. "You don't have a dog either? Don't your parents love you?"

Marcus touched his chin, the way he had seen Daddy do when he was bantering with Mommy. "I think so."

"You *think* so, Baby Boy?" Daddy asked with mock outrage. "You'd better know they love you. They love you more than anything."

"Mmm-hmm," Marcus replied, like Mommy. He must have done it just right, because Daddy laughed loudly. "But you haven't got me a dog yet," Marcus went on. "Or a cat." A cat was definitely the fallback position. Marcus wanted a dog. Actually, he wanted a puppy. A *big* puppy that would grow into a big dog.

"Yet," Daddy said, still smiling, but concentrating on his driving just enough to make a left turn. "We haven't got you a dog *yet*, Baby Boy. Once it's the right time, and you're big enough to take care of a dog by yourself, you will have you the biggest, baddest dog you have ever seen."

"I want a puppy," Marcus said, making sure there was no confusion on this point.

Daddy nodded his approval of the clarification. "The biggest, baddest *puppy* you've ever seen."

"Like Scooby Doo?"

Daddy grinned. "Maybe not that big and bad, but close."

"Can I call him Scooby?"

"You can call him anything you want, Baby Boy. It will be your dog. Your puppy, I mean."

"I'll take care of him."

"Yes, you will," Daddy said, nodding. "You will take him for walks. You'll clean up after him—"

"He'll play fetch."

"Absolutely, and you'll talk to him."

"Will he talk back?"

"Not in so many words, Baby Boy. He'll lick your face. He'll wag his tale. He'll perk his ears. He'll sniff your butt."

Marcus laughed. "He'll bark!"

"He'd better not bark in the house, if he knows what's good for him."

Marcus laughed again.

"But," Daddy said, "as I was saying, talking to a car is a lot like talking to your puppy." Daddy drove with only his left hand on the wheel, his right hand on his thigh. "You're the one doing most of the actual talking, but you're also listening, and looking. You listen for what the engine's telling you. You watch it run, or you just stare at it while it does nothing, and you pick up the little cues and clues. You hear what the car's telling you."

"What are cues?"

"And it's not just what the car is telling you, but what it's not telling you, when it should be. Just like a woman, the car might be telling you one thing, but she means something totally different. You know what I mean, Baby Boy?"

Marcus had no idea. He nodded, though, because Daddy seemed to expect him to.

Daddy fell silent, and Marcus looked up at the windshield again, thinking of the puppy he was going to get.

He never got the puppy. He grew and got bigger and the "right time" crept closer and closer over the next year, then Daddy died and Marcus stopped asking.

8

TALKING TO NOVA WAS NOTHING like talking to any dog or cat Marcus had ever met. It was more like trying to talk to Alvin, of *Alvin and the Chipmunks*, after a double espresso, while simultaneously watching every car chase in every movie ever made. The rush of mileage calculations, tire changes, odometer readings, fuel tank refillings, garage servicings, and towings combined with an avalanche of moving images, most of them speeding along at headlight level above the pavement, turning left and turning right, fishtailing and curb jumping, and nearly scraping his nose on the asphalt during sudden stops. Car doors opened and closed in his mind and hatchbacks slammed, over and over, the air pressure change popping his ears and threatening to push his eyeballs out of their sockets—

Marcus stumbled backward and sat down on the pavement, face to bumper with the angular front end of the 1985 Plymouth Omni that called herself Nova. Because that's what the Driver called her.

Not Nova's first Driver, not even her second. Nova had had a number of drivers before *the* Driver.

Marcus blinked against the unblinking stare of Nova's headlights, trying to keep track of what were his memories and what were Nova's. Everything the car had...

Said seemed like such a small, unimposing word for the Niagara Falls sensation that had swept over him.

But everything the car had said, or transmitted, or pushed into his brain, had been in the first person. And at very high speed.

The blast of a car horn hit him in the side of the head, reminding him that he was sitting in the middle of the road.

"Sleep it off somewhere else, asshole!" a man's voice yelled.

Marcus staggered to his feet. He took more time than he could have, if he had been willing to brace himself on Nova. She seemed more than willing to let him use her bumper to pull himself to his feet, but he didn't want to touch her. Not again. Not yet, anyway. She understood, though, and didn't take it personally.

He was still dealing with the first-person image of a massive dragon head leaning down at him, the tongue coming out to lick his face when the small, Jeep-like vehicle that had been waiting for him drove past him with another blare of the horn and another shout of, "Asshole!"

Marcus stared as what had to be one of the few remaining Suzuki Samurais as it leaned around a sharp turn and drove out of sight.

Keeping his hands close to his body so he didn't accidentally touch Nova again, he stood next to the car, looking down at her.

The Driver. That's what Nova called Thara-with-an-h. He could see the woman's face from a variety of angles in his mind. The images that stuck in his mind the most, though, were from below. As if someone had put a camera in the center of the steering wheel and aimed it up at the woman's face, so he mostly saw her chin, and up her nose. Then he realized he could *feel* her too. Her hands gripping him. Her feet on his pedals. Her ass on his lap—

He ran his hand over his bald head, feeling the rough stubble beginning to grow back. He shook his head and shuddered.

He could almost see Nova trying to apologize in the gleams of the sun on her windshield.

"Yeah," he said. "That was pretty intense."

Nova was sorry. Really, really sorry.

"I know, I know."

Really, really, really sorry.

"It's OK. It's OK."

It was just that she was so excited—

"I get it. It's OK." He patted Nova softly—and quickly—on the driver side rearview mirror.

He looked up and saw a dark-haired woman watching him as she took the long way around him and Nova to reach a car parked in the center of the lot. He smiled at her, then reached into his pocket and took out his phone. He pretended to poke at the screen then held it to his ear. The woman looked unconvinced, then looked away.

"So," Marcus said, keeping his phone to his ear. "Yeah."

Nova agreed. She was still sheepish.

"It's OK. Don't worry about it. It was my fault. I... let's try this again." He paused. "I wanted to ask you about the dragon."

The Driver.

"No," Marcus said. "The dragon. The one that licked me... that licked *you*... on the face. Or the windshield."

The front end of the car remained perfectly still as Nova nodded vigorously in Marcus's head. The Driver.

Marcus frowned. "Why are you calling the dragon..."

The Driver. Nova wanted him to touch her again. She could explain faster that way. If he touched her.

Marcus didn't touch the car. He pulled his hand back just in time. He stood straight and looked around. He was alone in the parking lot. Except for all the other cars watching him talk to Nova.

None of the cars were facing him. They were just... parked. They hadn't moved.

But every car in the parking lot seemed to be focusing on him. Watching. Listening. Especially the 1964 Beetle, the 1979 Bobcat, and the green-and-white Silverado pickup. The pickup actually seemed to be panting.

Marcus looked down at Nova. He hadn't felt this nervous talking to a girl since high school, when he had asked Delann Wiley, cheerleader, to their Senior Prom in front of the whole cross-country team. After another quick look around, just like he had then, he ignored everyone else. They weren't important. He focused on Nova.

He reached out and placed his left hand on Nova's hood.

Nova's voice still had that sped-up, caffeinated chipmunk sound, but she made an effort to speak slower. The avalanche of moving images came slower too, and focused on Thara. Thara getting into the front seat. Thara opening the hatchback. Thara lifting the hood. Thara shifting from park into reverse, then from reverse into drive. Thara driving. Thara turning left—sometimes without signaling, Nova pointed out. Thara turning right—see? There she did it again. Turning without signaling. Thara looking over her shoulder as she drove the car in reverse. Thara setting the hand brake. Thara exiting the car.

Nova kept up a running commentary as the images came and went. *This is the Driver driving to work. This is the Driver driving home from work. This is the Driver parking me next to Howie. This is the Driver driving to work. This is the Driver driving home from work...*

Marcus tuned out the voice as best he could and focused on Thara. In the images, her hairstyle changed rapidly, as did how she applied her makeup, especially her eye shadow and eyeliner. In the first images, she looked younger than she did now. Closer to Marcus's age. It was hard to be sure, though, with how often she changed her hair. She had gone through a 90s grunge phase in her early 20s, Marcus figured. And a pink-and-blue post-punk phase. And a hairspray-heavy poofy bangs phase. Permed. Sunstreaked. Razor cut. Almost imperceptibly, though, Thara's face matured, the roundness in her cheeks flattened to expose her cheekbones and create the angular planes that Marcus recognized. Her gold-brown eyes, though, never changed.

Again, the images were more than just visuals. They came with the sensation of Thara's fingers gripping the steering wheel and flipping the signal switch up and down—when she remembered to do either. Her hands on the transmission shifter and the door handles and stroking the fenders. Her feet on the pedals. Her ass in the seat.

Marcus didn't pull back this time, despite the uncomfortable intimacy. He did notice one thing, though. "What? She never gave you a bath? No carwashes?"

The sensation of cold water hitting him in the face startled him. Then Nova treated him to a high-pressure wash and blow dry.

"OK, OK. I get it. There were baths."

Not enough, though. Nova was beginning to feel the itches of rust on her undercarriage.

"Right."

The later images of Thara had all been outside the car, doing little more than checking in, as the sky flickered through seasons behind her.

"How long has it been..." Marcus stopped. Asking Nova how long it had been since she was last driven suddenly seemed like a very personal question. It couldn't have been that long, except—

Nineteen years, six months, and eleven days.

Marcus shook his head. Nineteen years? That couldn't be right. Unless Thara-with-an-h had been some kind of driving prodigy at the age of six or seven. Ten, at the oldest, and that required him to adjust his estimate of her age from midtwenties to at least thirty. And, at the tender age of ten, had somehow looked about twenty. Which seemed to be her age in Nova's earliest memories of the woman. The mental contortions to make the math work made Marcus's head hurt.

He changed the subject. "I thought you were going to show me the dragon."

The Driver.

"No, the dragon—"

The Driver. Nova was most insistent.

Nova didn't have as many moving images of the dragon as she did of Thara-the-driver, but she had more than just the cars-eye-view of the windshield-licking action shot Marcus had already experienced. The images of the golden dragon's head with its pointed crest were also external shots. The dragon never seemed to have gotten in the car.

No, that wasn't right. Nova showed him the dragon, noticeably smaller than in the videos, exiting the car. Once through the driver side door. Once through the hatchback.

"Hold on. Back that up. How did the dragon get inside?"

Nova showed him Thara, looking stressed and pale, her lips pressed together, getting into the car. Driving. Pulling over. Changing.

Marcus sat on the hood of the 2003 Hyundai Elantra parked next to Nova. He ignored the Elantra's offering its name and engine and transmission statistics. He no longer had his hand on Nova, but he couldn't stop seeing Thara's face contort. Her head grow and almost split in half as she opened her suddenly huge mouth. Her fingers stretch and form golden claws that flailed at the door handle to let herself out of the car.

Thara-with-an-h was the dragon.

Again, Nova remained perfectly still as she nodded vigorously.

The Driver.

5. Spicy Dragon Ribs

The Queen

THE QUEEN PAUSED, PANTING, IN Her daily labor of secreting the day's seasoning.

A worker scurried forward to dab the Queen's Face with a towel, to remove the unseemly perspiration that was a result of the effort involved in Her daily labor. She ignored the worker's efforts, instead expanding Her awareness of the World around Her.

Something had changed.

A tooth of the ratchet that was Her Plan to Consume the World, to bring an End, had caught.

A tumbler had fallen into place within the combination lock that spun back and forth just below the visible surface of the World.

The final ingredient had been found.

The worker, misunderstanding the smile that spread the Queen's mandibles, bowed, handed the towel to the next worker in line, and jumped into Her maw.

Surprised by the unexpected offering, the Queen nevertheless managed to maintain Her composure. She also managed to chew and swallow the offering without choking.

Still panting, but also smiling, she resumed Her daily labor. Her Work was almost complete. The End was coming.

The Confused

THE CONFUSED HUNG BY HIS left hand on the shadowed side of the tallest structure from which he could see the lair of his new enemy. The Confused had let the claws of his hands extend so he could climb the external face of the building, pushing his claws into the concrete to create handholds as he needed them. He had wrapped himself in shadows as best he could, but as it was nearly noon, he knew he was at least partially visible to anyone below who might happen to look up.

He stared at the squat structure of his new enemy's nest, wishing he could see through the brown walls. The Child had returned to the enemy's lair again today.

What thrall could his new enemy have cast over the Child that she served it so willingly? Was she so blind that she could not see the signs? Or was she just so young she did not know who her enemies were?

The Confused again considered forcing himself into the nest of his new enemy. But the ugly building looked so harmless, and he had detected no overt threat. Perhaps the new enemy was as young and naïve as the Child. Could they really be unaware of each other?

The Confused felt the Sun moving through the sky, working His way into a position from which He would be able to see the Confused. The Confused had, so far, managed to stay out of the Sun's view. The Moon, however, had almost certainly reported his movements. The Confused hoped the Moon had received something equally valuable in return, but he doubted it. The Moon was always being bested by the Sun. So it had been, and so it likely always would be.

The Confused did not want to confirm his presence, though. Not yet. He preferred to remain a rumor.

He relaxed his grip and slid down the face of the building, using his claws to manage his speed. The five parallel scratches he left in the concrete would be all the sign that he left for the Sun to see.

The Bug

THE BUG WANTED HIS CHANCE to talk about the Driver. The Second Ugly Replacement, relative newcomer that she was, hardly knew the whole story.

Bland and late to the party, that was story of the Second Ugly Replacement.

The Bug, though, had been with the Driver since the beginning. Since the Driver's father had given her the Bug, anyway, which was the only beginning the Bug cared about.

1

STILL STARING AT NOVA, MARCUS let the hand with his phone drop from his ear.

Yesterday he had been paid fifteen thousand to look for a dragon. Today he could claim another fifteen thousand for finding a dragon. But only if he called August Neuland.

He looked at the phone in his hand.

Why didn't he make the call?

Two days ago, he had thought the whole "dragon hunting" thing was a joke. What else could it have been except a joke? There were no such things as dragons. There might be a few forty-something women who still looked twenty-five the way Thara-with-an-h somehow did, there might even be more people like Daddy—or, it seemed, himself—who could talk to cars, but the nonreality of dragons had seemed a lot more certain.

He focused on the display of his phone without seeing it—and without starting a call. He jumped when the device buzzed in his hand and the display lit to show him Morgan's name. He realized he had been worried that it was August Neuland calling him and was relieved it wasn't. He answered the call.

"Did you find your dragon, Baby Boy?" Morgan asked. The same question he had been worried August Neuland would ask. Morgan's voice was teasing, though. She had used the same tone last night when he tried to convince her that he had, in fact, been given a fifteen thousand dollar retainer as a dragon hunter.

"Yeah," he said, deciding she couldn't believe him any less today. "I did. Her name is Thara," he added, looking at Nova. "With an 'h.' She's a waitress."

"So you are some kind of recruiter," Morgan said with a told-you-so tone.

"That's not—" Marcus stopped and shrugged. "Well, I guess I could be, but that's not what I expected when I took the job."

"Don't tell me you were expecting to find a *real* dragon?"

"I didn't *expect* to find anything. Or anyone."

"Wait," she said, excitement in her voice. "Does that mean you've been paid the rest of your outrageous fee? I was just going to ask if you were available for lunch, but now I want to know if you're available for Cancun."

"Cancun? What? No, I haven't... told anyone... yet. Just you."

"Me? I'm not going to pay you fifty thousand dollars to find a waitress."

"I'm not sure I should tell anyone," Marcus said. "It doesn't feel... right."

"Taking his money?"

"Telling her secret."

"What secret? I don't get you. She's just a waitress, Baby Boy, even if she does spell her name funny. Tell the man, take his money, and run away with me. We can be making love on the beach by this time tomorrow."

"You want to know the really funny thing?" Marcus asked. "She already works there."

"Are you hearing yourself, Baby Boy? I'm talking sex on the beach with money in the bank— What do you mean she already works there?"

"She's a waitress, or whatever, at the Yellow Sign Buffet. She was hired yesterday, same as me."

"Shit," Morgan said, then fell silent. After a few seconds, she asked, "Do you think he'll still pay you if you point out that he's already hired the person he hired you to find for him?"

"I think so."

"I mean, you have a contract with him, right? He can't back out?"

"The money part was more of a handshake deal. It's not written down."

"Marcus Nelson," Morgan said, saying his name—and probably shaking her head—the same way Mom Nelson would have, if present.

"He already paid me the first fifteen thousand. So even if he doesn't pay me the rest, I'm hardly hurting."

"Still, you should have insisted on a written contract."

"Are you my lawyer now?"

"There's a big difference between fifteen thousand dollars and *fifty* thousand dollars."

"I'm just not sure," Marcus said. "This isn't what I expected."

"I don't see your dilemma. All I see is your lucky weekend."

"Is that all you think about?" he asked, trying to change the subject. "Getting lucky?"

"And money," she said. "I say, as soon we finish talking, you call your ridiculously generous boss and tell him you've found his girl. His dragon waitress or whatever," she added, before he could correct her. "Then we cash in and disappear for like, a week, at least. In case he changes his mind."

"I don't know."

"What's not to know?"

"For one thing, the banks aren't open today or tomorrow, so we wouldn't see the money before Monday."

"Monday is early enough for an additional thirty-five thousand dollars, Baby Boy. The fifteen you've already got should hold us till then, don't you think?"

"It's not just the money. Mom needs her car back before lunch tomorrow."

"OK. So we drive down today, after lunch, and give Mom Nelson her car back. Then we go buy you a new car. One that won't shame you in front of your highly successful, up-and-coming girlfriend."

"I don't want a *new* car," he said, thinking about Lilith, his father's old Lincoln Continental, and a certain blue Pontiac GTO. And, for some reason, thinking about little Nova. "And not tonight. I want to talk to her first."

"What's there to talk about?"

"It's her secret. Her life."

"I swear, Baby Boy, I do *not* understand you sometimes."

Marcus wasn't sure he understood either. He didn't say anything.

After a minute, she said, "Where are you? I'll pick you up and we can talk about this over lunch."

He wasn't hungry, and he couldn't see any value in continuing to talk about it. Morgan wasn't going to understand him because she would never believe Thara was a dragon, or believe him when he told her how he knew.

What he really wanted to do was to drive back to the Yellow Sign Buffet and ask Thara-with-an-h some questions. Like, how she could be a dragon. And how she managed to look as good as she did when she was at least as old as Mom Nelson. Older, probably. Except he didn't want to ask her those questions at the Yellow Sign Buffet. August Neuland might be there, and the man would almost certainly want to ask Marcus how the hunt was going. If he went to lunch with Morgan, though, he could come back and find Thara after her shift.

"Baby Boy?"

"Lunch sounds great," he said, trying to sound convincing. "You want me to meet you somewhere?"

"Driving your Mom's car? No. You just come back here, and me and my new Camry will take you out in style. That is, so long as you don't smell like a stale waiter. And you pick up the check this time."

Marcus assured her he hadn't even set foot in the restaurant today, then told her he would be there in twenty minutes and ended the call. As soon as he did, he wished he had told her longer. He looked at the VW Beetle and the Mercury Bobcat that had also been identified as Thara's cars. He wondered what stories those two cars could tell him about Thara Gold, dragon.

His phone buzzed with another call, this time from a number he didn't recognize.

"Good morning, Marcus," August Neuland said, sounding enthusiastic. "Have you found us a dragon yet?"

"Yes," Marcus said before he could stop himself. "No! I mean, I might be getting close." He forced himself to stop talking. He swallowed nothing, because his mouth was dry and there was nothing to swallow. "Very close."

"That sounds promising. Very promising, even. I knew I was right about you, Marcus. Fate brought us together. How about you come into the restaurant and you can tell me all about it over lunch? The buffet is particularly good today."

"I'd love to," Marcus lied, "but I just made a lunch date with my girl-friend."

"Well, now, all right then," August Neuland said. Marcus could imagine the man's big grin. "How about lunch tomorrow?"

"How about Monday?" Marcus countered. "There are some leads I want to run down," he added, because that sounded like something he might be doing with the extra day. "And I have some running around I need to do tomorrow."

"I suppose tonight is out of the question?" August Neuland asked. "More plans with the girlfriend?"

"We are going dancing," Marcus said, which might or might not be true, depending on how Morgan responded to his current plans.

"OK, Monday it is," August Neuland said. "I can't wait to hear your progress."

Marcus ended the call. He leaned against Nova. He wished he knew Thara-with-an-h's phone number so he could call and ask her when her shift was over.

Nova didn't know the Driver's phone number.

"That's OK," Marcus told the car absently, patting her on the fender.

He had fifteen thousand dollars in the bank. He hadn't even had a chance to spend any of it. He could have doubled his money, then headed home to tell Mom Nelson another twenty thousand was on the way, and that he and Morgan were on their way to Central America.

He wasn't sure there was a lot of repeat business in dragon hunting, so he would still have to find a "real" job after that, but he wouldn't feel so left behind by Morgan's new lifestyle. Especially if she would be coming with him.

So why didn't he want to do it?

2

SATURDAY LUNCH WAS BUSIER THAN the day before. Fortunately, two more employees showed up, a man and a woman. They arrived together, and Keenan and the so-called Mr. Lampley always referred to them together as Hogan and Sally, but Thara was never certain which was Hogan and which was Sally. The two weren't twins. They weren't related or even the same height. They looked nothing alike. The woman, Hogan—or maybe she was Sally—was at least six inches taller than her opposite number and thirty pounds lighter. Dressed in the same brown and yellow uniforms, though, with those ridiculous hats, the two managed to be almost indistinguishable when standing next to each other. When Keenan joined them by the double doors to look out at the dining room, Thara noticed that he became less distinct, as well. Almost blurry around the edges, and hard to focus on as an individual.

As soon as the first dirty plates and empty chafing dishes started coming back from the dining room, Thara assigned herself the dive station again. Holding her breath while taking the chafing dishes from the conveyor belt in the back to their slots in the steam tables made her lightheaded, and seeing people eat food she couldn't visually identify made her nauseous. Plus, each time she pushed open the double doors, she found herself looking for Marcus Nelson, dragon hunter. The booth closest to the front door still had the Reserved placard on it, but he hadn't come in. She didn't like how she was both relieved and disappointed that he wasn't there, not eating.

She tried not think his absence almost certainly meant he was back at her apartment, talking to Nova.

She distracted herself by tipping a stack of dirty plates into the water. The heavy ceramic plates rattled against each other and clanged into the stainless-steel sides of the sink with enough noise that the trio of Keenan, Hogan, and Sally, the look-a-like food haulers and table bussers, stopped to stare at her. Nothing had broken, though, so they went back to watching people eat through the windows of the double doors.

For some reason, the smears of so-called food left on the ceramic plates and the gobs clinging to the sides of the stainless-steel chafing dishes didn't smell—or look—as bad as the fresh heaps exposed when taking the lids off the chafing dishes. Or maybe the pungent chemical scent of the industrial-strength dishwashing liquid overwhelmed her nose while the suds hid the leftovers.

Within a few minutes of filling the sink with hot, soapy water, the so-called Mr. Lampley appeared, called her Gold, and told her she needed to stay in the back and wash the dishes. So he hadn't given up his hopes for the title of World's Worst Manager. She didn't know whether she should hate him for trying, or cheer him on. Ricky so obviously wanted to be a manager, and just as obviously wasn't cut out for it. He was a manager for the same reason she might be the highest-paid dishwasher in Rio Cruces: August Neuland worked in mysterious ways.

She pretended she didn't hear what the so-called Mr. Lampley said, turned around quickly, and doused his shoes with a splash of hot, soapy water. Then made him repeat it one last time, while he stood there with his pant cuffs dripping on the tile floor.

"I just wanted to make sure I heard you right," she said. "Wash the dishes. Thank you. I'll get right to that."

She turned her back on him. She clearly heard his wet, squishy foot-steps as he walked away.

Mr. Neuland had been in the manager's office when Thara arrived, but he had only smiled and nodded at her through the big window. He had disappeared soon after, presumably leaving the so-called Mr. Lampley in charge. Very mysterious ways.

After the lunch rush, when the last few dirty plates, cups and trays had been brought back from the dining room, she noticed Keenan, Hogan and Sally—or maybe it was Hogan, Sally, and Keenan—standing near her. She forced herself to focus, to see them, and picked out Keenan's spotty face.

"What?" she asked him.

"Aren't you going to tell us what to do?"

"No." She nodded toward the manager's office. The so-called Mr. Lampley sat the desk, pretending to write something while studiously not looking up. "That's his job."

"Can we take our break now?"

Thara pointed this time. "His job."

"I know we're short staffed," said the male half of the Hogan-Sally pair, "but we haven't had a chance to eat anything since we got here."

"So go ask *him*."

Keenan looked doubtful. None of the three made any move toward the manager's office.

Thara frowned. Yesterday, Keenan had been more than happy to tell her what to do. As he should have been. He had seniority. She had just been hired, quite literally, to help him out. She had resented it every time he did, but that was both their rights. His to be bossy, hers to resent it. But here he was waiting for her to give him permission to eat.

"Fine," she said. "Take your break. Eat something."

"All of us?"

"Yes, all of you."

"Can we go to the bathroom?" Keenan asked.

Thara stared at them. She looked down at herself and wondered if it was because she wasn't wearing that horrible uniform. She had made one foray into something management-like, back when Jimmy Carter was still in the White House, and decided she didn't like it. Since then, she had stayed away from anything resembling authority. "I just want to wash dishes, guys. Go ask him."

None of them moved.

She sighed. "Sure."

She turned her back on them before they could ask permission for anything else.

After a few minutes of additional scrubbing, she decided it was time for her break, as well. She hung her brown apron on its hook, then grabbed one of the cups she had just washed and took it into the dining room. As she fill her cup with soda she tried not to see Keenan, Hogan and Sally piling their plates with whatever was left in the steam tables. Instead, she thought of the cold pizza slices she had waiting for her at home.

After the others had taken their plates of so-called food into the back, Thara followed them.

She had to step between Keenan and the female half of Hogan-Sally, as the three of them had stopped just past the double doors. They ate standing, holding their plates with their left hands and shoveling food with the forks in their right. As they did this, they watched the empty dining room through the porthole windows.

Thara held her breath until she was past them. Then she walked past the silent conveyor belt with its ominous, plastic-curtained windows, and into the manager's office. She smelled the faint whiff of eau de chicken coop again as she sat in the chair closest to the door.

The so-called Mr. Lampley looked up, uncertain, and maybe a little bit scared. "Yes? Gold?"

"These are the two seats in the back," she said, and took a sip of her drink. "I only need one of them."

The so-called Mr. Lampley picked up a pen, looked at it, then put it back down on his desk. "I," he said. Then, "We."

"Ignore me," Thara told him. "I'm on my break and needed to sit."

He stared at her.

"Go on," she said. "Do what you were doing. You won't even notice me."

He started to say something, then stopped. Then he stood and walked around the desk past her. He paused at the door. "I, uh, we... we need you to work the dinner shift again tonight. Gold."

Thara shrugged and nodded, but he was already gone to give the same bad news to the others. She heard him give his uncertain orders, then go through the doors into the dining room.

She made herself as comfortable as she could in the office chair. Which was not very, but at least she was off her feet. With judicious sipping was able to stretch her soda through two attempted returns by the so-called Mr. Lampley. She considered moving to the padded leather chair behind the desk, but decided that might be pushing it. The so-called Mr. Lampley wouldn't say *boo* to her about it, but he might say something about her to Mr. Neuland. Especially if she put her feet up on the desk and took a nap.

This was the weirdest restaurant she had ever worked for, but it was also the one paying her the most she had ever earned to show up and wash dishes. So she stayed in the office chair until she heard the so-called Mr. Lampley come from the front for the third time.

She took her cup with her, instead of leaving it on his desk, because she was feeling in a better mood after her break. Which might have been the caffeine and sugar as well as the time spent off her feet. She dropped the cup into the sink and nodded at the so-called Mr. Lampley as she passed him. He wasn't looking at her.

The Keenan-Hogan-Sally trio, looking more indistinguishable than ever, had finished their lunches, but they still stood by double doors. They looked at her as she approached.

They looked at her *expectantly*.

She stopped walking and looked back at them.

The female half Hogan-Sally asked, "Should we start?"

The male half added, "Prepping for dinner?"

Thara swiveled her head to look at the shelves full of trays, plates, and bowls, then at the office again. The so-called Mr. Lampley seemed to have forgotten he was supposed to be telling people what to do.

"Yeah," she said. "Do that."

The Hogan-Sally pair walked past her, leaving Keenan by the double doors. He watched them, uncertain, his eyes flicking from the pair, to Thara, to the manager's office with the World's Most Unambitious Manager, and back.

"What did the so-called Mr. Lampley tell you to do yesterday?" Thara asked.

"The drink station? Check the soda fountain syrups?"

Thara nodded. "Sounds good. And brew some fresh tea and coffee, while you're at it."

"How do I do that?"

She started to make a sarcastic remark, then remembered that there was no coffee maker in the drink stations, just glass urns on warmers, and gas ranges for heating water were as absent from the back area as clocks. And that she had seen where the coffee and tea came from.

"The tea and coffee come up on the belt," the female half of the Hogan-Sally pair said as she passed them with an impressive stack of ceramic plates.

"Right." Thara shuddered, then made a mental note to warn the so-called dragon hunter about the tea.

She followed Keenan through the double doors and into the empty dining room.

Thara had worked in restaurants that closed their dining rooms between lunch and dinner. The Yellow Sign Buffet didn't seem to need to. The front door was unlocked and the sign there still presented its message of openness to potential visitors, but the dining room had no customers. Only employees preparing for dinner. And her.

The Hogan-Sally pair were prying the last of the chafing dishes from the steam tables to take them back to the sink, and Keenan was inspecting the various parts of the drink station. Thara stood out of the way and watched them. Now that they had orders, or at least permission to do what they knew needed to be done, the three employees were going about their tasks with an efficiency that could almost be admired.

Almost. And not for very long.

After a minute, Thara walked past the soft-serve yogurt machine and around Keenan, then across the front to the counter.

She went behind the front counter for the first time since she had been hired. The red LED display of the cash register was dark, but she could hear it was still running. Next to the register, the credit card reader's display scrolled a digital greeting. Other than those two bits of technology, and the cords and cables that connected them, the counter was bare. No basket of complementary dinner mints. No toothpick dispenser. Not even a stack of free Penny Pincher "magazines" advertising used cars and rental properties.

Neat. Tidy. Bare.

August Neuland seemed to be a very different kind of small restaurant owner. The Yellow Sign Buffet would have a hard time being even less typical of any kind of restaurant—sit-down, take-out, or buffet. Thara had seen food trucks with more garnishes, and more attempts to make money from more than the food.

The yellowing photographs on the wall drew her eye.

She had noticed the largest photograph when she first entered the restaurant. It was a simple photograph, taken from street level. The cars parked around the restaurant dated it to the early 1950s. Except for the sign mounted on top, the restaurant looked the same today as it did about sixty years ago. Thara wondered which owner had decided that simply having a yellow sign with "Buffet" on it wasn't obvious enough. She noticed a man standing by the front entrance of the restaurant, waving for the camera. His features were too indistinct to make out, but the smile on his face and his posture were dead ringers for August Neuland. There was also a glint on the man's left wrist from a gold watch face. His grandfather, maybe, August Neuland III.

A collection of three smaller photographs arranged vertically next to the large one showed the restaurant in various stages of its construction. First, the foundation, then the cinderblock walls going up, and, finally, the installation of the plate-glass windows. Still curious about the restaurant's kitchen—it had to have a kitchen, even food trucks had a kitchen—Thara peered at the first photograph with some interest. A large excavator with its scoop resting on the ground was parked in the back of the image, beyond the foundation. The primary walls had been clearly marked on the empty slab of concrete, and she could pick out where the restrooms and dive station would eventually be located, as well as the main wall dividing the dining room from the back. The southwest corner of the slab, though, had no obvious plumbing or power fixtures. Just bare concrete.

Or mostly bare concrete.

Thara leaned forward until her nose almost touched the glass covering the photograph. Besides three chickens standing on the freshly poured concrete—as if in anticipation of a coop going up around them—Thara could make out some kind of design drawn on the concrete. Small triangles inside larger triangles, creating a shape that wasn't exactly triangles anymore. Whatever the shape was, it was all straight lines. The chickens and the age of the photograph obscured the rest of the details.

In the other two photographs, that portion of the foundation and interior were obscured, so she couldn't see anything else. There were more chickens, though, scattered through the construction site, both inside and out.

She spotted August Neuland III in the third photograph. His back was to the camera as he supervised the installation of the windows, but his posture was unmistakable. And he had the same male pattern baldness as his grandson. A chicken pecked the dirt at his feet.

The next photograph was even older and showed a wooden frame building, roughly the same size as the current one. The "Buffet" sign was mounted in the center of the front, above saloon-style swinging doors. A serious-looking man wearing a suit stood by the doors. His posture was more rigid, but because the picture was taken closer, and because the man was directly facing the camera, Thara could see that this version of August Neuland—Junior, maybe?—looked even more like the current August Neuland, than the grandfather had. The chickens in this photograph perched on the boardwalk in front of the door, and a couple were visible inside the dining room.

The final photograph was of a tent with no doors, but with a large "Buffet" sign propped near the entrance. The photograph looked to be a late-nineteenth-century print. Again, there was only one Neuland visible, standing near the door and looking even more serious. Chickens of dark and light varieties all but surrounded the tent.

Thara leaned back, eyeing all the photographs at once. For a family that prided itself on keeping the family business in the family, they didn't seem to take pictures of the next generation. Or maybe those photographs were in the family archives somewhere.

"Gold."

Thara jerked back from the photographs and turned to see the female half Hogan-Sally standing next to her.

"Call me Thara," she said, hoping to prompt a narrowing of the woman's name options.

"Mr. Lampley—"

"Call him Ricky."

"—said to tell you the belt has started."

The front door of the restaurant opened. A man held the door open for a woman and a collection of four children of ever-increasing height, ranging from toddler to teenager. The man and the woman were smiling blandly, as were the three youngest children. The teenager, a girl, looked blandly sullen.

"Who would bring their kids here?" Thara asked, but the Hogan-Sally woman was already walking toward the back of the restaurant. The male half of the pair emerged from the back with a covered chafing dish.

Thara smiled her best hostess-smile for the couple. "Welcome to the Yellow Sign Buffet," she said with only the slightest hesitation. She didn't say anything else, because the man and woman only glanced at her, their smiles faltering for an instant, then they walked down the aisle. The sullen teenage girl stared at her.

"What are you supposed to be?" the girl asked. "A waitress? This is a buffet. How useless."

Thara left her smile in place as the family went to stand in line at the steam tables.

Seeing additional customers about to enter, and not wanting to continue smiling, she left the front counter. She went to the back, pausing at the double doors to let Keenan barge past her carrying a heavy chafing dish. Once in the back, she found a pair of oven mitts, took a deep breath, and picked up the next chafing dish on the conveyor belt.

After closing, she and the so-called Mr. Lampley were again the last to leave the restaurant. This time, though, there was another car parked behind the building. A Ford Focus.

Marcus the Dragon Hunter sat on the trunk, his feet braced on the rear bumper. He had his phone out, and was staring at the screen. He wore a leather sports coat, unbuttoned. He looked up and gave her an incline nod as she stepped out, then he put his phone away and slid down.

The so-called Mr. Lampley had already asked her if she wanted a ride back to her apartment, and she had already said no. So of course he asked her again as he looked at Marcus. To his credit, he didn't stammer any more than he had the first time. She told him no, again, then stood and looked at him until he got into his Corolla and drove away.

"What do you want?" she asked Marcus when the Corolla's taillights disappeared around the corner of the building.

"We need to talk," he said.

"About what?"

He shrugged. "This. That. Dragons."

"There's no such thing as dragons," she said automatically. "I'm tired. If you're not going to offer me a ride, why are we talking?"

"No such things as dragons?"

"Nope." She turned away to start walking the same way Ricky's Corolla had gone.

"That's not what Nova says," Marcus said to her back.

Thara stopped and shook her head. She sighed. "That little tramp."

3

"You can't go get a drink like that either," Marcus said, standing near the front door of Thara-with-an-h Gold's apartment. He pulled his eyes away from the nearly naked white girl to glance at the deadbolt on the front door.

Her, said the voice in his head, sounding smug.

Thara had locked the door when she closed it behind them, declared that she wouldn't go anywhere dressed as a soggy waitress and would be taking a shower, then started unbuttoning her shirt as she walked across the living room. He had stopped by the door and watched as she took off her shirt, revealing an athletic figure with a narrow waist and nicely curved breasts held in place with a sports bra. Her skin was smooth and had an unusual sheen, almost a luster, reminiscent of the gold scales he had seen in the images of the dragon Nova had shown him.

Ignoring his comment, Thara tossed her shirt on a pile of similar clothes next to a wall covered with a large mirror. With no visible hesitation, she peeled off her sports bra, letting her breasts hang free, threw the bra on the pile too, then started kicking off her shoes. Each kick, every movement she made, made her breasts jiggle in a way Marcus couldn't ignore.

"Depends on the bar, doesn't it?" Thara asked.

She didn't turn to face him, but she didn't have to. The mirror showed him everything.

Her her her.

"We were just going to have a drink, right?" He felt his face get warm. He also felt stirrings in his boxers and tried to distract himself from her breasts—

She unbuttoned her pants and pushed them down over her hips. "I asked if you wanted to wait in the car."

Her.

The voice in his head wasn't helping. It was like he had to look at her. He had to resist the urge to point and agree.

"Yes, you did." His leather jacket suddenly became too warm. He started to take it off, but the act of taking off his jacket at the same time she was taking off her clothes seemed too... intimate. He turned his body so that his growing erection wouldn't become obvious.

"You still can."

"I'm cool," he lied. "You do what you got to."

Marcus looked away. Or tried to. He noticed the TV for the first time. And how reflective the screen was. She took off her panties and her pants at the same time, her bare bottom swaying back and forth in his peripheral vision as she did.

Her.

Thara-with-an-h Gold was still not his type. But something about her was definitely working for the voice in his head.

"No tattoos, huh?"

"I used to get a new tattoo every few months." She stepped out of the legs of her pants and panties. "Before rent started going up."

"Temporary tattoos?"

"No," she said, turning to face him, standing there in black ankle socks. "They just didn't... stick."

He turned the long way around to look at the sofa. Clothes, folded and not, were piled on the sofa, and there were more clothes scattered around the living room. Neither the clothes nor the sofa reflected anything. Certainly not the naked figure in the far corner.

"Have a seat." She turned her back to him again, then kicked her pants and panties onto the same pile of dirty clothes. "Watch some TV, if you can find the remote. Or see if there's anything to drink in the fridge. I'll be out in a few minutes."

She went into the bathroom and closed the door. Then she came back out, took off her socks, and went back in. After the door closed, Marcus heard the distinctive click of the thumb lock being engaged.

Marcus stared at the bathroom door, wondering what Morgan would say. Remembering how Morgan had looked at him, with her eyes almost squinting and her lips pressed together when he mentioned wanting to talk to Thara after her shift, he tried to push the images of a naked Thara-with-an-h out of his head. It was probably best if he *didn't* mention this part of his evening to the girlfriend he had not gone dancing with.

Not gone dancing with *yet*, he protested to no one present. The night was still young. Ish.

He shook his head and blew out a breath, then took off his jacket. He looked for a place to put it, and settled for draping it across the back of the sofa.

"A few minutes" turned out to be fifteen. Marcus had time to find the TV remote beneath a pile of clean white button-down shirts on the sofa, and to discover that, no, there wasn't anything to drink in the fridge. There was nothing in the fridge except a pizza box with a half-eaten large pepperoni pizza.

As he did these things, his eyes kept going to the bathroom door. He noticed the three deadbolts on her bedroom door, but didn't want to stand that close to the bathroom door to see if they might be locked.

He sat on the sofa between a pile of clean underwear, not folded, and a stack of carefully folded black trousers. He turned the TV on, but he couldn't focus on it long enough know what was on.

So, yes, there was more to Thara-with-an-h than just her golden eyes. She still wasn't his type. Not really. Seeing her naked, though, did highlight her better points—

Morgan was going to kill him. But not before she flayed him. She would know. As soon as she saw him again. He didn't know how she would know. He sure as hell wasn't going to tell her. But she would know he had been in the same room as a naked woman that wasn't her. And then she would peel off his skin and kill him. She might even hang his carcass from her third-story balcony. A warning to future black boyfriends of the penalty for lusting after naked blonde white girls.

He glanced at the bathroom door. The player in his head—and the one in his pants—kept replaying the sight of her bare ass swaying back and forth—

He forced himself to look at the TV screen and the banal, nonerotic car dealership commercial playing there. And to remember—to hear over and over—the *click* of the lock engaging on the bathroom door. He shifted his position on the sofa so he was sitting between clean white shirts and clean black trousers, as far from the tangled collection of clean bras and panties as he could get.

There had been no invitation in her stripping, or in her nakedness. She hadn't taken off her clothes because he had been there, or because she had known he would watch. She simply hadn't cared that he was standing there, or that he was watching her.

He jumped to his feet, his heart racing, when the door to the bathroom unlocked with another distinctive *click*, then opened. Then he made himself sit back down, with only a single glance, as nonchalantly as he could manage, at the naked woman with the large bath towel draped over her shoulders. She had towel-dried her hair, and it stuck in all directions but mostly straight up, like some kind of old school punk rock Mohawk. She must have reapplied her eyeliner before she left the bathroom. The heavy black lines helped him focus on her eyes.

Her.

She met his glance, but her eyes held no more invitation than before. She took the towel from her shoulders and tossed it into the corner. Then walked into the living room, and past him—she had to go around his out-stretched legs—to the pile of underwear.

He tried to focus on the TV while she bent over, picked a pair of panties, and pulled them on. He really tried. But his peripheral vision kept shouting at him that there was a naked woman—*Her! There! Right there!*—getting slowly unnaked.

He glanced at her as she pulled the sports bra over her head, then stretched it cover her breasts. "You—" He stopped to clear his throat. "You look pretty good for a forty-five year old dragon-woman."

"You're so sweet." Something about her tone reminded him of the *click* of the lock on the bathroom door. She picked up the top pair of worn blue jeans and bent over to pull them on. As she buttoned them around her hips, she said, "Sixty-seven."

"You were born in 1967?" He did the math. "So you're forty-eight?"

"No," she said. She stood there in blue jeans and a gray sports bra, looking down at him with an amused expression. "I was born in 1948. I turned sixty-seven in March."

Marcus stared at her as she turned away from him to survey the more colorful shirts scattered around the living room.

The voice in his mind still wanted him to know that, well, *her.* Now that she had clothes on, though, the voice was less... insistent.

"I guess you only talked to Nova." She walked in front of the TV and bent over at the waist, in profile. The bright display of the TV screen high-lighted her narrow waist. "My roommate moved out yesterday," she said as she picked up tee-shirts and tank tops. She stood up with an armful.

"She made a mess of my clothes. She thought I had stolen one of her camisoles."

His mind was still trying to reconcile the smooth, naked body he had clearly seen with the numbers 1948 and sixty-seven. His mouth answered for him. "Had you?"

"I don't think so." She brought the collection of shirts to the sofa and dumped them on top of the pile of underwear. She picked out a plain black tee-shirt and pulled it on. The curved shape of her breasts and the slender line of her waist disappeared beneath the loose-fitting shirt. She picked two nearly matching black socks from a pile, then sat on the pile of shirts and underwear to pull them on.

He turned to face her. "Sixty-seven?"

She nodded. "Sixty-seven and a half, I guess." She stood up from the sofa and walked to the mirror wall. Her reflection lacked the punch it had had before, but Marcus couldn't stop himself from thinking about what he knew she looked like under the clothes. She ran her fingers through her hair, pushing the strands into something resembling a part and a style. Then she pushed her feet, one after the other, into a pair of short, black biker boots, and turned around. "You ready to go?"

"You're sixty-seven."

"And a dragon-woman," she said. "Though usually only four nights out of the year." She bent over at the waist again, rooted around in the pile of dirty clothes, and stood back up with her phone and a ring of keys. "There's a bar and grill a couple blocks away," she added, pushing the phone into a pocket of her jeans. "Do you want to take your car?"

Marcus stood as she walked past him to the front door. "Sixty-seven."

She opened the door, then turned around to peer up into his eyes. "I guess we had better walk."

He moved to follow her out the door.

She pointed at something behind him. "Your jacket."

"Right." He turned back around and leaned over to retrieve his jacket. Walking was probably the best idea. He didn't know about her—Her!—but he needed to clear his head. He noticed her short sleeves as he shrugged into his jacket. "What about you? Won't you get cold?"

She looked at him. She blinked once, slowly.

"Oh, right," he said. "Dragon-woman." Something she had just said finally registered in his mind. "Why only four nights out of the year?"

"Why does the Sun come up?"

"What?"

"Or are the stars merely pinpricks in the fabric of night?"

It was Marcus's turn to blink at her.

"Never mind," she said. "Just take my word for it. Let's go."

4

Marcus followed Thara out the door, into the breezeway. He glanced back at her as she locked the door. The voice in his head still insisted on reminding him, *Her*, every time he looked at her, but it was manageable now.

He looked away from her, down the breezeway toward the parking lot. The solitary sconce that illuminated the breezeway seemed to be struggling to provide more than a yellow stain on the darkness. Beyond the breezeway, the streetlamps in the parking lot seemed to be having the same problem pushing the darkness out of the way.

"Whoa," he said. "It got dark."

"It was dark when we got here."

"Not this dark."

"Do you want me to hold your hand?" Thara asked as she walked past him.

He fell in step beside her. "Would you do that for me?"

The extra darkness receded as they walked and seemed to disappear as they left the breezeway. The streetlamps flared as they resumed their normal, unimpressive illumination. Marcus glanced back at the breezeway, expecting to see a black cave. Instead, he could see all the way to Thara's door at the end. He started to point out the change in illumination to Thara, but she had stopped in front the VW Beetle parked facing the breezeway.

"This is Louie," she said. "If you've already talked to Nova, I can assure you that Louie *really* wants to talk to you."

"Louie," Marcus said, and started to reach out his hand.

"Not now, though. I'm not going to stand here while you two gossip about me."

Marcus took back his hand. "So you believe I can talk to cars?"

"That's not the strangest thing that has happened today." Thara pointed to the Mercury Bobcat parked next to Louie. "And this is Howie."

Marcus nodded to the Bobcat. "Howie."

"You've already met Nova, of course. These are my Outdoor Babies."

"Your Outdoor Babies."

She sighed and nodded. "Someday I'll have a garage where I can park them."

"So they're project cars?"

"No," Thara said. "They're *my* cars. All the cars I've owned, except poor Niwanda. And I want them kept safe."

"So you don't plan to fix them up?"

"How would I do that?" she asked, glaring at him. "I'm a waitress, not a mechanic." She walked between Louie and Howie, her hands outstretched so she was touching both with her fingertips. "And I like them just the way they are."

Marcus followed. "Wouldn't they be more useful if they actually ran?"

Thara turned to glare at him again. "They don't need to be useful. They're my Outdoor Babies."

"OK, OK. I'm just making conversation."

She didn't respond.

"I don't know about the Bobcat or the... I mean Howie or Nova," he corrected himself as she looked at him from the side of her eye. He looked over his shoulder toward Louie. "I don't know about those two, but the Beetle, Louie, you could probably find parts for."

"So you're a mechanic?"

"I could have been," he said, thinking of Daddy. "Maybe I still could."

They walked across the parking lot, then between buildings. They walked on the sidewalk the old man had been examining, following the tracks of a dragon. He mentioned the old man to Thara.

"He's Jimmie the Wrangler," Thara said. "He works for the city."

"How do you get a name like Jimmie the Wrangler?"

"His name is Jimmie, and he wrangles."

"That's not what I meant."

"When you've been around as long as he has, maybe people will be calling you Marcus the Mechanic. Or maybe Marcus the Dragon Hunter."

He looked at her, and she met his glance with a smile.

"So you know about that?"

She shrugged. "Was it supposed to be a secret? I was there when you were hired, remember?"

"I remember you dropping that pan of mashed potatoes and... whatever it was."

"That's the life of a waitress," she said. "If you do your job right, no one remembers you. They only pay attention when you screw up."

Something dawned on Marcus that had been bugging him all day. "1964. That's what you meant. You've been a waitress since 1964. Fifty-one years? And you're still dropping pans?"

"That wasn't an accident," she said. "That was me protesting your job title, and how much you were being paid. And I was doing the world a favor by sending whatever that mess was straight to the trash. Which reminds me," she added. "Don't drink the tea anymore." She held up a hand. "Don't ask. You don't want to know."

They reached the entrance to the apartment complex, Thara led him to the right, along Fifty-first Street. As they walked, Thara craned her neck to look at the sky overhead. He looked too, but saw nothing unexpected.

Movement in the corner of his eye drew his attention behind them, looking back the way they had come. He saw only the apartment complex's entry sign, parked cars under streetlamps, and the looming buildings. Most of the apartments had lights on. He saw nothing moving, though.

He turned back to Thara. "Were you always a dragon?"

Thara nodded. "All my life. Well, not *all* my life. I had my first Episode when I was ten." She told him about becoming a lizard in the birthday bubble bath. Then about Nancy Chisum's pajama party. She pantomimed claws by curling her fingers and swiping at the air. "It was horrible," she finished. "I hid in the bathroom until morning, when Poppa picked me up."

"And here I thought growing body hair was the most traumatic part of puberty."

"It wasn't puberty," Thara said. "I was ten. But body hair was still plenty traumatic," she added. "High school was bad enough, but then I started growing hair in odd places. I was only eighteen. I was not prepared for that."

"Eighteen?"

Thara glared at him. "For a guy who stared so hard at a naked sixty-seven year old—"

"I wasn't staring."

"You were totally staring. At least your mouth wasn't hanging open. I'll give you points for that."

"Points? Thanks, I guess?"

Thara smiled at him. "I age... slowly. At least, I have since I was ten. Which I would think is obvious."

Marcus considered several responses. He settled on, "How slowly?"

Thara shrugged. "Slow enough I didn't start getting breasts until I was almost twenty. Nancy quoted Song of Solomon at me all through high school. 'We have a little sister,',", she said, pitching her voice higher, "'and she hath no breasts: what shall we do for our sister in the day when she shall be spoken for?' The guys in school were less kind about it."

Marcus kept his eyes on her eyes, though she wasn't looking at him. "I guess you grew out of that."

Thara smiled, but it wasn't for him. "Nancy thought that little verse was the funniest thing in the world. She might have been a bit jealous, though. I could run cross country without hurting myself. In the dark days before sports bras," she added, glancing at him, "the small-chested woman ruled the arena."

Walking along a city street after dark, with a girl, on their way to a restaurant, reminded Marcus of his time at the university. Except this wasn't a date. And the "girl" was a woman three times his age. And a dragon.

"Why aren't you a dragon all the time?"

"I don't *look* like a dragon all the time," she said. "In here," she added, tapping her forehead, "I'm always a dragon."

"Is that why you don't like people? Because you're a dragon? Or because they're not dragons?"

"What makes you think I don't like people?"

Marcus shrugged. "My mistake."

"I like people fine," she said. "So what about you? Are you a dragon hunter all the time?"

"Only since yesterday. So why don't you look like a dragon now?"

"I'm only a dragon during my Episodes," she said. She explained about solar equinoxes and solstices.

"Then what happened the other night? This is October."

"I was late." She nodded at a large, brightly lighted sign ahead of them. "That's where we're going."

"Jose O'Reilly's?"

"The best Tex-Mex Irish food in Rio Cruces." She led him across the parking lot toward the main entrance of the restaurant. "I used to work here. Twice. A few years in the eighties. Another couple years in the late nineties. I might come back here after this new job craters. Most job applications only ask for the last ten years."

"Tex-Mex Irish? I didn't know that was a thing."

"Two days ago, you had never met a dragon."

"That's true."

"On the other hand, neither had I. It's been a busy week for both of us."

Before Marcus could ask her what she meant, his phone buzzed. He didn't have to see the display to know who it was. "I have to get this," he said, taking his phone out of his pocket. "You go on in and get us a table."

She shrugged and went inside.

He took a deep breath, pushed all the images of a naked Thara-with-an-h out of his mind, then thumbed the button to answer the call on the third ring. "Hey, Morgan."

5

"I THOUGHT YOU WOULD BE back by now," Morgan said. "It's ten thirty."

"I had to wait until she got off work."

"Uh huh."

Marcus stepped away from the door of Jose O'Reilly's so a man and woman could enter. "And then she insisted on taking a shower."

"A shower."

The woman entering the restaurant glanced sideways at Marcus, her expression very similar to the one he imagined on Morgan's face.

"Maybe you're not the only one that doesn't like stale waiters," Marcus told both Morgan and the door closing in his face. "Maybe she doesn't like *being* a stale waiter."

"So now she's all clean and not stale?"

"Yes?"

"You'd better not be ditching me to hang out with your 'dragon.' After what you told me, though, I think she's more like a cougar."

"I'm not ditching you. We're just having a drink—"

"Leaving me at home to go have a drink with some other woman is ditching me."

Another man, alone this time, strode out of the night and up the cobblestone sidewalk of Jose O'Reilly's. The man wore a black trench coat, the tails billowing behind him dramatically as he walked. Darkness seemed to follow the man, fluttering in the night air like the tails of his trench coat.

Marcus noticed the man looking at him.

231

Their eyes met briefly, just long enough for the voice in Marcus's head to say, *Him.* Then Marcus turned away.

"It's not like that," he said. He was going to say more, to sweet talk her back from the ledge she seemed to be standing on, but the voice in his head distracted him.

Him, said the voice again when Marcus turned to see the man pull open the door of Jose O'Reilly's far wider than was actually necessary. The man didn't look back as he entered. The door took its time closing, as if to make sure the man had all the time he needed.

Marcus remembered the man in black armor and sword he had seen outside the Yellow Sign Buffet the day before.

Him, agreed the voice in his head.

"It looks exactly like that from where I'm sitting," Morgan was saying. "All dressed up, but still at home. Not dancing. Drinking by myself while my supposed boyfriend is out with another woman old enough to be his mother. I don't know why you have to have a drink with her. Just give the man her name and collect your money."

"It's not that simple," Marcus managed to say as he stared after the man. The door closed. So did his chance to say anything else to Morgan.

"Yes, Baby Boy, it *is* that simple. You don't know this woman. You don't owe her anything."

"Look, I'll be back by eleven. Eleven thirty at the latest, that's still plenty of time—"

"You have until eleven."

Morgan ended the call before Marcus could respond.

6

THE HOSTESS GREETED THARA WITH a smile and led her to a booth by one of the front windows. The hostess looked to be about sixteen and wore a short black dress with a green sash belt tied around her waist. The waitress that appeared as soon as the hostess was gone was at least twenty and wore, of course, a white and black outfit almost identical to what Thara had been wearing less than forty-five minutes before. Though not sweat-soaked and steaming from a long night of washing dishes.

Thara told the waitress she was waiting for someone and the young woman left her alone.

She could see Marcus through the window. He was pacing back and forth in front of the door to the restaurant as he talked on the phone. His expression was hard to read, switching between smiling enthusiasm as he spoke and increasingly pursed lips as he listened. The net effect was one of not enjoying the conversation.

She looked at the menu she had been given, deciding that her leftover pizza would still be a viable breakfast in the morning. Tonight would be the dragon hunter's treat. Dublin Chili would hit the spot, and maybe provide additional leftovers.

Movement outside the window drew her attention, and she looked up to see a man in a black trench coat approaching the restaurant. He had long, wavy black hair that looked as if it had been styled and blown dry just before he appeared. His lean face was Asian, with broad cheekbones, a straight nose, and a distinctive chin line, but his skin was unusually pale. His eyes were tilted, but round. He never turned his head, but Thara saw he and Marcus exchange a glance as he strode past. Two males sizing each other up. Thara shook her head, then looked back at the menu.

She looked up again as the man in the black trench coat sat in her booth, in the seat across from her. He wore a black suit under his trench coat, with a black shirt and a silver tie. His skin looked less pale under the yellow light hanging over the table. She saw his eyes now, and they were as silver as his tie, though flecked with white and black. His face was ageless. She was certain he was older than her, but the skin of his face was smooth. The skin of his hands was smooth, as well, but neither face nor hands looked soft. She could smell him now, too. Beneath the scents of new clothes and freshly applied cologne and hair products, she smelled something... different. Something at once familiar, and that she had never smelled. Something not just *male*—

Something *dragon*.

"You are here with the hunter," the man said. "Leave with me now." His voice echoed in her mind the same way it had two nights before when he had told her, *Run away, little one! Hide!* His accent was like his face, Asian, but not typical. She couldn't place it. His tone, though, was unmistakably paternal and chiding.

Her excitement at meeting another dragon—a *male* dragon—was overcome by unexpected thoughts of Poppa and irritation at the man's presumption.

She smiled an unfriendly version of her that's-really-sweet-but-I-never-date-customers smile, and tried to make that her only concession to the overwhelming presence of the man. Besides the tingling sensation in her fingers and the base of her neck. And the warmth growing in her belly.

She balled her fists in her lap, out of sight, and said, "My date will be here soon. You should go."

Marcus wasn't her date, and she didn't want the man to leave, but she wanted to say something to disturb the man's calm.

The man's calm remained annoyingly undisturbed. "Are you toying with him? Is this some childish game?"

Annoyance joined forces with irritation and removed the smile from her face. "Who are you calling childish? My date will be here soon," she repeated, "but he's not the one you have to worry about."

"I do not concern myself with the hunter. My worry... is only with you." The chiding in his tone lessened, replaced with something warmer. The macho paternalism, though, was still there.

Thara leaned forward. She had so many questions. She had never met another dragon, and here he was. Except he was being kind of a dick. "Who are you?" she asked. "What's your name?"

"I am the Only—" the man started. Then he closed his mouth.

"The only what?" Thara asked.

The man's calm was still in place, but there was a hint of something... slightly lost... behind the silver eyes now. He glanced away, then back. "Forgive me," he said. "It has been a long time since someone asked me that. Especially someone..." The man's voice trailed off, but his eyes remained fixed on hers.

She liked his eyes. She liked his face. She had no doubt he could leave the restaurant with any woman there, and more than a few of the men. With fifty-one years of waitressing behind her, though, there was no way she was going to be that easy. Even if he was the last male dragon in the world. "Leave now," she said, "and all is forgiven."

Not that she wanted him to leave, whether he gave her his name or not. Still, she tried to keep the warmth from spreading to her face. She couldn't remember the last time she had blushed, though it had probably been in response to something Poppa had said—

This hardly seemed the time to be thinking of Poppa. She dug her fingernails into her palms to help her focus. The pain worked better than expected. Her fingernails seemed longer—and sharper—than they should have been.

"Who are you?" Marcus asked.

Thara looked up. Distracted by the man across from her and by her own thoughts, she hadn't seen Marcus approach. He looked taller than he had walking beside her a few minutes before. His leather sports coat added some bulk to his shoulders and made him almost intimidating. She couldn't decide whether he was trying to protect her, or was just upset another man had moved in on him. Not that she cared either way, but she wanted to be able to properly tease him about it later.

Marcus's apparent tallerness and added bulk dissipated as the man in the black trench coat stood and showed her what *taller* and *bulkier* really meant. Thara gave Marcus a few extra points for not backing away. Maybe she wouldn't tease him.

"I am the Eldest," the man said.

"The oldest what?" Marcus asked before Thara could.

The man stood only slightly above eye to eye with Marcus, but the difference in heights seemed much greater. The man didn't answer Marcus. Silver eyes looked down into brown with an intensity that made

Marcus seem more substantial. As if he existed more now that the man looked at him.

Thara felt left out. She wanted the man to look at her like that. To make her more real. Except, no, she didn't. She wanted him to leave. Then she wanted him to come back, introduce himself properly, and maybe she would—

"I see," the man said, interrupting her thoughts. "I did not expect... this." Then he looked at Thara. Instead of looking at her the way he had looked at Marcus, though, he pressed his lips together and lowered his brows.

Thara's fingernails stabbed into her palms. She was disappointed to realize she didn't feel more substantial from his gaze. She felt he was trying to figure her out. She decided that was a victory, of a sort. She hit him with her would-you-like-to-try-one-of-our-amazing-appetizers-tonight smile. He didn't seem to notice the smile, or the irony behind it. Which took the fun out of it.

"You didn't expect what?" Marcus asked, standing straighter than before and squaring his shoulders.

The man continued to look at her. His eyes never left her eyes, but she wasn't sure he was even seeing her. Something about the look on the man's face reminded her of Poppa again, as if he were about to tell her something important, but didn't know how. Or as if he wanted to protect her from something, and knew he couldn't. Still paternal, but no longer patronizing.

"Just say it," she said.

The man looked away from her and looked down at Marcus again.

"You do not have to be a hunter," the man said. "There are other options."

Marcus's mouth opened, then closed. "What other options?" he asked after a few seconds of glaring back at the man.

The man ignored that question, as well. He turned to face Thara again. His expression had resumed the extreme calm and confidence from when he first sat down.

He gave her a slight bow from the waist. "Please accept my apologies for this intrusion. Good night, child."

Paternal or not, something about the way he said *child* did *not* remind her of how her father used to call her *Goose*.

The man turned and Marcus stepped aside.

"Wait," Thara said before the man could walk away, the only other dragon she had ever met. "You didn't tell me your name."

The man looked back at her and smiled. The parts of Thara that had been growing warm almost melted. "When I think of it again, child, I will be happy to share it with you."

No, Poppa had never called her Goose the way this man called her child.

He turned and walked away, leaving only his scent and the lingering impression of his presence. Thara was sure he must have walked to the front of the restaurant and left through the front door, but she realized after he was gone that she hadn't witnessed that. What her mind thought she had seen was him taking a single step away from her, then disappearing into the shadows between the tables and the hanging lamps. She noticed the other women in the restaurant, patrons and staff, were all doing the same thing she was, staring after the man with their nostrils slightly flared.

"Why are you glowing?" Marcus asked.

"I'm not glowing," Thara said in spite of the warmth she felt all over. "You're glowing."

Marcus took off his jacket, folded it and tossed it into the corner of the booth. After he was seated, he twisted around to stare after the man too. Then he leaned over to look out the window. "I didn't think I was gone that long."

There was no sign of the man outside. Thara had already checked. Her fingers were still tingling, so she kept them in her lap.

"Stop glowing," Marcus said, not looking at her. "It's distracting."

"Does he make you hot too?"

Marcus shifted in his seat. His eyes met hers briefly, and she grinned at him. Then he looked down at the menu on the table in front of him. His face might have become a shade darker than normal. "I don't know what he makes me." He picked up the menu, but didn't open it. "All I know is I look at him, and some part of me says, 'Him.'"

Thara nodded. "Me too."

She lifted her left hand to where she could see her fingers. Her fingernails were longer, golder. Hooked. She felt an odd urge to gouge something. She curled her fingers back into a loose fist and rested her hand on the tabletop.

"And you too," Marcus added, letting the menu drop. He looked at her again, and didn't look away this time even when she smiled. "The same thing happens when I look at you. Even when you're not glowing."

"Some part of you says, 'Him?'" Thara asked. "When you're looking at me?" She looked down at the front of her shirt. "I know they're not the biggest boobs in the world, but I would think they indicate something. I mean, after all, you've seen them. And more."

This time his face definitely became a shade darker, and his ears too, but he didn't look away. He smiled a lopsided smile.

"There's nothing wrong with your boobs," he said. "No. In your case, that part of me says, 'Her.'"

"Good. That makes more sense. I think." She let her fingers spread on the tabletop and glanced down at them. Her fingernails were still gold, but they were no longer hooks. "But which part of you are we talking about? Just so I'm sure."

"No," he said, shaking his head. "None of this makes sense." Then he sighed and picked up his menu again. He opened it this time. "Morgan is going to kill me."

Hearing the woman's name made Thara want to tease him, to make him blush again. "Why is she going to kill you?"

"We were going dancing," he told his menu.

"And you stood her up for me?" Thara asked. "That was shortsighted of you. We are not on a date."

He looked up at her. He had the same lopsided smile as before, but he wasn't blushing now. "No, you're not my date. You're my job."

Thara put both her hands on the tabletop. All her fingernails were gold. She didn't remember that ever happening before, not even before an Episode. She decided she liked the look. "Your job?"

"I'm a dragon hunter. And you're a dragon."

She waved her right hand, gesturing to indicate the restaurant. "So this is you hunting me?"

"No, I did my hunting yesterday, and this afternoon. Me and Jimmie the Wrangler both, I guess."

She put her hands back on the tabletop and leaned forward. "You talked to Jimmie the Wrangler? About me?"

"No, I just meant he seemed to be hunting you too."

"He's been hunting me since before you were born." After a second she added, "I might have eaten his dog."

"A collie?"

"Maybe. I forget."

"I'm not even sure why I asked that," Marcus said, squeezing his eyes closed and shaking his head. "I really didn't want to know."

The waitress arrived. She looked at Thara, smiling, her eyes wide and glistening. "Are you two ready to order? Or do you still need a minute?" She looked willing to wait as long as required. Thara noticed that the top buttons of the woman's shirt had come undone. The woman had been fully buttoned up before. Thara understood. She was still feeling a bit warm under the collar, as well.

They ordered and the waitress left. She had never even looked at Marcus. Thara wondered if the girl thought she knew the man's phone number and was hoping she would give it out. Then she remembered the tingling sensation at the back of her neck. She pretended to adjust her hair while she touched her neck. She felt only skin. No scales.

"I told you," Marcus said. "You're glowing." He glanced over his shoulder. "Or maybe she likes you."

"Don't presume to know the sexual orientation of waitresses," Thara said. "Or waiters."

"The way you're glowing, I don't think her usual orientation matters."

"I'm not glowing."

"Uh huh. So what about dragons?"

"What about them?"

Marcus raised one eyebrow in silent question.

"Same deal. If they haven't told you, you don't know."

"Anything you need to tell me?"

Thara shook her head. "No. Remember? This isn't a date."

"So what is this then?"

"You tell me, dragon hunter. What is this? Why are we here?"

7

MARCUS DIDN'T ANSWER RIGHT AWAY. He looked out the window. He more than half expected the man in the trench coat to be out there. He wasn't. When Marcus faced Thara again, she was looking out the window. Her glow took on a disappointed tint that made him oddly jealous.

Her, said the infuriating voice in his head.

After their brief, odd encounter with the man in the trench coat—with the voice in his head shouting *Him!* over and over—Thara had developed a golden sheen that was at once difficult to look at and hard to look away from. Her eyes were more gold than ever. Even the black eyeliner around her eyes had become gold, as well as her fingernails. Looking at her was like looking at the sun. Too bright to see clearly, and burning Thara-shaped impressions on his vision. Marcus kept wanting to squint when he looked at her, except the effect was only his mind. Like the voice that kept saying, *Her*.

Marcus could tell he wasn't the only person effected by her new corona. Men and women throughout the dining room kept glancing at their table. At her.

He tried to clear his head. Why had he wanted to talk to her?

"Maybe it's Fate," he said. Which sounded lame even as he said it, but it was all he could think of.

Thara looked at him. "What is that supposed to mean?"

Before he could answer, their food arrived. Marcus used the distraction to consider his answer while the waitress arranged Thara's steaming bowl chili in front of her. The waitress also gave him his beer, but not with the same attention to detail and outright fawning. Thara didn't seem to notice the waitress, or the attention of the other patrons in the restaurant. She had eyes only for her chili, when she wasn't glancing out the window.

"Well?" she asked as waitress walked away. She picked up her spoon and stirred her chili. Her golden fingernails flashed the light in his eyes.

"A week ago," he said, picking up his pint of beer. He paused and took a sip. He put the beer down. "No, not even a week ago. I was looking at job listings, and I saw one that had to be a joke. 'Dragon Hunter wanted. No experience necessary.'"

"No experience necessary? I'm not sure how I should take that."

He shrugged, then watched her crumble crackers into her chili. It was hard not to find even her most banal movements endlessly fascinating. He squeezed his eyes closed and thought of Morgan. He tried to think of Morgan smiling at him, but all he could conjure was a squinting glower over a glass of wine. He turned his head so he would be looking out the window again when he opened his eyes.

"It had to be a joke, right?" he asked her reflection, which was also glowing and glittering, but not with the same intensity. "Dragons don't exist, so dragon hunters aren't going to see a lot of action. But I called the number anyway. Why wouldn't I?" he asked, as if she had challenged him on it and not just taken another slurp of chili. "I'd made lots of other calls for jobs that turned out not to exist. How would this be any different? At least it might be funny." He shrugged. "That was Monday. And here we are."

"I thought you were hired yesterday."

Marcus nodded. "Right. They asked me... August Neuland asked me, I mean, to come in Friday morning. Yesterday. But only if the world hadn't ended by then."

"The world didn't end," Thara said. She pursed her lips and blew on a spoonful of chili, then put it in her mouth. "What?" she asked when she noticed him staring at her lips.

"Nothing." He looked away again. "So, anyway, when I'm driving up yesterday morning, I'm still thinking it's a joke. Though it's beginning to be kind of a long joke. Except, it's still not a joke. I get hired. I get paid more money than I've ever seen to find something that doesn't even exist. And why?" he asked, turning to face her again.

Her.

"Fate?" Thara offered over another spoonful of chili.

He nodded, trying not to stare this time. "That's what August said, yeah. Fate." He picked up his beer and took a drink.

"August, eh?" Thara asked as she chewed. "You two are on a first name basis already? Everyone else calls him Mr. Neuland. And they keep calling me Gold."

Marcus nodded. "I can see that."

"You can see what?"

"Nothing." He shook his head and blinked. "August... Mr. Neuland... told me he only took one phone call off his internet job posting. Mine. Because he believes in Fate. I thought that was a weird thing to say—"

"It is a weird thing to say."

"—but the money was good," he went on. "Too good, I guess. I just couldn't make myself argue with a man willing to pay me fifty grand to look for something that doesn't exist. Then I find you."

"I guess I made it easy for you," she said. "Getting a job at the same place on the same day."

"Yeah," Marcus said. "I was thinking that. Maybe that's Fate too."

Thara drew back from the table. "Are you trying to turn this into a date again?" she asked, pointing her spoon at him. "I'll call Morgan myself, and tell her."

"You don't know her number."

"I don't need to know her number."

There was a flash of gold that streaked across the space between them. Her spoon moved from her hand to rest in her bowl of chili and his phone appeared in her hand.

It was his turn to pull back from the table.

"How did you do that?"

"Fingers." She wiggled the fingers on her right hand as she held the phone and thumbed the display alive with her left.

"No. How did you do that so fast?"

"I didn't do anything fast," she said as she peered at the password screen on the phone. "And I'm not going to call your girlfriend and rat you out." She put the phone back on the table and slid it to him at a more normal speed, one he could actually witness. She picked up her spoon again. "I'm too hungry, and you didn't seem upset enough about the prospect to make it any fun." She shoveled another spoonful of meat and beans into her mouth with a complete lack of grace.

Her golden glow had dimmed significantly. Yet the voice in his head still said, *Her.*

He smiled and shrugged. "You think I didn't learn anything in college? You live with enough roommates, you learn to password protect everything." He let the smile fade into another sigh. "Here's the deal, Miss

Thara-with-an-h. This is why I wanted to talk to you." He took a breath. "Yes, I was hired as a dragon hunter, and it turns out dragons do exist. Sort of."

"Sort of?"

"It's not like you're a dragon all the time. I'm going to go with 'close enough.'"

"Close enough? Come back around the winter solstice, you can follow me around during an Episode. You can tell me how 'sort of' that is. Tell me if that's 'close enough' when I light up the Christmas trees with a bit of high-octane gaslight."

Her face remained human as she spoke, except for her eyes, which grew rounder and larger. Her golden irises expanded, and her pupils took on a penumbra like a total eclipse of the sun. A small gust of her breath came across the table, smelling of chili and as warm as a desert breeze at noon.

He held up his hands, palms facing her. "My bad. I take it back. I didn't realize I was insulting your dragonness. I'm sure you're all the dragon I need to find."

"I'm all dragon," she said, jabbing at him with her spoon. "Even if I only show it four nights of the year."

Marcus thought about pointing out how much dragon she seemed to be showing at the moment, but even as he thought the words, her eyes resumed their regular shape and size. More of her glow dissipated too, making her easier to look at. "Why only four nights a year?"

She shrugged. "I don't know. I don't even know why I'm a dragon. I'm not even adopted. So, anyway, you found me. Congrats. Now what?"

"I don't know," Marcus said. "That's the question I keep asking myself. What do I do now that I've done the impossible?"

She rolled her eyes. "It sounds so... so... typically *male*, when you put it that way. Especially considering you've now met *another* dragon, also without even knowing it."

"What? Who?"

Thara looked out the window.

"Him," Marcus said, at the same time the voice in his head said the same thing.

"Yeah," Thara said, sighing. "Him."

"How many dragons are there?"

"How would I know? Until two nights ago, I was the only one I'd ever met."

"Fate." The word sounded less like a joke this time.

"Or something."

"No, really," he said, leaning forward. "Why was I hired to find a dragon? Why did all this happen now?"

Thara shrugged. "How would I know? Especially when they had already found one, sort of. They could have saved themselves a lot of money."

Marcus rubbed his hand on the top of his head, feeling his scalp. "My dad used to say that he charged the same hourly rate for a simple fix as a hard one. It's knowing where to apply the simple fix that you're charging for."

Thara shook her head. "How does that even apply? You didn't think dragons existed. So what were you charging for?"

His player smile came back. "But I still found you, didn't I? So I'm obviously worth every penny. But you're still missing the point."

"Enlighten me, oh mighty dragon hunter."

"Why did a buffet restaurant hire me to find a dragon?"

Thara shrugged. "Maybe they need a new mascot? Or do you think they want to put me on the menu? What did August Neuland tell you when you asked him?"

"He didn't. That's what worries me."

"I'm touched by your concern for my well-being," she said, her sarcastic tone at odds with her words. "Here's a thought, though. Split it with me."

Marcus looked at her. "Split what with you?"

She rolled her eyes and shook her head again. "The money, you moron. Pay me half whatever they're paying you, then turn me in. I go quietly, and as a bonus, I can stop washing dishes or even waitressing for a few months. Maybe even find me a new place to live. One with a garage."

8

"No," Morgan told Marcus, "you are *not* going to split anything with her, you moron."

Morgan had been dressed to go out when he returned to her apartment, but she had made no move in that direction. As soon as he was in the door, she steered him back to the dining room table, made him sit, and demanded to know what had happened.

There was an open bottle of wine on the table, but only a single, half-full wineglass. Morgan picked up the wineglass as she sat. Then she crossed her legs and leaned back to look at him. She looked good in her tight gold top and black leather skirt, but she projected more the air of an interrogator than a dance partner. So he told her everything. Except about Thara getting naked in front of him. Then, after her shower, getting unnaked. He also left out the glowing and the bit about the man who was also a dragon.

"What you are going to do, Baby Boy," Morgan said, "is call August Neuland first thing in the morning and tell him you found his dragon." She took a sip of her wine. "Then, as soon as his money hits the bank Monday morning, you hand her over." She leaned toward him and placed the glass on the table in front of her, punctuating her declaration.

"Hand her over? It's not like she's stuffed in the trunk of my car."

"You know what I mean."

"I just wish I knew why they wanted me to find them a dragon."

"She's not really a dragon, Baby Boy. She just meets the criterion they gave you."

Marcus nodded. "She meets the criterion, alright."

Morgan looked at him.

"Did I say that out loud?" he asked, turning on his player's smile and letting his eyelids droop just enough.

"Mm-hmm. You think you're cute."

"I know I'm cute."

"Mm-hmm. Some player you are. You're letting this little white girl play you."

"She's not playing me."

"Oh, she's playing you, alright," Morgan said as she stood. "Did she flash you a quick glimpse of her 'criterion?'" she asked, leaning over. She bunched her breasts with her arms, and shook her cleavage in his face.

"No," Marcus lied, genuinely enjoying the view while trying not to let the tight gold fabric of Morgan's blouse remind him of Thara's white-gold skin.

Morgan stood straight and let her arms fall back to their sides. "Split the money with her." She shook her head. "Sometimes I do not understand you, Marcus Nelson." She picked up her wineglass again and drained it. "Get my keys, Dragon Hunter," she said as she placed the glass on the table. "You're taking me dancing."

6. Sesame Dragon

The Queen

THE QUEEN SANG AS SHE Worked in Her Kitchen, calling to Herself Her scattered seeds and seasonings, Her children, Her workers.

Her Daughters joined Her, Their Voices muffled within Their cocoons, weak but growing stronger.

The Queen had never sung Her Song before, but She knew the Words and the Melody. Like Her Daughters, She had known Her Song since before Her Birth over a century before. The Song was part of Her.

She had been Born to Sing the Song. Her Song. The Song of the World's End.

The final Dinner Bell.

The Queen sang. She sang the World a Song, with Her Daughters, in Perfect Harmony.

The Nameless

THE NAMELESS SAT ON THE peak of the roof of the Child's apartment building, his legs dangling over the edge, in full view of the pocked, battle-scarred half-face of the Moon, and wondered what had happened. How had he lost control of the encounter so quickly?

His first meeting with the Child had not gone as anticipated.

She had shown him no deference. She had offered no explanation of her actions. She had not even recognized him.

She had treated him like an ill-prepared, blundering suitor. He, the Nameless, who had courted—and won!—the Black Queen of Kemet, had stuttered and stammered and fled in the face of a single, simple question.

What's your name?

Centuries spent as the Only, the last of his kind, had robbed him of his name. "Use it or lose it" applied in this case, as it did in so many others.

The Nameless looked up to see the Moon had set in the west. If the Moon remembered his name, it was too late to ask. Typical. The Moon always managed to be absent when the really important questions needed answering.

The Nameless looked over his shoulder to the eastern horizon. The Sun would know, of course. The Sun did not know everything, but He forgot nothing. The Sun would be more than happy to remind the Nameless of his forgotten name, when He Rose in a few hours. All the Nameless would have to do is ask, and endure the response.

The Sun would be a right bastard about it. The Sun was always a right bastard about everything.

As the Nameless waited for the Sun, he heard a new Song of the World's End rising into the night.

The Nameless stood on the peak of the roof, listening, considering. Another possible Ending, so soon after the last. What did it mean? Was the World so determined to End? Had the World existed so long that it *wanted* to End? The Nameless could understand that.

The Bug

THE BUG HEARD THE NEW Song of the World's End and wondered if there would be another earthquake. An earthquake wouldn't be as much fun as a tow trip to the impound, but combined with the End of the World, the view should be incredible.

The Bug noticed the First Ugly Replacement was getting scared that the World might really End this time. If the Bug had been able to shake his head in condescension, he would have.

Silly First Ugly Replacement. The World had never Ended *before*.

1

THE LAST PERSON MARCUS EXPECTED to see standing just off the dance floor was August Neuland.

In the near-darkness, under the pounding beat of the house music, the flashing lights illuminated the man in bursts, from a variety of directions and in a variety of colors. The man had appeared between bursts of sound and flashes of light, standing there as if he had been there all along, smiling, looking at Marcus, but otherwise not moving. The lights distorted his bland, white bread features, melting them and spreading them left, right, up, down, coloring them purple, blue, green, red, as if the lights were punching his face in retaliation for not even *trying* to dance.

Marcus stopped midmove, creating a rupture in the rhythm of bodies on the dance floor, beginning with Morgan, who backed into him and bounced off. He managed to get his arm around her waist before she pitched forward onto the floor. Around them, the other couples staggered as if the floor had shaken or the music had skipped a beat.

He helped Morgan regain her footing, then apologized with a look and a shrug because she wouldn't have heard anything he tried to say. He left her standing on the dance floor, looking after him with an expression of mixed confusion and affront. Her mouth moved as if she were saying something, but he couldn't hear her.

He walked to where August Neuland waited. Under normal circumstances, he would have danced his way off the dance floor, but just the sight of the man had knocked the beat out of him, so he had to repeat his nonverbal apology multiple times as he wove his way through the other dancers. He felt like a salmon swimming downstream, disrupting the upstream mating dances of the other fish.

Between white and blacklight flashes, just before Marcus stepped off the dance floor, August Neuland disappeared.

Marcus pulled up, frowning.

As the overhead red and purple spotlights spun, throwing search-light-like beams across the people in the bar, Marcus saw August Neuland sitting at a tall table.

The man wore the same yellow shirt and brown trousers he had been wearing when Marcus first met him, or close enough. Same articles of clothing or not, the cut and fit, the colors—the man himself—looked so out of place, so incongruous, that Marcus's mind was still struggling to actually perceive the man as he walked to the table.

Marcus took the man's outstretched hand and shook it once, quickly. He leaned forward.

"Hey!" he shouted into the man's ear. "What are you doing here?"

August Neuland didn't respond except to smile wider. Marcus pulled back. August Neuland took his amazing phone out of his shirt pocket, activated it, and started thumbing a text message. Marcus looked back and forth from the phone to the man's face. After a few seconds, the man looked up again.

Marcus's phone buzzed in his pocket as the text message arrived.

"Hello, Marcus!" the message said. "Fate has brought us together again." No abbreviations, and proper punctuation made the text message as weird as the man himself.

"Fate?" Marcus shouted. "What are you talking about?"

Before August Neuland could finish responding with another text message, Morgan arrived, appearing on Marcus's left. From her eyes and the line of her mouth, she still looked confused and affronted, though the mixture had definitely tilted away from the former and toward the latter. She pulled on Marcus's arm to bring his ear close to her mouth.

"What's going on?" she shouted. "Who is this?"

She turned her face, presenting him with her ear.

"August Neuland," he shouted.

She looked at him without fully turning her head. Her lips moved, shaping the words, *Your boss?*

He nodded, then his phone buzzed with the arrival of a new text message.

"Can you step outside? I cannot help but think it would be easier for us to talk."

Marcus caught August Neuland's eye and nodded, then leaned down to shout into Morgan's ear. "We're going to step out. I'll be right back."

She shook her head and grabbed his arm. He shrugged as best he could. They retrieved their jackets, then followed the here-again-gone-again form of August Neuland out the front door of the club. As late as it was, there was no longer anyone waiting behind the velvet rope to get in. The bouncer still sat on his stool by the door, though, so the three of them walked around the corner to the parking lot where Marcus had parked Morgan's Camry.

Morgan put on her jacket as they walked and wrapped it around her. Marcus left his draped over his arm.

"What are you—?" Marcus started to ask, then realized he was still shouting. He lowered his voice. "What are you doing here, August?"

"Please," the man said, "introductions first." He offered his hand to Morgan. "I am August Neuland."

With a glance at Marcus, Morgan took the man's hand and shook it. "Morgan," she said. "Morgan LaVoi."

"Very nice to meet you, Miss LaVoi," the man said. Before he released her hand, though, he paused. "LaVoi? Are you by any chance the... let me see, you would have to be his granddaughter, I'm sure... of Lawrence LaVoi?"

"No," Morgan started to say, then stopped. "You mean my grandfather? Larry LaVoi?"

"A wonderful man, your grandfather. Lawrence and I had some business dealings back in the... hmm... it must have been the early 1960s. It is indeed an honor, Miss LaVoi." He put his left hand over their joined hands and shook again before releasing.

Marcus looked from August Neuland to Morgan. She was smiling, an improvement in her mood Marcus had not expected. Still, when he looked at August Neuland again, he couldn't believe the man was old enough to have had business dealings with anyone in "the early 1960s." Except maybe a babysitter or a school teacher. Before Marcus could ask him about that, though, the man was talking.

"I told you, Marcus," August Neuland said, still smiling, "it's Fate. Fate has brought us together this week in so many ways."

"Why are you here?" Marcus asked.

"We need to talk."

"How did you find me?" Marcus thought of the phone in his pocket. "Did you track me here? You could have just called."

August Neuland held up his hands in a placating manner. "No, no, Marcus, I didn't track you here. You mentioned you were going dancing when we spoke earlier today."

"That doesn't tell me how you found me. Or why."

"I told you, Marcus. Fate brought us together. I needed to speak with you, so I came straight here, to you. I hate to interrupt your date," he went on, "but there have been... developments. The Song has begun, and we need to move quickly."

Marcus wanted to ask why the man hadn't just called him, but he knew the answer. The short answer would be Fate, again. The longer answer being that if August Neuland had simply called, or sent a text message, Marcus wouldn't have answered or responded, not before tomorrow. The logic of Fate made Marcus's head hurt. As if the man knew what Marcus was thinking, he grinned and winked.

"Wait," Marcus said. "Just wait. What developments? What song?"

"You told me you were close to finding our dragon," August Neuland said. "Very close, even." When Marcus nodded in response, the man went on. "Well, we're going to call that 'close enough.'"

"Close enough?"

"Close enough?" Morgan echoed. "What does that mean?" She squinted her eyes as she peered at August Neuland. "Does he still get the full fifty thousand?"

Marcus looked at Morgan. "Wait—"

"Every penny, Miss LaVoi," the man said. He pulled an envelope from the breast pocket of his shirt, where it had been behind his phone. He held out the envelope. "I have a check for the remaining thirty-five thousand dollars right here."

Marcus looked around to make sure no one was near enough to hear. Morgan took the envelope before he could. She ripped open the top and peered inside.

"That's a very pretty check," she said. "All nice and round, but we can't cash it until Monday."

"Would you prefer cash?" August Neuland asked.

"If you could."

August Neuland held out his hand to take the check back, but Morgan held onto it. "We'll trade you the check for the cash," she said, smiling.

August Neuland smiled back. "You said you were going dancing with your girlfriend," he said, still smiling at Morgan, "but this young lady is obviously your business manager."

"Oh, I have many talents."

Marcus felt left out of the conversation. "Wait. Hold on. I'm not even sure I found a..." He couldn't make himself say the word for some reason. "I'm not even sure I found what you're looking for."

"Marcus," August Neuland said, gripping Marcus's shoulder with his right hand. "Marcus, Marcus, Marcus. It's Fate, I assure you. I had no doubt when I took your call the other day. And no doubt I hired the right man for the job. You are a dragon hunter, the first in..." He bit his lower lip and his eyes looked past Marcus for a second. "Let's call it fifty generations. Maybe more. Fate brought us together, you and me. Believe in yourself, Marcus. I do."

"He found a woman," Morgan said.

Marcus turned to look at Morgan. "Wait—"

"Her name is Thara," she went on. "With an 'h.'"

"Thara." August Neuland's smile became larger than his face for an instant. His grip on Marcus's shoulder became tight and hard, almost painful, then he let go. His face and his smile went back to normal. "With an 'h.'" He winked at Marcus again.

"What did I tell you, Marcus?" He pointed at Marcus with his index finger. "Fate. When you've been around as long as I have, and heard as many prophecies, and seen them come true, you learn to believe."

Marcus didn't know what to say.

"So how about that cash?" Morgan asked.

"We will need to go back to the restaurant," August Neuland said. "If that's OK."

"That'll be just fine. You know, I had forgotten until you mentioned Papa Larry, but I've been to your restaurant before. He took me."

"Well, Miss LaVoi, we'll be happy to see you walk through our door again. We like to think of our customers as our family."

Marcus didn't remember starting to walk, but they had reached Morgan's Camry. Parked next to it was a beige 1992 Cadillac Eldorado that showed no signs of its age. There had been no open space next to the Camry when Marcus parked it there. August Neuland walked to the driver side door of the Eldorado.

"We'll follow you," Morgan said. "Get in, Marcus. I'll drive."

Morgan and August Neuland opened their separate car doors in unison. Marcus hesitated before opening the passenger side door of the Camry. His hand went to his pocket with his phone. His fingers touched the cool glass of the main display, but he didn't pull the phone out.

He wanted to call Thara, to tell her... what? To warn her? Except he still didn't know her number.

"Get in, Baby Boy," Morgan said.

2

MARCUS DIDN'T TALK AS MORGAN drove. She followed the taillights of August Neuland's Cadillac Eldorado as they turned left, right, and around, leading them out of downtown Rio Cruces. She had her left hand on the steering wheel, and her right hand on the shifter, as if the Camry were a stick shift. She kept her eyes locked on the car in front of them, keeping as little distance between the two vehicles as possible.

Marcus stared out the windshield, seeing nothing. A succession of automobile statistics streamed through his mind. Their speed, to three decimal places, the current ratio of atomized gasoline to air mixture in the computerized fuel-injection system, estimated fuel efficiency in miles-per-gallon, also to three decimal places, cabin temperature versus climate control settings, pounds per square inch of pressure in the tires, and more. The level of detail was greater tonight than it had ever been. More digits after the decimal place, more systems. He wondered if talking to little Nova had opened his mind, so he could even talk to newer cars. He could almost feel the Camry ready to start a mental dialogue—or establish a connection—as if his mind were some kind of wi-fi router for cars. He didn't want to talk, though. Not now.

"Even if he doesn't come up with the cash," Morgan was saying, "we still have his check. We take that to the bank first thing Monday morning, before he has time to cancel it. You were right. I don't think he would cancel it, but just in case. Then we're off, Baby Boy, just you and me. I call work and break it to them that I am *not* coming in this week, and we go straight to the airport. I've always wanted to travel with no luggage, and just buy what I need when I get to my destination..."

Marcus tuned out both Morgan and her Camry. He took his phone out of his jacket and stared at the blank display. He didn't want to talk about vacation plans or how they would spend August Neuland's money. He wanted to talk to Thara. To tell her... what, exactly?

He still didn't know. Some part of him wanted to warn her, but what would he be warning her about?

Plus, he had already done that. Sort of. She wasn't concerned. August Neuland didn't frighten her. She just wanted Marcus to split the money with her.

August Neuland was beginning to frighten Marcus.

Fate.

He could almost hear August Neuland saying the word.

When you've been around as long as I have... you learn to believe.

He activated his phone and brought up the number pad.

How did one use Fate to find a telephone number? Was it like getting in your car and driving, trusting that Fate—or whatever—would lead you to the proper destination? Did you just start punching numbers at random, get to nine digits, and press Send?

He wasn't even sure he could press random numbers. He had to keep his eyes open to use touch screen number pads, otherwise he had no idea what he was pressing—

He closed his eyes. He held the phone in his left hand, and punched four times with his index finger. He made no attempt to adjust his aim. If Fate was going to work, it was going to have use the motion of the Camry, the lean of the turns and the lane shifts. Maybe even the spinning of the Earth as it orbited the Sun, as that star hurtled through the Milky Way Galaxy—

He opened his eyes and stopped thinking about the movement of celestial bodies. It made him dizzy. It took his eyes a second to focus on the phone again.

As far as he knew, he had punched the same number four times. Or maybe he had punched the Send button already, and was about to hear the message for an incorrectly dialed number.

"Damn," he said before he could stop himself.

He had dialed a "1" and the first three digits of a Rio Cruces phone number, the area code: 918.

Now he really felt dizzy.

"What are you doing?" Morgan asked. "Are you calling her?"

She reached over and took his phone. She dropped the phone on her lap, then put her right hand back on the shifter. She batted away his attempt to get the phone back.

"No," she said. "I'm not going to let you screw this up."

"So you're going to save me from myself? Is that what you're doing?"

"You need me, Baby Boy."

"I didn't need you to get this job. I didn't need you to find Thara."

"That was blind luck," she said. "You told me that yourself. Well, now the blind luck is over. I'm going to make sure you don't screw this up. You're not going to tell her to run away or whatever, and you sure as hell aren't going to split the money with her."

"It's my money."

"It's our money, the foundation of our future together."

"After a short vacation?"

"Absolutely."

Marcus looked at her profile. "I guess it's just Fate."

"Now you're getting it." She glanced at Marcus, then locked her eyes on the taillights in front of her again. "Can you believe it?" she asked after a minute. "We've hit every light perfectly since we left the club. It's like the stoplights work for us. And all the other cars just move out of our way."

Marcus turned to look out his window at the darkness. He could almost hear August Neuland saying it.

Fate.

3

THARA'S PHONE RANG ON THE floor next to her.

The white goose down comforter she had wrapped herself in when she laid down for the night did nothing to muffle the jangling sound, so she extended her left hand out of the folds to feel around on the floor to find the phone.

Her encounter with the other dragon—the *male* dragon—had left her jittery. And horny.

The warmth in her belly had not dissipated on the walk home. The Dublin Chili from Jose O'Reilly's might even have made it worse.

She had managed to keep her hands—and claws—to herself, though. She had ignored the waitress's continued attempts to flirt and kept Marcus at arm's length on the walk back to her apartment. Not because she wouldn't have gladly done either of them, separately or together—and maybe even one after the other—but because she was worried about... breaking them.

The three times she had partially transformed during sex had been as traumatic for her as for her partners. Lots of screaming had been involved, though no blood had been spilled. Where possible, apologies had been made.

This time, though, tonight, she had actually *wanted* to transform during intercourse. To make that part of the experience. And there was only one viable partner for that, and she had sent him packing. Which, in retrospect, seemed like a hasty move on her part. Even if he did remind her of Poppa more than was comfortable.

That she had already had her Episode and additional transformations shouldn't be possible for at least two months didn't dissuade her from wanting it to happen. The fear of it maybe not happening—combined with the fear that maybe it would—left her... confused. And more than a little unsatisfied.

The only certainty was she wanted something she couldn't have.

She sent Marcus away—back to his girlfriend—then parked herself under the shower and let cold water wash over her, steaming, until her internal temperature and more violent desires finally ebbed. Then she wrapped herself in the white goose down comforter, curled up in the corner of her hoard, under the window, and fell asleep to dreams of impure thoughts.

Her phone rang again before her fingers found it. She pulled the phone into the comforter, accepted the call without trying to read who it was from or what time it was, and pressed it to her ear. She could hear voices on the other end, men and women, not talking to her or whoever held the phone on the other end of the call. She thought she heard Marcus's voice, but that made no sense. She definitely heard August Neuland's voice. Behind the voices, just loud enough to obscure whatever was being said, was some kind of buzzing that went up and down in pitch. Something in the buzzing harmonized with a similar sound in her head. As if the buzzing and a long-forgotten song were working together to annoy her.

"If this is some kind of booty call," she said, "you had better be up to it."

"Uh," said the so-called Mr. Lampley. His voice cut off the background sounds. "I, uhm, we—"

"Damn it, Ricky." Of all the booties in all the world— "Do you know what time it is?"

"I'm sorry," he said. "We... I... we... need you to, uh, come in."

"That wasn't a rhetorical question, Ricky. I have no idea what time it is, but I do know that it's too damn early."

"It's, uh, three thirty."

"Good-bye, Ricky."

"Wait! Mr. Neuland... he said you—you need to come in."

"Why do I need to come in, Ricky?"

"Mr. Neuland said it was... important?"

"What? Some kind of Sunday Brunch Special?"

"Do you, uh, need me to come over? To give you a ride?"

"Do I get paid overtime, Ricky?"

"What? No, I mean, wait. I'll, uh, ask Mr. Neuland."

"You do that."

The background voices and the buzzing resumed as she heard the so-called Mr. Lampley do exactly that. She heard August Neuland's voice as he responded. The owner of the Yellow Sign Buffet sounded as excited as a man in a maternity ward. She heard the words she needed to hear.

"He said—"

"I'll be there in fifteen—no, twenty—minutes," Thara said. "Or thirty."

She thought she might have heard Marcus shout her name, but she had already ended the call. She wasn't going to call back. If Marcus had something to tell her, and he was actually there, at the restaurant, she would see him in a few minutes. Or forty-five.

With one last, impure thought, she threw off the comforter.

4

DRESSED AS A WAITER AGAIN, Thara left her apartment. The apartment complex was unusually still, and the night seemed especially dark beyond the weak illumination that hung from the parking lots' streetlamps. It had been a long time, nearly a decade, since she had had to walk to work, or the bus stop, in the predawn hours, but she was pretty sure it was supposed to be quieter.

The Interstate that passed behind the complex never slept and roared along at nearly rush-hour decibels all day, every day, but there was far more traffic on Fifty-First Street than she expected at four in the morning. Plus, she could still hear the buzzing in her head.

She didn't feel hung over, which made sense. She hadn't had anything to drink at Jose O'Reilly's. Just the Dublin Chili, and some water. The Dublin Chili had never let her down before, so she was suspicious of the water. She wondered if that waitress had slipped something into her glass.

When she reached the entrance to the apartment complex there was a lot of traffic on Fifty-First Street—but only going one way—her way—and going that way slowly. Both lanes of westbound traffic were full. The opposite side of the street, though, was empty enough to lie down and take a nap.

She yawned and made a right. She walked beside the slow-moving river of red taillights and brake lights, with headlights illuminating her from behind. Each step she took, a dozen shadows took the step with her, radiating away from her.

The river of cars turned left at Harvard Avenue, the same way she wanted to go, and merged with cars coming from the east and north. There didn't seem to be any cars come from the south. Six lanes of slow-moving traffic from three directions merged, braided together to create a double stream that crept south. The stoplight for the intersection blinked a regular sequence of yellow-red-green, but the drivers of the cars and trucks and SUVs weren't paying attention. They were following the tail-lights of the car in front of them, not the traffic signals. The movement of the cars, start-and-stop, start-and-stop, seemed synchronized with the buzzing in Thara's head.

She surveyed the vehicles congesting—swamping?—the intersection. They were all going her way, but none of them looked as if they were willing to yield to a pedestrian. She could see the drivers and passengers of the cars, but no one even glanced at her. They seemed to be staring fixedly toward their shared destination.

She almost turned around and went back to her apartment, her hoard, and her white goose down comforter. She saw no way to cross the inter-section without having to walk between the bumpers of unpredictably moving multi-ton vehicles.

Then she saw a white Chevy S-71 Sierra pickup coming up to the intersection from the north, inching along at walking speeds. The truck was in the near lane, and its bed looked empty.

She walked across the two empty northbound lanes of Harvard Avenue to the side of the pickup. The driver, a man in a cowboy hat, never looked at her, not even when she climbed the back bumper and into the bed of the truck.

She rode the pickup through the confluence of the intersection. When another, smaller Toyota pickup pulled alongside the Chevy, she jumped from one pickup bed to another. She glanced at the windshields of the cars behind the trucks, but she couldn't see through them. Too much yellow glare. She didn't pause in the Toyota pickup bed. She jumped out the far side and landed on the sidewalk.

Once she was walking on the western side of Harvard Avenue, heading south toward the bright yellow sign above the Yellow Sign Buffet, she could see the river of red taillights extended only as far as the restaurant. Beyond the restaurant, on the other side of the five-lane street, was a separate river of headlights. Both rivers were coming together as the cars pulled into the parking lot of the Yellow Sign Buffet one after the other, taking turns in the same way they had done back in the intersection.

She wondered what kind of Sunday Brunch Special could be *that* special.

As she walked closer, she saw that the restaurant parking lot was nearly full. Cars were parked in tight lines, bumper to bumper, with only enough room between them to open one set of doors at a time and shimmy out. The parking lot behind the restaurant was full, and along the north side. People who had parked had exited their cars and stood in the narrow spaces between the cars. They looked at the restaurant—

No, they were looking up. At the blazing yellow sign on the roof.

Thara glanced at the sign, then looked away again immediately with a floating brown afterimage clouding her vision. The sign was so bright the words "Yellow Sign Buffet" were no longer visible. The brightness of the sign wasn't constant, though. The light didn't flicker, but throbbed, in time with the buzzing in her head.

She really, *really* wished both the light and the buzzing would stop.

She realized she was walking faster, her hands at her sides, finger-tips tingling with the urge to tear the whole place down, down, down, below the concrete foundation, until only a smoking crater remained. The shadows of her hands ahead of her had become wickedly pointed. And the breath in her chest was getting warmer, steaming in the cool, night air.

She stopped walking, and stood panting, staring at the restaurant. She held her hands up where she could see them. Her fingers had grown. There was no sign of scales, but for the second time that night her finger-nails had become golden, hooked claws.

She curled her fingers to hide the claws. Or tried to. It was hard to make a proper fist with her fingers that long. She hunched her neck in case it had grown too.

She glanced at the nearest car, to see if the occupants had noticed her sudden elongations. The car, a four-door Hyundai Elantra of recent vintage, was driven by a woman, with a man in the front passenger seat. Both were dressed as if going into the office. The man even wore a tie. Neither of them, though, was looking at Thara. They were staring straight ahead, up, and to the right. The extreme brightness of the sign reflected in their eyes so their eyes seemed to glow yellow. The reflected light throbbed to the same tempo as the buzzing in her head.

Thara wondered if she allowed her transformation to continue, if she became a full twenty-five-foot dragon next to their car, would they notice her then?

She was tempted to find out. There must have been some Episode left unfinished from the other night, because she was pretty sure she could do it. If she just let go.

She didn't let go. Nearly six decades of trying to avoid having an Episode in public kept her human. Or at least *mostly* human.

She stared at her semiclenched fists until her fingers pulled in on themselves and became fingers again, and her claws had retracted to slightly long fingernails. She left her fingernails gold, though. She never planned to paint her fingernails again. If she didn't think it would threaten her socks and her favorite pair of sensible shoes, she would do the same with her toenails, right now. She would conduct experiments in dragon pedicure later. After work.

She looked up at the Yellow Sign Buffet again, keeping her eyes focused on the building, averted just enough to avoid looking at the blazing sign. When she started walking again, it was like driving into the sun, but with no visor she could drop down.

She hoped more of the "lost" staff had come back. There was no way just she and the Hogan-Sally-Keenan trio could handle this much business by themselves. Or maybe the so-called Mr. Lampley would help.

Thara snorted. As if.

Of course, she had no idea where the employees would park if they did show up. The last two available spaces in the parking lot were taken by a car making a right and another car making a simultaneous left.

Like water hitting a dam from two sides, both rivers of cars, the bright red and the brighter white, sloshed to a stop. The cars in the front stopped. The cars behind them pulled up as close as possible, then stopped. This created a ripple effect toward her and away from her on the far side of the restaurant. The red river of taillights flared as brakes were applied, then disappeared as cars were turned off. The white river became splotchy as some of the headlights went off and others stayed on.

Another wave passed through the cars, as doors opened and people stepped out. Then a wave of car door slammings like an explosion of metallic applause in time with the buzzing in her head. The people standing between the cars, though, didn't walk toward the restaurant. Instead, they stood and stared at the bright yellow sign.

Once again, Thara considered turning around and walking back to her apartment. Sure, she had already talked to her so-called manager and said she would come in. He would know she had cut out on him. If he wanted to fire her tomorrow, that would be his right.

She glanced back over her shoulder.

The glowing yellow eyes of the faces looking past her and over her head shown brighter than the headlights. None of the people were in her way, though. They still stood in the street.

She made up her mind. She turned around to walk back to her apartment. The world had become too weird. The Sunday Brunch Special would get along fine without her. Or, more likely, go to Hell just as quickly without her as with her. She would go visit Jose O'Reilly's tomorrow, and see if they needed any experienced wait staff. Or bus staff. Maybe the flirty waitress would put in a good word for her.

She had taken only two steps back along the sidewalk, though, her eyes averted from the headlights and the glowing eyes, when the people standing in the street began to move.

First, all the eyes shifted. Hundreds of tiny yellow spotlights swung across the sky and the tops of the cars and the road and the sidewalk until they locked on her. The people no longer looked past her or over her head. They looked at her, as if all the stars in the heavens had paired up, come to Earth for Sunday Brunch, then decided to stand around and stare at her.

Thara resisted the urge to look away. She confronted the closest starers with a stare of her own and kept walking. She was a waitress. If she couldn't handle people staring at her as she walked, she would have changed careers long, long ago.

The men, women, and children started walking. Also toward her. They filed around their cars, through the narrow gaps between bumpers, and onto the sidewalk.

The buzzing in her head became louder. Then the mouths of all the people fell open and the buzzing erupted into audibility.

A wave of white noise and yellow static and stale, toothpasty morning breath roared and hit her in the face and the body. She stumbled and coughed and blinked against the smell as the noise and sound continued to push at her. She tried to keep walking, but the noise and the sound combined to create a current of unintelligible static that wanted to wash her down the sidewalk and across the parking lot, to tenderize her with repeated slams to the concrete and against the metal fenders of parked minivans and four-door sedans and, finally, into the Yellow Sign Buffet. Through the windows, if necessary.

Thara caught her balance and managed to lean into the onslaught. Her sensible shoes let her down, though, and the worn rubber soles slipped on the concrete. Still leaning forward, she stumbled backward.

The rush of the sound pressed against her and prevented her from falling on her face.

She spread her arms and extended her fingers, letting her claws grow. She spread her legs, and let her toes grow as well. Her sensible shoes became cramped, then she felt the claws that had been her toenails shredding her socks and piercing the leather uppers of her shoes. She gripped the concrete with her long, clawed toes—

Her calves first, then the back of her thighs, hit the side of a car, knocking her legs from under her. She fell backward over the sloping white hood of an Impala. Her claws left scratches on the fender, then the hood, as the wave of noise pushed her headfirst across it.

Her head dropped into the gap between vehicles and she flipped, feet arcing high, over the gap, to land on a Charger's hood, face down. She hit hard enough to push out what little breath she had managed to retain, but the flip left her in better position to grab with her hands. Her golden claws punctured the thin metal of the Charger's hood. She could feel the heat of the engine on her torso, but the engine was off and the heat wasn't painful. Her toes flexed and she tried to catch hold of something with those, as well, but her feet dangled over the side of the car, in the empty air of the next gap.

She bowed her head against the continuing onslaught of the sound and wind. Her short hair whipped around. The car she laid on shook and she could hear the metal of the hood she held groaning. She thought she also heard Marcus's voice. Like her, his voice was fighting an upstream battle against the overwhelming river of sound. Also like her, his voice was losing. She had no idea what he might be trying to tell her.

She opened her eyes. She tried to look over her shoulder, toward the restaurant and toward where Marcus's voice seemed to be coming from. She was distracted by the Impala.

The Impala she had been blown over shook and shivered from the rush of noise and wind. As she watched, it rose on its driver side wheels, then settled back with a crash.

The wind and the sound shifted, focusing on the Impala. The car rose on two wheels again. This time it didn't stop.

Thara released her grip on the hood of the Charger and scrambled backward, away from the rolling, falling white wall of metal and glass the Impala had become. She fell between the Charger and a Toyota Sienna minivan just as the Impala crashed down on the Charger, hood on hood, windshield smashing windshield, side windows shattering and cabin roofs crumpling together.

The noise changed again.

The Charger shook. The Impala trembled, shedding bits of broken rearview mirror and sparkling gems of safety glass as it began to slide across the Charger.

Thara crawled on her hands and knees, trying to get out from between the hard place of the Sienna and the multiple, ominous rocks the Impala and Charger had become. Her first choice, to head away from the Yellow Sign Buffet was cut off by the front end of a Nissan Altima that slid and bumped into place. So she went the other way, just before the Sienna, Impala, and Charger came together with a crash.

She scooted along, crouched between cars to stay out of the wind and the noise, and to be able to move fast enough to avoid the cars, trucks, SUVs and minivans slamming together with no especial regard for the laws of gravity or physics, and seemingly little regard for her lifetime record of no broken bones. She wondered where the people had gone, the ones she had seen standing in the parking lot. She seemed to be alone in the crushing maze of parked cars.

She dodged forward before the grill of a Chrysler LeBaron could pin her against the rear end of a Chevrolet Suburban. She collided with Marcus, who had been coming from the opposite direction. She pushed him backward as he pulled on her. They fell, pushing and pulling, into the gap between an Oldsmobile Supreme and a GMC Jimmy, then pushed and pulled each other into a clear space, where they fell, before the Supreme and the Jimmy became shatteringly intimate. She landed on top of him, her hands on his chest, her overlong, clawed fingers dangling past his shoulders, her face nose-to-nose with his.

"I saved your life," she shouted at the same time he shouted, "I tried to warn you."

He grabbed her shoulders. "Why did you come here?" he shouted as the overwhelming noise and the pushing wind stopped.

The groaning, crashing, shattering sounds of parked cars being pushed together stopped, as well. The buzzing in her head, though, continued unabated.

"Why did you come here?" Marcus asked again, no longer shouting but still gripping her shoulders.

"They called me in to work," Thara said. She would have shrugged, but her shoulders were immobilized in his hands.

"And you came?"

"I always have before. Unless I decided to quit."

"You should have quit."

"Now you tell me."

His eyes searched her face. His expression was very serious, but not in a way that invited the kiss she almost gave him.

"Are you going to let me up?" she asked, instead.

His eyes locked on something above her.

Thara twisted her head around to follow his gaze and saw they were on the sidewalk just outside the front door of the Yellow Sign Buffet. Through the tinted window of the door she saw August Neuland smiling down at her. Next to him stood a black woman in a tight gold lame top and a black leather skirt. The woman wasn't smiling.

"Morgan," Marcus said.

His hands released Thara's shoulders and Thara rolled off him with his suddenly enthusiastic, if slightly distracted, assistance.

"Oh," she said, pushing herself to her feet, "is that the girlfriend?" She wiped at the front of her white shirt. The smudges from dusty car bodies that she had crawled over—or been pushed over—and the dirt from the parking lot and sidewalks, didn't budge. There was also a tear across her left shoulder. Her black trousers hadn't fared much better. "Damn it," she added, when she saw what was left of her favorite pair of sensible shoes. Her toes had become normal human toes again, clearly visible through what was left of her socks, but the damage caused by her claws was irreversible. She sighed, then held up her left foot and wiggled her toes. Her new golden toenails, though, gleamed in a way that made her happy.

"We need to go," Marcus said, taking her elbow. He started to pull her away from the front door of the restaurant.

As he did, the lack of a smile on his girlfriend's face behind the glass became a brow-furrowing frown, and the noise and wind started again. Both sound and wind went from nothing to roaring in the space of a heartbeat, hitting them and pushing them against the door of the restaurant. Thara held up her hands so she wouldn't hit the glass face first.

5

August Neuland pulled the door open easily, as if there wasn't a hurricane-force gale pushing on it at the same time, and held it open as Marcus and Thara fell through, very much pushed by the hurricane-force gale. Morgan stepped back to avoid colliding with them.

The wind and sound disappeared as they slipped on the tile floor and stumbled bodily into the front counter. August Neuland closed the door.

"Nice shoes," Morgan said, glancing at the torn shoes on Thara's feet. Then she looked Thara up and down. "She doesn't look sixty-seven to me. I was expecting a cougar. Not a minx."

"Minx?" Thara said. "Who says minx anymore?" She looked at August Neuland. "What the hell, boss? What's going on?"

"Miss Gold," August Neuland said, smiling even wider than before. "How good of you join us." Then, looking past her at Marcus, his smiled faded. "I am disappointed in you, Mr. Nelson. Your prowess as a dragon hunter notwithstanding, your behavior has been less than exemplary."

"What prowess?" Thara asked. "I just fell in his lap. Not unlike how I just fell through your door, but with less pushing." She looked up at the fluorescent lights, then squeezed her eyes closed with a grimace.

"Was that your idea of a lap dance?" Morgan asked.

Thara opened her eyes again, but she was still grimacing. "Why not?" she said with a shrug. "He got the strip show earlier."

"What?"

"She's just kidding," Marcus said, feeling his face get warm.

"Kidding about what, Baby Boy?"

"Mr. Lampley," August Neuland said, raising his voice. "Please escort Miss Gold to my office."

"I don't need escorting," Thara said. "I know where the chicken coop is." She looked around and appeared to notice the empty dining room for the first time. "Where is everybody? I thought this was all hands on deck." She glanced at the front door. "You're definitely going to need more than me and the Hogan-Sally-Keenan triplets to handle that crowd. The National Guard, maybe."

"Everyone who could make it is already here," August Neuland said. "They are in the back."

"Oh."

The younger manager, the one Marcus had never met, came through the double doors from the back. Marcus realized he had never seen the back of the restaurant. He had seen what the kitchen produced, though. Which was as close as he wanted to get.

"What's up, Ricky?" Thara asked as the younger manager walked up.

Ricky looked unsure, but said, "The, uh, End is coming. I think. For real this time."

"So it's not just Sunday Brunch?"

"What?"

"Don't forget our deal," Thara said to Marcus. She made an elaborate gesture of sniffing in his direction. "I have your scent now. I can find you." She touched her nose, then pointed at him.

"You can smell me?"

Thara didn't answer. She crooked an elbow at Ricky. "Escort me to the office, Ricky."

Ricky looked at her elbow. His right hand came up, as if he were going to put his hand through her elbow, then he blushed and walked away from her. Thara relaxed her arm and followed.

"I smell something," Morgan said as the two walked away.

"Were you attempting to renege on our deal, Mr. Nelson?" August Neuland asked when Ricky and Thara disappeared through the doors to the back.

"No," Marcus lied, shaking his head for extra emphasis. " I just don't want anyone to get hurt." He looked out the window toward the parking lot. "What was all that, anyway—?"

He stopped talking. The overflowing parking lot was no longer visible through the men, women and children standing just outside the door, and outside the plate-glass windows along the front. The people stood still, looking into the restaurant. There were hundreds of them. Their expressions were relaxed, bland, but their eyes glowed yellow, the same color as the sign on the roof.

"A commendable thought, most nights," August Neuland said. "On the night the World Ends, though, it is a bit naïve. Many, many people will be hurt tonight, Mr. Nelson, and there's nothing anyone can do about it. In fact, I would say that's part of the point."

Marcus continued to stare at the people beyond the windows. "The World... Ends?" He glanced at Morgan. "Are you seeing this?" he asked, pointing to the windows.

Morgan glanced at the window, then looked away with a shudder. "Reminds me of when I used to work fast food," she said. "When buses arrived. I am so glad I went to college. Unlike your cougar, I guess."

"She's a dragon," Marcus said, "but that's beside the point. Their eyes are glowing."

Morgan didn't look at the window again. "Don't be ridiculous."

"You are free to leave, Mr. Nelson," August Neuland said. "You and Miss LaVoi both. You have been paid, and your services are no longer required."

As he spoke, the people standing on the other side of the door shifted, creating a narrow corridor through their midst all the way to the street and the cars still parked in midturn.

"Hey," Thara said, pushing her way back through the double doors. "I thought we were going to split the money."

Ricky came through behind her. "Gold, please."

"Stop calling me Gold, Ricky. Don't forget, Marcus," she added. She touched her nose again and pointed at him. Then she let Ricky pull her back, out of sight.

"Come on, Baby Boy," Morgan said. She reached out to take Marcus's hand. "We've got our money, they've got their cougar-dragon." She eyed the doors to the back. "Even if she doesn't look like much. It's time for us to go."

"The End of the World?" Marcus said. He ignored Morgan. He looked at August Neuland.

"As a start, yes," August Neuland said, "but you know what they say. 'The dinner of a billion worlds begins with a single bite.'"

"What?"

August Neuland smiled as Morgan shook her head.

"Let's go," Morgan said. She held her hand out more emphatically. "This place gives me the creeps. No offense."

"None taken, young lady." August Neuland gestured toward the door.

Marcus took Morgan's hand, but didn't let her pull him forward. "Wait." He kept his eyes on August Neuland. "What's the point of leaving, if the World is going to End?"

"You have played your part, Mr. Nelson, delivering Miss Gold to us. You have your reward, and, I might add, a diminishing amount of time to enjoy it."

"The world isn't going to end, Baby Boy," Morgan said. "Now come on." She pulled Marcus toward the door.

"The World won't End right away, Mr. Nelson," August Neuland said. He looked at his watch. "But the clock is ticking. If you hurry, you should have time to fly to some remote corner of the Earth, to enjoy yourself with the lovely Miss LaVoi. Until the End comes."

Morgan pulled the door open with her free hand. "Come on. We've got a vacation to figure out, and we can do that while we're vacating it."

Marcus let her pull him out of the restaurant. None of the people pressed around them looked at them. The men and women had glowing eyes only for what was in the dining room. None of the people talked, or sniffed or coughed. The silence was... incomplete. There was no silence. Instead, there was the sound of a thousand people breathing in unison, in a rhythm that was, somehow, slightly off. Once he was aware of their breathing, Marcus couldn't stop hearing it. The sound became more than obvious, it became oppressive. He struggled to keep from breathing to the same rhythm. Then he was struggling to breathe, as if he were drowning while walking. He looked at Morgan, but she seemed undisturbed. She kept her eyes forward, averted from the people.

Marcus stumbled as he emerged from the narrow corridor through the crowd. The sound of the crowd's breathing was still there, but it no longer surrounded him. He felt like a drowning man stumbling out of the ocean and onto the beach. He could breathe again. He wasn't going to die.

He shook his hand free of Morgan's vise-like grip and turned to look back at the restaurant. The corridor to the front door had disappeared. He was tall enough to see over most of the crowd, but he could no longer see August Neuland in the dining room. He looked left and right. The crowd of people wrapped around the sides of the building.

"Something weird is going on here."

"You think?" Morgan asked. "The more reason to get out of here. We have fifty—" She stopped talking with a glance at the crowd. She pulled him close to her. "We have fifty thousand dollars, Baby Boy," she went on in a lower voice. "Thirty-five thousand of it in cash." She patted her handbag with the wrapped stacks of bills. "Should we go back to my apartment? Or just go straight to the airport? If a flight isn't leaving right away, we can charter one."

She didn't wait for an answer. She took his hand again.

Marcus let himself be pulled across the two empty southbound lanes, then through the cars parked in the middle of the street. August Neuland had told them to park on Fifty-first Street, not at the restaurant. At the time, Marcus had thought it odd. Now, though, seeing the streams of motionless cars that blocked traffic, he realized the advice had been prescient. If they had parked at the restaurant, there would have been no way to escape—

Was that what they were doing? Escaping?

On the eastern side of Harvard Avenue, past the cars parked in front of the restaurant in midturn, there was no traffic. The other side had become a two-lane parking lot that extended past the intersection with Fifty-first Street in three directions. Gridlock had taken over the streets for at least half a mile in all directions. He looked back toward the restaurant and its thick wall of people.

"What did I do?" he asked.

"You did good, Baby Boy," Morgan said. "Now let's go enjoy the fruits of your labor."

Above the restaurant, the yellow sign blazed as bright as the Sun, wiping out the stars. The Moon wasn't visible, either, as if it had already fled the night sky.

Marcus let her pull him along. He turned his back on the restaurant.

As they walked, the ground beneath their feet began to vibrate.

6

"So WHAT DO YOU NEED a dragon for, anyway?" Thara asked the so-called Mr. Lampley as she followed him through the swinging doors and through the standing crowd of nearly identical-looking employees dressed in yellow and brown polyester uniforms. She was surprised to see so many employees. She wanted to ask where had they been the last few days while her and Keenan and Hogan-Sally did their work? She didn't ask, though, because they weren't talking to each other or even looking at each other. They were just... standing there.

She counted thirteen employees besides herself and the so-called Mr. Lampley. She tried to pick out Keenan's spotty face, or even the Hogan-Sally twins, but in a group, somehow, a skinny, redheaded twenty-year-old male was impossible to distinguish from a thirty-something, plump brunette female.

"Keenan?" she said, raising her voice.

Every face turned to look at her, including the so-called Mr. Lampley.

"If you're not Keenan," she said to the faces, "then I didn't just call your name. So you can... look away. At someone else."

The blurry faces continued to look at her. The faces weren't blank, or expressionless. Rather, they seemed expectant, as if Thara might say something amazing any second now.

"Never mind."

The faces still didn't look away from her, so she looked away from them. She noticed the so-called Mr. Lampley stood beside her, looking at her the same way, as if he too were waiting for her to say something amazing. Or anything at all. His yellow button-down shirt and brown trousers were losing their definition, somehow becoming almost identical to the polyester uniforms worn by the others.

"What?" she asked him, blinking and trying to focus on him for the first time since she had known him.

He blinked, as well, and he came into focus again.

Thara shook her head. She was definitely never coming in to work here again. In fact, she was going to walk home, now. She walked the rest of the way to the manager's office. The so-called Mr. Lampley followed her.

She walked around the big desk to the back door of the restaurant.

"You can't leave."

Thara started to tell the so-called Mr. Lampley to watch her do exactly that as she pushed on the emergency exit latch. The latch didn't budge. She pushed on it again, but the latch refused to acknowledge either her intention or the printed order of the Rio Cruces Fire Marshal mounted on it that said, "This Door to Remain Unlocked At All Times When Building is Occupied."

"Mr. Neuland wants you to take a seat."

"Fine," Thara said. She spun the leather desk chair around and sat. She leaned back, examining the fire-code-violating, not-always-unlocked exit from this vantage. Then she spun herself in the chair as hard as she could.

The so-called Mr. Lampley's face showed surprise and disapproval each time it came into view. She kicked the floor with her ruined shoes to keep the chair spinning. She wondered which would happen first: bored or dizzy?

She never got to find out. Between one revolution and the next Mr. Neuland replaced the so-called Mr. Lampley in the door of the office. Even after an additional five revolutions, Mr. Neuland still looked amused, so she put down a foot to stop spinning. Before she got dizzy.

"I want a raise," she said.

Mr. Neuland smiled. "No," he said, "that will not be possible."

"How about you pay me for my hours worked, then fire me? Or vice versa?"

Still smiling, he shook his head. "No, that will not be possible either."

"I'm pretty sure I can make you fire me," Thara said. "But I would rather you paid me first. My rent is coming due."

"Now that you are here, Miss Gold, your rent will no longer be an issue."

Thara felt the restaurant vibrate. Outside the office, in the prep area, she heard the conveyor belt come on. She saw the amorphous collection of employees turn to face the conveyor belt.

"So it's time for the Sunday Brunch Special to begin?"

Mr. Neuland nodded. "Something like that, yes. This is indeed the Beginning, Miss Gold. Perhaps, if Fate continues to smile on us, even the last Beginning." He smiled, then added, "Every Ending needs a Beginning."

Before Thara could ask what he meant, the floor shook and the office wall next to her lurched. The photographs of Mr. Neuland, the so-called Mr. Lampley, and the other employees, past and present, fell away as the wood paneling that covered the wall bowed outward and the wall behind it moved down. The paneling split with a loud crack, spitting tiny wooden splinters, then crumpled as if it were being pushed down by the hand of a giant.

7. Pasta with Dragon Sauce

The Queen

STILL SINGING THE SONG, THE Queen's Daughters burst through the husks of Their cocoons. The shattered bodies of the drones that had given themselves that Her Daughters might be Born fell away and Their Beauty was revealed.

Each in turn, her Daughters approached the Queen and, after She chose not Consume Them, to stave off the raging hunger the Song had awakened inside Her, She regurgitated into Their mouths the royal jelly.

The Song did not stop. Rather, each retching vomit of the Queen, each muffled gagging of a Daughter, each gurgling scream as They were transformed from larvae to infant queen, fit the cadence and added to the overall harmony. And as each Daughter became a Sister-Queen, She took up the Song, singing for Herself and Her Sisters.

Finally, as the Queen rejoined the Song She had never left, adding Her Voice to the Voices of Her Daughters, the Queen became a Goddess.

The End of the World was so close She could Taste it. The Queen's Tongue flickered forth to confirm this.

She was a very hungry Goddess.

The Angry

THE ANGRY CONSIDERED LETTING THE World End, since the World seemed so desperately to want to End.

This was not the Angry's World. The Angry could recognize neither himself nor what the World had become while he slept.

In the Angry's World, a child dragon would never have been allowed to enter the lair of an embryonic, enemy goddess, let alone to labor for that embryonic, enemy goddess. Nor would that child dragon have been allowed to consort with a known dragon hunter.

In the Angry's World, the embryonic, enemy god would have been served raw, on a half shell, with a side of flambéed hunter, and the Child might have been allowed a nibble.

Perhaps the Angry should never have awakened. Then he would never have had to see how messed up things had become. He could have Ended along with the World, peacefully, in his sleep. Not Angry. And not, when the time came, screaming.

The Song of the World's End began to get on his nerves.

The Bug

THE BUG DID WHAT HE could to comfort the First Ugly Replacement. The silly, scratched-up, faded-brown lemon of a car didn't share the Bug's faith in the World. Probably a holdover from when the First Ugly Replacement had been ridiculed and rebranded, right off the assembly line.

The Bug had survived earthquakes, missile crises, smog, glam rock, oil shortages, acid rain, and hair metal—which the current Song of the World's End most closely resembled.

After a few more decades, the First Ugly Replacement would come around. Assuming, of course, there were a few more decades available for coming to full maturity.

The Bug glanced over at the Second Ugly Replacement, but she was busy preening for the green-and-white pickup truck that had been panting over her the last two days.

A change in the Song of the World's End made the Bug's antenna quiver, as if an overstimulated, post-Townsend guitarist had just smashed an electric guitar on a solid state amplifier.

Another earthquake was coming.

1

THARA PUSHED HERSELF AND THE office chair backward, away from the crumpling wall just as one of the black, four-drawer metal filing cabinets fell toward her. She looked at the wall, the fallen filing cabinet, then at Mr. Neuland.

"What the Hell?"

Mr. Neuland only smiled in response. The wall continued to crumple. She looked back at the wall.

She didn't know what she expected to see behind the wall. Maybe some kind of bizarre kitchen full of blue flames and filthy cook-slaves chained to their stations, mixing and churning out incomprehensible, inauthentic cuisine that was dumped into chafing dishes and pushed onto the conveyor belt.

That's not what she saw.

She blinked, squeezing her eyes closed—hard—before reopening them. It didn't help.

The only light came from the office, and it was, at best, tentative. The light didn't want to illuminate what was on the side of the wall any more than her eyes wanted to see it. Certainly no more than her brain wanted to make sense of it.

She focused first on the stacks of sparkling clean chafing dishes and pitchers, because those made perfect sense. She had cleaned most of those a few hours before and sent them into the back on the conveyor belt. They had been stacked next to the conveyor belt on this side of the wall. Next to the chafing dishes, pushed out of the way under the conveyor belt was a suitcase Thara had seen before too, though not in months. Not since Tina had moved in.

It was just a green suitcase, hardly noticeable, with a retractable handle and wheels for pulling it through airports. It didn't *have* to be Tina's suitcase. Her mind didn't *want* it to be Tina's suitcase. Because if the suitcase was Tina's, then the skinny, twitching creature crouched, cowering, between the conveyor belt and the abomination that dominated the rest of the space had to be Tina.

Thara focused on Tina.

In less than four days, Tina had gone from mousy to bedraggled. The girl still wore her brown-and-yellow polyester uniform, complete with hat. Her hair hung in strands that had fallen free of the confinement of the hat, obscuring her face, but not her eyes. What Thara could see of the girl's face had become pale, jaundiced, and smudged with brown...

Thara's brain offered no meaningful word for what was smudged on Tina's face. And on her hands. And on her arms up to her elbows. And on the front of her shirt and down the front of her trousers. If there were such a thing as a brown rainbow, with a spectrum running from pale, pastel yellow to dark, oubliette brown, and that brown rainbow had taken physical form, Tina looked as if she had found the pot at the wrong end.

Thara opened her mouth to ask, again, what the Hell, and why, but nothing came out. The abomination she had been trying to avoid looking at pulsed and drew her attention.

The abomination was, for lack of a better phrase, a prep station. The stainless-steel surface was as clean as the chafing dishes Thara had sent back. The shelves and cavity beneath that surface, though, and around it, were covered in the same substances that had begun to coat poor Tina.

Poised above the gleaming surface of the prep station was a...

Thara's brain offered the word *spout*. Or maybe *spigot*? She tried to avoid the word *sphincter*, but failed. She didn't want to think that the spout-spigot-not-a-sphincter was pressed together into a twisted, bemused-looking smile.

She tried not to see the pulsing, knotted tube that was terminated by the not-a-sphincter. Or the way the tube sagged from a series of hooks on the ceiling. She failed.

The end with the please-don't-be-a-sphincter was the narrowest point. It grew steadily wider as it went... wherever it went. The tube was opaque, but organic looking, the color of the darkest brown on the rainbow-of-brown spectrum, but gleamed a glossy, urine yellow in the lights from the office. The tube piled up in coils in the darkness beyond Tina and the prep station in a way that Thara did *not* want to think of as *intestinal*.

As Thara watched, a portion of the tub bulged. The bulge traveled around and around through the coils and knots of the pile, up and over and between the hooks, until it stretched the bulbous end just behind the—

The twisted smile became the most obscene pucker Thara had ever witnessed. There was a squealing, bubbling hiss.

Thara failed to hold her breath fast enough. The mixed smell of not-quite-food that permeated the Yellow Sign Buffet, the air outside, and Thara's clothes the past few nights washed over her. Her eyes watered and she tasted bile in the back of her throat.

Some part of her mind, though, interpreted the smell. *Stand-ready-to-receive the-Seasoning.*

As Thara sat in the leather chair, clenching her fists and trying hard not to stand-ready-to-receive *anything*, Tina stood. The girl stepped to the stacked dishes, took a stainless-steel pitcher from the tower of them, turned, then placed the pitcher on the prep station directly below the...

"Spigot," Thara said through a tight throat.

Tina kept the pitcher steady with her right hand, and put her left on top of the...

"Spout."

Thara heard August Neuland chuckle—much nearer than she expected—but she didn't take her eyes off Tina.

She tried not to notice as another bulge appeared and worked its way through and up and across and down. This time the twisted smile straightened into a curve. The... Thara didn't want to think of them as *lips* either... parted, and a stream of dark liquid streamed out. Steam rose from the top of the pitcher.

Before the pitcher could overflow, Tina pulled it back. At the same time, she pushed the... end of the tube away from her. The excess fluid splattered on the tiled floor on the far side of the prep station. The pucker repucked, stopping the last, dribbling flow of liquid, then the twisted smile returned. Tina released the end of the tube as a slight bulge ran in reverse down the length of the tube and out of sight. Thara didn't want to think of it as *swallowing*. The liquid that had spilled on the floor flowed down the tilted tiles, past Tina's encrusted shoes to the drain that Thara realized the girl stood on.

Tina picked up the pitcher with both hands and turned to face Thara. The still-steaming liquid inside had to have made the pitcher hot, but Tina showed no sign of discomfort.

"The Seasoning," the girl said, and offered the pitcher to Thara.

"The Seasoning," intoned a chorus of voices.

"The Hell you say." Thara spun the chair to look at August Neuland, to ask him what the unholy fuck was going on, and almost collided with him. He had moved from the door of his office to stand behind the chair.

Surprised, and not liking the way the man loomed over her, she stood and stepped away.

Beyond, August Neuland, outside the office, pressed up against the plate-glass window, was the so-called Mr. Lampley and as many of the other brown-and-yellow uniformed employees as would fit. Noses and cheeks were pressed against the glass, leaving smudges and warm fog. Everyone was staring at Thara.

Except the so-called Mr. Lampley. He was staring at Tina.

"Make yourself at home, Miss Gold," August Neuland said, gesturing to indicate that she could sit again, if she wanted.

She didn't want to.

Somehow, he stood close enough again that Thara felt his breath warm on her face. She pulled away from him, then asked him, loudly, as she had planned to do when she stood, "What the unholy fuck is going on?"

"I think you would be more comfortable in your natural form," the man said. He had not raised his voice. He spoke in his typical conversational tone. "Don't you?"

"My what?" Her tone was hardly conversational.

He smiled again. "You are a dragon, Miss Gold. Be a dragon."

She wanted to deny she was a dragon, but she knew he knew. Marcus had told him. Instead, she said, "It's not that easy." She took a breath to give him the lecture on Episode preconditions, including the position of the Sun relative to the Earth's Equator, the same lecture Poppa had given her all those years ago. Turning into a dragon wasn't something she controlled, she wanted to say. Not really. It was more something that happened to her, and that she usually tried to keep from happening when others were watching—

August Neuland interrupted her before she could say anything, or even point at the ceiling.

"Of course it is, Miss Gold. It is the nature of Fate that what needs to happen, will happen, when it should happen. That makes everything easy. You are the dragon we require, tonight, right here. And here we are. All that remains is for you to be the dragon you have always been."

"It's not that easy..." She repeated the words automatically, but let them trail off.

As if August Neuland's words were some kind of trigger, as if tonight were the night of the Winter Solstice, the longest night of the year, after the day when the Sun reached its lowest noontime point, instead of that night being nearly two months in the future, as if there were no audience of restaurant employees, Thara felt the transformation begin.

2

THARA FOUGHT THE TRANSFORMATION. SHE didn't like the thought that August Neuland, middle-aged white man and congenial restaurant owner—and dragon hunter employer—had somehow caused it to happen. She also had more than fifty years of habit trying *not* to have an Episode in public. The back office of the Yellow Sign Buffet was hardly public, but there were a lot of people looking on. Nudity in front of people didn't bother her. Turning into a dragon in front of them, though, was different. That was personal. A level of intimacy she wasn't ready to share.

"You should not fight who you are, Miss Gold," August Neuland said, almost speaking the words into her ear. "That kind of personal and emotional constipation never ends well."

Thara thought of a snappy response, about how he could examine his own constipation up close, but said nothing because her jaw was clenched and her teeth were grinding from the effort to keep her jaw from stretching and her teeth from becoming long and curved.

"Plus, this is Fate, Miss Gold. You might be able to fight who you are, but you cannot fight Fate."

Fate or not, Thara continued to ignore him and continued to fight—

Then, with a start, she realized he was right. She was fighting herself. Because becoming a dragon was exactly what she *wanted* to happen. To become a dragon and tear the Yellow Sign Buffet down brick by brick, starting with the hideous, obscene, organic lump of not-bricks that piled and looped and dangled in front of her. August Neuland might have—

somehow—triggered this Episode, but how it ended could be completely up to her. Besides, her favorite pair of sensible shoes were already ruined.

Her point of view rose to the ceiling as her neck extended, then divided as her face lengthened and her eyes moved to the sides. Her crest brushed against the dirty drop ceiling. Her torso expanded and extended, as well. Her spines ripped through the back of her shirt as her expanding chest burst the plastic buttons on the front. Her sports bra stretched to match her changing shape, then reached the end of its elasticity and snapped. Her tail grew and curled against the wall behind her. Her legs became as thick as tree trunks, split the seams of her trousers and splayed to support her suddenly much bulkier bulk. Her arms swelled and finished off her shirt. She fell forward and caught herself with her oversized, over-clawed dragon hands. She landed with her left front claw on the desk and the other on the spilled file cabinet. Her right front claw pressed a five-pointed dent into the side of the file cabinet.

"That's better, Miss Gold," August Neuland said. He must have stepped around her as she transformed. He stood near the back door, but gave no indication of an intent to leave. Unexpectedly, he wasn't smiling at her. The look in his eye, the line of his chin, the way his lips were pressed together, all of it indicated he was judging her. "Accept who you are, and what you are."

"And what am I?" Thara asked, looking at August Neuland with her right eye and allowing more than a little growl into her voice.

"Is it not obvious, Miss Gold? You are the Wyrm of the World's End. If a bit... smaller than expected."

Through it all, Tina had simply watched, still holding the pitcher of steaming whatever-it-was. She had lifted her head so her eyes remained on Thara's face, but that had been the only concession to seeing her former roommate become a twenty-five-foot dragon right in front of her.

"The Wyrm of the World's End," intoned the chorus of voices from outside the office.

Thara swiveled her left eye to look at the so-called Mr. Lampley and the other now completely indistinguishable employees. They were all staring at her, which she expected, with what looked and smelled like religious awe. Which she had not expected at all.

"Who are you calling a worm?" she asked the gathered employees. When none of them answered, she swung her head to point the wedge of her nose at August Neuland. "And what do you mean 'smaller than expected?'"

"You are not as large a dragon as I was expecting," August Neuland said. "I expected the Wyrm of the World's End to be... bigger."

A week ago, Thara would have protested that she was the biggest dragon she knew. A lot had happened in the last week, though, so she just glared at him. She had not expected body shaming to make the leap to dragons.

August Neuland leaned to his right and spoke past her. "Mr. Lampley, if you would, please."

Outside the office, the so-called Mr. Lampley said, "Line up, in reverse seniority." Then she heard the shuffling of people moving around, the rustling of polyester uniforms. She turned her head just enough so she could watch the employees with her left eye. They were lining up at the door of the office. She could almost recognize the person at the front of the line, since she stood by herself. Or himself.

In front of her, Tina lifted the pitcher. "The Seasoning," she said again.

Thara shook her head back and forth. "Not a chance—"

Tina drew back the pitcher, then tipped it and threw both the pitcher and its contents into Thara's mouth, which was open in middenial.

Thara fell back, sputtering and spitting and trying not to crunch the steel of the pitcher between her jaws. In spite of her efforts, she could taste the Seasoning crawling across her forked tongue.

There was no single, distinct flavor. Sweet, sour, salty, and bitter—and umami, offered the memory of another chef she had dated more recently—combined and broke apart, creating flavors that disintegrated and/or morphed before she could identify them. She gagged as the Seasoning started crawling down her throat.

She stopped falling with her back against the wall, her right front leg on the toppled filing cabinet, holding her up while she hung her head next to the desk, spitting and trying to push the dregs of the liquid out of her mouth with her tongue. She scraped her tongue across the palm of her left claw, then wiped her claw on the old-fashioned blotter that covered the desk.

She was vaguely aware of August Neuland still standing by the door to the rear parking lot. "If you would, Mr. Lampley," August Neuland said.

Thara dropped her head, then extended her tongue and dragged it across the tile floor, hoping for some dirt or chicken shit or anything that could have been tracked in on a shoe that might clean the taste off her tongue. The floor beneath the desk was remarkably clean, unfortunately. She spit and sputtered some more, but it didn't help.

"That was not cool—" she said as she raised her head. She stopped when her nose collided with someone.

Her eyes crossed as they focused on Keenan standing directly in front of her. Since he was by himself, Thara could make out his red hair and spotty face. Behind him, Tina stood at her prep station, filling another pitcher. Thara's tongue flicked out and back in, very nearly licking Keenan in the face. She tasted his fear, but it was an unusual flavor of fear. Religious fear. He was scared, frightened almost beyond the point of bowel control, but he was also ecstatic. He *quivered*.

She focused on him with her left eye, so her right eye could keep tabs on August Neuland. The man hadn't moved, but she didn't trust him.

"Keenan?"

"Eat me," Keenan said, his eyes wide, his whole body quivering. He said the words, but he no longer sounded like a cook in training.

"What—?"

As soon as her mouth opened to speak, Keenan leaped, throwing himself between her jaws.

She fought the reflex to immediately bite down and opened her jaws as wide as she could. She fell backward—or would have, if there had been room. Her claws scratched on the surface of the desk and on the tiled floor, trying to push away from Keenan. She remained where she was. More than a few of the teeth on her lower jaw caught in Keenan's uniform and scraped against his skin as the fabric tore. She tasted warm, metallic blood as a rivulet dribbled down one curled tooth. Keenan fell on the desk. She pushed on the desk and sent it and him toward Tina.

Keenan rolled off the desk and landed on his feet with shaking, nervous energy. "Eat me!" he shouted, and climbed on the desk to throw himself at her again.

She caught him with her left claw, her long fingers wrapping around his torso. She had to use a surprising amount of strength to keep him from breaking free.

"I'm not going to eat you!" The wind of her shout blew the hat off his head and the heat of her breath chapped his cheeks.

He was undeterred. "Eat me!"

Behind him, Tina stepped up carrying another full, steaming pitcher in both hands.

"Eat him," August Neuland said in a quiet voice.

"Eat him," intoned the so-called Mr. Lampley at the office door in chorus with the other employees who stood in a line.

"EAT HIM." The words shook the walls of the Yellow Sign Buffet as the people standing outside took up the mantra.

"Eat him," Tina said, reaching up to pour the contents of the pitcher over Keenan's head. The liquid steamed and where it touched Keenan's skin, raised a red rash.

"No!" Thara said. She pulled the squirming Keenan away from Tina so the last drops fell on the floor.

Tina turned and walked back to her prep station.

"You must eat him," August Neuland said. "And the rest, if necessary."

Thara had her left eye keep watch on the so-called Mr. Lampley and Tina as she said to August Neuland, "The rest?"

"To reach your full growth," he said. "To seize your full potential. Also, you need to be properly Seasoned and Marinated, and this is the fastest way." He smiled at her like a doting father. "You cannot grow up big and strong if you do not eat."

"I'm not going to eat Keenan."

August Neuland shrugged. "There are many other options." He gestured to the so-called Mr. Lampley, who looked less than eager, then the other employees, who were quivering the way Keenan still did. "They are here to serve, and to be served."

"To serve, and to be served," the line of employees said.

The so-called Mr. Lampley just bit his lower lip.

"This is crazy," Thara said.

She threw Keenan at Tina, then spun to her right, letting her tail whip around to block the so-called Mr. Lampley from entering the office. August Neuland stood in front of the other door, still blocking it, but dragons could make their own doors.

Thara's claws tore away the paneling on the wall and left deep gouges in the exposed cinder blocks. Left, then right, she ran her claws across the old bricks, creating a gray cloud of cement and mortar fragments.

"Eat me!" Keenan shouted again and jumped on her from behind.

"Eat him," intoned the chorus.

From outside came another wall-shaking, "EAT HIM!"

She shrugged and sent a ripple through her body to shake Keenan loose, but the distraction allowed the so-called Mr. Lampley to get past her tail. He grabbed at her right foreclaw with more bravery and disregard for his personal safety than she expected.

"You cannot leave, Miss Gold," August Neuland said from where he stood by the rear door. His voice was still cheerful, unaffected by all the shouting and violent, attempted deconstruction of his office wall.

"Watch me." Thara pulled her right arm back so the so-called Mr. Lampley would be out of harm's way, then slammed the top of her head against the wall.

The force of the blow crushed multiple cinder blocks, exposing their hollow interiors.

Thara staggered back, blinking. She had felt the blow more than she expected, as if something more than old concrete had reflected the force of her blow.

More uniformed employees came into the office and joined the so-called Mr. Lampley. She felt hands on her forelegs and the weight of more than just Keenan on her back. They weren't hurting her. They were hindering her. Subduing her. Or trying to crawl past her shoulder to shove themselves into her mouth.

Thara roared, letting a tiny tongue of flame erupt from her throat to splash against the broken cinder blocks. The fire blackened the cement and the roar pressed against her own eardrums in the enclosed space, but none of the people grabbing her seemed to notice. A hand grabbed her tongue. She felt what had to be Keenan grabbing her crest and putting his feet on her spines for traction. She shook her head, but he kept his grip. So she shook harder. He was whipped off. He hit the doorframe, hard, but made no sound of pain. He just rolled over and fell to the floor.

"Stop!" she shouted with an undertone of roar and overtone of more fire. Cinder blocks, unfortunately, despite their name, didn't burn. The edge of the paneling she had torn away, though, did catch fire this time. The air in the office became smoky. A fire alarm went off.

Thara didn't want to seriously injure anyone. She certainly didn't want to kill anyone or burn down the restaurant on top of herself. But she was going to leave. She raised her head to smash into the wall again.

A cold, white, powdery blast erupted in front of her. First it took her breath away, then it burned in her throat in a way totally unlike her inner furnace. She coughed and snorted, but couldn't seem to clear her airways. Her left eye swiveled and she saw August Neuland standing, calm as always, holding a fire extinguisher in his arms, aiming it at the wall.

Then he shifted the nozzle and the blast hit her full in the face. Her eyes' nictitating membranes closed and her nostrils squeezed shut, but not before some of the burning chemicals clouded her vision and burned in her nasal passages.

In contrast to the chemical burning, an unexpected sensation of cold flared deep in her chest as the potassium bicarbonate she had inhaled quenched her internal fire. That had never happened before.

Panicked, she swung her left claw, intending to sweep August Neuland off his feet, but she missed. He had stepped back the instant before she struck. He sprayed her again. She heard coughing and gagging from the other employees. He was not sparing his employees in his efforts to stop her leaving.

Thara tried to roar in frustration, but could only cough and sputter and gag. With the extra carbon dioxide from the fire extinguisher in her lungs, she couldn't hold her breath. Dark bubbles swelled and popped around the edges of her vision. In desperation, she smashed her head against the wall, using all four feet to push herself forward like a battering ram.

The impact condensed her vision to a narrow tunnel, but at the end of that tunnel she could see she had finally managed to burst the wall out. She shook her foreclaws free of encumbering coworkers and attacked the wall, wedging her claws into the cracks and pulling.

She heard a crash of metal and glass, as if a ten-car pileup had just happened, but without the squealing of rubber tires and screams, and without the usual need for a highway of moving cars. Then came a roar.

She felt the roar before she heard it, then it was all she could hear or feel. The roar shook the foundation of the restaurant and the walls and rattled the drop ceiling over her head. The roar was a blast that erupted through the cracks in the wall to hit her in the face. Then came the sound of metal groaning in protest, then screaming as it gave way and was bent and broken.

The rear door of the office disappeared, pulled out, complete with frame and a few partial cinder blocks, and thrown away by an unseen force.

The pointed ends of silver claws the length of a man's arm appeared in the gaping hole, gripped either side, and pulled away chunks of wall. Fragments of cement and mortar and broken cinder blocks clouded the air but couldn't fully obscure what was happening outside.

Coils of silver scales writhed over the wreckage of a dozen automobiles as men and women and children dressed for Sunday Brunch ran back and forth and jumped and grabbed and held on, all without a word.

Another roar became words in Thara's head. *Go, Child! Flee! This game is over!*

A silver dragon's head the size of a Cadillac Escalade appeared in the absence of the rear door, one eye swiveling in its socket to see inside.

August Neuland, who had turned to face the hole, lifted his fire extinguisher again and let loose a new conical white cloud. The dragon roared and pulled his head back.

August Neuland looked over his shoulder at Thara. The bastard was *smiling.* "I see I paid Mr. Nelson too soon," he said, "and for the wrong dragon. Fate sent you to us, Miss Gold, but I let myself get too excited. I got ahead of myself. And ahead of Fate."

Beyond August Neuland, in the parking lot, a gale force wind erupted as the silver dragon leaped into the air, wings beating. Thara saw a man in olive slacks and a navy blue blazer fall out of the sky and bounce off the crumpled hood of a Honda Accord.

"You were not the dragon Fate promised us," August Neuland shouted. "You are not the Wyrm of the World's End. You are bait! Fate bait!" He laughed at his rhyme. "I am humbled," he added, still smiling and not looking at all humble.

Thara decided that the new hole was bigger than the one she had been working on. She closed her eyes and her mouth, then twisted herself and charged August Neuland. She hoped she would trample him, but he managed to step aside again. She felt herself dragging at least a few employees, but they too fell away as she burst out into the parking lot. She opened her eyes to look for the other dragon—

Wind hit her from behind just before huge, silver claws gripped her torso.

You must go, Child! I will fight this End for you, but you must go!

Then she was lifted, her neck and tail drooping like that of a surprised kitten who has just been picked up by her scruff. She was no kitten, though, and she needed no one to fight her fights for her. Or her Ends. Even if she had no idea what fight or Ends he was talking about.

She twisted in the dragon's grip. She bared her teeth up at the dragon's huge face. The other dragon had perched on the flat roof of the restaurant, in front of the blazing yellow sign. The tips of her claws scraped against the scales of the other dragon's long fingers and wrists, creating a shower of gold and silver sparks.

"GO!" the silver dragon roared, out loud and in her mind, then threw her over the heads of the converging crowd.

Behind her, the yellow light of the restaurant's sign exploded, creating a new sun that cast the shadow of the silver dragon ahead of her, as if to catch her. She fell into the shadow as the silver dragon roared again.

3

"WE SHOULD GO BACK TO my apartment," Morgan said as she walked. She still had a tight hold of Marcus's hand, pulling him along. "We can decide where we want to go on our way there, then buy the tickets. We can use my Amex, and you can pay me back. We don't want to be buying airline tickets with cash. They would probably put us on some kind of terrorist watch list or something, even if we bought round-trip tickets."

Marcus didn't say anything. She didn't seem to need him to.

The night around them felt... wrong. The streetlights were on, but their light was only visible when Marcus looked directly at them.

What was happening behind them also felt... wrong. When he was tempted to look back, though, at the wall of cars, trucks, and SUVs and its throng of... Sunday Brunch enthusiasts? Buffet worshipers?... he remembered the Sunday School lesson of Sodom and Gomorrah and Lot's wife turning into a pillar of salt.

He didn't look back. Not even when a mighty chorus of voices shouted, "EAT HIM!"

Morgan winced, but she didn't look back either.

Marcus *wanted* to look back. He wanted—he needed—to know that Thara was safe. But something about the yellow light casting his shadow in front of him—something about how the light seemed to be trying to wrap itself around him, looking for his eyes—something about hundreds of people chanting, "EAT HIM!"—warned him that he shouldn't look back.

Through it all, Morgan kept talking, and kept pulling him along the strangely—wrongly—empty street.

He didn't look back. Not even when the wind picked up and pushed on his face. After a few seconds, the wind passed over him, then it was behind him, pushing him away. He still didn't look back.

"We don't have to go to Central America," Morgan was saying. "Spain or the south of France would be just as—"

Keeping Lot's wife firmly in mind, Marcus didn't look back when the night air exploded into a roar that shook the bones in his flesh.

Visibly shaken this time, her lips pressed together in a tight line of irritation at being interrupted, Morgan turned and looked back before he could stop her.

Morgan's lips parted, as if she were about to say something. Maybe she had meant to express her opinion about loud noises or fast food restaurants she would never eat at again, but she said nothing. Instead, her face relaxed. Her hand released his and dropped to hang at her side.

"Morgan—?"

Her eyes started glowing.

He dropped his eyes to avoid looking into the light coming from her eyes and saw the gold lame of her top reflecting the light of the sign against his chest. He could *feel* the reflected light trying to crawl up the front of his leather jacket, trying to reach his face and the windows of his soul—

Another roar hit him from behind.

They had been walking along Harvard Avenue, on the sidewalk. Marcus decided it was time to start cutting—directly, and very quickly— across the empty parking lot of the shopping center on their way to Morgan's Camry.

He took Morgan's hand. Her fingers were limp in his grip. "Come on," he said, and pulled.

She stumbled along in his wake. She didn't protest, she didn't try to stop him, but her constant looking back meant she was all but walking backward in her pumps, slowing him and keeping him from running.

He resisted the urge to look back. He didn't want to look at her, at her eyes, and especially not at the glowing yellow sign. He knew if he looked back, he wouldn't see Thara. He wouldn't know if she were safe or in danger. If he looked back, he might not be able to look forward again.

If he didn't look back, he could save Morgan. Maybe.

He wondered what he was saving her from. August Neuland had said the End of the World was Beginning. But that hadn't made any sense.

Though, with the wind, and the roaring, and the blazing yellow light, it was beginning to make more sense than before. A scary amount of sense.

Still looking forward, he focused on Morgan's Camry. It would be locked, of course, but Morgan had the keys in her purse. A quick, averted glance more down than back confirmed that she still held the purse in her free hand. Enraptured by the light of the Yellow Sign Buffet, she retained enough of her own mind to keep a tight grip on her purse, which bulged with three full stacks of hundreds and one full stack of fifties.

His quick, averted glance also showed Marcus what walking backward in six-inch pumps was doing to Morgan's ankles. He winced, then looked forward again and pulled faster.

They reached the Camry, and stumbled to a stop. He released her hand to reach for her purse.

As soon as he let go, she turned and started walking back the way they had come.

He managed to look down at the stripes on the parking lot before the yellow light could do more than leave a brown streak across the periphery of his vision.

He kept his head down and walked directly behind Morgan, using her body to block the light as he caught up with her. He put his left arm around her waist and lift her off her feet. Fortunately, her legs stopped moving once her feet were off the ground. Still using her body as a shield from the light, he turned and carried her back toward the Camry.

She twisted in his arms as he walked, the smooth lame of her top and her leather skirt making the experience almost erotic, especially the way her breasts pressed and brushed against him. Then bulged in front of his face as she squirmed, trying to keep her eyes on the light. He had to use both arms to keep her from wriggling free.

He put her down, then pinned her against the side of her car to keep her from escaping, holding her with his right arm while he took her purse with his left hand. Or tried to take her purse. Her grip didn't yield.

"Come on, Morgan," he said, pulling on the purse. "It's time to go. We have to get out of here."

He grabbed the purse with both hands. She let go, then stepped around him, headed back to the restaurant.

"Damn it, Morgan."

He risked a quick, side-of-the-eye glance as he fished in her purse for her key fob. She wasn't walking any faster than before. He could catch her again. First, though, he would open the car. He pushed the button on the key fob twice and the car locks opened with an audible click.

He pulled the driver's door open and tossed the keys and the purse inside. Then he ducked his head and put his left arm across his face as he ran after her.

"Morgan!" he shouted. "Wait for me!"

He almost tackled her—and himself—when he caught up with her and put both arms around her waist, but he kept his balance. He lifted her off her feet. Since he knew it was coming this time, he let her twist in his arms as he turned around, lifting her as she did so he was carrying her over his left shoulder in a fireman's hold. He had his left arm across her butt and his right arms secured her legs. Tight leather and stretched nylon tried to get his attention again, along with the yellow light.

"Any other time," he told her as he walked, "I would be enjoying this."

Morgan didn't tell him she knew he was already enjoying it. She said nothing.

Another roar, and the light flickered. He felt more than heard Morgan moan.

The yellow light behind him suddenly burned as bright as the setting sun. He could feel its heat on his back through his jacket and on the back of his legs through his pants. Where the light touched the bare skin of his neck and scalp, though, he didn't feel heat. He felt an almost physical caress.

He was a few steps from the car again, planning how he would heave Morgan through the open door, over the gearshift and into the passenger seat when another roar hit him from behind and tried to push him over.

Then a twenty-five-foot golden dragon passed over his head close enough he felt the wind of its passage just before it slammed into the Camry with a crash and a roar.

4

THE CAMRY'S CHASSIS BENT AT the point of impact, slid and flipped over.

White fire erupted in coughs and gasps from Thara as she flipped with the car, her body twisting and her claws scrambling to find purchase on the smooth metal so she could land on top.

Thara righted herself as the car came to a crunching, grinding halt, ending with her perched on the canted undercarriage, head up, tail curling and uncurling as it dangled past the inverted rear bumper. She shook her head to clear the impact fireworks still going off on the backs of her eyes, then she faced the way she had come. She squinted as her nictitating membranes snapped into place to protect her eyes from the glare of the yellow light.

Her internal fire sputtered back to life as she coughed out the last of the bicarbonate and cleared her lungs. She felt the fire explode within her, fanning it with a long, deep inhalation. Her neck arched, then extended as her mouth opened and released a jet of white flame back toward both the Yellow Sign Buffet and the overprotective silver dragon perched on the restaurant's roof—who was suddenly a lot less sexy and reminding her even more of her father.

She didn't notice Marcus until he ducked and scurried to get out of the direct line of fire. She had no idea why he was carrying his girlfriend and didn't care. She still had some ire fire she needed to spit.

Neither the silver dragon nor the yellow star seemed to have noticed her previous effort—and Marcus had moved himself out of the way—so she took in another deep breath, and locked her eyes on the new, yellow

star that burned over Yellow Sign Buffet. She hated that new star as much
as she hated the old restaurant, and she could feel the return enmity of
the star in the light it kept throwing at her. She didn't hate the silver
dragon. She didn't know him well enough to hate him, but he had just
picked her up and thrown her a quarter mile. She breathed another—
longer, hotter—breath of white fire—the longest and hottest breath of
fire she had ever breathed—the length of five Cadillac Escalades, at least.

Her fire burned the yellow light out of the air and caused the silver
dragon to turn its huge head to face her.

She smiled as she took another deep breath, fanning her internal fire
even higher.

As she inhaled, the rear walls of the Yellow Sign Buffet burst out,
showering cinder blocks over the nearest parked cars and the people
gathered around. The people only moved if they were hit, otherwise they
seemed unimpressed. Then the roof the silver dragon stood on collapsed
beneath it. White fire erupted, then disappeared as the silver dragon fell
out of sight.

Go!

The silver dragon's word echoed in her mind, the word fading with
the last silver light.

She let out her breath and her fire, but with more of a startled grunt
than the geyser of flame she had intended.

Craning her neck as high as she could, she watched as nearly identical men and women in brown and yellow uniforms stumbled free of the
wreckage at the back of the restaurant. Then they turned around and
walked back in, picking their way over the debris. They didn't even dust
themselves off first.

5

MARCUS DUCKED INVOLUNTARILY, THEN RAN to his right, out from under the first gout of flames. The heat of the flames was hotter than the yellow light behind him, but had none of the *wrong* feeling. The flames would turn him to ash if they engulfed him, but they weren't trying to possess his soul. Which was only partially reassuring.

The golden dragon paused to take another breath, then roared and breathed more fire toward the restaurant. The dragon seemed focused on the yellow sign. If the light from the sign had any effect on the dragon, Marcus couldn't see it.

After a third long, white-hot breath had ended, the dragon drew back, its neck curling, its broad chest expanding and contracting like a golden-scaled bellows as it panted. Only then did the dragon seem to notice Marcus.

One eye swiveled to look at Marcus while the other still looked past him, back the at the restaurant.

At that moment Marcus realized the difference between seeing a dragon in a blurry Web video—or even in the firsthand memories of a secondhand car—and seeing a dragon almost close enough to touch. And more than close enough for it to breathe fire on him. Or rush him, grab him in its yard-wide mouth, jerk him to snap his neck, then swallow him in one, toothy gulp.

The ancient, reptilian part of his brain admired the dragon, while the more recent mammalian part gibbered nonsense in his head and wanted him to run. Run. *RUN!*

He managed not to run. Then to swallow. "Thara?"

The dragon glared at him with both eyes. "Have you met?" the dragon asked, still panting. "Any other? Gold dragons? In the last few minutes?"

The voice was Thara's, but more so. Not deeper so much as... *more.* A lot more. Amplified, condensed, and in high definition. If she could somehow fit into a sound booth, Marcus was sure Thara Gold, dragon, could have a long career in commercial radio. Listeners would buy whatever she told them to buy, go see the movies she told them to see, and wait to listen to whatever music she told them was coming up next. He was surprised he couldn't see her words glinting gold in the air between them. Or striking sparks off the asphalt.

"I never actually met you," he said. "As a dragon." He paused. He wondered if there were a different, more deferential way he was supposed to talk to a dragon. Then said, "I thought you only changed..." He didn't say *into a dragon.* "During the solstice?"

"Yeah," Thara said, and it was the most definite, most substantive *yeah* Marcus had ever heard. "Me too." Then she added, "We have to go back. We have to..."

"We?"

Thara was looking past him again. Marcus had to resist the urge to turn around and see what the dragon—he knew it was Thara, but his mind wasn't completely willing to connect her name with the creature in front of him, not yet—was looking at. He knew what the dragon—she—was looking at. Maybe the dragon—Thara-with-an-h—could look back, but he could still feel the wrong in the light coming from behind him.

He could also feel Morgan's weight beginning to drag him down. Except he couldn't put her down yet.

"What's going on?" he asked. "Back there?"

"They got him."

This time, in spite of knowing better, Marcus turned to look. Fortunately, Morgan's waist and hips blocked his view in that direction.

"They got who?" he asked, facing Thara again.

Thara's dragon lips—did dragons have lips? he had to admit they had something at least similar—pressed together in the same way her human lips would have. "I don't know his name."

"Whose name?"

"The other dragon."

"He's here?" He would have looked back again, but Morgan's hips saved him one more time.

Thara's huge head moved up and down in the dragon equivalent of a nod. The gesture caused the overturned car beneath her to rock forward then back with a crunching sound. More bits of glass fell from the shattered windows.

Marcus had never seen a dragon's face express confusion. He decided he didn't like it. It made the mammalian part of his brain indignant, as if the dragon were hesitating to eat him, but for all the wrong reasons.

6

THARA LOOKED DOWN AT MARCUS. His eyes were wide, looking up at her. He was talking. He was asking questions. But she could tell he was having a hard time. He was doing better than some people she could tell him about, but there was no time for congratulations or commiseration. Not now. Time, she could feel, was suddenly running out. She started to tell him that, but stopped. She focused on him with both eyes again.

Marcus was carrying his black-and-gold leather-and-lame attired girlfriend over his left shoulder. The girl was obviously not unconscious. Her back was arched, and she held her head up, staring back at the yellow star that blazed above the Yellow Sign Buffet.

Thara glanced at the sign again. The words Yellow Sign Buffet were no longer visible. Neither was the rectangular shape. The light had expanded beyond the confines of the physical sign. It was nearly as wide as the building beneath it.

The silver dragon was nowhere to be seen. There was no sign of him in the smoking crater the rear of the restaurant had become, and he wasn't flying or swooping through the air above it or around it.

She noticed the sky above her—the entire night sky—was as empty as the void of space. It was as if the Yellow Sign Buffet had opened up and swallowed the stars and the silver dragon.

She didn't know about the stars, but the silver dragon still lived. She could sense him, somehow. She inhaled through her nose. She could smell Marcus, of course, since he was right in front of her. He smelled of fatigue and fear and confusion. The girl on his shoulder, though, smelled... wrong. Perfumed, shampooed, and ready to party, but also... wrong. Off. No scent at all remained of the silver dragon. There was only the overwhelming, nonspecific scent of the Yellow Sign Buffet, and the Seasoning Tina had tried to make her drink. But she knew the silver dragon was still there. Somewhere. Just out of reach of her eyes and her nose.

She could still hear the silver dragon shouting into her mind. *Go, Child! Flee! This game is over!*

Something about how the silver dragon spoke to her reminded her of her father more than ever. Not specifically Poppa, though. Like the way adults spoke to children, expecting the children to already know what the adults were getting upset and shouting about, though the adults had never once brought it up before. What game was over?

"What game?" Marcus asked, echoing her thought.

"I don't know," she said. "Did you hear him too?"

"No. I heard you. Just now."

Thara's left eye focused on Marcus, while her right eye took in the girl's rump and legs. "Why are you carrying... what's her name?"

"It's a long story."

Thara decided she didn't care that much. "OK. *Where* were you carrying her?"

"Her car," he said, and nodded to the overturned Camry Thara was perched on. "I thought we might be able to get away... from... here... or whatever."

Thara looked down at the wreckage beneath her. "Oh. Sorry."

The car made additional metal-crunching and glass-breaking sounds as Thara climbed over the front end to the ground. Her weight caused the car to tilt that way, raising the rear end behind her. When her tail was clear, she faced the car again and nudged it with her nose. It tilted back the other way.

The girl on Marcus's shoulder said nothing. She hadn't moved that Thara had noticed, except to continue staring at the light over the restaurant when Marcus shifted her weight on his shoulder.

"She's taking it well," Thara said. She made an effort to remember the girl's name. "Morgan, right?"

"Yeah. Morgan. I don't... I don't think she's noticed the car yet." He added, "I don't think she's noticed you yet, either."

Thara wasn't sure how to take that, so she glanced at the yellow light again.

She wasn't sure what to do now. She wanted a—

"Drink," Morgan said, and Thara heard the voices of the people packed around the restaurant say the same thing, as if in response. "Drink."

"Thara," Marcus said, pulling her attention back to him. "What's going on?"

Thara shook her head. "I don't know. I don't think it's the Sunday Brunch Special, though."

"Drink," Morgan said again. And in the distance, "Drink."

"The Queen is coming," Morgan said, her voice taking on a singsong quality. The people around the restaurant provided a distant chorus as they singsonged the same words in response. "The Queen and Her Sisters are coming."

Morgan twisted in Marcus's grip and slid down, somehow keeping her eyes fixed on the yellow light as she did. Her leather skirt hiked up, exposing the top of her panty hose and the rest of her posterior. How she managed to land upright on her golden six-inch spikes defied physics and should have sprained at least one ankle. Thara winced in empathy.

"The Queen and Her Sisters are coming to Consume the World," the girl said, and pushed past Marcus, walking toward the restaurant. She gave no indication she had almost twisted an ankle or was aware her skirt was still bunched around her waist.

"Damn it, Morgan."

Marcus ducked his head, covered his face with his right arm and went after her. He caught up with the girl after two long paces. He pressed his face against her back as he wrapped his left arm around her waist and hoisted her up. She twisted in his grasp as he turned around and positioned herself on his shoulder so she could still see the light. Her legs kicked a couple times, but he didn't release her.

"What are you doing?" Thara asked as he walked back.

"What does it look like I'm doing?"

"I asked the wrong question. *Why* are you carrying her?"

Marcus looked at her as if she were crazy. "If I don't carry her, she'll walk back... there."

Thara shrugged. "She seems to want to. Why don't you let her?"

Marcus shook his head. "Look. She didn't know they were going to End the World. She just..."

"Uh huh."

"I have to. She's my girlfriend."

"Fine," Thara said. "How much further do you think you can carry her?"

Morgan threw her arms wide. "The Queen and Her Sisters are coming," she sang-shouted, "to Consume the World for the Glory of the Queen!"

"Not far enough," Marcus said. He stumbled, then caught his balance. He started to pull her skirt back over her exposed posterior, but had to give it up when she almost wriggled free.

"How about my apartment?"

"The Queen is becoming!" Morgan shouted with additional arm movement and what might have been jazz hands.

"Maybe," Marcus said. "But what are we going to do with her there?"

"Lock her in the bathroom?"

"The Queen and Her Sisters are becoming!"

"Then what?" Marcus asked as he walked past Thara.

Thara shrugged, then followed him. "Ignore her pleas to let her out? Stuff a sock in her mouth?"

"The Queen and Her Sisters are becoming the End!"

"That's not what I meant. What are we going to do about that?" he asked, jerking his head to indicate what was happening behind them. "About August Neuland and the Yellow Sign Buffet? And about the other dragon?"

Thara looked back. The yellow sun seemed to be getting bigger.

Morgan sang-shouted, "The Queen and Her Sisters are becoming the End of the World!"

"Do you think it's really the end of the world?" Marcus asked.

"The End of the World!" Morgan shouted, correcting Marcus's capitalization.

I will fight this End for you, the silver dragon had said. Thara could see no sign of fighting. She couldn't even sense the silver dragon's presence any longer. His impression in her mind had faded. All that remained was the hope that he was... not gone.

How did one fight the end of the world?

"The End of the World!" Morgan shouted, correcting her capitalization, as well.

Thara wondered if fighting the End of the World was something she would have learned in Dragon Kindergarten, if she hadn't grown up human and missed her invitation. Then she turned away from the light. She fell in step beside Marcus, so her head was even with his shoulder.

"What are we going to do?" Marcus asked again.

Thara thought of Tina, and Keenan and the so-called Mr. Lampley. She thought of the silver dragon. "I don't know." She wanted to go back and help him, but he had told her to go. To *GO!*, in fact. And she wasn't sure how she would help him. She was only half his size, and she had no idea how small a fraction of his age her sixty-four years comprised. "I'm hoping we'll think of something on the way to my apartment."

"The Queen is hungry!" Morgan shouted. In the distance, the chorus answered, "Mmm, mmm good!"

7

THARA WALKED OVER THE CARS parked bumper to bumper in the two westbound lanes of Fifty-first Street, taking out some of her frustration and confusion on the hoods, trunks, cabin roofs and windshields of the empty vehicles. That was one advantage of having four legs and being twenty-five feet long. She could cover a lot of ground and bring a lot of weight to bear on her frustrations. Marcus, though, was forced to walk between the cars. The cars were parked so close he had to twist sideways more than once. When he did, Morgan always reoriented on his shoulder so she still faced the Yellow Sign Buffet, even if that meant she was trying to see the light through Thara's golden body. The girl kept up her singsong call-and-response litany with the people behind them. The Queen was hungry, the End was coming, blah blah blah, complete with jazz hands and heel kicks.

Off to the east, at the far end of the double line of parked cars, a car with an actual driver in it was leaning on his horn, as if audible irritation would miraculously clear the street. The honking happened in time with the buzzing in Thara's head, and in time with the girl's stupid song about the Queen, Her Sisters, and Their dinner plans.

"The Feast of a Billion Worlds begins with a Single Bite!"

Distracted by the honking, singing, and the limited emotional release of denting hoods, scratching fenders, and smashing windshields, Thara nearly ran over the man standing very still on the sidewalk on the far side of the street. The man wasn't looking at her, or at Marcus with his shoulder-bundle of tightly wrapped T&A. Instead, the man was looking at the sidewalk in front of them. The bill of the ball cap on his head was pulled down so Thara couldn't see his face. He leaned on a ten-foot catchpole, its rope loop dangling above his head. The weary posture of how he leaned on the pole made him look old. And familiar.

Jimmie the Wrangler wasn't wearing his oversized, wrinkled Rio Cruces Animal Control Center uniform. The casual clothes he was wearing, though, looked almost identical. Blue work shirt, worn blue jeans, baggy leather gloves, and dirty work boots. All that was missing were the hand-sewn patches and his name stitched on the left breast.

"I thought I might," Jimmie said. "Find you here. Eventually. Probably." He still wasn't looking at Thara, but there was no doubt he was talking to her. "Been following your tracks." Then his head bobbed down and back up in a single nod unmistakably meant as a greeting to Marcus, who responded with a single incline nod.

"The Queen and Her Sisters are Coming!" Morgan shouted.

Jimmie the Wrangler shook his head. "Kids today."

There weren't a lot of people old enough to include Thara in that comment. Jimmie the Wrangler was one. Thara decided he was talking about Morgan, though. Not her. Or at least, not entirely about her.

"The Queen and Her Sisters are Coming to Consume the World!"

Jimmie took the glove off his right hand and scratched his scalp by pushing his fingers under the ball cap. "Should've known," he mumbled. Then he rubbed his nose. "What did you do?"

He was talking to Thara again.

"What did *I* do?" She drew back her head. Behind her, her tail took out another windshield. If Jimmie the Wrangler noticed how dragon she was being right then, staring down at his tiny, wrinkled old man self with her two eyes focused on him, he didn't give any indication of it. Marcus flinched at the sound of the breaking glass. Morgan was as oblivious as Jimmie.

"The Queen and Her Sisters are Coming to Consume the World to Satisfy the Hunger of the Queen!" In the distance, her chorus of white people repeated her words while Morgan took a breath.

"Must've done something," Jimmie said. "The World is Ending. Again."

"The Seasoning has begun!"

Thara glared at Marcus, since he was the one carrying Morgan, but he didn't notice this time, even when she punctuated her glare with another tail-busted window. He was focused on Jimmie the Wrangler.

"The World is Ending?"

Jimmie the Wrangler gave another singular nod as he pulled the glove back on his hand. Then he lifted his head to look at the sky overhead. He shrugged. "It's done it before."

"The Seasoning has begun! The Final Ingredient marinates!"

Marcus shifted Morgan on his shoulder. Thara watched him start to look back, then stop himself. "The World has Ended before?"

Jimmie shook his head, left, right, center. Then he said, "Kids." He glanced at Marcus's shoes, then over at Thara's foreclaws, then went back to looking at the sidewalk in front of him. "Tried to, probably. Never done it. Yet."

"The Seasoning has begun! The Final Ingredient marinates! The Queen Salivates!"

"How often has this happened?"

Jimmie held his right hand in front of him and counted on his gloved fingers. When all five fingers were extended, he sighed. "This week? Well, it's Sunday now. So it's a new week, probably. Just this once."

"So what are we supposed to do?" Marcus asked while Thara was still trying to parse Jimmie's math. She remembered the night she had first seen the silver dragon. The world had certainly looked as if it was trying to End then, too. Had the silver dragon fought that End for her too? What was she supposed to do when the world was trying to End?

"Stop it, probably?" Jimmie said to the sidewalk, as if she had asked the question aloud. Then he shrugged. "Up to you, I guess. Kids. The future. All that. I would think. Probably."

"The Seasoning has begun! The Final Ingredient marinates! The Queen Salivates! The Mandibles of the Queen's Sisters click in anticipation!"

There was no rhyme in the woman's rantings, but there was a definite rhythm that gave Thara a headache. She looked around for something—anything—she could stuff into the woman's mouth. Unfortunately, her socks had been destroyed already, back at the restaurant.

"How?" Marcus asked. "How do we stop the End of the World?"

"Ask her," Jimmie said, glancing at the sidewalk in front of Thara. "She knows. Or should. Probably."

"The Mandibles of the Queen and Her Sisters click click click!" Morgan punctuated each *click* with a hand clap.

"Ask her what?" Marcus asked at the same time as Thara asked the same question, but in first person.

"She's the Wyrm," Jimmie said. "The Wyrm of the World's End."

"Click click click! Click click! Click-click click!" Morgan shouted and clapped. Her legs bent at the knees, waving in time in front of Marcus. Her spiked heels flashed in front of Jimmie's face, but he didn't seem to notice, since his eyes were protected by the bill of his cap. In the distance, her chorus did a much less precise copy of her clapping.

"I'm not a worm," Thara said.

"A wyrm, probably."

"No, I'm not a *wyrm* either. Changing one letter doesn't make it more accurate."

"The Wyrm of the World's End Marinates! The Wyrm of the World's End Marinates in the Seasoning! The Wyrm of the World's End waits to be Consumed!"

"Great. Now you've got her saying it." Thara heard the distant echo. "And them."

Marcus was staring at Thara. "You're going to end the world?"

"End the World, probably," Jimmie corrected him.

"The Queen and Her Sisters will Consume the Wyrm!"

"No!" Thara said. "At least, I don't think so." She twisted her head around to look back at the Yellow Sign Buffet and its new star. "The End of the World is happening over there, and I'm over here."

"Distance doesn't matter, probably."

"The Queen and Her Sisters will Consume the Wyrm and the World!"

Thara thought of August Neuland calling her the Wyrm of the World's End, then changing his mind when he saw the big silver dragon. "What if they've got the wrong wyrm? I mean, the wrong dragon?"

That got Jimmie's attention. Maybe. He might have shifted his weight from one foot to the other. "Another dragon?" he asked Thara's foreclaws.

"You didn't know?"

Jimmie shrugged. "Doesn't leave tracks, probably. Doesn't burn down biker bars?"

"You weren't even there."

"Got the calls, probably."

"So what if he's the Wyrm?"

Jimmie the Wrangler shook his head once, left, right, center. "Nope." "Nope what?"

"You're the Wyrm. No probably," he added. "No doubt."

"I have doubts."

"Doesn't matter, probably."

"So they've got the wrong dragon?"

"Sounds like. Maybe." After a few seconds of silently contemplating the sidewalk, he shrugged. "Might make a difference. If the wrong dragon is eaten. Probably."

"Eaten?"

Marcus had been looking back and forth. "So the world isn't going to end?"

"Still going to try, probably." He nodded in Thara's direction. "The Wyrm." Toward the restaurant. "The End. All that."

Marcus looked like he had more questions, but didn't know which to ask first, so Thara focused on Jimmie. The old man was back to staring at the sidewalk. He offered no further probablies of wisdom.

In the silence that followed, Thara noticed the silence. She glanced at Morgan's butt, then saw the girl had twisted at the waist and was staring at her. Her eyes glowed a staticy, flickering yellow, like miniature versions of the new star that burned over the Yellow Sign Buffet.

"The Queen is Displeased," Morgan said. Her brow furrowed and her lips curled back to expose her teeth. "The Queen and Her Sisters Snarl. The Queen and Her Sisters Growl in Fury."

In the distance, the voices of the chorus didn't repeat the words. Instead, a growl torn from a thousand throats shook the ground.

"Should have left her," Jimmie said. He looked at Morgan's butt, then back at the sidewalk. "Behind. Probably."

8. Honey Glazed Dragon

The Queen

THE QUEEN PAUSED, MIDBITE.

In spite of Her whetted appetite, in spite of the silver dragon's haunch already in Her mouth, in spite of the bloody Flavor that already dripped on Her tongue, the Queen did not Eat. Her Sister-Daughters, arrayed around the dragon, each with a chosen morsel ready to Rend and Tear and Eat, also paused.

The knowledge came to the Queen, as all knowledge did, since the Queen knew all, if sometimes only just in time.

This dragon was not the proper, prophesied Final Ingredient. To begin Their Feast now would be to postpone the Feast. This dragon would not be the Appetizer of the Final Meal. Instead, the dragon would spoil Their Appetites.

The Queen withdrew Her teeth. Her Sister-Daughters did the same, though with Whining.

The Queen understood Their complaint. She did not *wish* to withdraw Her teeth, either. The dragon might be old. It would almost certainly be stringy, tough, and full of gristle. But the dragon had been Seasoned and allowed to Marinate, if only the minimum amount. More important, the dragon would not taste, in the slightest, like chicken. The Queen had become very tired of chicken. After decades of subsisting on chicken—with only the odd worker or drone for variety—the dragon represented a feast such as She had never known.

But the *wrong* feast. Not *the* Feast.

The Queen trembled at the thought of properly Seasoned dragon, but pulled Her Tongue back into Her Maw.

The Queen refused to eat until the proper Final Ingredient was brought to Her.

The Entree

THE ENTREE THREW HIMSELF AT the Goddess's oversized maw, to force Her to eat him, to save the Child and the World.

The Goddess snapped Her maw shut, and turned Her huge head so he collided only with Her for-lack-of-a-better-word-he-called-it-Her-cheek.

The Goddess twisted her he-decided-to-call-it-her-face away from the Entree, then pushed him away.

Frustrated, the Entree scooped up and swallowed one of the baby goddesses that surrounded him and the Goddess. He ate it raw, which was the best way, and, in fact, the only way. The Goddess and Her Brood of tiny, half-formed baby goddesses had already proven to be impervious to his fire. But even a Goddess could be eaten. Too bad She had foolishly been allowed to mature until She was too big to swallow hole.

Before he could eat another, the Goddess reached out with two overlong limbs and swept Her newly hatched baby goddesses behind Her, out of his reach. Then the Goddess did... nothing. She seemed to be waiting.

The strength of the baby goddess he had swallowed invigorated the Entree. And reminded him he had not eaten since awakening. He was not there to eat, though. He was there to be eaten. To be the Entree.

The Entree charged the Goddess again, climbing her bulk to stand on Her head and shoulders. He brought his foreclaws to bear, to force Her to open Her mouth. She shook Her head back and forth, refusing. The wound the Goddess had made in his right foreleg dripped on Her face. Below Her and behind Her, the tiny goddesses made pitiful noises of frustration, fear, and anger. One of the tiny goddesses scrambled forward to lick his blood, but the Goddess knocked the tiny goddess back and away.

Beyond the new yellow star that blazed overhead, the Entree heard the Child roar. The Child was coming to rescue him.

Below him, in his grip, the Goddess perked up. She heard the same thing. She opened Her maw in anticipation.

The Entree roared again, louder than before, wordlessly, but with all the meaning he could muster to communicate that the Child should not, under any circumstances, come to his aid.

His death in the gullet of the Goddess would not stop Her, but it would thwart Her current plans. That might give the Child time to mature, and to stop Her more permanently.

Then, once more, the Entree threw himself into the mouth of the Goddess.

The Bug

THE BUG HEARD ALL THE roaring back and forth, and decided it was time for one last trip out of the parking lot. He had been saving this trip for an emergency, and the possible End of the World seemed emergency enough.

The Bug started his engine, then engaged his transmission and reversed out of his favorite parking space. He shifted into first and headed out to meet his destiny—

Behind the Bug, the First Ugly Replacement stopped shivering, then clicked and rattled and wheezed as it also started its engine. Rusty cams struck rockers whose lubrication had dried out long ago, creating a raucous crescendo that became a merely painful clicking after several long seconds.

The Bug stopped and waited. He hadn't realized the First Ugly Replacement still had a self-sparking start left in it. He would have winced if he could have managed the facial expression as the First Ugly Replacement ground gears and eventually found reverse.

The First Ugly Replacement paused after backing out of his space and ground more gears. His clutch wouldn't disengage, and the old gears couldn't be forced any longer. The First Ugly Replacement was stuck in reverse. After what looked a lot like shrug, the First Ugly Replacement came around the long way, backward, and pulled up behind the Bug.

The Bug sighed and led the way, the First Ugly Replacement following, backward.

The Second Ugly Replacement started to follow them, but the Bug and the First Ugly Replacement both told her to stay, and to take care of the Driver for them.

1

MORGAN TWISTED IN MARCUS'S ARMS and tried to push herself off his shoulder. He resisted, holding her tighter even as he stumbled. He wrapped both arms around her thighs. He was still trying to process what Jimmie the Wrangler had been saying. He wanted to ask—

"Morgan!" he said. "Stop it!"

She didn't stop.

"Morgan!"

She shifted her weight again, as if trying to crawl down his back and escape that way. Wrapped in golden lame, her breasts moved smoothly down his back as her hands grabbed his belt and pulled, giving him a wedgie such as he had never experienced. Just before he was forced to drop her, she released her grip on his belt and lifted her torso at the waist.

"Look out—!" Thara roared.

What had to be Morgan's left elbow hit Marcus at the base of the skull and everything went dark—or at least darker—as he fell to his knees. Morgan's legs slid down his chest until her feet touched the ground, then his face slid down her legs on his way to the sidewalk.

2

THARA BACKED AWAY FROM MORGAN as the woman stepped over Marcus's prone form and advanced on her. Twenty-five-foot dragon or not, Morgan looked... wrong. And very, very angry. Her yellow eyes flared. Even Jimmie the Wrangler took a step back, and Morgan was ignoring him.

"The Queen will not be denied!" Morgan shouted. She would have shouted in Thara's face, but Thara continued to back away and kept her face out of harm's reach. "The Queen and Her Sisters will Feast!"

The word *Feast* seemed to echo as the chorus in the distance took it up as a chant. *Feast! Feast! Feast!*

Morgan came to an abrupt halt as the loop of Jimmie's catchpole came down over her head and shoulders and went taut across her chest, pinning her arms to her side. Morgan didn't turn around. Her glowing yellow eyes remained fixed on Thara. She strained to walk forward, but Jimmie held her back. Somehow. The old man didn't look as if he weighed enough to stop the progress of a drugged Pomeranian.

"The Queen and Her Sisters will Feast on this World and All Worlds!"

"Feast!" shouted the chorus, louder than before.

"The Queen and Her Sisters will Feast on you, Wyrm."

"Feast! Wyrm!"

"Stop calling me that," Thara said. She looked back toward the restaurant. The chorus wasn't just getting louder. It was getting closer. The crowd from around the restaurant was walking toward her, chanting.

"Feast! Feast! Feast!"

"A wall of fire would be useful," Jimmie said. "Probably. Since you're a dragon. Maybe that's something you could do?"

Thara nodded, agreeing. She did a bow-legged scramble back over the double line of motionless cars. She made no special effort this time, and did only minimal damage. The scraggly hedge that lined the far side of the street had caught her eye.

She perched on the roof of a white 2002 Chevrolet Tahoe. She gripped with all twenty claws, creating footholds in the metal shell. She took in a breath, felt the fire blossom in her chest, and let breath and fire out in a tight stream. Or as tight as stream as she could manage. Her dragon lips didn't seem to be designed for high-precision puckering. White fire poured across the two empty lanes and onto the sidewalk, engulfing the bushes. Leaves withered and branches caught fire. She blew the fire to the left and the right, creating a low, burning wall about fifty feet across.

Which was not wide enough by what looked like a hundred yards or more when compared to the width of the oncoming, chanting crowd. Also, the bushes burned too quickly. Within a few seconds, the wall of fire had become a line of fading embers and blackened sticks. Only a few bushes were substantial enough to provide lasting fuel.

"Feast! Feast! Feast!"

Thara looked at Jimmie, who still held back a straining Morgan.

"Any other suggestions?"

Jimmie shrugged.

Morgan seemed unaware of how easily she could push the loop of the catchpole over her head. Or how easily she could turn around, grab the pole, and almost certainly—probably—wrench it from the old man's hands and beat him with it. Morgan was still focused on Thara. Snarling.

"The Queen and Her Sisters will Feast!" Morgan shouted. She would have thrown her arms wide, but the tight loop of the catchpole kept her elbows pinned to her sides. "The Queen and Her Sisters will Feast on the Wyrm of the World's End!"

Beyond Morgan and Jimmie, Marcus had pushed himself into a sitting position. He rubbed the back of his head.

"What do I do?" Thara asked Jimmie.

As if in response, a roar split the night.

3

THE ROAR SHOOK THE GROUND and rattled the windows of the cars near Thara that still had windows. The bits of glass on the asphalt shook and jumped, like drops of water on a hot frying pan.

There were no words in the roar, only rage and frustration.

None of these emotions were directed at Thara, but she felt them. They touched her soul and squeezed dragon tears from her eyes. She raised her head and roared in response. The hot fire from her belly lit the night sky, temporarily creating a white star that flared in defiance of the growing yellow star over the ruins of the Yellow Sign Buffet.

It was the greatest roar of her life, but only a firecracker on the sidewalk compared to the roar that answered.

More rage. More frustration. And this one was definitely directed at Thara.

The meaning was clear, even without words. She was supposed to run away. To flee. To by-all-fucking-means *go*.

She didn't go.

She launched herself off the Tahoe and across the two empty lanes of Fifty-First Street. She ran through the coals of her attempted wall of fire, directly at the advancing crowd—who were surprisingly unaffected by the sight of a roaring dragon charging them. They continued to chant and march.

"Feast! Feast! Feast!"

Not having wings, unlike some dragons she knew, Thara lowered her head and hit the front line of the crowd like a four-legged, gold-crested snowplow. She swung her head back and forth, pushing and tossing men and women out of her way. The indescribable, indistinct smells of the Yellow Sign Buffet's so-called food were thick, and threatened to make her gag. She wasn't smelling people, she was smelling entrees. Or hors d'oeuvre. Appetizers.

"Feast! Feast! Feast!"

Thara realized the chant wasn't their intent. They weren't coming to eat her or Marcus or Jimmie the Wrangler. They were coming to be eaten. The nearest ones were throwing themselves at her mouth with the same enthusiasm Keenan had demonstrated a few minutes ago.

She kept her mouth closed and stepped over the bodies that fell off her face to land in front of her. She didn't want to hurt anyone, and she certainly wasn't going to eat anyone. She swung her head left and right, knocking people sprawling. She just wanted to get the people out of her way. A few bruises wouldn't kill them. So long as the people didn't do anything stupid—

A man jumped on her back while a woman wrapped herself around Thara's left foreleg.

Stupid. But not stupid enough she was going to seriously hurt them. She sent a ripple through her body to throw off mountain climbers and shook her leg to free it of cling-ons.

"Let go!"

A man in a tweed jacket—complete with leather patches on the elbows—grabbed Thara's lips and pushed himself into Thara's mouth.

"Feast!" the man shouted down Thara's throat.

Thara used her tongue to prevent the man from following his words, then threw her head side to side in an effort to shake him loose. She recognized the flavor of the Seasoning where her tongue touched the man's skin. Her tongue recoiled and she gagged. She reared back, getting her head above the crowd, then hawked up a hot loogie of dragon snot the size of the man's head. In the exact opposite manner of an iguana using its tongue to snatch a dragonfly out of the air, and in much greater scale, Thara's tongue extended fifteen feet and deposited both the steaming snot and the slightly singed man on the heads of a family of four who were surprisingly well dressed for four in the morning on a Sunday.

Thara stumbled as her tongue retracted with more force than expected, then closed her mouth tight, regained her footing and continued to push through the tide of people. Hands grabbed her legs, heavy soled shoes stepped on her long claws, and the voices around her kept chanting, "Feast! Feast! Feast!"

Wings would definitely have been useful in this situation. In addition to flying, having two extra appendages with which to knock some sense into mobbing, chanting, seemingly suicidal restaurant patrons would have been handy. She made a note to ask the big silver dragon when her wings might grow in. After she saved him.

She pushed her way out of the crowd of crazy customers. She shook free whoever it was that grabbed her left back leg, knocked over as many as she could with a last slap of her tail, then launched into a full speed lizard run toward the Yellow Sign Buffet.

She was going to save the silver dragon, whether he wanted her help or not. Then she was going to kick his fifty-foot, silver ass for a growing list of offenses, including, but not limited to, butting into her life, throwing her at a Camry, and existing her entire life without telling her.

4

Marcus stood—slowly, so as not to startle the sidewalk, which seemed a bit jumpy—and watched twin Jimmie the Wranglers holding matching catchpoles and preventing identical Morgans from following double dragon Thara back toward the Yellow Sign Buffets two locations. The smoke in the air made his eyes water and he blinked. The blink reunited the Jimmies and the Morgans and allowed both Tharas to get away. He blinked again, which let Thara get even further away. The dragon woman could move fast when she wanted to.

The gap Thara had created in the line of oncoming restaurant enthusiasts disappeared as the line coalesced into an amorphous blob, blocking his view. The blob oozed back toward the restaurant and the blazing yellow star that hovered it. With the base of his skull still throbbing from the impact of Morgan's elbow, he found it hard to focus on the light—

"You don't want to be looking at that, probably," Jimmie the Wrangler said.

Marcus closed his eyes and nodded in agreement. He turned his back on the light and waited until he could no longer feel the light prying at his eyelids before opening his eyes.

When he did, he saw the line of Jimmie's catchpole pointed at the light behind him like a compass, with Morgan as the arrow.

"Maybe we should," Jimmie said. "Let her go. Your girlfriend." He might have been looking at the sidewalk, but the line of his ballcap suggested he was at least keeping one eye on Morgan's butt. "Seems to want to."

Marcus started to shake his head in dissent—she was his girlfriend; he couldn't just let her go back to whatever—then stopped before his head fell off his shoulders. He held his head in place with both hands and asked, "Which one? Morgan? Or Thara?"

"Have to let one go, probably, to save the other."

"You think we can save Thara?"

"The Queen and Her Sisters will Consume the Final Ingredient!" Morgan said without turning her head. She leaned toward the Yellow Sign Buffet. She stood on her toes, the spike heels of her shoes quivering inches above the sidewalk.

Jimmie managed a shrug. "Not standing here, probably."

"What about the world?" Marcus asked. "Who saves the world?"

"The Queen and Her Sisters will Consume the World!" Morgan pulled against the catchpole and dragged Jimmie a few inches before the old man shifted his grip and reset his heels against the sidewalk.

"Need to make a choice," Jimmie said. "Probably."

Marcus almost looked back at the restaurant, into the light. He stopped himself and looked at Morgan. The yellow light was splashing off the shiny gold fabric of her top like sparks, but none of the drops of light landed near him. Morgan's hands were feral claws held at her side. She hadn't realized she could just pull the rope of the catchpole over her head. He almost said that aloud, but stopped himself. Morgan only seemed to be not listening, until she was.

He pointed to the metal fence behind Jimmie that even now, in the face of pending world doom, pretended it was somehow making the apartment complex more safe.

"What if you hang the pole on the fence?" he asked.

Jimmie glanced back at the fence. "Going to need help, probably."

It took both of them pulling on the catchpole to force Morgan to moonwalk back far enough so Marcus could lift the pole while Jimmie looped a wrist strap over the pointed top of one of the fence posts. With a nod to coordinate their timing, both men released the catchpole, ready to snatch it up again if it came loose.

The catchpole jerked taut as Morgan strained at her end, still on her toes, her eyes still focused on the light, her arms still down at her sides, but it held.

Jimmie ducked under the pole and stood beside Marcus, looking down at the sidewalk.

"Now what?" Marcus asked the top of Jimmie's head.

He heard the rattletrap sound of multiple, poorly maintained car engines just before a pair of round headlights appeared from inside the apartment complex. He turned to see a faded blue Volkswagen Beetle driving toward the entrance of the complex. A pair of red taillights followed the Beetle. Someone was driving backward.

The Beetle swerved to its right as if to drive straight at Marcus and Jimmie, then braked with an ear piercing sound of old brake pads and the dull squeal of old, worn-out rubber sliding on asphalt. The other car's taillights did a little leap as that car's engine and transmission revved to new levels of metal-on-metal torture. The other car had an all-glass hatchback that flashed the reflected light of the Yellow Sign Buffet's overachieving sign, causing Marcus to look away before he could identify the make and model. All he could tell was that the car was old, though probably not as old as the Beetle. Definitely more 1970s than 1960s.

The car drove backward at ever-increasing and ever-more-painful-to-hear speed, aiming its back bumper at the two lanes of parked cars that blocked the way in and out of the apartment complex. Specifically, it aimed itself at the small gap between a Toyota Prius and a Honda Element. The Element's hood sported a five-pointed dragon claw impression left by Thara a few minutes before.

Just before impact, the car's brake lights blazed bright red and its rear end dipped. The car didn't stop, though. Its tires were too bald. Instead its rear bumper slid beneath the rear bumper of the Element as it plowed into both the Prius and the Element.

Marcus winced and looked away at the same time Jimmie did. Morgan didn't seem to notice.

The crash was loud enough to drown out the horrible sound of the car's engine, but only for a few seconds. Then the squeals and bangings of poorly lubricated metal parts became louder as the little car kept trying to force its way through.

Marcus looked at the crash. He knew there were no drivers or passengers in the cars parked on the street. Then he saw there was no one visible in the little car with its two back tires spinning out and creating a stinking cloud of burning rubber smoke. The glass of the hatchback had shattered and fallen into the back of the car's cab. Its rear end was under the rear end of the Element and smashed into the front end of the Prius. With more burning of rubber and moaning of metal and crunching of glass, the Prius and the Element were being pushed against a 1990s-model Volvo in the far lane. The Volvo slid, rocking on its wheels.

Then Marcus recognized the empty, pushing car as one of Thara's three Outdoor Babies. Howie, the 1979 Mercury Bobcat.

"How is that possible?" he asked, shouting to be heard over the noise.

An odor of stale gasoline joined the acrid smell of burning rubber.

"We should step back," Jimmie told the sidewalk and Marcus's shoes.

"Probably." He nodded toward the Bobcat. "Might be called a Bobcat, but it's still a Pinto."

When Marcus didn't move, Jimmie's gloved right hand gripped his elbow and pulled him back, away from the street, toward the Beetle and its unblinking headlights.

Marcus shook off the man's hand, but followed him. He turned to look at the Beetle that had pulled over. The two round headlights were pointed at the Bobcat as if the car were watching, waiting. Marcus couldn't see through the windshield past the headlights. He turned to look back at the Bobcat, and saw Morgan was still where they had left her, held in place by Jimmie's catchpole and her unthinking need to return to the restaurant.

Marcus started to run to her, but Jimmie's gloved hand snagged his elbow again. Marcus struggled to get out of the man's grip in the same way Howie the Bobcat struggled to push three cars with an underpowered 2.3 liter four-cylinder engine that had somehow not rusted solid. Marcus was pulled up short by Jimmie's grip, and almost off his feet.

Howie's engine noise dropped to a low rattle, followed by a grinding of gears that should have caused bits of metal to fall to the pavement. The clutch disengaged and the car drifted back—forward?—from the point of collision. It rolled ten feet, then the back tires squealed and there was a sound like a chorus of rhythm-impaired carpenters trying to strike a stainless-steel roof with claw hammers all at the same time, and failing. The Bobcat lurched backward again and struck the Prius and the Element with renewed force, this time with no last-second breaking.

The Prius and Element were pushed further, creating a vee with enough separation the Bobcat could almost fit through. The Volvo rocked from the new impact, and its rear end was pushed across the yellow line.

The Bobcat disengaged its clutch again, with even more noise than before, and drifted back, its rear bumper falling to the pavement as it did. Then the car repeated the hammering, lurching reengaging of the clutch. The small car's tires spun out on the asphalt, then pushed it forward again. The fallen bumper went under the tires as the car shot forward, creating sparks as it was pushed and dragged across the asphalt and scraped against the underside of the car. The Prius and Elements were brushed aside and the Bobcat struck the side of the Volvo.

Howie's punctured gas tank exploded on impact.

5

MOST OF THE FORCE OF the blast went forward with the rolling red fireball created by atomized gasoline, but enough of it hit Marcus to knock him backward into Jimmie the Wrangler and cause them to fall. He lost sight of Morgan as he fell.

His ears ringing, his vision obscured by the green afterimage of the blast, his arms and legs tangled with those of Jimmie the Wrangler, it seemed to take forever for Marcus to regain his feet. When he did, he saw the explosion had thrown the severed front end of Howie the 1979 Mercury Bobcat, past him. The smoking, mangled remains of the car had come to rest alongside the idling Beetle. The Bobcat's windshield, somehow, was intact. Not a crack or a scratch marred the glass. The smoke inside the cab swirled, revealing the continued lack of a driver. And the lack of a driver's remains between the front seat and the steering wheel.

Marcus stared at the car, dazed.

As he watched, the Beetle's front tires turned in place, then the car moved, ever so slightly, and gently bumped its left front fender against the fender of the Bobcat. The headlights clicked off, as if the Beetle were closing its eyes. With the headlights off, Marcus saw there was no driver in the Beetle either.

"A hand, probably?" Jimmie the Wrangler said, lifting a gloved hand.

Marcus helped Jimmie to his feet, then remembered Morgan. He turned to look for her, fear for her safety clenching his gut. If she was hurt—

She didn't appear to have been hurt. If she had been knocked down by the blast, she had been able to get to her feet faster in her six-inch heels than Marcus had been in his dress shoes. She was already walking between and around parked cars that had been pushed around by the blast, headed toward the yellow light that looked even bigger now in Marcus's quickly averted, peripheral vision. The catchpole loop was still tight across her chest, and the pole dragged behind her. He would have run after her, but Jimmie snagged his arm again.

"I'll get your missus," Jimmie said, still shouting to be heard over the ringing in Marcus's ears. "I think this is your ride, probably. You being the Hunter. And all that."

"What?"

Marcus turned to see the Beetle pull up next to him and Jimmie. The Beetle's headlights were on again. The passenger door swung open with a loud click of its latch, and a screech of its long-unlubricated hinge.

There was very clearly no driver sitting in the driver's seat. For an instant, though, Marcus thought he saw his Daddy sitting there, leaning back in the seat, left elbow propped against the far door, the fingers of his left hand casually touching the steering wheel, right hand gesturing for him to get in. He could almost hear the man say it.

Get in, Baby Boy.

But it wasn't Daddy talking. It was Jimmie the Wrangler, shouting as he pushed Marcus toward the open door. "Get in, Hunter. You got somewhere to be, probably."

"Who's driving?" Marcus asked, because the vision of his father had faded, and there was still no one there. "Why did you call me 'Hunter?'"

"Not sure it matters, probably."

"It matters to me," Marcus said, but he ducked his head and stepped into the car.

Louie, said a voice in his head as he sat back in the worn and split vinyl of the passenger's seat.

The car door closed on its own. At the same time, the steering wheel turned, the break disengaged, the clutch engaged, and the car pulled forward.

The car aimed for the gap created by the Bobcat. The Prius and Element had been pushed out of the way, and the Volvo had been knocked back and on its side by the blast, leaving just enough room for the Beetle—

Call me Louie.

—to fit through.

Louie the Super Bug, the car added as it nudged Howie's bent and blasted bumper out of the way, then navigated between the cars. *Poor Howie. That was his only superpower.*

Marcus watched the gearshift move on its own as the car shifted into second gear, speeding across the two empty lanes of traffic and into the nearly empty parking lot of the supermarket and strip mall.

Marcus saw Morgan, still dragging the catchpole, stepping from Fifty-First Street to the curb of the parking lot. She was still staring fixedly on the light—

In front of Marcus, the visor dropped and blocked his view of the light. Then the glove box dropped open. In the glove box, Marcus saw crumpled maps, old receipts, something bulky wrapped in dusty canvas, and a pair of huge women's sunglasses that had probably last seen the Sun in the years between the original recording of Bruce Springsteen's "Blinded by the Light" in 1972 and the more popular cover by Mannfred Mann in 1976, both versions of which were suddenly playing in the back of Marcus's head.

"OK, OK," he said. "I get it."

He took the sunglasses out of the glove box, and unfolded them. They had heavy, plastic tortoiseshell frames and large, round brown-tinted lenses. As he examined the glasses, the glove box snapped closed. After a moment's hesitation, he closed his eyes and put the sunglasses on. If either Morgan or Mom Nelson saw him wearing these, they would first mock his manhood—then steal them to wear. Keeping his eyes slits, just in case, he raised the visor enough to risk a quick glance at the bright yellow light that hung in the sky over the Yellow Sign Buffet.

He could *feel* the yellow light hitting the lenses of the sunglasses and pushing against them. The light tried to spill around the edges of the lenses, but the thick tortoiseshell frames kept that from happening. Marcus almost took off the sunglasses to get a better look at them. Almost. Instead, he pushed the visor fully out of his way and looked at the source of the light.

"What the Hell?"

Even with the sunglasses, he couldn't look directly at the tiny star that hung above the restaurant. It was too bright. But he could see around the light, and below it. The Yellow Sign Buffet's eponymous sign was gone, as was most of the building that had been beneath the sign. The front of the restaurant looked intact, its plate-glass windows dark but unbroken. The rear section of the building, though, had all but disappeared. The roof was gone. The cinderblock walls had been pushed out far enough for cement blocks to fall on the closest parked cars. A smoky haze rose from the fallen cinder blocks and from the darkness at the center of the destruction.

Louie the Super Bug leaned on its horn—

His, man. His. I'm a dude.

—his horn, Marcus corrected himself, as the car caught up with the mass of people returning to encircle the ruins of the restaurant. None of the men, women, teenagers, and children even turned to look.

Maybe it's my California childhood speaking, Louie said, *but I hate pedestrians.*

The steering wheel spun and Louie pulled to the left.

Going to have to take the long way round. Probably just as well, though. There's someone who wants to talk to you.

Marcus lost sight of the destruction at the rear of the Yellow Sign Buffet as Louie drove behind the wall of people. Only the new yellow star was visible over their heads. Marcus tried to see through the people, but the sunglasses let him down. No X-ray vision. He hadn't seen any sign of Thara. He finally registered the words Louie had been speaking in his head.

"Talk to me?"

Yeah, man, just a second.

The car swerved around a small, enclosed ATM kiosk in the middle of the parking lot. *I just hope the curbs we have to jump are low, and the sidewalks are wide. I haven't driven the streets of Rio Cruces since before you were born, and my few tow trips have always been north. So I have no idea what to expect. We might have to off-road it a bit to get past this foot traffic.*

Marcus reached behind his head for the seat belt, then remembered how old this car was and reached down between the seat the door. He found nothing there either.

"Where's the seat belt?"

Louie didn't answer. The car shifted itself—himself—into third gear and pointed them at where the parking lot ended and the sidewalk began. The curb there did, fortunately, look to be low. Louie hit the curb with only a slight bump, then they were speeding past cars on the narrow, empty strip of concrete between the street and the wooden fence of a residential neighborhood.

Both Harvard Avenue's northbound lanes were bumper to bumper with parked cars, extending south ahead of them as far Marcus could see. The sidewalks, unfortunately, didn't seem to go that far.

Marcus braced himself against the dash.

The Beetle reached the end of the sidewalk and the world around Marcus tilted and changed.

6

THARA RAN AT FULL DRAGON speed across the parking lot, until she reached the confluence of the two rivers of parked cars, one from the north and one from the south. She stopped as only a reptile can, freezing in place, transitioning from full speed to complete immobility in an instant, perched on top of a white Dodge Ram pickup, her front half on the cab roof, her back half draped through the pickup bed, her tail dangling off the end. Her eyes swiveled to see in all directions and her tongue flicked out and back in, enhancing her sense of smell. Not that she could smell—or taste—anything except the Seasoning that permeated the air. She licked the windshield of the truck to get rid of the taste. It didn't help. She pulled her tongue back into her mouth and squeezed her nostrils closed, as well.

The chanting crowd—*Feast! Feast! Feast!*—followed her, but at much slower, more human speed. Beyond the crowd, between the chanting, she heard a squeal of tires and a collision that involved at least three cars, maybe four. Beyond that, she could hear someone still leaning on their horn, honking in time with the chanting.

The plate-glass windows that stretched across the front of the Yellow Sign Buffet were intact, but there was no light behind them. No light reflected from the windows either, making them appear to be windows into the empty blackness of space.

The pulsing yellow star that hung in the sky above the restaurant lit the world in stark black-and-yellow highlights. Shadows were sharp enough to wound and as deep as the Void. Yellow smoke and steam wafted from the ruins, drawn into the light in swirling arcs, as if the light were constantly inhaling.

Splashing water, spraying from broken pipes, and the sound of someone—some*thing*—gagging was all she could hear from the pit that had once been the back half of the Yellow Sign Buffet.

Thara launched herself forward again.

Her claws brushed over the hoods or fenders or windshields of the intervening cars, pushing herself off again so fast her weight scarcely had time to register. Her tail balanced her and counterweighted her as necessary so she flowed more than ran over the tops of the cars. She stopped as suddenly as she had started, perched on the broken cinder block wall which had been the backsplash of the dive station, where she had been standing only hours before, washing dishes. Cold water geysered from the bent and broken pipes, spraying water into the pit the tile floor of the prep area had fallen into. At the top of the arc of spray, some of the mist was pulled toward the yellow light.

She kept her mouth closed, resisting the urge to sniff or taste, and used only her eyes to perceive the scene in front of her.

The yellow-and-brown uniforms of the employees standing around the edge of the pit appeared white-and-gray under the yellow light. She spotted the so-called Mr. Lampley and August Neuland standing where the manager's office used to be with another uniformed figure she hoped was Tina. The ecru shirts of the two men appeared to glow. Neither managers nor employees turned to look at Thara. They stood transfixed by the scene in the pit.

Thara stretched her neck to see over their heads.

The silver dragon gleamed a sickly yellow as it wrestled with something Thara's brain recoiled from even considering. Not only were insects *never* supposed to get that big, *insect* as a word was never meant to be ascribed to something so alien, so huge, so...

Thara thought of the bilious brown coils and the sphincter she had seen before, and the gases and liquids that had bubbled through and leaked from the nauseating s-shaped smile, taking mental solace and comfort in the hideous familiarity those represented compared to what she was looking at now.

She closed her eyes, but she couldn't stop seeing what she was seeing and what her mind did not want to describe or consider or contemplate or acknowledge or in any way continue to gyre and gimble or slithy mimby mome...

Above her, the sucking yellow star thrummed into ever-brighter existence, illuminating the beast in the pit—the GODDESS-QUEEN THAT WOULD CONSUME THE WORLD—in black-and-yellow relief that penetrated every layer of Thara's eyelids.

Brillig toves wabed and uffishly manxomed inside her head, seeking exit through her ears and nose.

Behind her, she felt one of her Outdoor Babies explode and die.

Her overwhelmed mind latched on to this distraction, this pain of loss. She extended her neck to its fullest and twisted to face back the way she had come. She saw the smoke from the explosion as it rolled and rose into the night air, pushed by the wind and pulled toward her by the influence of the yellow star.

"Howie!"

She twisted in place as she roared, letting her tail swing so it slapped against a section of cinder block wall that had not been toppled.

She breathed angry white fire across the cars parked near her. Paint blistered and peeled. Glass blackened and drooped. Interiors caught fire.

She started to rush back, to investigate who or what was about to die a horrible, flaming death, but stopped when she heard a sound she hadn't heard in more than three decades.

"Louie?"

She scrambled over the cars she had just set alight, ignoring the flames and the molten glass, until she was on the roof of a Honda Odyssey and could stretch her neck to see over the heads of the amorphous crowd still following her. She saw her faded blue Volkswagen Beetle driving across the parking lot, coming up behind the people, honking and swerving to go around the stragglers. The light of the yellow star above and behind her reflected off the windows of the car, so she couldn't be certain, but she thought she saw a passenger. And a complete lack of a driver.

She knew who the passenger was. Who else could it be?

First Nova, now Louie. Her Outdoor Babies were being far too accepting of—and helpful toward—Marcus Nelson, dragon hunter.

Nova had never talked to her, no matter how much Thara talked while driving. Louie had never driven her around of his own volition. Hell, the car hadn't even turned over its engine the last time she tried to start it. What else was the little car hiding?

Another roar and the renewed sounds of struggle pulled her attention back to the pit.

7

THE PHRASE *DÉJÀ VU* POPPED into Marcus's brain. Not because it applied. It didn't. Nothing he was experiencing at that moment came close to being a repeat of anything he had experienced before. He thought of *déjà vu* because he realized he had no word or phrase to describe the sensation of experiencing two very different events—two completely separate *realities*—simultaneously, and in such a way as to be unable to distinguish which was real and which was hallucination. Because one of them had to be a hallucination.

In one reality, he bounced about in the cracked and worn front seat of a driverless 1964 Volkswagen Beetle as that car raced through the night on a thin, uneven strip of landscaping between parked cars on one side and alternating fences and hedges on the other. Sometimes swerving into shallow ditches to avoid telephone pole support wires. Sometimes edging far enough the other way the sideview mirrors of parked cars rushed by close enough to scratch paint or cause serious damage. Louie the Super Bug laughed inside Marcus's head whenever they had a particularly close call, and made sure Marcus was aware of how few fractions of an inch of rubber were actually making contact with the concrete below the passenger side tires versus how many inches were dangling over the edge of the curb.

At the same time, Marcus sat—perfectly still—in the same front seat. The seat wasn't worn, there were no splits or tears in the vinyl and no bits of off-white padding leaked out, but there was no question it was the same seat. Louie assured him it was. The interior of the Beetle wasn't showroom perfect, but it was clean and smelled as fresh as clothes hung to dry on a clothesline in the summer. The black steering wheel gleamed. The dashboard was dust-free and the carpet beneath Marcus's feet looked factory fresh. None of the interior paint had faded, and it was the same color blue as the afternoon sky visible through the crystal-clear windows.

In spite of the reality trying to buck him out of the seat and throw him through the windshield with sudden, jerking turns and changes in speed, Marcus released his grip on the door handle with his right hand and reached up to touch the window next to him with his fingertips. He had to know if this was real. The cool glass certainly *felt* real, but no halos of moisture formed on the glass around his fingertips.

I'm real, man, Louie said. *Real as real can be!*

Then Louie the Super Bug was laughing maniacally again and offered no further explanations or contradictions. That other reality, though, where Marcus was offroading in a driverless VW Beetle, faded.

Only then did Marcus notice the car was parked at a drive-in restaurant he had never seen on any of his visits to Rio Cruces. The drive-in was all sparkling glass and shiny stainless-steel with a double line of partially covered, herring-bone parking spaces. Fresh-faced white girls, teenagers, smiling, with their hair pulled back in ponytails and wearing white button-down blouses and pleated skirts, skated back and forth between the two lines of cars carrying folded-over paper takeout bags or trays with drinks and burgers on them, but Marcus hardly noticed. He saw only the cars.

All the parking spaces Marcus could see were occupied with Chevrolets and Fords, Chryslers and Oldsmobiles, all from the mid-1950s and early 1960s. A Bel-Air, an Impala. A Starfire. A Skyliner. A Windsor. Two doors, four doors, hardtops, a convertible. Parked next to Marcus was a 1961 Checker Marathon, green with a brown hardtop.

Marcus couldn't help but think of his father, and how much Daddy would have enjoyed seeing all those cars—especially the Checker Marathon. They weren't shiny show cars, or kit cars, or project cars kept in hermetically sealed garages and only brought out for parades and car shows. They were working cars and family cars. They weren't in mint condition. They were in *original* condition. Pure as pure could be.

"Beautiful, isn't she?"

Startled, Marcus jerked his hand back from the window and turned to see that he wasn't alone in the car.

He more than half expected to see Daddy sitting there, smiling, leaning back from the steering wheel, nodding to indicate the Checker

Marathon or looking around and gesturing to make sure Baby Boy noticed the remarkable, pristine condition of this 1964 Volkswagen Beetle more than fifty years after it—*he*—had rolled off the assembly line.

But it wasn't Daddy. A middle-aged white man Marcus had never met sat in the driver's seat. He was relaxed, leaning away from the steering wheel, but not in the same way Daddy would have been. The driver side window was rolled down, and he had his left elbow propped there. His right hand was on his thigh. He wasn't looking at Marcus or the beautiful vintage cars. He was watching a carhop with golden blonde hair skate past in front of the Beetle's hood.

The girl looked too young to be a carhop. She looked... maybe twelve? She was as tall as the other girls, who were clearly teenagers, but looked much younger. Her face was round, not yet stretched by puberty so her nose still seemed a bit bigger than it should be. Her figure was athletic, almost boyish in its lines. Marcus didn't recognize her until she skated back by, this time flashing her golden eyes and a bright white smile at the man in the car with Marcus. When Marcus had first seen that smile, it had been more mechanical, less childlike and with less joy, but the shape of it remained. The girl was Thara-with-an-h Gold.

Before he could stop himself, Marcus thought of the girl all grown up. And naked.

"She's my baby," the man said.

Marcus felt his face grow warm and he stopped following teenage Thara's flowing, back-and-forth progress. He tried to focus on the cars again, then at the dash in front of him. He risked a sideways glance at the man in the driver's seat. The man—was he Thara's father?—was also watching her, though very differently from how Marcus had been.

"I don't know your name," the man said.

Marcus reached across with his right hand, slowly, coolly. "Marcus—"

"I'll leave that for her." The man never even looked at Marcus. Not even when Marcus raised his hand and waved it. "I'm sure she'll think of a good name for you."

Marcus took his hand back. He twisted in the front seat so he was facing the man. "You're Thara's father?"

The man continued looking through Marcus. "She's the Wyrm of the World's End."

"You knew that?" Marcus asked. "Why didn't you tell her?"

The man sighed. "That's what the prophecy said, anyway, but I love her. Wyrm or not, World Ender or not, she's my Goose. My Goose from the Golden Egg."

"She hatched?"

The man stopped looking through Marcus and looked around at the interior of the car. "I'm not going to be around forever, certainly not until the End of the World, so you're going to have to take care of her for me."

"Thara? Take care of her? Did she even let *you* do that?"

Shh! said Louie in Marcus's head. *Just listen.*

The man gripped the steering wheel as if he were gripping the shoulders of some young man. "Keep her safe," he told the steering wheel. "Be there for her."

The man fell silent. After a second, he relaxed. His left elbow went back to the window, his right hand dropped back to his thigh. He smiled as the teenage Thara skated past again, delivering a tray with two root beer floats in frosty mugs to a 1960 Dodge Polara with a hotrod paint job that would have made Marcus's Daddy shake his head and sigh.

Marcus waited for the man to go on. He and the man both waved at Thara as she skated back by. Thara's smile seemed to falter as her eyes left her father and swept over Marcus. As if she might have seen him. Then she was gone again.

"She didn't see you."

Marcus said nothing as he turned to look at the man again. This time the man's eyes were waiting for his.

"You can see me?"

The man shook his head. "You're not there. Not here. Not yet." He broke eye contact and leaned forward to look at the world outside the Beetle. "You're probably not even alive yet. But you're coming. The prophecy gave us her, so the End is coming, and so are you."

"Fate?"

"It's not Fate," the man said after a short pause, still looking out the window. "Not really. But it sometimes feels a lot like it, doesn't it? I'll bet a week ago you thought you had it all figured out—"

"Not really, no."

"—you probably had a good job, maybe a nice wife—"

Marcus snorted.

Shh! Louie said.

"—and then all this... shenanigans... just started *happening*." The man turned to look at Marcus again. This time, though, their eyes didn't quite meet. The man seemed to be focusing on Marcus's right cheek. Marcus shifted so they were eye to eye again. "One day you're what? A mechanic? Or some kind of engineer?"

Marcus gave the man an incline nod in response. Close enough.

"And the next day you're the Hunter, looking for..." He sighed. "Dragons. How much of a shock was that?" The man smiled and shook his head. The smile faded, and he sighed again. "Except... you were Hunting my baby girl. My Goose. And you found her. Because of course you did. You're the Hunter, it's what Hunters do. And that's how prophecy works." The man's expression became harder. "It messes with your life."

The man's right hand went to his shirt pocket and tapped on it, then fell away. "I haven't wanted a cigarette this much since the war." His expression relaxed and he smiled a wistful smile. He looked past Marcus again. "I had mostly stopped smoking before Goose was born." There was only a slight hesitation before the word *born*. "We decided it was best, though, to minimize the number of matches and flammables around the house once we brought her home. We bought an electric range. We don't even have a fireplace or a backyard grill. Just seemed... safer that way. And wouldn't give her any ideas."

For the first time in his life, Marcus wondered if a cigarette might be exactly what he needed.

No smoking in the car, man. Driver's rules.

"Prophecy," the man said, shaking his head. "It's a bitch."

"Fate," Marcus said, thinking of August Neuland.

"You might be thinking it's Fate," the man said. "But you're wrong, Hunter. It's not Fate, no matter what... some people... might say. Fate and prophecy aren't the same thing. There's a difference, though it might seem only semantic, or a matter of where you stand looking at it. Fate doesn't give you a choice. It happens whether you want it to or not. Prophecy, though, even if it doesn't sound like it, there's always a choice."

Marcus tried to think of the last choice he had made. Had it been when he decided to call about the dragon hunting job, no experience needed? Or had it been when he let Morgan tell August Neuland about Thara?

The man went on. "We knew she was coming, we knew what she was prophesied to be, and we chose to let her be born. We were in a position to... to prevent it. But we *chose* her, Momma and I. We chose to let her... hatch. We chose *her*. She was our little Goose. Some people might think we were destined to make that choice, but... we were there. We know what... could have happened." His right hand clenched on his thigh, then relaxed.

The man turned to look at Marcus again, and Marcus shifted so the man was looking him in the eyes and not at his forehead.

"We didn't," the man started, then stopped. "We couldn't let the dragons die, Hunter. Not when there was a chance they could come back. What's the point of saving the World if you have to strip away all the beauty to do it? If you do that, what have you saved?"

The man's expression was identical to the one Thara had whenever she asked Marcus a question. His eyes were brown, though, not gold.

"The World is a better place because it has my little Goose in it," the man went on, "but it's also on a collision course with you and..." He paused. "And the rest of the prophecy. She is the Wyrm of the World's End, after all. That became her destiny when we... when she... was born. But it's not her Fate, Hunter. You can save her from that."

"How am I supposed to save her?" Marcus asked.

"Just don't expect her thank you for it."

Marcus smiled a lopsided smile. "OK. So you do know your daughter. But that's not a useful answer—"

"You're the Hunter," the man said, interrupting him. "You're also in the prophecy, though I doubt you've ever heard it."

"You could tell me."

The man seemed to think about it for a second, as if he had heard Marcus, then he shook his head. "No. There's no time to tell you the whole prophecy, and the Hunter only appears near the end, anyway. It's a single line, and you've already fulfilled that part, I have no doubt."

"How was I supposed to know—"

"Prophecy loves amateurs. They never know the right questions to ask. It's hard not to believe in Fate when you're in the middle of it and everything just seems to be... happening. What you need to know, Hunter, is that you *could* have chosen differently."

"You don't know Morgan. She—"

"You know you could have. You were there. I don't blame you, Hunter, I just ask you... now... to do what you can to save my Goose."

Marcus felt as if he had just been given a pop quiz for a class he hadn't signed up for, and his grade would determine whether he passed or failed. "How am I supposed to do that?"

"Your part in the prophecy makes you the Hunter," the man said. "*Be* the Hunter."

"What does that mean? I didn't get much of a job description when I was hired. 'Find me a dragon,' the man said. I didn't get an employee's manual."

The man didn't answer. He looked out the windshield and sighed.

Marcus reached out to poke the man in the shoulder. His hand passed through shirt sleeve and flesh as if they weren't there. He snatched his hand back. "You can't stop there. What do you mean 'be the Hunter?'"

Thara skated in front of the car again, carrying a tray with a single drink in a tall glass. Instead of continuing past, though, she spun to her left and toe-braked to a stop beside the driver's side window.

"Hi, Poppa," she said as she hung the tray on the door. She picked the straw up from the tray and dropped it in the glass, then picked up the glass and took a sip. "Have you been talking to yourself again?"

The man smiled up at her. "Excuse me, miss, but isn't the customer allowed to imbibe his own beverage in this establishment?"

"This isn't your drink, Poppa," she said, taking another sip. "It's mine. But I'll share it with you." She handed him the glass. When he had taken the drink, she leaned over to peer past him into the car. "You've been talking to yourself since you got here. Is there someone hiding in the back seat?"

Marcus thought her eyes met his for an instant, but her eyes moved on immediately and she was scanning the interior roof and the back seat.

"What do you think?" the man asked. "Will she do?"

"She?" Thara asked. "Poppa, you need to have your eyes checked. This car is most definitely a *he*."

You know it, Louie added, his voice in Marcus's head from both past and present creating an unusual mental stereo effect.

"For Momma, though?" Thara looked doubtful. "I know she wants something smaller, but this might be taking it a bit far, don't you think?"

"But do *you* like it? I mean him?"

"Of course I like him, Poppa. He's as cute as a button."

"I'm happy to hear you say that, Goose, because he isn't for Momma. He's for you."

Thara squealed in a way Marcus had never expected to hear Thara-with-an-h Gold squeal. She nearly spilled the drink all over her father and the front seat of her new car as she tried to hug her father through the open window.

The other carhops came to see what was going on. They gathered around Thara and her new 1964 VW Beetle.

The girls, the other cars, Thara's father, the sunlight, all faded and Marcus was again sitting in the dark, in a worn vinyl seat. This time, though, he was speeding up the wrong side of Harvard Avenue toward the glowing yellow star that hovered over the smoking ruins of the Yellow Sign Buffet.

8

As SHE TURNED BACK TO the pit, Thara wondered if keeping one eye closed would let her keep half her sanity. Because watching a fifty-foot silver dragon trying to shove itself down the gagging gullet of a—

Her brain still didn't want to fully classify what her eyes resisted looking at. When she tried to focus on *It*, her eyes refused. Her field of vision slipped off sideways, leaving only an impression of cold and slime. It was like trying to pick up cold tapioca with her bare hands, except the chill and the slime touched her mind and not her fingers.

She struggled to comprehend what she was seeing. What was happening around her. She was more accustomed to being the source of any weird shit happening than being the one experiencing the weird shit and having to deal with it.

She remembered her first glimpse of her own left leg in its golden and scaly dragon form, with its dragon foot and long, drooping dragon toes and golden claws. Since then—and since rising up out of Nancy Chisum's wading pool to scare the bejesus out of her grade school friends—she had encountered nothing that scared her as much as herself. Until four nights ago, when the silver dragon roared at her from the sky and sent her running. And now this... It... whatever *It* was...

—THE GODDESS-QUEEN THAT WILL CONSUME—

No.

Thara stopped her mind from joining the gibbering chorus of words forcing their way into her head. She clenched her jaw closed to keep the words from escaping that way, then forced her eyes to see what was in front of her, and forced her mind to consider the possibilities.

Was It a cockroach crossed with a tree toad?

Was It the offspring of a spider and a chicken?

Could It be the love child of a weevil and a salamander, birthed in Hell, decanted in ooze, and plopped down on a pile of Its own guts with the twin urges to Feed and Propagate?

Was It—

A feeling of EXTREME RESENTMENT OF THESE CHARACTERIZATIONS pushed against her mind, hitting her mentally hard enough to interrupt her tally of odious possibilities and make her stumble backward a step.

Then there was a wet, snucking sound, like a giant with a head cold sniffing at full strength to avoid dripping snot from a nose the size of a 1972 Fiat 126. The bloated body of the It shook and shivered and seemed to draw in on itself.

The muscles of the silver dragon's rear legs bulged as he pushed himself slightly farther into It, eliciting a gag and a choke that shook the night and threatened to send Thara's mind back to its earlier, more gibbering-inclined state.

It convulsed. First a tremor, barely a ripple, then an explosive cough-sneeze-retch. The silver dragon flew backward, away from It, in a gusher of slime, to slam and splash against the far side of the pit. Where the slime touched the cinder block walls or dripped to the broken concrete floor, hissing smoke rose. The smaller its hiding behind It would have scattered at the outburst, but Its various appendages of varying length held them in place.

The silver dragon twisted to right himself. The slime dripped as he spread his wings wide. He roared and breathed fire that reached across the length of the pit and engulfed the It and Its offspring. The flames rolled off the It and the smaller its the same way the slime had slid off his scales.

Then the silver dragon turned to face Thara. Silver lips curled back to expose the broad, curved sabers that were his teeth.

The dragon's voice roared in her head. *Damn you, Child! I should eat you myself!*

Thara's mind, still reeling from It, reeled further, unspooling inside her skull. That had not been the response she expected.

"I'm trying to save you!" she shouted back, loud enough—she hoped—that he could hear the words inside his thick skull.

The silver dragon roared again. There were no clear words, though, only fire-sharpened points of emotions including anger, frustration, and desperation.

Anger striking anger, frustration sparking confusion, fire feeding fire, Thara ignored the *It* and focused on the silver dragon. In a blind rage and—for some reason, thinking of her father and all the bits and pieces of the world and life he had forgotten to mention before going away—Thara threw herself into the pit at the silver dragon.

9. Marinated Dragon

The Queen

THE QUEEN WIPED HER FACE when none of Her Workers rushed forward to do it for Her, then wiped Her claw on the burned and broken floor of Her ruined Kitchen. She stopped one of Her Sister-Daughters from rushing forward to lick the smear, then She turned Her attention to the Final Ingredient.

The Final Ingredient had not been properly Seasoned.

The Queen decided She did not care. Her Appetite was Whetted. The World would not Consume Itself.

The End needed to Begin.

The Frustrated

THE FRUSTRATED DID *NOT* UNDERSTAND the Child.

He had clearly told the Child to run, to go, to flee to safety. He, the Frustrated, would fight this fight for her. Prevent this End.

He did not think he could have shouted this information any louder.

The Child had not run. She had not gone or fled. She was not now a safe distance away. Instead she was here, at the center of the End of the World, fighting *him*. Roaring nonsense and breathing fire.

The Frustrated wondered why he had ever discontinued the ancient tradition of eating newly hatched dragonlings. Children were such an incredible pain in the ass.

The Bug

THE BUG HELD IT TOGETHER—ENGINE, drivetrain, the whole rusting, friction-wearing shebang—as he ferried the Hunter up the wrong side of the street to the End of the World.

The heat building in the Bug's engine block as the pistons did their little up-and-down dance with the valves and rockers was reaching critical levels. It felt as if both engine and transmission would go molten and melt into a solid lump. He had little doubt this was his last drive.

The Bug had no complaints, though. He had always known he would go out with a bang. That it might be a Reverse Big Bang only made it more interesting. And somewhat made up for all the years he had spent in Oklahoma. So did driving on the wrong side of the street. Empty or not, it was surprisingly fun and satisfying.

He only wished this particular End of the World had opted to happen during daylight hours. It was hard to sight-see in the dark. The growing yellow ball of fire he was driving toward was hardly proper illumination. The yellow light made everything look ugly.

At the last instant, the Bug accelerated, then executed a tight emergency brake turn so he was facing back the way he had come, and so the passenger side door could pop open—to impressive dramatic effect—in front of the Yellow Sign Buffet.

It's time, man, the Bug told the Hunter, who was pretending he hadn't just squealed in fright. *Time to be the Hunter.*

Then the Bug let his engine seize.

1

His heart racing, his left hand braced against the dash, his feet pushing against the floorboard so his back was tight against the back of his seat through the squealing arc of the emergency brake turn, Marcus still almost fell out of the car when the passenger door opened.

The car lurched, its rear end popping up, as its engine seized and its transmission attempted to come through the firewall behind the back seat. Then the car settled on its shocks and went quiet.

"Louie?" Marcus asked. Reluctantly, he took his left hand off the dash, and used both hands to reseat the oversized sunglasses on his face. "You still with me?"

There was no response.

He leaned forward, putting his hands on the dash and listened, with his ears and his mind. He wanted to ask the car what "be the Hunter" meant.

"Louie?"

The glove box fell open, startling him, but there was no other response.

Marcus blinked, then sighed. If Louie was gone, Thara was going to kill him.

Assuming he survived. And she survived. And the World didn't End.

He looked deeper in the glove box, wondering if there was anything else—

The bulky bundle wrapped in canvas had a curved impression of what was wrapped inside. The shape reminded him of a tooth. He took out the bundle and unrolled it on his lap, exposing a collection of knives, blades inserted into pockets to protect them. The hilts of the knives were dark-stained wood, with three rivets each. The longest knife looked to be an eight-inch chef's knife. There were other knives of varying length and blade shape, but beyond the chef's knife and a paring knife, Marcus didn't know their names. Somehow, it seemed completely appropriate that Thara would have a collection of kitchen knives in the glove box of her car.

He quickly surveyed the rest of the glove box's contents, but nothing else seemed useful. He didn't need a map of Rio Cruces circa 1968 or a stack of long-expired insurance verification forms.

Marcus rerolled the bundle of knives and put it back in the glove box. When he tried to close the glove box, though, it popped open again. And again. He took out the bundle of knives and tried again. The glove box closed easily. And refused to open again when he pushed the button.

"Louie?"

There was still no response from the car.

Holding the bundle of knives in his left hand, he stepped out of the car onto the sidewalk. Louie's crazy turn had deposited him at the end of the sidewalk that led from the street to the darkened front door of the Yellow Sign Buffet.

The crowd that he and Louie had driven around was beginning to filter through the frozen streams of parked cars. Their eyes glowed yellow in pairs. None of them seemed to be looking at him. They were staring up, at the light, not even watching where they were going. Somehow, though, they never stumbled or placed a foot wrong, even when stepping off the curb into the street. They stepped around the front and rear fenders of cars without taking their eyes off the light.

Beyond the crowd, visible because of her bright eyes and her gold lame top, Morgan walked, still dragging the catchpole. The shuffling form of Jimmie the Wrangler was coming up behind her.

Marcus turned to face the restaurant again. He adjusted his leather jacket on his shoulders, then pulled on the cuffs on his sleeves. He started to put the knives away in the breast pocket of his jacket, but the wrapped bundle was too big. So he turned to toss the bundle back into the car. The car door closed on its own before he could.

"You could have just said 'here, take these.'"

Louie didn't respond.

Turning back to the restaurant, Marcus made sure the sunglasses were in place. He could see the huge yellow light that hovered overhead but he didn't look at it. He walked to the front door of the restaurant and pushed it open with his right hand.

Like the intact plate-glass windows, the dining room looked as if nothing had happened, as if the restaurant were merely closed for the night, waiting for the opening crew to show up and prepare for Sunday brunch. The silence in the dining room was complete, as if the World wasn't Ending only a few feet away. As if the dining room were in some other World, separate.

No lights were on. Even the old electric cash register was dark, its red digits extinguished. In spite of the darkness, Marcus didn't remove the sunglasses. He could see well enough to navigate.

He walked past the booth where he had been hired—where he had accepted the impossible job of dragon hunter and became the Hunter, whatever that meant—and across the front of the dining room. He turned right and walked toward the double doors that led to the back. The soda fountains and the soft serve machines were quiet.

Beyond the double doors, through the smudged round windows and around the edges of the doors, Marcus could see lights moving, white and yellow, but he could hear nothing.

He paused with his right hand on the double door.

"Be the Hunter," he said—not because he knew what it meant, but because everyone else had said it and maybe the meaning would become clear if he said.

No meaning came to him, clear or otherwise.

He shrugged and pushed through the doors.

2

THE DARKNESS AND SILENCE OF the dining room shattered and fell in hot, yellow shards around Marcus as he opened the double doors. In spite of the sunglasses, he brought up his left arm to shield his eyes. Yellow light thrummed and pushed on him from above. White fire roared and crackled. Smoke swirled, carrying heat and bits of ash, creating a haze. The doors swung closed behind him.

He had only glimpsed the prep area in the back of the restaurant before, so he didn't know what it was supposed to look like. He was pretty sure it had never looked like this.

He stood just inside the double doors. The floor extended about five feet before becoming a ledge of broken floor tiles. The ledge continued around an irregular oval pit that had swallowed the rear half of the restaurant. Broken pipes sprayed water in a glittering arc to splash on the tiles and spill over the edge into the pit. Standing on the lip of the ledge, evenly spaced around the circumference—even when that meant standing in the spraying water—were the uniformed employees of the Yellow Sign Buffet. None of the employees, not even the two men—or were they women?—closest to Marcus seemed to notice him. Their heads were bowed as they stared into the pit. Across the pit from him, he saw August Neuland and the other yellow-shirted manager. They ignored him too.

Admitting to himself that he was avoiding actually looking into the pit, in spite of the roaring and thrumming and crackling and thrashing that should have been drawing his attention, he focused on the nearest woman?—man?—employee?—

He stopped. Blinked. Then, with an effort of will he focused on the *person* to his right.

Never in his life had Marcus struggled so hard to determine the gender of a person standing only a few feet away. The shapeless uniform hung on the person's frame, creating an impression of ageless... lack of fitness. And uneven skin tone. Someone... of some age... getting... rounder? And, presumably, older?

His eyes refused to focus on the facial features beyond the obvious, probably human indicators of eyes, nose, mouth and hat hair. Anything that might have made the person distinct could not be discerned. Eye color would have been impossible to see under the thrumming yellow light, but the shape of a nose should have been obvious. As easy to see as... the nose?... in the middle of the... person's?... face?

Marcus's head hurt from the effort and his eyes watered. He blinked away the tears and turned to his left.

The same thing happened when he tried to focus on the person there. He was pretty sure it was a person, at least. What other options were there?

And again when he tried to focus on the next person in the line. And the next. And the next.

His eyes and focus slipped from one employee to the next around the edge of the pit until he found he was looking at August Neuland looking back at him.

Despite the distance between them, the man's incredibly detailed and specific face registered surprise for an instant, then the corners of his lips pulled up and he smiled. His lips moved, and Marcus saw him say, *Mr. Nelson.* Then the man gestured for Marcus to behold what was in the pit.

Marcus shook his head. He didn't want to. Some part of his mind, even without looking and confirming, knew it didn't want to know what was in the pit. Or what it might be doing.

August Neuland repeated his gesture of invitation. The man's expression seemed to be telling Marcus to behold what he had helped bring forth.

Marcus responded with an incline nod and still didn't look.

The man's lips moved. There was no way Marcus could have heard what the man said, but the words were clear.

Welcome to the End of the World!

August Neuland's smile became a grin, and he spread both hands, taking in the pit, the ruined restaurant, the yellow star over their heads, and the universe beyond.

Then the man looked down into the pit again. Something he saw there made him laugh.

Before Marcus could stop himself, he looked down, as well.

3

THE SCENE IN THE PIT slapped Marcus, hard, right across the face, and the mind.

He wanted to blink, but he wasn't allowed to. He couldn't even lift his arms or put his hands in front of his face to block the view. He felt his nose begin to bleed in a warm rush over his upper lip. He couldn't lift his hands to stanch the flow of blood, either.

The pressure of what he witnessed pushed against the lenses of the sunglasses and bent the frames. The temples of the sunglasses seemed to be trying to twist down and sheer off his ears. He wasn't sure which would happen first. Would the lenses pop out? Or his ears come off?

He didn't remember dropping the bundle of knives.

He didn't remember stepping up to the edge of the pit, where he fell to his knees and almost toppled in. He stared at—

Overcooked Cream-of-Wheat.

A particularly slimy pea salad from a church potluck.

"Pink stuff"—the bowl of whipped cream and Jell-O with bits of chopped fruit from that same potluck that had haunted his nightmares for days after he had recovered from the food poisoning.

Marcus remembered getting sick another time, after eating too much oily, salty popcorn at a movie—he could never remember the name of the movie, but it probably starred Will Smith; Mom Nelson was a huge Will Smith fan—he had vomited partially digested popcorn and Coca-Cola all over the tiny kitchen of their apartment. Heave after heave. Two more heaves as Mom Nelson hauled him by the back of his shirt through the small living room, down the short hall, and very nearly threw him at the toilet in the apartment's only bathroom. The last heave splashed all over the seat of the toilet, staining the seat cover.

"You are definitely cleaning this mess up your own self," Mom Nelson had said as he stared at the bits of chewed popcorn and stringy snot that hung from the toilet seat. "You know where the towels are."

It had taken him over an hour, and every clean towel in the apartment. Then another hour scrubbing the carpet and the toilet seat cover with disposable wipes.

None of that—bubbling grain cereal, whirled peas with chunks of cheese, pink stuff with tainted fruit, or popcorn vomit—described what he saw. Rather, they described what his mind felt like as it sloshed behind his eyes, trying to escape comprehension through any available orifice. All his mind seemed capable of at the moment was assuring him there weren't enough clean towels or disposable wipes in the world to clean this mess up.

His vision became yellow static. Yellow noise filled his ears while yellow smells and yellow tastes tried to suffocate him.

He wondered if he had fallen into the pit yet. He wondered if he would know. Would he feel the impact of hitting the bottom of the pit? His mind had put additional knowing past the current moment on a strictly-definite "maybe" status.

Somehow, he didn't fall in.

Slowly, painfully, his mind adjusted to the overloaded reality in front of him, aided—protected and slightly balmed—by the lenses of the sunglasses. As if he had rubbed on SPF 10 sunscreen on an SPF 30 kind of day and the sunburn wasn't as bad as it could have been. The tinted glass blunted the impact and allowed his optic nerves to do their jobs. Even if they didn't want to.

An impossibly huge silver dragon, twisting and writhing, wrestled with a gold dragon—Thara—that he had already come to grips with. Thara's presence gave him something to anchor on, something to compare the rest of the scene to. A sense of scale, so to speak—pun unavoidable in his current circumstances.

Claws slashed and scraped, sending up sparks but doing no damage that Marcus could see. White fire erupted from gaping maws lined with curved teeth ranging in size from karambits to scimitars. The fire washed over both dragons, doing as little damage as the claws. Thara's teeth might have been more effective, but clawed silver hands with long silver fingers held the teeth at bay. Despite first appearances, the two dragons didn't appear to be trying to kill each other—

No. That wasn't it. The smaller dragon—Thara—wasn't holding back. She was being held back. Her lethal intentions were being kept at bay by the much, much larger silver dragon.

One of the silver dragon's eyes swiveled around to look at Marcus. The gleam off the black orb as it *saw* him, and the word *HUNTER* that suddenly echoed in his head made his brain try to scamper away again. His mind had nowhere to go, unfortunately, and found itself forced to follow the gaze of the silver dragon's eye as it swiveled again and pointed him at the part of the scene in the pit Marcus realized he had been avoiding all along.

Lurking in the shadows at the far end of the pit, under the over-hanging edge of the floor, was a capital-n Nightmare forest of stabbing, articulated legs the length of telephone poles and tipped with black barbs the size of college biology textbooks. Bulbous, black eyes as big as disco balls but as smooth as oil slicks that swallowed more light than they could possibly see watched the dragons fight. Marcus was sure he would have lost his last, tenuous hold on sanity if the Nightmare had been looking at him. Unfortunately, that left him sane enough to see the salivating man-dibles dripping and clicking. And the splashing, sizzling spittle that flew in drops as large as Marcus's hands and created craters the size of his head in the blackened concrete floor.

Beyond the capital-n Nightmare, in the murkier shadows behind it, additional nightmares squirmed, smaller, but equally horrific. A bucket of nightmare crabs clicking and pulling and grabbing and getting in each other's way as they tried to claw and crawl past the Nightmare and into the yellow light.

The silver dragon had its back to the Nightmare, using its wings to keep the Nightmare and its miniature nightmares at bay. The huge wings buffeted the stabbing, clicking, salivating darkness back as it tried to reach past and grab Thara. For her part, Thara was not making that easy.

HUNTER.

The word shook Marcus's brain inside his skull again, contributing to the continued liquefaction of his gray matter. Marcus's eyes bulged in their sockets from the pressure of the word, and from his eyes' increas-ingly desperate attempts to escape and stop seeing what they were seeing. His eyes fled the Nightmare held in check and locked again on the nearest eye of the silver dragon. The dragon's mouth had not moved beyond spewing another dribble of white fire across Thara's golden scales, but both Marcus's jostled brain and his near-bursting eyes agreed that the word had come from the silver dragon.

YOU ARE THE—

The silver dragon's words were cut off, as Thara suddenly threw herself in a new direction, pulling the silver dragon with her, and bringing the silver dragon's sinuous neck within striking distance of her jaws. She struck.

Her teeth struck sparks off themselves, upper against lower, as her jaw came together on empty air mere inches from the silver scales of the other dragon's neck. The silver dragon's neck had curved and pulled away from her just in time.

—HUNTER. BE—

The Nightmare lunged closer, taking advantage of the distraction, skirting along the wall of the pit to Marcus's right.

With a roar, the silver dragon forced itself between the Nightmare and Thara again, wrapping her in his wings. The Nightmare came over the silver dragon's back, legs and claws stabbing, seeking weakness, grabbing for Thara.

Marcus fell backward, away from the lip of the pit and its roiling, hungry Nightmare darkness. He scrambled away until his back hit the double doors. The doors no longer swung. They held him there, refusing to let him escape. Across the boiling blackness of the pit, he saw August Neuland standing with arms upraised again, smiling, laughing.

The head of the Nightmare rose into view, black hole eyes sucking in the yellow light, mandibles gaping and dripping. Only the combination of the sunglasses still on his face and that the Nightmare's eyes weren't looking at him prevented Marcus from shitting his pants in fear. The Nightmare's mandibles somehow opened even wider, dripping viscous slime. Then the head disappeared as it struck down.

The silver dragon roared, this time in pain, and Marcus could feel the creature's pain. He could feel the mandibles of the Nightmare on the back of his own neck, just above where his wings would have been, and feel the stabbing pain as the proboscis penetrated his skin—

BE THE HUNTER!

The force of the words knocked Marcus back hard enough that he bounced off the double doors and landed on his hands and knees on the broken floor tiles.

Between his hands, on the floor in front of his face, was the canvas-wrapped bundle of chef knives he had brought with him, and dropped at some point in the distant past, when the universe had only been a little mixed up and he was pretty sure he had still been sane. The universe—and his mind and maybe the rest of him—had become a lot more fucked up since then. The bundle of knives, though, gave him something to focus on. Something that almost made sense.

Within inches of his right hand, a black handle protruded from the bundle, one of the knives knocked loose when he dropped the bundle.

"Be the hunter," he said—or thought he said, since he couldn't hear his voice over the noise—and grabbed the knife.

He pushed himself to his knees wondering how the hell he thought he was going to help the silver dragon save Thara with a kitchen knife, but he would do what he could. Maybe he could be a distraction, to get the Nightmare to release its bite on the silver dragon's neck, or—

He stared at the knife in his hand. The straight blade was double edged and pointed, but only about three inches long. An oyster knife.

He dropped the oyster knife and bent over to retrieve the bundle of knives. He knew there was a longer knife in there.

The double doors behind him burst open, knocking him forward. Or maybe someone came through the door and pushed him from behind, hard. At this point, either possibility seemed as likely as the other.

As he rolled over to see what—or who—had hit him, a golden, spike-heeled shoe came down on his chest and pressed him to the floor. He couldn't see her face, only her eyes, glowing in the silhouette created by the yellow light that blazed over her head, but he would know Morgan's shape anywhere. As an additional clue, though, the catchpole still trailed behind her, the tail end preventing the double doors from closing fully.

"You should be more careful, Baby Boy," Morgan said, her voice somehow piercing the din. As she spoke, she pressed down on his sternum with the sharp heel of her shoe. "You are the Hunter. You could hurt someone with that thing."

Marcus grabbed Morgan's ankle with both hands to relieve the pressure. Her ankle and calf felt as strong and silky as always, but pushing on her leg felt like trying to push an ornate, cast-iron streetlamp. As if to prove the point, Morgan smiled, shifted the pressure from heel to toe, and pushed down just a bit harder.

"Morgan," he wheezed, then stopped talking, before he lost all the air in his lungs.

He felt the bundle of kitchen knives beneath him, between his shoulder blades, helping Morgan achieve the rock-and-a-hard-place effect slowly overcoming him.

In the pit beyond his head, he heard the silver dragon moan, then felt its convulsion as it succumbed to the Nightmare's poison and collapsed.

Thara's victory roar and geyser of white flame were choked off as the double doors behind Morgan swung open, pushed by a man and a woman in matching brown turtleneck shirts, pulling Jimmie the Wrangler between them. The old man's ball cap had been knocked off, and his white hair was a wispy, windblown fog around his head. He saw Marcus on the ground.

"About what I figured," Jimmie said in the sudden near-silence, nodding once. "Probably."

Before Marcus could protest that Morgan had surprised him—that she had attacked from behind—Jimmie looked past him, into the pit. If the sight of the Nightmare holding up a wriggling, snarling gold dragon disturbed the old man in any way, the expression on his face told Marcus nothing.

"I guess this is the End," Jimmie said. He didn't nod this time, just glanced around and shrugged. "About what I figured."

4

THE *IT* HAD CRAB-LIKE PINCERS on the end of *Its* legs. One pincer gripped Thara's neck, just below her head, as if the creature were considering beheading her. Two more claws gripped her torso, just below her front legs and just above her back legs. The last claw gripped her tail.

Thara had always wondered if she had the salamander-like ability to grow back severed limbs or a severed tail. She was pretty sure, though, even salamanders couldn't regrow heads.

She struggled against the creature as it held her aloft and retreated backward to the shadows It had come from. All her anger at the silver dragon she now focused on the *It*. For all the good it did. Again. Her claws proved no more effective against the chitinous outer shell of the creature's legs as they had against the silver dragon's scales. She was beginning to wonder what good hooked, golden claws were if she couldn't claw anything. She couldn't bring her teeth to bear, and her tail was only whipping uselessly back and forth or wrapped around the leg of the claw that held it.

She wasn't adjusting well to *not* being the biggest, baddest predator on the planet, which she had previously thought she was, starting about age thirty in the late 1970s when she was finally larger than the alligators and crocodiles at the Rio Cruces Municipal Zoo.

She decided to call it a victory that the *It* was no longer biting the silver dragon on the neck and had instead grabbed her. There. She had saved the silver dragon. She would tease him about that later, when this weird-as-shit, End-of-the-World, *It* business was over. Assuming there was a later.

The silver dragon lay in a heap against the wall of the pit, silver blood leaking from the wound on his neck to mingle with the puddles of slime still burning holes in the concrete floor. The sight made her wonder if her dragon blood was gold. Her human blood, which she saw about four times a year, seemed red, normal. She had never seen her blood as a dragon, though. She had drawn blood as a dragon more than a few times, but she had never met anything with the tools to pierce her skin and show her her blood. Until now, it seemed.

She took in a breath to roar fire into the mandible-clicking, slime-dripping face of the *It*. She knew her fire wouldn't hurt *It*, but she wanted *It* to know how she really felt. Unfortunately, she only managed a hot gasp-choke, leaving her mouth open, before the pincer on her neck tightened.

The spray of so-called Seasoning hit her in the face like sewer water from a pressure hose, driving the liquid up her nostrils and down her throat—which was suddenly unsqueezed. The force of the spray kept her mouth from closing, and when she turned her head to her left, then her right, the dangling, looping, intestinal hose followed her, a spiteful, vindictive fire hose of ick. She couldn't raise her foreclaws high enough to do more than scatter the spray some. Even when she twisted her neck all the way around so she was facing away from the *It*, *It*'s gaping sphincter was waiting for her. She couldn't help but swallow. The Seasoning forced its way down her throat, muscled its way past her gag reflex, and splashed into her stomach.

Through the spray and the nausea and the increasingly desperate need to breathe, she saw Marcus laying on the broken tiles of what was left of the floor of the prep area, his catchpole-wearing girlfriend standing over him with one foot on his chest. A small knife lay on the floor next to him, but he had both hands on the girlfriend's leg, failing to lift her foot off his chest. She wondered what had made him think an oyster knife would come in handy at the End of the World. It was almost funny. She would have laughed, but she couldn't even breathe.

Then she saw Jimmie the Wrangler held by indistinguishable Yellow Sign Buffet customer bookends and nothing was funny anymore. If they had captured Jimmie the Wrangler, maybe the World was going to End after all. Probably.

5

MARCUS TRIED NOT TO TASTE the drops of whatever-it-was the Nightmare was spraying from Its he-didn't-want-to-know that splashed on his face. He felt fortunate that he lay on his back with his head toward the pit and none of the he-tried-to-think-of-it-as-fish-sauce went up his nose.

Marcus still held Morgan's ankle and pushed up against the downward force she was applying to his chest. He didn't seem to be making any difference, but he didn't want to let go and find out how much harder she could be pressing down.

"Morgan," he managed to wheeze without actually exhaling. "Please."

She didn't respond.

Blinking against the stinging mist droplets, he looked up Morgan's leg, past her bunched-up skirt and the tight gold fabric covering her breasts to her face. She was still in silhouette, so he couldn't see her face. Only her eyes. But he could make out she was no longer looking down at him. She watched, enraptured, as Thara twisted and squirmed, held in the air above the pit by the Nightmare.

Marcus tightened his grip on her ankle and pushed harder—

And continued to have as little effect as before.

He no longer wondered that Jimmie the Wrangler had failed to stop her from walking back to the restaurant. He began to wonder how he had managed to pick her up earlier and carry her around on his shoulder. In the intervening minutes she had become as strong as iron, and just as unyielding.

"Be still, Hunter, and enjoy the view," Morgan said. Her toe lifted and tapped on his chest for emphasis. "Or I will sting you again and send you back to your place among the stars."

She smiled as she spoke, but she didn't look at him. Her voice had changed, picking up the cold edge of iron, as well.

He wanted to ask her what that meant, beyond the obvious, but he had no extra breath left for anything as frivolous as trying to talk. He was curious, though. More curious than he expected, considering his current circumstances.

You are the Hunter, she had said before, when she first put her foot on him. *You could hurt someone with that thing.*

Your place among the stars...

Marcus looked past Morgan's face, then past the new yellow star that hung in the night sky right above them. His sunglasses let him see the edges of the star, then past the star, to see the sky beyond. The yellow star had washed away most of the real stars in a flood of light pollution, but three stars, forming a line, were still visible.

Once he had seen those stars, his eyes adjusted further and he began to pick out more, until he could see the other four stars that made up the bow tie constellation of Orion. He tried to remember the names of the stars, but all he could think of was a smirking ghost in a striped suit and a snarling woman with a mound of a black hair and a wand. It wasn't the individual stars that mattered, though, it was what the stars signified.

Orion. The Hunter.

Then he was able to see the small line of stars and the nebula that made up Orion's dagger and he remembered the oyster knife he had dropped. The pitiful thing was probably still on the floor near him. He was lucky he hadn't fallen on it and stabbed himself on its tiny blade—

You could hurt someone with that thing.

He tried to remember the story of Orion the Hunter. Beyond the part about being killed by a scorpion and turned into a constellation. Unfortunately, he couldn't recall anything about the Hunter having ninja-like hand-to-hand combat skills. Being the Hunter, whatever else it might mean, didn't seem to include being able to stop End-of-the-World-possessed girlfriends from standing on his chest.

The spray stopped, but Marcus continued to resist the urge to lick his lips. Thara stopped gargling and sputtering and began coughing and spitting, which caused a new spray and convinced Marcus he had made the right choice about not licking his lips.

Morgan let out a very un-Morgan-like cheer that was echoed first by the indistinguishable employees around the edge of the pit, then by hundreds of voices beyond the broken walls. The cheer had no words. It was only a shout that continued longer than a shout should, and got steadily louder. Like a roaring heavy-metal singer with no regard for the future use of his vocal chords. It made Marcus's ears hurt. And his throat.

Thara stopped coughing and seemed to be about to say something. Then the spray started again and she could say nothing. Just gargle and spew.

Morgan shifted her weight as she watched Thara twist and squirm, easing the pressure on his chest, though only slightly. The handles of multiple knives beneath Marcus still dug into his back, reminding him of how close they were, and how far out of reach. Except, maybe, the oyster knife. That couldn't have fallen too far away. If he could find that and grab it, he could stab Morgan in the leg—

No. He wasn't going to stab Morgan. In the leg or anywhere else.

But he needed to get out from under her spike-heeled shoe.

He shifted his right hand first, as quickly as he could, so he was gripping the six-inch heel. Then he moved his left hand, wrapping it around the sole of the shoe and her foot. Like his hands, the shoe was wet and hard to grip.

Above him, Morgan stopped shouting-cheering and looked down. He couldn't see the frown he knew was pulling at the corners of her mouth. He felt her weight shift, and she began to press down harder. After taking as deep a breath as he could manage without puncturing his abdomen, he pushed with his right hand and pulled with his left.

The spike heel tore free of the sole of the shoe and dragged painfully across his abdominal muscles—

Morgan's toe hit him under the chin, distracting him from the stinging pain of his abs. He couldn't be sure if she had kicked him on purpose, or if it was his own fault for pulling on her foot. Intentional kick or not, her knee buckled, she lost her balance and fell. He barely had time to roll to his left.

She landed on his hip, hard, taking his hip bone in the flesh of her glutes, then she fell off to his right as the impact pushed him away. The catchpole clattered on the tiles as she rolled.

His right hand came down on the hilt of the oyster knife, but since he still held the heel of Morgan's shoe in a death grip, he couldn't grab the knife in the two seconds he had to scramble to his feet on the slick tiles before Morgan could grab him with stiff, curled fingers.

Hands from behind grabbed his arms and pulled him to his feet. The turtlenecked couple who had been holding Jimmie the Wrangler had stepped forward to grab him.

Marcus jerked his right arm free of the woman in the turtleneck and she stumbled backward and away. Her partner in the matching turtleneck, unfortunately, had a better grip, and stood behind him. Marcus flipped the spike heel over in his hand, so he gripped the wide end and the narrow end extended two inches from his fist. He twisted in the man's grip, then jabbed fist and heel at the man's solar plexus. The man grunted and Marcus was able to free his left arm.

Neither move was in any way ninja-like, so Marcus had no idea if he was properly "being the Hunter," but at least he was on his feet and unencumbered—

Jimmie the Wrangler stepped in front Marcus and delivered a short, powerful jab to the turtleneck man's jaw, right on the joint. Turtleneck man's head jerked. His eyes barely had time to get wide with surprise before he crumpled.

Likewise, Marcus barely had time to feel inadequate before the woman he had shaken off jumped on his back and wrapped her right arm around his throat. He staggered and ran into Jimmie from behind. The three of them stumbled, almost tripping over the catchpole that swung back and forth as Morgan freed herself from the loop of rope.

Marcus couldn't shrug the woman off his shoulders as she had her legs wrapped around his torso and both arms high around his neck. He dropped the broken heel and grabbed her forearms with both hands to pry them off his neck. The woman squeezed tighter, threatening his larynx.

He felt Jimmie's hands grab the woman's waist before he fully realized the man had moved behind him. Jimmie the Wrangler could be very quick for someone his age. Then Marcus had to focus on not falling backward—and not having his head pulled off his neck—as Jimmie yanked the woman away.

He managed to brace himself and keep his feet. He touched his neck, wincing. The fingernails of the woman's right hand had dug furrows in the skin of his neck.

He stood there, panting, his left hand on his neck, feeling the warm sticky blood from the parallel scratches, and his right hand feeling oddly empty. He was facing the pit. Somehow, he still had the sunglasses on, so the sight of the Nightmare holding Thara aloft and spraying her in the mouth as she struggled didn't overwhelm him in the few seconds it took his eyes to slide off the Nightmare and focus on Thara.

Morgan had regained her feet and stood unevenly on the edge of the pit. She was off balance from her broken shoe and standing half on tiptoes. He could see her face now. Her frown and her glowing yellow eyes looked unpleasant. Unfriendly. But she didn't come at him. Instead, she reached her hands to either side. The uniformed employees who also stood on the edge of the pit turned around then. They looked at Morgan, then at him.

"Go!" Jimmie the Wrangler said from behind him, just before the old man put something in his right hand.

Marcus looked down and saw Jimmie had given him the oyster knife.

"You couldn't have grabbed a bigger one?"

"Size don't matter," Jimmie said. "Probably."

Marcus wanted to say it mattered sometimes. He wanted to ask what he was supposed to do with a tiny knife against a Nightmare the size of a landmark. Before he could say or ask anything, though, Jimmie had pushed him forward, toward the edge of the pit.

"Be the Hunter," Jimmie shouted after him, as he stumbled between Morgan and a Yellow Sign Buffet employee as they tried to join hands.

The hands grabbed him, so he teetered on the edge of the pit. Their hands and his arm, though, were slick from the Nightmare's spray, and they couldn't hold him. He fell into the pit.

6

MARCUS LANDED ON THE PRONE form of the silver dragon. The taut but giving surface of the leathery wing broke his fall and prevented him from breaking his neck. Somehow he managed to hold onto the oyster knife—and stab neither himself nor the big dragon—when he landed and rolled and slid down and off the wing. The silver hide of the dragon seemed to have lost its luster, and begun to tarnish. The dragon hadn't moved, even when he fell on it. He wondered if the beast was dead.

The spray from the Nightmare fell like rain in the pit and soaked him further. There was no way he couldn't taste it now. He could feel himself marinating. Become moister and tastier. Perfect for raw consumption.

He shook his head to clear it and pushed himself to his feet. He looked up at Thara. The sunglasses protected his eyes from the spray, but the drops on the lenses made it hard to see. Which he was OK with. Not being able to see clearly had never seemed such an attractive worldview.

He looked up to the edge of the pit where he had been standing a few seconds before. Morgan had regained her feet and stood at six o'clock to August Neuland's twelve o'clock. The indistinguishable employees in their nondescript uniforms stood at regular intervals around the edge. Jimmie the Wrangler wasn't visible, neither standing on the ledge, nor did he seem to have been pushed into the pit with Marcus. As Marcus watched, more people arrived to stand around the pit. They perched on the brink, staring down at him or up at Thara with their glowing, yellow eyes. The spray soaked them as much as Thara. They didn't seem to care.

Marcus pulled his eyes from the people not helping him, to take in the enormity of what he stood on the edge of. He had no idea what he was supposed to do now that he was in the pit. A single man, armed with an oyster knife, alone in a pit with two dragons and a Nightmare. "Be the Hunter" hardly seemed adequate instruction—

A smaller version of the Nightmare—merely a nightmare—only the size of a small car, like Louie or Howie or Nova, with oily black eyes and claws—leaped from behind the dark forest and coils of the true Nightmare and skittered toward Marcus. The nightmare held up its forelegs, displaying pincers the size of dinner plates. Its mandibles clicked together in time with the stabbing, scrabbling footsteps. The black eyes gleamed, unblinking.

Be the Hunter, my black ass, was all his mind offered as his overwhelmed nervous system gave up considering all the horrible ways he was about to die and he stood there, watching the creature come at him.

The hard ridge of a silver wing hit him from behind and swept his legs from under him and swept him out of the path of the smaller nightmare just before it pounced on the spot he had been standing in. The wing carried him in an arc toward the pit wall.

Marcus rolled backward over the surface of the wing, away from the point of impact with the wall. He rolled onto the soot-blackened, spray-drenched concrete of the pit floor just before the wing hit the wall with a bone crushing thud. He saw the nearest eye of the silver dragon close as he got to his feet. The dragon shook its massive head just enough to express disappointment. Then the dragon's wing relaxed and the dragon stopped moving.

Then the smaller nightmare had spun and was running at Marcus again.

Marcus still had no idea what he was supposed to do, but he was no longer frozen in fear. He had only a brief instant to wonder whether that had been the silver dragon's plan, then he tightened his grip on the oyster knife and crouched. He hoped he at least *looked* as if he knew what he was doing.

As it had done before, the smaller nightmare leaped at him.

Marcus rolled forward, under the creature. The barbed ends of the creature's legs brushed him as it arced over him. He came out of the roll sloppily, slipping on the slick floor, but he managed to turn around before the creature did. He leaped on the creature's back. With his left hand, he gripped a ridge created by two overlapping chitinous plates. He stabbed with his right hand, half-aiming for a similar gap between another two plates while hoping that was actually a weak point.

The three-inch blade of the oyster knife disappeared into the black body of the creature, as did his hand, and his arm up to the elbow. It would seem he had found a weak point.

The creature gurgle-screamed, spewing slime that hissed and burned new craters into the concrete of the pit floor.

Marcus screamed and pulled his arm free. He let go and slid off the back of the creature as it ran away squealing in pain. He again—somehow—managed to hold onto the knife as he rolled, ass over grimace, envisioning his right forearm being dissolved into red-black goo—

He came to rest on his back, his right arm held over him, his right fist still gripping the oyster knife. His arm felt hot, but that was all. His skin didn't seem to be melting, nor was his flesh dissolving. Brown ichor dripped from the blade, and from his elbow.

He heard more screaming, then crunching. He turned just in time to see the silver dragon, head lifted, neck bulging and extended, swallowing the injured nightmare. Whole. The silver dragon's eyes opened. Silver light blazed in the huge eyes as if the dragon's internal flame had just been rekindled.

The Nightmare above them screamed and Its scream broke the air and shook the ground.

Thara's golden dragon body fell, writhing and roaring, to the pit floor much too close for comfort, especially since she was coughing and gagging splotchy, marinated fire. Marcus rolled away from her reflexively. Then everything went silver-dark, as the huge wing that had saved him twice already, saved him a third time by slamming down on top of him and pinning him to the floor and very nearly crushing his skull.

He felt and smelled the viscous fluid retched and sprayed by the screaming Nightmare as it gushed and flowed over the wing. He smelled burning, boiling concrete and, for some reason, a hint of fried chicken. He pulled himself into the smallest possible fetal position under the wing, just in case a hand or foot might be too close to the edge. Then he focused all his energy on not screaming again as the lava-like avalanche of caustic goo continued.

Be the Hunter. The words bounced around inside his skull. *Be the Hunter.*

7

THARA CAUGHT ONLY THE TAIL end—literally—of the silver dragon wolfing down the smaller it that Marcus had—somehow—stabbed. Both sights—stabbing and swallowing—aroused confused feelings of elation and frustration and jealousy.

Elation because the silver dragon was still alive. Frustration and jealousy because not only was she too small to duplicate the silver dragon's culinary feat—her mouth was too small, her throat too narrow—but she had no idea how Marcus had been able to hurt one of the creatures. Whatever the creatures were—roach-toad or spider-chicken or weevil-salamander—they had, so far, proven impervious to her fire and her claws. Were her claws too big? She preferred to think Marcus had been lucky—

Then she was falling. All four claws of the *It* had released her. *Its* spraying-thing had stopped spraying her in the face and the mouth. And *Its* huge mandibles had stopped slavering and click-clacking and splattering spittle everywhere.

There was still a lot of spittle, though. The mandibles opened wide enough to swallow Thara whole, then erupted. A volcanic, spittle-infused scream hit Thara in the face, stunning her so she made no attempt to get her feet under her. She landed hard enough to knock her breath out in a soggy burst of flame.

She twisted and scrambled back to her feet, coughing, as the silver dragon moved to cover the prone form of Marcus with a wing.

She took in a breath to spew pointless white fire at the *It* just as *It* stopped screaming and started vomiting.

This was no marinating high-pressure spray. This was the *It* emptying *Itself* of digestive juices. Turning *Itself* inside out.

Thara's scales protected most of her, including her eyes once she had shut them, but there were no scales lining her nostrils or coating her mouth. Foul-smelling and worse-tasting bile burn her nasal passages before she could squeeze them closed. The fork of her tongue and the inside of her cheeks burned from the initial onslaught of the viscous liquid, before her own fire had burned the liquid away and she was able to close her mouth.

With her eyes closed, she had no idea what the hot, wet, pliable thing was that struck her face and wrapped itself around her like a blanket, covering her from her nose down past her shoulders. She decided she didn't want to know, and that she could probably hold her breath as long as it took—

The hot, wet, pliable thing stiffened and *pulled* and yanked Thara off her feet and into the belly of the *It*, swallowing her in one gulp, almost exactly like the silver dragon had done to the smaller it.

Thara wasn't sure she could hold her breath *that* long.

10. Dragon Links

The Queen

THE QUEEN CONSUMED THE FINAL Ingredient all by Herself.

Her remaining Sister-Daughters immediately protested.

The Queen promised Her Sister-Daughters that She would share. In a minute. The Queen was Busy. Digesting.

The Only

THE ONLY COULD NOT BELIEVE he had just intervened to save the life of the latest incarnation of the Hunter for a second time. Granted, the Hunter had lured one of the baby goddesses from the protection of the Goddess, then wounded the baby goddess sufficiently for the Only to eat it and regain at least some of his strength. But that had probably only prolonged the inevitable.

Because the Only had not only just saved the latest incarnation of the Hunter, he had also—at the same time—allowed the Child to be consumed, thus triggering the End of the World.

The Only hated prophecy. Even when the prophecies didn't mention him, by name or inference, they got him involved.

And Fate. The Only *really* hated Fate.

If he had known he was going to trigger the End of the World anyway, no matter what he did, he would have stayed away, licking his emotional wounds. Hell, he would have stayed asleep on his mountaintop, wrapped in his blanket of snow, kept company by an ever-increasing number of dead mountain climbers and their cleated boots.

He hoped the Child was happy. She had totally ruined his life. And gotten herself eaten. And kicked off the End of the World.

The Only hoped the World finished Ending before the Sun came up and could see what had happened.

The Bug

THE BUG WONDERED IF HE might get one last tow before the World Ended.

He doubted it. World's might take a long time to get *started* Ending, but once started, they tended to just go for it.

That had been his experience, anyway.

The Bug hoped the Second Ugly Replacement wasn't too scared. Maybe she should have come along, then neither of them would have been alone at the End. No help for it now.

It would all be over soon.

1

THARA THRASHED AROUND INSIDE THE tight-and-growing-tighter space of the *Its* stomach. She felt her claws, left, right, front, back, sliding ineffectually over the slick—and apparently indestructible—stomach lining. She could feel only the slightest resistance to her attempts to rip and tear, as if she might be leaving scratch marks in the lining, but little else. She couldn't open her eyes to see, though, because she liked her eyes and wanted to keep them.

She was no longer sure which way was up, or down. She wasn't sure it was all that important at the moment.

Where her eyelids came together, she could feel the acid burn of digestive juices. Her inner eyelids would prevent any real damage. At least for as long as she could hold her breath. Which would probably be longer if she would stop thrashing around.

Except she could feel the same burn in her nostrils, and her lips.

Which way would she drown and die? Would the *Its* stomach acids of doom burn their way through her defenses? Or would she eventually have to take a breath and die from inhaling those same acids?

She didn't want to find out. So she continued thrashing about and hoped she might—eventually at least—cause the *It* an ulcer. She didn't seem to be digesting all that fast. Maybe she could outlast the stomach lining.

The first impact hit her lower back. Something hard, with rough edges.

The second impact hit the same place, but heavier, and harder, and with a lot more rough edges. And a lot more pain. The blow almost made her gasp, but she managed to hold it in and not swallow stomach acid and die.

There was a third impact, but it was blunted by whatever had hit her the first two times.

She couldn't see what had hit her, but it felt like a wall. Or part of a wall.

Had *It* started consuming the World already? Or just the cinder block walls and concrete foundation of the restaurant?

More impacts shifted her position, twisting her around under pressure. The stomach had become considerably more crowded in a matter of seconds. Her claws still reached the stomach lining, but she had no room to move her legs. Her tail could only twitch.

Jagged bits of concrete ground against her, like cracked molars. She could feel the stomach acids already wearing down the edges of the debris, but the debris itself was also beginning to wear her down.

It had swallowed her whole, without chewing. The chewing had begun.

2

As soon as the huge silver wing lifted away, Marcus scrambled to his feet. He amazed himself by still having the oyster knife in his grip—and again when he realized he hadn't cut himself with it in spite of all the falling, landing, and jumping.

He crouched and looked around to better inform himself of which way he should start running should the need arise again. He stood on a patch of smooth concrete foundation surrounded by a steaming swamp of pitted, acid-washed gray. In some places the concrete had been eaten away, revealing rusting rebar and black earth.

There was no sign of Thara. She had just... disappeared. The Nightmare had reared back and away, but a quick glance up told Marcus the Nightmare hadn't picked up Thara again. At least, not with its claws. Had the Nightmare stuffed Thara, whole, into Its mouth?

The silver dragon had backed itself into a corner of the pit, facing the Nightmare. The dragon stood on all four legs with its neck held high. The dragon's wings extended in either direction, almost lining the walls. The dragon held its left wing lower than the other, the wound on its neck limiting the range of motion, but it seemed to have recovered enough to look nearly as menacing as before.

Marcus felt exposed. Being the Hunter was sucking more every second.

He didn't want to run across the still-steaming gray sludge, but he also didn't want to be standing this close to the Nightmare. Or between the Nightmare and the dragon. He ran toward the dragon.

Marcus aimed for the bare bit of floor between the dragon's feet, and hoped the soles of his shoes would hold up better than the concrete.

The Nightmare's stomach acid seemed to have oxidized itself into complacency. Mostly. His shoes survived long enough for him to reach his goal. As he grabbed the thick leg of the silver dragon to steady himself, he could feel the cool, smooth concrete he stood on with his toes. He looked down. From this angle, his shoes just looked muddy. He picked up his right foot and saw that though the rubber heel was mostly intact, the leather soles were as thin as newspaper, as if he had spent the last five months walking to his job interviews. He couldn't see his foot, but he could see his toes wriggling inside.

The silver dragon flexed its leg, forcing him to let go and stand on his own. He looked up to see the silver dragon's truck-sized face almost nose to nose with him.

The Hunter does not usually run from his quarry.

The dragon's lips separated as the words hammered their way into his brain. No sound came from the dragon, though. Just wisps of sulfurous steam.

Marcus impressed himself by not jerking back and cowering further under the dragon's torso.

"What quarry?" He also wanted to ask what he was supposed to do against the Nightmare when it had already kicked the scaly asses of two dragons, present company included, both bigger than him and better armed.

The earth shook before he could ask the additional questions and before the silver dragon could respond to the one he had asked.

Marcus fell into a crouch again, brandishing his unimpressive oyster knife and wondered if he would survive long enough to tease the big, bad dragon for flinching. The dragon's face twisted away and he and the dragon watched as the Nightmare slammed itself face down—for the second time—and scooped up an excavator-sized pile of rubble. Then tilt itself back to swallow the broken, acid-pitted bits of concrete and rebar.

Marcus could see the rubble distending the Nightmare's torso from the inside. Then he saw an impression of a five-pointed claw press out between the distensions of the rubble.

"Thara!"

The Nightmare bent over for a third helping of concrete, this time scooping it from the wall of the pit nearest it.

Save the Child, Hunter.

The words boomed in his head at the same time as the dragon's leg next to him bent and a claw the size of Mom Nelson's apartment grabbed him and flung him at the bulging torso of the Nightmare.

3

MARCUS FLIPPED OVER ONCE THEN slammed in a vertical belly flop against the bulging, brown-black torso of the Nightmare. His left hand slipped, finding nothing to grab on the smooth, hard surface, but his right hand embedded itself up to his wrist and kept him from sliding down the lumpy front of the creature. He dangled from his right hand as his left hand and both feet tried to find purchase. Above him, the creature reared back to swallow its latest mouthful of rubble.

The surface of the Nightmare bulged against his legs and steadied him. Previously swallowed bits of concrete foundation were pressed outward by the newly swallowed bits of wall. Or maybe pushed toward him by Thara, still thrashing around on the other side of the stomach wall.

Behind him, the silver dragon roared and white fire sprayed. Marcus braced himself for incineration, but the fire hit the head of the Nightmare, yards above him. Still close enough, though, that the heat washed over him and he worried about his exposed skin. And his clothes. And the rest of him.

Steadying himself against the Nightmare's—abdomen? thorax? he had no idea; his Computer Information Systems degree had included no life sciences requirements—he pulled his right hand free. There was a sucking sound, then a small gout of the same brown ichor that had covered his arm after stabbing the smaller nightmare. He teetered on the still-shifting ledge, then thrust his hand forward again, going deeper this time—

Deeper?

He felt the short blade of the knife penetrate layers of what he somehow, in spite of his woeful lack of advanced biology classes knew were muscle, subcutaneous tissue, and... fascia? He felt the tiniest triangle of the blade's tip prick against what had to be the Nightmare's stomach before he jerked his arm back.

He panted and hugged the surging, bulging belly of the Nightmare as best he could as the Nightmare thrashed about and clawed at the silver dragon. The Nightmare screamed—audibly and mentally. Unintelligible sounds backed by graphically violent images of what the Nightmare intended to do to the silver dragon washed over him. He held tight and considered his options.

The brown ichor coating his hand and forearm didn't seem to be acidic or especially deadly—though it smelled like fecal-coated death rot. But he had already witnessed what the Nightmare's stomach acid could do to concrete. He had no urge to see what it would do to his arm. Or the rest of him.

Except if he didn't, Thara—golden dragon and impossibly old twenty-something white-girl—was going to die. Then the World would end. Or End. One of those.

Neither of those options, capitalized or fully lowercase, seemed good—

With another roar—no fire this time, but with breath hot enough to chap skin—the silver dragon interrupted Marcus's thoughts. The same silver claw that had thrown Marcus at the Nightmare hit him from behind and closed around him again. Five silver claws as big as backhoe scoops, one to his left, the other four on his right, scraped along the smooth hide of the Nightmare, doing no damage at all. The tip of one claw snagged on the small knife wound Marcus had made and tore a short section, but that was it. Then the claws were sliding under Marcus and pulling him away from the Nightmare. Marcus's first thought was to scream and try to get away. Then he realized his best option at the moment was probably to just go with it. He and the silver dragon were, presumably, even demonstrably, on the same side. At least to a point.

The claw jerked Marcus back, then tried to snap his spine as it shifted its grip on him and flicked his right arm out. Before he could ask what the hell was going on, the claw thrust him toward the Nightmare again. Headfirst, arm extended.

His left hand came up, joining his dragon-extended right hand more in surprise and borderline panic than any real attempt to save himself. His hands struck the Nightmare, hard. The impact stung his left palm and jolted his left elbow and threatened to dislocate his left shoulder, but his right hand, still holding the oyster knife, plunged into the belly of the Nightmare up to his shoulder. It might have gone further but his face stopped his forward momentum.

Bright lights lit up the back of his eyelids and red pain erupted from his nose as it broke.

The Nightmare's body shook, an earthquake of obscene pudding, like the pink stuff at the potluck dinner, but brown, and with chunks of concrete instead of rotten fruit.

Marcus felt the grip of the silver dragon's claw shift again and knew the silver dragon was about to pull him back and stab him forward again.

Then he felt the four front claws of the Nightmare grab the silver dragon.

The silver dragon released him, leaving Marcus dangling again.

Brown ichor burst from the wound, spraying him in the face and drenching him. The skin of the Nightmare became too slick for his feet to get a grip. He twisted the knife around with his wrist, hoping it would catch on something. But the blade moved with no resistance. Pressure inside the wound began to force his arm out.

He wanted to ask—someone, anyone—why the oyster knife was able to cut the Nightmare's skin while the silver dragon's huge and obviously sharp claws wouldn't even leave a red mark, but there was no time—or breath—for questions. Or anyone to ask. His arm had already been squeezed out up to the elbow.

He also wanted to ask—again, anyone at all—how he *knew* the wound had missed anything vital. All the silver dragon had managed to do by stabbing the Nightmare—with Marcus serving as both hilt and very tiny blade—was piss the beast off. The blade had missed the stomach that held Thara and—even with his twisting the blade in the wound—anything that might have slowed the creature. And now he was held up by only his wrist.

He opened his eyes in spite of the warm fluid still gushing over his face, looking for something—anything—he could grab with his left hand. All he could see was the wound with his right hand in it.

He pushed the fingers of his left hand between the edge of the wound and his right wrist.

The slipping progress slowed, but didn't stop until he stopped twisting the knife.

He dangled from the wound, left hand gripping viscera of some sort—or maybe that fascia thing his mind somehow knew about without his ever learning about it—his right hand gripping the hilt of the knife.

His feet, though, continued to slip and found nothing to press against. He risked a glance down and saw he was at least twenty feet above the floor of the pit.

He didn't see the incoming claw until it latched onto his left wrist and pulled. He looked up and saw one of the smaller nightmares face to face and eye to eye. The creature had crawled up and over the Nightmare's body. Movement to his right proved to be a second smaller nightmare. This one had stuck the pointy ends of its butt into the earlier stab wound Marcus had made and was filling it with a yellowish fluid. The tightening grip pulled his attention back to the closer nightmare, the one trying to gnaw his hands off at the wrists.

He tried to bring his feet up, to kick at the creature. If the creature hadn't had been holding him as tightly as it was, he would have pulled free and fallen.

Behind him and above him—though not behind or above enough—the silver dragon continued to fight with the Nightmare. Claws slashed and grabbed. Wings buffeted and billowed and sometimes blocked the yellow light, leaving Marcus in the dark. Fire sprayed and slime splattered. The surface of the Nightmare expanded and contracted as muscles clenched and stomach contents shifted and pushed. Somehow, he managed to hold on. The distance to the floor provided some incentive.

A silver claw swung across his field of view and knocked the smaller nightmare away from him. And nearly knocked him off, as well.

Clinging as best he could, Marcus realized the silver dragon was protecting him. Distracting the Nightmare. Keeping the massive claws away from him. Mostly—

He ducked and flinched as best he could while dangling. The huge silver wings diverted the acid spews. Mostly.

Droplets of acid mist swirled around him. Where he was covered in the brown ichor, the droplets only beaded and rolled off. From the cleaner, less ichored parts of his shirt and pants, though, rose tiny wisps of smoke.

All this effort on his behalf probably meant the silver dragon expected him to do something besides hang there. For example, find and attack one of those vital spots he somehow knew he was nowhere near.

Not that he knew where any vital spots were. He had no clues about Nightmare anatomy, except a very general idea of where its stomach was, and that mostly from resting against it. He hoped he wouldn't be reduced to stabbing at random. Still, he had to try something.

He glanced up, ready to hide his face again if something hard, pointy or acidic was about to fall on him. He couldn't make out anything in all the movement and fire.

Maybe he could climb higher, up to the head. Then stab the creature in one of its eyes. In movies, the guy with the sword was always stabbing the slobbering, indestructible monster in the eye to kill it.

Maybe he would find a sword on the climb up. Wouldn't that be an interesting twist of Fate? He would even choose to use it.

He shook his head sharply and squeezed his eyes closed. He needed to focus.

He opened his eyes and tried to get a better grip with his left hand, to start pulling his way up, but the effort caused his hand to pull free of the wound. Before he could thrust his fingers back into the wound, his right hand slipped.

His left hand joined his right hand in holding the hilt of the oyster knife before the sudden addition of all his weight on his right wrist twisted the knife out of his hand. He held onto the knife, but even pushing his feet against the bulging surface of the Nightmare's stomach he couldn't stop him from sliding down.

As he slid, the knife blade carved a widening vertical slit in the surface, but didn't seem to be slowing him. He was falling and sliding at full speed. Only his sense of time was slow, so he could watch the floor coming at him with all the time in the world.

His feet hit the floor at an awkward angle. His left ankle refused to take his weight and the entire leg folded under him. He fell backward, his head hitting the acid washed concrete floor between two huge dragon toes. Dazed, he could only watch as a waterfall of gleaming, steaming brown ichor washed over him.

4

THARA HAD NEVER HELD HER breath for so long. The air in her lungs had gone past stale and now burned her lungs with nearly the same intensity as the stomach acids were attacking the mucous membranes of her eyes, nose, and mouth. And a couple other places that she had become aware of. Normally, holding her breath this long would have raised her internal temperature to the bursting point, but the *Its* stomach acids also seemed to be at least adequate radiator fluid.

She had no way of knowing what was happening outside the small, dark, churning, grinding, digesting universe of the *Its* stomach, but at least the *It* had stopped swallowing more rocks. The churning, though, had become much worse, as if the *It* had realized *It* was overeating and had taken up Sweating to the Elder Gods to compensate. Folding, stretching, confining, crushing. On the off chance she survived, she wondered what kinds of scars she was going to have.

She wanted to think the silver dragon was out there, fighting for her. Which was a big part of why she was still trying to escape on her own. Not just to breathe and continue living, but because she wanted to be able to see his face when she saved herself.

All stomach churning abruptly ceased with one forward, sloshing tilt. Her tiny, rocks-and-acid-filled world quivered, then began to shift, pulling her backward.

She felt *Its* scream in her bones.

5

THE DRAGON TOES MARCUS LAY between shifted and slipped on the brown ichor still leaking from the wound as the dragon foot they were attached to yanked back, away from what was about to fall on them. And him. Dazed from the fall and from the psychic and all-too-physical noise of the Nightmare's screaming, Marcus had only enough time to bring his hands up in front of his face before the vertical slit he had carved in the Nightmare's abdomen tore open and something bulbous and heavy succumbed to gravity.

A slow-motion avalanche of warm weight and slime fell on Marcus, climbing up his legs and torso and coming down on his face. Brown membranes stretched to dull, translucent yellow against him and over him and covered him like a suffocating comforter, blotting out the yellow light and at least some of the Nightmare's screaming.

The broken chunks of concrete and jagged ends of torn rebar—and maybe a section of squirming dragon tail—pushed against the membrane, and him. He couldn't decide whether he would suffocate first, or be crushed. With his arms crossed over his face, left arm bracing his right, he managed to keep the membrane off his face, but only just. He could feel the Nightmare moving, probably still fighting with the silver dragon, but the weight of the stomach contents meant the organ didn't shift much. Just enough to make him wonder how long it would be until his legs were fully crushed and ground away.

In the hot, heavy darkness, he pushed against the weight of the stomach, but it turned out the Hunter not only didn't have ninja-like combat moves, he didn't have super strength, either. Plus, the way he held the oyster knife in his right hand meant the blade was being pushed toward his left eye. He couldn't see the blade in the brown darkness, but he knew the point hovered only an inch above his eye on the other side of the sunglasses he still wore. If it weren't for the lens, he could stab himself in the eye just by relaxing. Which might be a better way to die than either asphyxiation or gradual pulverization. He was already feeling lightheaded and the weight on his chest allowed only shallow breaths

It seemed it was time for another of those choices he had been told about. Fate wanted him to die, but at least he could choose how. Of the three obvious options, none of them were of use to anyone else. He would just die slow, with either increasing panic or pain, or fast. So he chose the fourth option. He hoped it would be fast. Once again his college degree courses let him down. He had no idea how long it would take the Nightmare's stomach acids to dissolve him.

Keeping his grip on the oyster knife as tight as possible, he twisted his wrist around to bring the point of the blade to bear. When he felt the tip of the blade scrape on the sunglasses, he realized he had underestimated how close the point had been to his eye. He put all his strength into pushing against the stomach. He could only twist his wrist so far. He could feel the blade scraping slime, the tip barely pricking the skin of the membrane. He worked the blade back and forth, but made little additional progress. He was holding the knife wrong for proper stabbing.

He took as deep a breath as he could, which wasn't deep at all—and he was reasonably sure he could have counted the number of unused oxygen molecules remaining in his available air—and shifted the angle of his attack. Keeping the blade straight, he pushed his right wrist along his left forearm, toward the elbow. He felt the tip of the tiny blade bite into the membrane, a shallow cut. He pushed harder, twisting his wrist to the breaking point.

When he was certain—somehow—the blade had fully entered the membrane, he pulled his right arm down, carving an arc.

The membrane separated, pulling away from the point of the cut. He felt the hot fluids of the stomach coat his left shoulder and torso right before the blocks of unchewed, partially digested concrete settled on him. He might have grunted from the impact, but the membrane covering his face didn't allow any air to escape his mouth and nose. He wondered how long it would take him to black out, either from suffocation or from the shock of stomach acids digesting him. In the meantime, he continued the slow cut with his tiny knife. The weight pushed his arm against his chest, but he still move it, lubricated by ichor and acid.

The knife blade scraped against concrete and his wrist caught on something. He pushed against the resistance. Thara was going to need as big a hole as possible if she was going to escape the Nightmare's stomach. The resistance pushed back.

6

THARA FELT SOMETHING MOVE AGAINST the far end of her tail.

Something that wasn't concrete or rebar.

Something that moved on its own.

Something with at least a single tooth that bit her. Hard.

What had the *It* swallowed that could survive the acid bath and still have the gall to attack her? Would the *It* have swallowed one of the smaller its to aid in *Its* digestion?

She acquiesced to extensive bruising as she twisted and thrashed to pull her tail from the mouth of whatever had bitten her and to turn herself over and around within the accumulated rock and acid environs of the *Its* stomach. She shook off the biting creature, but the wound immediately started burning from contact with the stomach acids. That was going to leave a mark.

She "swam," pushing debris aside with all her legs and claws, pushing herself down to where the biting creature had attacked her from.

Her questing claws didn't find anything. She felt the tips of her claws sliding across the smooth stomach wall—

Until they snagged on something.

A snag was different. A snag was something she could work with.

She forced two clawed fingers into the snag, ignoring whatever it was that was pushing through the snag from the other side as it tried to bite her again. She pulled. The rip expanded.

The *Its* screaming crescendoed until the echoes threatened to shatter her skull.

She pulled on the rip with the claws of both her forelegs, pulling the stomach wall apart along a visceral seam. The seam opened down, but since the stomach rested on something hard, the contents—including her—were slow to settle out.

She bent herself double so she could bring her back legs into play.

Pressure from outside the stomach pressed down on her and threatened to crush her, just as she was about to claw her way to freedom. And fresh air.

Something grabbed one of her back legs. That leg stopped pulling at the tear and grabbed back.

Whatever it was, it felt... fleshy. And bony. Like an arm.

She continued to pull at the tear with her forelegs and pushing herself forward with her unencumbered back leg. She dragged along whatever— or whoever—she had grabbed. So she could deal with it in her own time. Once she was free—

The stomach walls that had confined her fell apart, torn from inside and outside and from the weight of their contents. She rolled forward. More bruises, but totally worth it.

She felt the rocks and the acid fall away from her. She opened her outer eyelids and blew out the stale, burning air from her lungs in a geyser of white flame. Then she took in the sweetest-foulest breath of her life and blew out even more fire. Not because it helped, but because it felt good.

The silver dragon towered over her. He stood on his rear legs, his wings extended, as his foreclaws and his teeth pulled on ragged tears and cuts in the hide of the It, ignoring the Its huge claws that struck and grabbed him. The smaller its swarmed over the bloated body of the It, attacking the silver dragon or trying to stitch the It back together with gooey strands excreted from their butts. The Its huge mouth hung open, emitting the ear piercing and mind splitting scream of Its pain and frustration.

Thara shook her body from nose to tail tip, shaking off the viscous bodily fluids and stomach acids that had coated her as well as scattering the debris that landed on and around her. She yanked the creature that bit her free from the gore around her feet and twisted back to grab it in her teeth to shake it and tear it apart—

She stopped with her teeth about to close on Marcus's head.

She swallowed her fire and shifted the young man to her front claws, as gently as she could. Had he been swallowed too? His battered body certainly looked both chewed up and spit out, but only showed a few spots of burns from the *Its* stomach acids. The blade of the ridiculously small oyster knife still clenched his right hand—even after she shook him; he had quite a grip—showed more acid damage than his body. Even his clothes seemed remarkably intact. She held him close to her left eye to see if he was still alive. She resisted the urge to shake him again.

He coughed and gasped and gagged as his eyes opened—then went huge. His hand came up with the knife. She pulled him away from her eye and held him at foreleg's length. His arm with the knife went limp as he recognized her and he coughed some more.

She swung the tip of her tail around so it passed in front of his face. So he could see what he had done and why she might be pissed at him, even if he had saved her life. Then she tossed him toward a wall of the pit, away from the struggling behemoths.

Something with a lot of legs and pincer claws jumped on her back. She twisted her neck and bit on the smaller it, grabbing it with her jaws. She pulled the smaller it from her back to where her foreclaws could also grab it. She held the smaller it in front of her face, both eyes swiveling to focus on it.

Unlike the *It*, she could actually focus on the smaller it. But she could sense the godlike potential of the squirming, clawing, clicking, spitting little bastard. It was disgusting. It was revolting. It was... oddly appetizing.

She wanted to eat it. No. She was *supposed* to eat it. That was her *purpose*.

The possibility existed, she realized, that she had taken the job at the Yellow Sign Buffet for the express purpose of gulping down this leggy salamander-weevil roach-toad. She just hadn't known it at the time. She had thought she only needed to pay the rent. And maybe find another roommate.

She sensed the silver dragon's attempt to steal her smaller it and twisted just in time to prevent him grabbing it with his mouth, his silver saber teeth sparking on empty air in front of her face.

She roared at him to get his own roach-toad, this one was hers, and she stuffed it into her mouth.

Before that instant, she had had no real idea of how wide her mouth could open. The strain on her cheeks was painful and she worried that she might have dislocated her lower jaw, but she couldn't stop herself. Her foreclaws pushed and she gulp-gagged-choked on the smaller it as she forced it down her throat.

She wondered if she looked like a python who had swallowed an elephant. She wondered if she were going to vomit the whole thing back up again when she felt the smaller its many legs squirming in her throat trying to crawl back up. She wondered if she would be able to vomit it back up, or if she would die with this stupid roach-toad stuck in her throat. She gulped-gagged-choked again. Her eyes watered.

She was definitely going to vomit.

7

MARCUS LANDED ON HIS BUTT and rolled backward, ass over stunned look, ending with his back against the wall of the pit, trying even more desperately to breathe as the impact knocked the stale air out of him. He couldn't believe he was still alive. But he still couldn't breathe.

He made fish faces, opening and closing his mouth trying to take in a breath. He thumped himself on the chest with his left fist because his right hand still had a death grip on the hilt of the oyster knife. He might have let go of the knife if he hadn't been so totally focused on taking a breath. He no longer had the willpower to spare for such trivial things as thinking.

His vision went fuzzy and dark around the edges before the pressure on his chest eased and he was able to take a breath. He kept thumping himself on the chest—because why stop what seemed to be working? Then he was able to see again. He finally stopped hitting himself and used his left hand to straighten the sunglasses on his face. His right hand fell to the floor beside him as he watched. He still didn't release the knife, though he was pretty sure his part of this fight was over. At least, he hoped it was over.

When he could finally see straight, he blinked. Because Thara looked like a python who had swallowed an elephant. Her long neck swelled in the middle, distended to the point where he wondered if her golden scales were going to pop off. She was clawing at the swelling with her front claws and her eyes protruded even more than usual. Her mouth opened and closed in much the same way his had a few seconds before. He wondered if there were something similar to a Heimlich Maneuver that could be administered to dragons. Was this another of the odd duties or abilities of "being the Hunter" that no one had let him in on?

Thara's entire body convulsed as if she were about to vomit.

8

THARA FORCED HER MOUTH TO close. She squeezed her eyes closed because she didn't want to see Marcus watching her struggle. She didn't want to see him see her throw up.

Her mouth was dry, but she swallowed anyway.

If stuffing the smaller it down her throat had been her purpose for existing, it seemed like she could have been better built for it. She would have roared in irritation, but there was a roach-toad stuck in her throat. She would have added a lot of white-hot fire to that roar, except—

She let her internal fire build. Maybe she could roast the squirming, choking little bastard from the inside.

The sudden increase in the scrabbling attempts to crawl up her esophagus let her know the smaller it had noticed the increase in temperature.

She gagged. She choked. She forced herself to swallow. Her throat squeezed around the creature, refusing to let it come back up.

The sound of the smaller its exoskeleton cracking, then shattering was muffled, but she felt the sound from the tips of her claws to her teeth, from the crest on her head, down her spine, and to the tip of her tail. She felt the jagged edges of the creature's shell as she swallowed it.

She didn't swallow the creature so much as she suddenly absorbed it. All at once. Broken shell, still-twitching legs, creamy center. All of it.

The still-stinging wound on the tip of her tail stopped stinging. She hardly noticed.

The fire in her belly went nuclear.

9

MARCUS FELT HIS EYES GO wide behind the lenses of his borrowed sunglasses as Thara—

Exploded?

All twenty-five feet of her sinuous body went rigid. Golden light—

Erupted?

From her eyes. Her mouth. From the tips of her claws and the end of her tail. Her crest stood up on her head and radiated a white gold brilliance that could have challenged the noonday Sun. If the glow hadn't been so bright, he might have been able to count every golden scale on her back as she—

Expanded?

Before Marcus could be sure he had seen what he thought he saw— which was a twenty-five-foot dragon growing, swelling, getting longer and thicker—Thara had thrown herself at the Nightmare.

The two dragons, silver and gold, tore at the shivering, twitching, clawing, gushing carcass of the Nightmare. White fire roiled and splashed. Metallic claws ripped and tore. The fires of the dragons no longer washed over the skin of the Nightmare without harming It. The edges of the wounds Marcus had cut—and that the two dragons had ripped wide—sparked and singed. Brown ichor flowed, then congealed in the heat.

Thara flickered across the body of the Nightmare, a golden ray of superheated sunlight, ripping and tearing, buffeting and flaming. When she encountered one of the smaller nightmares, she snatched it and stuffed it down her throat, whole, which made her glow and burn even brighter. And made her grow still larger. Marcus wondered if she had even realized she had grown a pair of golden wings.

The silver dragon focused on the Nightmare, leaving Thara the choice of smaller nightmares to grab and stuff into her face, like an indulgent uncle "sharing" a box of chocolates with a favorite niece. The silver dragon ripped open wounds and reached into the dark cavities thus created to pull out oversized organs and viscera, tear off chunks with his jaws to chew and swallow, then fling the remains about the pit. The Nightmare's forest of legs splayed, twitching.

Marcus looked up as the yellow light that had been illuminating the pit sputtered. He realized it had been sputtering like that for a while. First fluttering, the level jumping like a candle, then actually going dark for an instant, then coming back to uneven life. The pure yellow of the orb had developed brown spots.

Around the edge of the pit, the six o'clock and twelve o'clock positions were still manned by Morgan and August Neuland, but the fence of people standing around the edge had developed gaps. Each time the light blinked out then back on, another gap appeared or an existing gap became larger. Marcus never saw the people turn and walk away. They just vanished into the brown darkness.

In the pit, the silver dragon continued to pull apart the Nightmare and Thara leaped and grabbed the shadows that moved and tried to escape her light and teeth.

Then there were only men and, presumably, women in brown-and-yellow uniforms standing on the edge of the pit.

Then only a single, small employee and two men in dull ecru manager's shirts. And Morgan, on the edge of the pit above him.

Then Morgan was falling into the pit.

Marcus dropped the oyster knife and pushed himself to his feet to try to catch her. Even if it killed him.

From the corner of one eye he thought he saw one manager reaching toward the remaining employee as August Neuland dove from the edge of the pit in a smooth arc. He thought he saw Thara reaching to snatch the man from the air.

From the corner of his other eye Marcus thought he saw a shadow skittering along the bottom of the pit toward him in the stop-motion, strobe light animation created by the dying yellow star. Then the silver dragon rose up in a silver wave behind him and over him, blocking his peripheral vision.

He looked up--

Morgan landed on him like a golden comet and the diseased yellow star above them winked out.

11. Buffalo Dragon Wings

The New Queen

THE NEW QUEEN PULLED HERSELF through the cracks in the crust of the World She was Meant to Consume. She would find a new home, a new place to rest. A new place to grow and feed and give birth to Sister-Daughters of Her Own.

As she made Her Escape, the New Queen nibbled on the portion of Her Sister-Mother She had been able to grab and carry with Her.

The New Queen would Consume the World. She would Avenge Her Sister-Mother and Her Sisters. But not tonight.

The Elder

THE ELDER DECIDED HE HAD been awake too long.

He considered stuffing the Hunter and the Golden Scorpion into his mouth and eating them before the Child noticed he had scooped up the one and caught the other. But he had stuffed himself on the Goddess and the few of the smaller goddesses the Child had not pounced on and gobbled. He could not eat another bite. So he placed the two humans on the tiles at the edge of the pit, belched a white fireball into the night air where the ugly yellow star had been, then turned his attention back to the Child.

The Elder sighed. The Child was playing with her food.

The Bug

As HE WAITED FOR THE Driver, the Bug watched the dazed and confused people walk around him on their way home or to wherever it was people who had been hoping to midwife the End of the World went when the End arrived stillborn.

More than one of the people tried to open his doors, but he had locked his doors. This wasn't his first rodeo.

Though he did wonder if maybe he was getting too old for this sort of thing.

1

THARA REACHED OUT WITH HER left foreclaw to grab August Neuland when he dove over the edge of the pit. She slipped on some bits of the It the silver dragon had thrown about, and missed him. She attempted to correct her grab, but even with her new, longer-than-ever golden-hooked claws she grabbed only air. Though more air than ever before.

She had become huge! Not as huge as the silver dragon, who still dwarfed her. But if there was another dragon who was the same size as she had been when she first jumped into the pit, she would totally dwarf that dragon. She estimated she was at least as long as two Cadillac Escalades now.

And she had grown wings! If "grown" was the right word. She didn't remember when the wings had sprouted—or even if they had sprouted. For all she knew, the wings had just shown up. Her wingspan extended about a Cadillac Escalade to either side. She had no idea if her new wings would allow her to fly, though, since she probably weighed as much as all those Cadillac Escalades combined.

She was twice the dragon she had been, but she *still* missed August Neuland in his swan dive. She wondered if her new wings had thrown off her balance when she reached for him. Or her new mass.

Whatever. She could still get him.

She had been planning to hold him up to her left eye—very near her much larger mouth—to ask him if she was big enough now, and to tell him she quit. And that she still expected him to pay her for the hours she had worked—at the ridiculous hourly amount he had promised her. All she managed to say, though, was, "Got you— Hey!"

The man landed on his feet. Which made her head hurt, since he had clearly dived headfirst. And he didn't land so much as... step out of the air and onto the broken, blasted floor of the pit.

She reached for him again.

And missed him again.

Somehow he had evaded her. Ducking and/or moving faster—much faster—than she expected. So far as she could tell, he hadn't so much as glanced at her or tried to avoid her. He just... evaded.

And managed, somehow, to say, "I'm sorry, Miss Gold, but I believe you would be happier seeking employment elsewhere." He didn't even sound rushed. "We're going to have to let you go."

Growling something that she hoped sounded like "You can't fire me, I quit!" she went for him with both her foreclaws.

He dashed toward the nearest pit wall. He zigged where she expected him to zag and she missed him again.

Something about how he moved, or how his shadow moved, made him appear to have more legs than he should have. And he seemed to be both standing upright and running horizontally along the pit floor. Her eyes hurt from trying to focus on him.

She dove after him—

She hit her head on the wall of the pit wall as he scurried away.

He zigged or zagged, whichever was the opposite of her expectation and strategy, as she chased him along the seam of the wall and floor. She ran into the silver dragon from behind and pushed him out of her way.

Somehow August Neuland never quite emerged from the safety of the debris and gore. She never managed to grab him. Or smash him with an open claw. Then he was gone, having improbably squeezed himself into a crack in the wall of the pit and disappeared in a flurry of arms and legs that cast odd shadows.

She used her claws to dig at the crack, but the crack went deeper than she expected.

After a minute she settled back on her rear legs. She shook the dirt and rocks from her claws as she took in a deep breath. She roared white fire into the hole she had dug and the crack that continued deeper into the earth.

She sighed, blowing hot air out her nostrils. She looked around, taking in the torn bits of the *It* scattered everywhere in the pit, and the wreckage of the Yellow Sign Buffet above and around the pit.

Damn it. She was going to have to find a new job.

"Let it go, Child," the silver dragon said, resting his left wing across her shoulders.

She shrugged his wing off. What did he know about being fired? Or about having to find another job?

She spotted Tina and the so-called Mr. Lampley huddled on the edge of the pit near where the manager's office used to be. Or rather, the so-called Mr. Lampley seemed to want to huddle with Tina, but Tina was trying to keep him at arm's length. Maybe it was time for old roommates to get back together.

Thara walked around the silver dragon, who she just knew was looking down at her with a disapproving expression. She stretched up and leaned against the edge of the pit. She turned her head so she could get a clear look at Tina with her left eye. She must have moved faster than she expected, because Tina jumped, pulled out of the so-called Mr. Lampley's arms, and started to scuttle backward.

The so-called Mr. Lampley turned to face Thara. He looked as if he was mustering the nerve to be protective when Thara brushed him out of the way with her left foreclaw. Tina had stopped with her back against the dented bench of the preparation station.

"Thara," Tina said, her face pale, her hand on her chest. "You startled me."

"Sorry," Thara said. "Are you OK?"

Tina nodded. "I... think so. Are you..." She took in Thara's large head and the rest of Thara that was visible above the edge of the pit. "OK?"

Thara shrugged in a way that showed off her new gold wings, then nodded.

"I'm sorry," Tina said. "About..." She looked around at the wreckage of the restaurant. She saw what she was leaning against and pushed herself away from it. "It's... gone? I'm..." She looked at her hands. She smiled and tears streaked the brown on her cheeks. Then she looked at Thara. Her eyes went wide again. "You're a dragon."

Thara nodded. "I had been thinking about telling you."

"It's the sort of thing a roommate should know."

"Not always."

"No. I guess... no..."

Thara took a breath. "Your room is still—"

She spotted the young man in the yellow-and-brown uniform charging out of the shadows right before he shouted, "Eat me!"

Keenan jumped at her open mouth.

She knocked him aside so he landed on the so-called Mr. Lampley. The two men struggled to disentangle themselves, thrashing about with nearly as many arms and legs as she had seen on August Neuland just before he disappeared.

Thara spotted Tina's big suitcase in the wreckage. She picked it up with her left claw and set it down next to Tina.

"I was going to say your room is still available," she said. "If you want it. We're paid up through the end of the month. Maybe we can find something bigger before then."

"Bigger?"

Thara nodded. "Yeah. I don't think I fit anymore."

"Oh. Will you be... all the time?"

Thara twisted her head around to admire the new lengths and breadths of her dragonness. Her lair was definitely not going to hold her new size and her hoard. And she was definitely not going to give up either one. She turned back to Tina. "No. I can change back anytime now. I think." She paused. "Of course, we'll have to find new jobs too."

It was Tina's turn to nod. "I... I think I might know someone."

"Just so long as it isn't fast food," Thara said. "Or a buffet." Thinking about jobs, and money, reminded her. She looked around. "On the other hand," she said, "someone around here owes me money. Where are you, Dragon Hunter?"

2

MARCUS REGAINED CONSCIOUSNESS WHEN SOMETHING large poked him in the chest, hard. He opened his eyes to find Thara's dragon face looming over him and a claw poised to poke him again. The night was dark, but Thara's golden scales reflected and amplified the starlight, so the darkness did little to blunt the visual impact of a massive dragon face looming over him.

"Why are you wearing my sunglasses?" the dragon face asked, looking aggrieved. Her claws came toward his face as if she were going to take off the sunglasses. Or maybe his face. "Oh, man, you scratched them!"

He tried to bring his hands up to protect his face and discovered Morgan draped across his body, pinning him to the floor. The last thing he remembered was trying to catch her—

His near-panic at seeing a huge golden dragon reach for his face became nearer-panic that Morgan was hurt, or worse.

Thara took her claw back and watched him as he struggled into a seated position with Morgan's head on his lap. Morgan felt warm and she groaned as he turned her face up, transmuting a portion of his panic into relief that she was still alive. Her black leather skirt was bunched around her hips, her blouse had come untucked from her skirt, and her hair was a mess, but he didn't see any bruises or abrasions on her exposed skin. Which was most of it. Her eyes fluttered, but didn't open when he touched her cheek.

"So, Dragon Hunter," Thara said, her breath hot on his face and smelling of bad seafood. "I was just thinking about my half of your dragon bounty and how it might help with my current employment, lodging, and transportation issues. How much did they pay you, anyway?"

Marcus looked up at her. "Employment issues? You're not the only one who needs a new job, you know."

Thara's dragon head went up and down in the largest nod Marcus had ever witnessed. "There does seem to be a lot of that going around." She turned her head so she was looking at him with just her left eye. The eye swiveled in its socket and scanned him and Morgan both.

"I don't have it on me," he said. He remembered tossing Morgan's purse into her Camry, right before Thara landed on it. He decided not to mention that part. "But I know where it is."

Thinking of Morgan's demolished Camry, he remembered Mom Nelson's Ford Focus. How it was parked at Morgan's apartment, and where it was supposed to be in a couple hours. He eyed Thara's new wings. "You think you could give me a ride? Later?"

Thara pulled back and settled her wings against her back. Her expression was hard to read. "Maybe," she said. She turned her head and her left eyes swiveled to look at something on the floor near Marcus. She poked at it with a claw. "What are these doing in here?"

Marcus saw the canvas bundle of kitchen knives he had dropped.

Thara looked at him again. "Have you been stealing all my stuff?"

Marcus was spared answering by the double doors behind him swinging open. Jimmie the Wrangler stood there with his catchpole in one hand and a clamshell phone in the other. He nodded to them, then flipped the phone open with his thumb.

"I'm guessing you're not going to help clean this up," Jimmie said, looking to his left, then his right, then down at the broken tiles of the floor. "Probably."

"Probably not," Thara said.

Jimmie nodded a single nod that very clearly indicated his opinion of kids today and their End-of-the-World shenanigans. He thumbed a button on the phone, then held it to his ear. "Yeah," he said into the phone after a second. "We got another one." He paused. "Yeah." He paused. "Yeah. Right across the street." He paused. "Yeah." He flipped the phone closed.

Marcus and Thara looked at him, waiting.

Jimmie didn't return their gaze. He looked at the clamshell phone in his hand, then pushed it into a pocket. He took the gloves hanging from his waistband and tugged them on one at a time. When he was finished, he glanced at Thara's neck and a tile near where Marcus sat. "Go on," he said. "We'll clean this up. We always do. Always will, probably, at least until that last time. Whenever that happens."

Then he stepped to the edge of the pit and looked in.

"Last time?" Thara asked.

"You're still the Wyrm of the World's End," Jimmie said. "Probably."

"Probably? Am I or ain't I?"

Jimmie shrugged, but still didn't look at her. "Probably."

Marcus met Thara's gaze when Jimmie wouldn't. Then he saw a dirty, disheveled woman walking around the edge of the pit, pulling a wheeled suitcase behind her.

Thara followed his gaze. "Don't worry, Dragon Hunter. She's with me."

3

THARA WAITED UNTIL SHE WAS sure the silver dragon was about to get angry that she was ignoring him. Not that she was ignoring him. She just had a lot to deal with in the postapocalypse. Like how she was going to give Marcus a ride back to his girlfriend's apartment when one of her Outdoor Babies had blown himself up, one had probably turned what was left of his engine into a hot block of rust, and the other hadn't turned over in decades. The buses weren't going to start for a couple hours yet. She hoped Marcus didn't expect a dragon ride. That was not going to happen.

Behind her, the silver dragon cleared his throat in a way that caused broken tiles to fall off the edge into the pit.

"Wait a minute," she told Tina and Marcus, and turned around to look up the silver dragon.

He had pulled himself to his full height, standing on his rear legs. She realized he had grown, as well. His wings extended further and his tail was longer. But he hadn't grown as much as she had. If she climbed out of the pit and stood on the edge, she would be eye to eye with him. Almost.

The silver dragon looked like there was something he wanted to say. Or like he was waiting for her to say something. Thara couldn't be sure. She had no experience reading the facial expressions of dragons.

"Well?" It wasn't what she wanted to ask, but it was all that came to mind.

After a long minute, the silver dragon let out something between a sigh and a volcanic vent.

I... do not understand you, Child. The silver dragon's voice rumbled in her head. *Stay safe.*

Before she could think of something to say in response—or which of a million questions about life as a dragon she should ask first—the silver dragon crouched, then launched itself into the air. His wings spread and caught the air. The wind from his wings rivaled the gusts from a spring storm as he flew away.

"Bye," Thara said to his back. She got the distinct impression he was going to go back to sleep.

Thara turned to look at Marcus and Tina again. Marcus's girlfriend was still out cold. Thara pointed a claw at the unconscious Morgan. "I suppose you're going to want to bring her along?"

"We can leave her at your place—" He stopped when he saw her expression. "Or not. We have to go to her apartment, anyway. That's where my car—my mom's car—is."

"Hang on," Thara said. She turned and walked across the pit to the other side, then pulled herself out.

She spotted August Neuland's beige Cadillac Eldorado parked behind the ruins of the restaurant. As expected, no debris had landed on the old car, though the so-called Mr. Lampley's Toyota Corolla parked beside it had been hammered by a chunk of cinder block wall. The so-called Mr. Lampley, who had been sitting on the dented trunk of his car, looking lost, ran away when he thought she was coming for him.

She ignored him and considered her options. There was no way to drive the car out of the parking lot, which was still full of cars.

She tried not to scratch the vintage paint job as she picked up the car with her front claws. It was awkward, reaching over the car next to it, but once she had picked up the so-called Mr. Lampley's Corolla and tossed it aside, lifting the Eldorado was easier. Then she tried not to waddle as she hauled the car awkwardly over the other cars and around the pit. Once she burned a path through the hedge on the south side, she was able to put the car down on the parking lot of the commercial building next door.

She waved at Tina and Marcus to join her. She saw Jimmie the Wrangler had walked back through what was left of the restaurant and was standing near Louie. Both old man and old car appeared to be waiting. She was going to have to have Louie towed back from impound. Again. Then she and Louie and Nova would have a proper wake for poor Howie.

"A hand, maybe?" Marcus shouted back, indicating Morgan.

"She's your girlfriend," Thara said. "You carry her. I brought the car."

She watched as Marcus tried to get Morgan to wake up enough to walk beside him with his arm around her, but the girl seemed determined to be dead weight.

Thara went back and picked up the woman, then three-legged it back to the Eldorado. She gently—ish—laid Morgan on the pavement.

"We need to get her purse out of her car," Marcus said. "Unless you think thirty-five thousand in cash will still be there when we get back."

"Fine. Wait here."

Thara jumped into the air in a shaky, uncertain attempt to mimic the silver dragon. She beat her wings and—

It didn't work. She came down on the remaining section of roof that had covered the dining room of the Yellow Sign Buffet. In front of the restaurant, Jimmie the Wrangler turned around to see what had happened.

How do I use my wings to fly? There was a question it would have been useful to ask before the silver dragon left. She would figure it out, though. Later.

She extricated her feet from the holes she had punched into the tarred roof and ran the rest of the way back to the wreckage of Morgan's golden Camry. Her dragon senses quickly found the purse with the money. She stuffed the purse into her cheek for the run back.

What do dragons use for pockets? was another good question.

On her way back, she noticed the big buffalo still sitting on the ruins of the Buffalo Burger Pit. The events of the night, the near End of the World, didn't seem to have fazed it. The serene expression remained.

Back at the Eldorado, she spit out the purse. Tina was putting her suitcase into the car's trunk.

"Wait," Thara said. "I need to borrow some clothes."

She changed into a naked human woman—then back into a dragon again, just to make sure she could, since that was a question she could answer on her own—and startled Tina and Marcus. Then she changed back into a naked woman again.

She looked at Tina's uniform. "You should change too," she said. "And let me burn that crap you're wearing."

Tina glanced at Marcus, then blushed and shook her head.

"Suit yourself."

Thara pulled on the panties, jeans and tee-shirt Tina gave her while Marcus proved he didn't need keys to unlock a stranger's car and pushed Morgan into the back seat.

"Shotgun," Thara said as she pulled on the jeans, because there was no way she was going to sit in the back with Morgan. Tina just shrugged.

Marcus sat in the driver's seat. He smiled as the car started, seemingly on its own.

"Will that trick work for me?" Thara asked as they pulled out of the parking lot and drove south. The north lanes were still full of parked cars. There was no sign of their drivers. "For the drive to... wherever you live. Or am I going to have to drive your car?"

"His momma's car," Morgan murmured in the back seat.

The Yellow Sign Buffet smell clinging to every occupant of the car, especially Tina, was already making the air seem stuffy. Thara pushed a button and her window slid down with a purr. Fresh air hit her in the face and started the long job of scrubbing the scent of the Seasoning from her nostrils.

"He says he'll start for you," Marcus said.

Thara nodded, then looked over her left shoulder at Tina. "You OK with a road trip? I don't think we're going to be able to get back to our apartment until after a lot of towing."

"Yeah, that's OK," Tina said and shrugged. She was staring out the window.

Thara wondered if the girl was in shock.

Just before they reached Sixty-first Street, a caravan of vehicles with lights and sirens passed them going the other direction. Marcus had to pull over so a Humvee with the logo of the Rio Cruces Animal Control Center painted on its doors and an old white van with the same logo could get past them sharing the southbound lanes. Something made Thara try to see who was driving the white van, but she couldn't see past the glare of the headlights. A fire truck followed the animal control vehicles, then an ambulance and a hazardous materials truck.

They watched the vehicles pass without comment, then Marcus pulled back into the street.

"You like this car?" Marcus asked.

"It seems to run," Thara said. "But, no, I don't plan to keep it. Do you want it?"

"Him," said Marcus. "Not 'it.'"

Thara touched the dash. "My apologies. Does he have a name?"

"He says no."

"Probably just as well. Who knows what August Neuland might have chosen." She paused. "So you're not going to keep him? I don't think August Neuland will be back for him anytime soon."

"He is a handsome devil," Marcus said, patting the steering wheel. "But I've had my eye on a blue 1969 Pontiac GTO."

"1969? That was a good year."

"Yeah?"

Thara nodded. "Yeah."

At Sixty-first Street, Marcus turned right, heading for Riverside Drive and downtown.

Thara held her hands in front of her face. Her fingertips tingled as she caused her fingernails to become shining gold. Then she smiled and looked out the open window.

THE END
of
Now Serving Dragon

About the Author

David R. Michael is probably listening to some form of industrial and/or electronic music as you read this. Odds are good he is either writing or working on software, because he is boring like that. David lives in Tulsa, Oklahoma, which is located in the real world at the precise location of Rio Cruces in his imagination. He lives with his wife, kids, and cats, all of whom are more interesting than he is.

To know when new books by David R. Michael are available, sign up for David's email newsletter here: **www.gunsandmagic.com**

Strange things happen when Dillon opens doors. A cold, lifeless universe waits in the bathroom. A hideous creature that looks nothing like a puppy lurks in his closet. He doesn't remember what was in his toy box, but he still has nightmares.

In his job as night manager at the Buffalo Burger Pit, Dillon has found a use for his special gift: hazing the new hires. Like when he offers them a free vanilla shake. Or opens the door of the big freezer for them to see inside.

Soledad has been able to read minds since life hit her with the puberty stick. Not Dillon's mind, which is probably why they're still friends. She's always thought his trick with the vanilla shakes was stupid. She never imagined how stupid.